The Magical Bookshop No. 2

The Tale of Alexis & The Straitlaced Gargoyle

by

Ella Outlaw

ISBN: 979-8-9918378-4-2

Published by Uncommon Pages LLC

First Edition: November 2025

Book Cover by Lisa Austin

Dedication

———◄O►———

To all my fellow monster lovers!

But especially those who had their monster awakening
watching the Gargoyles animated TV show.
Wonder if those animators know what they've done?

Trigger Warning!!!

I want to reassure you that this is indeed a COZY romance. That being said, there are a few topics that I want to make sure you are comfortable with before diving into this adventure.

- Sexual content and acts

- Bondage

- Spanking

- Voyeurism

- Law enforcement surveillance

- Theft

- Bones/buried humanoid remains

- Discussions about a VERY old murder

- Mentions of death from childbirth

Chapter 1

Alexis

I'm so BORED! Bored with my job, bored with my hair, bored with my life. Heck, I'm even starting to get bored of my current hyperfixation, lock picking. I'd gotten deep into it after my brother, Marcus, gave me a lock pick set for my birthday. Turns out I'm a natural. It came so easily to me. Too easily to keep my attention for long if I'm honest. It's been my obsession for months at this point, but it just isn't hitting right anymore, ya know?

An admittedly weird hobby for a thirty-one-year-old Black woman, but then again most of my hobbies weren't really that normal to begin with. Yoga is the tamest, for sure. What woman hasn't tried that out? But it's good for staying limber, so I do it. The rock climbing phase worried my dad the most, so I only did the 'safer' in-house climbs. Though, now that he's passed I could get back into it. Finally test my skills out in the real world.

My ADHD-fueled hobbies have really kept my family on their toes over the years. When I was younger, my interests cycled through gymnastics, ballet, break-dancing, Judo, cross-country running, and swimming, just to name a few. I tried some team sports as well but I always felt I could do things better myself, so dropped those quickly. Thankfully, my dad was cool with anything that got my 'extra energy' out. My tall, lean, and lanky body was well suited to many physical activities. No, not lanky. Lithe. A much better word to describe my beautiful body.

Maybe I should pivot to safe cracking? It's still along the same lines as lock picking after all. Hmm, might be doing some research after work, or more likely during it. Pretty sure I'm not fully booked today.

Ugh, work! Yet another thing I am so over. But who isn't really? If it hadn't taken me so long to get my certification, I'd probably quit. Though most people wouldn't call a year and some change long, it had still been a lot of work and effort to become a licensed massage therapist. So my stubbornness will help me stick with it...for a little longer at least. I know I'm what some may call a 'job hopper,' but I'm okay with that. After all, 'a jack of all trades is a master of none, but oftentimes better than a master of one,' as the saying actually goes.

Speaking of hopping, the decision to hop off the bus two stops early so I could walk had felt like a good idea this morning. I had hoped it would liven up my day a little. Plus, I needed the cool breeze to help with my itchy noggin. Absently, I scratch at my scalp while walking down the weatherworn sidewalk. I hadn't put my wig on properly this morning because I plan to rip it off as soon as I am done with Mr. Jenkins. That old misogynist always tips better when I have long hair, so I wore my longest and most 'feminine-looking' wig. It's a gorgeous black water wave wig with curls that fall loosely and naturally to the top of my waist. But it's already driving me crazy! All I want to do is throw it away at this point. I won't though. It would be a waste of good money if I did.

Since I don't often get off the bus so far from the spa, I'm not too surprised I don't remember seeing this old bookstore. But it's not the store itself that draws my attention, it's the cat sitting in the window that makes me stop in my tracks. I've never seen a more uniquely beautiful cat in my life! I mean, sure, I've seen pictures of cats like this before, but never in person! It's a tortoiseshell cat with black, orange, and white fur, but half of its face is completely black, split down the middle in a perfect line. The black side of its face has a blue eye, while the tortie side has a green eye. This gorgeous little furball is peering at me like I'm some kind of peasant, and if a cat could arch an eyebrow this one totally would. Then, this haughty little thing gives me a slow blink, which is all I need to race into the shop, eager to pet this strange cat. If Jackson Galaxy has taught me anything, it's that a slow blink means it's go time!

Giddy with excitement, I backtrack to the old worn wooden door. The chiming song of a brass bell at the top of the door sounds at my entrance. Glancing quickly around the shop I don't see anybody, just loads of books and bookshelves. Perfect! No one else to monopolize the kitty but me. Turning to the left, away from the giant wooden checkout counter, I briskly walk toward the window the cat is sitting in. There's a snug little seating area in front of a fireplace over here, but I ignore its siren call and make my way around a tall bookshelf that looms in front of the shop windows. There I find my prey. This little guy hasn't moved so much as a whisker at my entrance, but as soon as I approach, his ear cocks towards me, eventually followed by his head.

"Look at you!" I start off. "If you aren't the most amazing cat I've ever seen." This earns me an 'R' heavy meow, almost as though he understood what I said. Logically, I realize it's because I talked to him and he's just responding to being spoken to, but that's not nearly as fun to believe. "Boy, I hope you are a ham for attention because I am about to give it to you," I warn as I kneel down onto the floor. The window sill doesn't have enough space for me, but I've never been opposed to a little floor time.

At this, the cat decides to stand up and, after a big stretch, saunters closer to me. I offer a loosely closed fist and immediately receive a head bump. I have been chosen! I pet his little forehead, scratch around his ear and under his chin, then give him a nice long stroke down the length of his body all the way to the tip of his tail. "What a soft little cutie you are," I croon over his loud motorboat purring.

"Indeed, he is," a melodic voice says, far too close to me. Startled, I whip my head in its direction to find a towering vision of a woman standing next to me. How did I not hear her approach?! These old floors, though covered by rugs, are still creaky and her long floor-length skirt must swoosh as she walks, yet I heard nothing. She smiles down, and I am instantly held by the intensity of her gaze. I feel trapped by her amber eyes. Completely stuck, unable to move, unable to breathe, unable to look away or even blink. It's as if my body has been petrified! Just as I begin to scream in my mind, she blinks, shifting her gaze away, releasing me from my mental prison. What the FUCK was that?!

Standing up quickly—with every intention of getting the heck away from this woman—she calmly glances at me again. However, none of the former intensity appears in her eyes. Now they are beautifully warm and almost kind with a hint of patience. This sudden change makes me pause, so I take a moment to fully drink her in. It's not often that I have to look up at a woman, but this lady has my six foot-one inch frame beat. Her mahogany waist-length hair has a slight wave that cascades down her back and over her shoulders like a slow winding river. Her porcelain skin is without freckle, blemish, or wrinkle. I couldn't even begin to guess her age because her appearance and presence seem to be at odds with each other. How can someone appear this young but feel so...old?

Normally a woman with perfectly proportioned full hips and breasts would have my full attention, if you catch my drift, but this lady feels off limits for some reason. Plus, I like my men taller than me, not my women. Not that I don't find taller women attractive, being one myself, but I do enjoy a shorter female partner. Men, on the other hand, oh, I like my men to tower over me, much like this woman is. Hmm, maybe this lady isn't as off limits as I had thought. I mean, slightly terrifying could be hot too.

"Is my feline partner what brought you into my bookshop so early this morning, or are you in search of something in particular?" Her tantalizing voice breaks me from my perusal of her body.

Instantly, I open my mouth with an, "uhhh," without any kind of answer prepared. Thankfully, the kitty comes to my rescue with a loud indignant meow, bumping his head into my hip, demanding attention.

"Sorry, Mr. Kitty! Or are you Miss Kitty?" I ask while getting back to the real reason I came in here, petting this cat.

"Harvey, my dear. His name is Harvey, and it seems he has taken quite the shine to you," she answers with a crooked smile on that perfect face of hers. I'm admiring her deliciously plump lips when her words sink in.

"Harvey? This cat's name is Harvey? The cat with his face split perfectly in two!" Looking back down at him, I hold his furry little face cupped between both my hands. "That is absolutely perfect! You're named after Two-Face," I practically squeal. This lady is getting more appealing by the moment. My nerdy little heart is thumping with joy and appreciation.

"Two-Face? Sorry, I am unfamiliar with that reference. Harvey came to me already named. But, from your reaction, I am guessing it's a perfectly suited epithet?" I barely manage to contain my disappointment.

"Oh, yes, it's the human name of a supervillain, before he took on the Two-Face moniker. So whoever named him must have been a nerd like me." I chuckle bringing my focus back up to her, still petting my new little furry friend of course. "And to answer your question from before, yeah, I did mostly come in here to pet Harvey. He more or less drew me in. Not that I wouldn't love to look around your bookstore sometime. I really would, but I've got work this morning." As if on cue, my phone dings in my pocket, letting me know I have a text.

"Speak of the devil," I mutter after reaching into the thigh pocket of my light lavender scrubs to inspect my phone screen. An audible, "What!" escapes me when I see the text from the spa. Mr. Jenkins has canceled his appointment. That son-of-a-bitch! He's the whole reason I'm up this early, the whole reason I have this damn itchy wig on. I sink down to let my butt sit on the slim lip of the window ledge, careful not to knock into any of the display books. With a mirthless chuckle, I stuff my phone back into my pocket.

"Not good news, I gather," the lady infers.

Taking in a deep breath, I rip off my long bothersome locks to reveal my natural close-cropped hair. The instant coolness is a relief to my scalp and helps calm my building frustration.

"Not bad really, just frustrating. And very disappointing. On the plus side, it does mean I have time to wander around your shop." Harvey, the dear sweet little guy, manages to crawl into my barely existent lap and settle himself there. I quickly wrap my arms around him to make sure he doesn't slide off.

"If I may make a suggestion?" the book store lady begins. "How about we get you both into a more agreeable seating situation, because that," she gestures at the pair of us, "looks truly uncomfortable. Then you can tell me what types of books you love, and I can bring you something while you continue to enjoy sweet Harvey's company. How does that sound, Miss..." she trails off waiting for me to supply my name.

"Alexis, but everyone calls me Lexi." I wait for her to offer up her own name, but she doesn't. Instead she swiftly moves to my side, lifts me by my elbow as I hastily hold Harvey tighter in my arms, and begins guiding me around the bookshelf, back toward the little seating area by the fire I clocked earlier.

As I finally glance at this bookshelf, in an effort to avoid running into it, I notice the books upon it for the first time. All new-looking, leather-bound tomes of varying sizes and colors, but all missing some key details. None of these books have any names or titles on the spines or covers. You'd think that at least the ones facing out would have some kind of text on them.

"Is this some kind of specialty bookstore or something?"

"Oh, yes," she replies in a somewhat mischievous tone. "It is indeed quite special." Okay, well, that's cryptic.

"Do you work here, or do you own it?" I ask in an attempt to get a straight answer from this woman.

"I own it, my dear, and run it. Harvey and I are the only employees, as it were. And given that you are my only customer at the moment, we can devote ourselves to you entirely." Great, the undivided attention of a somewhat intimidating yet gorgeous retail shop owner. Everyone's dream come true, if by dream, you mean nightmare. At least this means I get this cat all to myself. Setting me down in a wingback chair, she nudges an ottoman I didn't notice before near my feet.

"Why don't you put your feet up and make yourself comfortable while I fetch us something to drink. I've just acquired a new espresso machine and have been itching to make some for a guest. How does that sound?" She's looking down at me expectantly with her hands clasped to her chest, giving the impression that she really is just as eager as she said.

"Um, sure. Why not? Espresso is my preferred caffeine intake method after all. And I could really use some right about now. Thank you." I don't know why I'm so surprised by her thoughtfulness, or the fact that this quaint bookstore has an espresso machine, but I am. Maybe I was judging this lady too harshly? Maybe the initial trapped sensation I had upon meeting her eyes that first time had nothing to do with her at all but was instead a reflection of my own current state of mind? Whoa, that was deep, Lexi. Good job! Way to self reflect.

"Fantastic! Let me pop off into the back and whip us up some little shots of heaven. I keep it back there so as to not potentially damage any of my books with its steam. Oh, and I would advise you to enjoy Harvey's attention while you can as I've found he can only stand it for so long. He does have his own personal cuddle limit, I'm afraid." Advice given, she gracefully turns around, swishing her skirt as she makes her way behind the wooden cashier counter, then into a back room.

"Okay then," I mutter to myself. As suggested, I prop my feet up onto the ottoman and lean back into my seat. Dropping the wig on the floor next to the chair, eager to get it away from me, I turn my attention back to my new little friend. "You just let me know when you've had enough lovin', and I'll leave you be. But until then, I am not about to waste this opportunity." His purrs resume as I ply him with pets and scritches once more.

"It's been a long time since I've gotten some good kitty love," I begin, filling the near silence with chatter to my little companion. "I haven't owned a cat in a very long time. Not since Mr. Watson, my family cat, passed away. He was incredibly old and it was his time, but it was still really hard on all of us. I just haven't had the heart to get a new one since then. Kind of been waiting for the cat distribution system to bless me, which hasn't happened so far." Harvey, bless him, chooses that moment to start making biscuits in my lap.

"Oh, little man, you are too cute!" My voice, turning into full on baby talk, "Look at you, working so hard kneading that dough." His purrs increase in volume at my praise. "I might just have to steal you away, Harvey." I lean in closer to whisper conspiratorially, "What do you say, want to come home with me and be my little guy?"

"Are you in here trying to poach my only employee?" I involuntarily bring a hand to my heart. For the second time, this store owner has startled me with her sudden appearance. "Oh, for shame," she continues in a playful tone. "I leave to make you a tasty treat, and you try to abscond with my shop cat." We both laugh.

"Sorry, not sorry. He's just such a perfect little man. Can't blame a girl for trying." The store owner hands me a little cup and saucer, then artfully sits down in the loveseat that's across from me. I take a big whiff of the brew in my cup, giving a 'mmmm' of appreciation. I gently blow across the rim of the mini-mug, then take a little sip. The audible moan that escapes my throat makes my human companion chuckle. But I couldn't help it! This might just be the greatest espresso I have ever tasted. It's bold and intense with chocolate and nutty tones and a slight sweetness that pairs beautifully with the bitterness. She wasn't lying when she called it a little shot of heaven.

"Wow, lady, this might be the best damn espresso I've ever tasted. And you said I'm the first customer you've made it for? If that's true, you have a natural gift that needs to be shared with the rest of the world. If you advertised these and sold them here, I bet you'd have this place full of people." She's smiling indulgently at me over her cup. "I'm serious! You get these brewing, open those doors, and people will flock in here."

"Well, that's very kind of you to say. While I am glad you are enjoying it, I don't believe I would like to have droves of people in here all at once." She sets her now empty cup and saucer down on a little tea service cart. "I much prefer these intimate one-on-one exchanges. Really getting to know my guests. Their wants, woes, and desires. Then helping them choose the adventure that is best suited for them among my hoard of books. So tell me, Lexi, what kind of adventure are you after?"

The way she asks that question makes me feel...odd...strange...off balance? I can't quite put my finger on it, but it's definitely weird. Almost like it's resounding in my head. As though compelled, I blurt out an answer.

"I am SO ready for a change! My life is so boring right now, and I feel trapped by it. I just want to be free! To try something completely new, something exciting!" I pause, surprised at my own outburst. Not that I mind telling my business, but it's usually intentional. With this, I hadn't even decided to say anything before it erupted from my mouth.

"Go on, my dear. No judgments here. I believe we all need a change in our lives from time to time." She sits back into the loveseat and motions her hand for me to continue. So I do, because I really want to tell someone. Thankfully this time I feel a bit more in control of my words.

"That's the thing, I change all the time! Well more often than most folks anyway. I seem to only be able to give a job a couple years max before I'm searching for greener pastures. I don't know if it's my ADHD or if I just haven't found the 'right fit' for me?" I pause long enough to exhale my frustration. "I mean, other people find a thing they like and stick to it, so what's wrong with me?" I've asked myself this question many times before, and it makes me feel bad about myself every time. I know I should stop asking it, but it keeps popping back up in my life time and again like a weed.

"Now, we shall have none of that here," the shop lady sharply interrupts. "There is nothing wrong with you, and there certainly isn't anything wrong with change. Change is as inevitable as death, and more beings would benefit from a little more change in their life than not."

I can't help but stare at her a little wide-eyed. That is not a response I have ever gotten before. It's usually, 'oh, you'll find something one day,' or 'you just need to learn to stick with it.' Her little speech about change being inevitable does kind of make me feel a little better about my life choices.

"I thought the saying went, 'Nothing is certain but death and taxes.' Never heard change brought into the mix before. But I guess you're right, nothing stays the same if you think about it–"

"Exactly!" she says cutting me off. "Change is an ever constant and should be treated as a friend and teacher. So no more disparaging remarks about change from you young lady. I can see that change has been a constant companion of yours, and you should be proud of this aspect of yourself. It tells me that you are intelligent and fearless. Not everyone in this world is as open to change as they ought to be." She waves her hand gracefully through the air. "Now enough about that, tell me more about yourself. How am I supposed to ascertain what kind of adventure you need without learning more about you?"

Adventure? Oh, that's right, she owns this book store and wants to sell me a book. I'm more an audiobook girlie than a physical book one, but she has been nice-ish. I mean, I have been getting free kitty lovin', so I'll let her see what kind of story she can find for me.

"Well, since you're the expert, what do you need to know in order to find me a good book?" I regretfully take my last sip of heaven and prepare for my interrogation.

"Oh, just the basics, my dear." She's crossed her legs in front of her with her hands clasped together on her knee. "The genres you typically gravitate toward, things you like or expect in a good story, your interests or hobbies, your current family and friendship dynamics. You know, the usual."

Family stuff? Why would she need to know about my family to find me a book? That's kind of weird, but maybe she wants to make sure she doesn't give me a book that hits on any touchy subjects. I mean, there is one thing about my family that comes up a lot in books, especially fairytales, but I'm pretty used to that at this point. Guess I'll just jump right in and see where this goes.

"Let's see, as far as friends go, my BFF moved to New Zealand years ago. We still keep in touch, mostly. I'll probably end up going for a visit someday and just stay there honestly." I chuckle at the truth of it. I've never gone because I know if I do, I'm not coming back home. "I have three older brothers and seven niblings! The kids are really the reason why I haven't left yet. Didn't want to miss out on being the cool aunt and watching them grow up. Several are in high school now, if you can believe it. Time does fly." A small smile leaps to my lips as images of the horde of kids come to mind. Dad loved having them all around for holidays. I shake my head to clear those memories before continuing.

"Both my parents have passed, Dad last year and my mom while giving birth to me." I continue quickly so I don't get any pity statements, "Which probably explains why I grew up such a tomboy, only guys in the house and what not. But they treated me like one of the boys and I loved it! Not that I'd have let them do any differently, or ditch me. I followed them around so hard, proving I could do anything they could and probably do it better too. To this day, we still have epic D&D sessions together!" She stares at me quizzically with an arched brow right before asking.

"D and D? What is that exactly? I am unfamiliar with the term."

"Are you serious?! Wow! It's become so popular in recent years! How have you missed out?" Pulling myself together, I answer excitedly, "So, D&D stands for Dungeons & Dragons. It's a tabletop role-playing game where you get together with a group of people to tell a story. We call these collaborative stories 'campaigns.' It's full of adventure, mystery, and sometimes utter chaos! You can choose to be any kind of fantasy creature you want. I love being a sneaky little rogue." I give a tiny 'te he he' and steeple my fingers like the naughty little imp I am. "Players create their own character, and the DM, Dungeon Master, or GM, Game Master, puts together the world, tasks, and NPCs." She gives me another arched eyebrow in question. "Oh, it stands for Non-Player Characters. Basically everyone else in the world."

"How profoundly interesting. And you all contribute to tell this story in your own unique way? Playing as these characters you have created?" I nod emphatically in reply. "Sounds marvelous," she says with a wicked smile. "Do go on."

"Yes, it's so much fun! And everyone has their own stats regarding how good or bad they are at a particular skill. I mean, you don't want your character to be good at everything. For one, it's boring and two, doesn't make sense, ya know? Then, there's also this huge element of chance with the dice! You tell the DM what you would like to do in any given situation, and you roll the dice to see if you are actually able to do that thing. And even if you fail the roll, it's still fun because something happens either way, and the story will progress forward!"

At this final statement, I lose my cuddly companion. Seems like I have become too animated in my explanation for Harvey's liking. He jumps from my lap, sits down in front of the fireplace, peers at me incredulously, then begins to clean his paws and face.

"Oh, I'm so sorry, sweet kitty. Come back! I'll be more calm, I promise." But my pleas land on uncaring ears as he completely ignores me. The cat's owner chuckles sweetly at our antics.

"Told you he had a limit, and it appears as though it has been reached. Though I for one love to see a person who enjoys creating a good story as much as I do." She gives a 'hummm' while tapping her chin. "So you love an adventure, fantasy, and mystery while being a little sneaky and mischievous. It all sounds spectacular to me, but what exactly is a rogue in this game of yours?"

"Oh, they're often like thieves, spies, assassins, scouts, that kind of thing. They usually have high sneak and stealth capabilities. Good acrobatics, deception, and/or investigation too. They can be good or bad or morally gray. All depends on how you want to play them." The bookstore owner nods her head and gazes off into space, before snapping her gaze back to me.

"I believe I have just the thing for you. But before I know for sure, tell me a bit about your hobbies. Do any of them align with this rogue-type character you like to play as?" She's asked me so earnestly that I reflect a moment before I give her the most truthful answer.

"Funnily enough, yeah. I kinda do. Or have had at one time or another. Huh, never really put that together before...." I shake my head, deciding that's something I might need to examine further. "Let's see, I've had so many hobbies in my life, but the ones that pop into my head when related to a rogue are: lock picking, several martial arts, rock climbing, gymnastics. One summer I taught myself to read lips; don't ask me why. Oh, and I can hold my breath for a really long time thanks to my swimming! I bet that would be helpful when it comes to being quiet."

"Goodness, my dear! It is as if you have been preparing for this all your life. You are too perfect!" she says with a genuine smile. Quickly rising from her seat, she claps her hand together in an audible slap! For some reason, I unintentionally stand up too, caught up in her excitement. She seems surprised, but only for a moment. "Come, follow me, Lexi dear, and I will give you such a grand adventure." Wow! I can't believe how excited this lady has me for reading a book! But I just know that whatever it is, it's going to be awesome!

She takes my hand and almost drags me through the rows of bookshelves. My long strides having trouble keeping up with hers. An unusual experience for me. Coming to an abrupt stop, I almost run into her but save myself at the last second as she reaches to take a book from the top shelf in front of her. Turning while releasing my hand, she passes the volume to me with reverence.

I grasp it with both hands, noting its weight. Glancing down, I discover that it is also without title. The cover is a shade of purple that reminds me of midnight, with silver box borders in the front and horizontal lines on the spine, almost as if it's just waiting for the title to be embossed upon it. Holding the spine steady in my right hand, I let the book fall open with the crackling of fresh pages within a new spine. Definitely the sound of a book that's never been opened. A book that has completely blank pages inside?

"Um, I think you handed me the wrong book by accident. This one doesn't have any text in it," I say to her like she isn't also staring down at an open book with glaringly white pages.

"Oh, is that so? Maybe you should check again? Just to be sure." Well, that sounds like gaslighting to me. The smirk she has on her face doesn't help either. I let out an exasperated sound, my former excitement quickly dwindling, but I comply.

"Here, lady, see!" I flip a few more clearly empty pages. "No words at all! No pictures, no colors, no lines. Just bright, bright white...very bright actually." In fact, the pages seem to be getting brighter as I look at them. Well, as I try to look at them, anyway. As we stand here, it's becoming increasingly harder to see. Even squinting my eyes isn't helping with the blinding light that's coming off these pages.

"What the hell?!" I yell as wind kicks up all around me, flipping the pages at a furious speed. I instantly drop the book onto the floor where it falls wide open.

"See you on the other side, my dear." I hear her words clearly over the sounds of wind and flapping paper. On instinct, I bring my hands to cover my face.

My final thought before my world turns upside down...what the actual fuck!

Chapter 2

---◆◇◆---

Alexis

I think I'm going to be sick. No, I'm for sure going to be sick! After being tossed around in a blindingly bright maelstrom, I come to a hard fall onto my hands and knees. Ouch, that's going to bruise for sure. Even though I'm touching the solid ground under me, it still feels as if I'm moving. My vision is dotted with light blindness, like a camera just flashed right in front of my cornea. And why does it feel like my ears need to pop?

Shakily, I stand, trying to get my bearings, while bringing my fists up ready for a fight. I don't know what the fuck just happened, but I'll be damned if I go down without swinging!

"Be calm. You are safe and sound," says the irritatingly tranquil voice of that shop lady a few feet in front of me. "I do apologize for the nausea and the bumpy ride, but traveling here isn't always an easy trip. You'll be right as rain in a few moments."

"Bumpy ride?!" I practically yell at her. "It felt like I fell into some white water rapids that had no water at all!" I can hear my voice sounding both heated and hysterical. "And what do you mean traveling here? Where the fuck am I? What the fuck did you do to me?" My alarm and panic increase the longer I sway on my feet still unable to make out my surroundings. I think I'd feel better if I could at least see properly.

"Alexis, compose yourself." It's not said angrily, it's not said in warning, but it is said with such a cool commanding tone that I feel my body instantly obey. My mind soon follows, though not as completely. "Take some deep calming breaths for me. That's a good girl. Close your eyes and give them a moment to recover." I stand, following each of her orders, fists still raised at the ready. "There, that should do the trick. Now, open those lovely golden eyes of yours and take in the world around you."

I snap open my eyes, desperately needing to see where I am. Blinking a few times, just to be sure, I stare open-mouthed at the glittering wonder around me. Treasure! I am surrounded by piles and chests filled with gold, coins, jewels, glittering weapons, and other expensive-looking things. I notice that the floor, walls, and high domed ceiling of this room are made out of gray flat stones with black grout between them. I'm left utterly speechless, turning around again and again, trying to take it all in.

"Did you drug me?!" My first question comes out in a high pitched voice that reverberates in an unpleasant way.

"Oh, goodness, why does everyone ask that?" comes her exasperated response. "As if I had no superior means of altering someone's perception should I wish to. Honestly."

Her reply further horrifies me. One, everyone?! How many people has she done this to, whatever this is? Two, she has better ways of fucking with someone's head than drugging them? I can feel my throat swallow involuntarily. And three, how and when did she get even taller? Here, in this space that is by no means small, she towers over me, even more than she did back in the bookshop.

How?! How is any of this even possible? This can't be real...there's just no way. I seem to have become a statue, frozen in place, staring at her with wide unblinking eyes.

"Oh, dear. Seems as though I made things worse. Here, let us have a little sit and a little conversation." She gestures to a chair and footstool that I know for sure weren't here before. Gracefully, this Amazon plants herself in the chair and motions for me to take the ottoman. With somewhat rigid movements, I comply.

"Now," she begins once I'm seated, "I do realize this is a lot for you to take in. So I'm going to explain it to you, then allow you to ask as many questions as you need to, alright?" All I can manage is to nod my head while continuing to stare at her.

"Fantastic. I believe your first questions pertained to traveling here and what I had done to you, quickly followed by where we are, so I'll start with those. You, my dear, have traveled into that lovely blank book I handed you back in my shop. This book is now your adventure, the grand one I promised you in fact. We have been transported into your very own Fairytale!" she says with emphasis, throwing her arms out wide.

It seems she has paused for dramatic effect, so I finally manage an "uh-huh" in reply. She appears somewhat disappointed, but only for a heartbeat, before she continues.

"As you go about your life and adventures here, the book will fill with your thoughts and actions as words printed upon its pages. Then once your story is complete and you reach the book's conclusion, I shall whisk you away back into the world you know and love. Having, of course, learned a valuable lesson with many a thrilling tale to recount to your various niblings." Once done with that confusing explanation, she leans forward with an almost concerned expression on her face.

"That is, if you actually want to stay here for a time and have a bit of fun? I'm currently wondering if you were as ready for this as I thought you were back at the shop." Giving me a long perusal with furrowed brows, she leans fully back into her chair, hand resting under her chin in contemplation. Finally finding my voice again, I quickly interject into her noticeably doubtful thoughts.

"Hold on, hold on! Give me a second to take it all in. You gotta realize that what you're saying sounds ridiculous. This," and I gesture wildly, "doesn't happen in real life. This only happens in movies, books, or to people high off their ass! So excuse me for needing a little time." Weird that her dismissal of me has gotten me all fired up, but it most certainly has. Mentally, I quickly piece together everything she just said.

"To recap, you've transported me into this fairytale book to make some kind of story out of whatever it is I'm supposed to do here, yeah? Then once the story is complete, I just go back home all hunky-dory? So what kind of book is this? What exactly did you drop me into that I'm supposed to complete?" I take a look at my surroundings once more, then freeze as the pieces click into place. We were talking about D&D, about fantasy and adventure, and now I find myself surrounded by mounds of treasure.

"Is this...is this a dragon's hoard?" I ask softly in an unbelieving and shaking voice. "Am, am I here to slay a dragon or something?!" The panic I begin to feel is palpable. Her loud laugh startles me as it echoes off the damp walls.

"Ha ha! No! Oh no, no, no. This is far too small for a dragon's horde. Well, maybe if it were a terribly young dragon, but even then…" She continues to laugh at my apparently foolish question. Rude. I mean, I thought it was a logical assumption. Dabbing a bit of moisture from the corner of her eye, she finally fills me in on where I actually am.

"We currently find ourselves in the treasure hold of a thieves' guild. The Avenston Thieves Guild to be exact."

"Excuse me, what?!"

"Well, you said you like playing the character of a rogue, who is often sneaky. And many of your hobbies align quite nicely with that of a thief, with a little training up, of course." Once more, I see the mischievous smile play across her perfect face. "So, what do you say? Are you up for the challenge?"

She just leaves that question hanging in the air between us, and I don't know what to say. I don't know what to do, what to ask, or how to reply. Jumping up to my feet, I begin pacing around. I can't think sitting still. I've got to move around and work this out.

"How long do I have to decide?"

"Only as long as we stay here in this room," comes her calm reply.

"What if I say I'll stay, but end up not liking it? Or what if I leave, but decide I want to try my hand at having this adventure? Can I leave then come back, or can I stay now then quit later?"

"I'm afraid not, my dear. This is your one chance, your only opportunity to say yes or no."

"Ugh, damn it!" I continue to pace. "So what kind of quest are we talking about here? Obviously to train to become a thief in this city, but to what end?"

"That is entirely up to you, my dear. I am merely your entrance, your beginning, the 'call to adventure' as it were. What you decide to do after I leave is your choice. You could join an adventuring party on their quest, work for the town in some way, help strangers in need, solve a mystery. You don't even have to train to become a member of the Thieves Guild if you don't want to. I merely assumed you'd like it, so I brought you here." Leaning closer to me she adds, "Nothing like breaking into the Guild's innermost treasure store to get an automatic invitation to join their thieving ranks," then winks before sitting back.

She's got a good point there. Plus, I mean, of course I'd want to join the Thieves Guild. She wasn't wrong in assuming it'd be right up my alley. Gamer me has been a member of many a thieves' guild across loads of platforms. Mind almost made up, I have one big burning issue left.

"What if I die? What happens to me? Will I respawn here in this room or back in your store? Or will I really be dead? And even then, what will happen to my body?" I'm beginning to talk myself out of this all together with all these death questions, when this lady begins to laugh at me again. At least it's a pleasant laugh, I guess.

"Oh, Lexi, the main character doesn't die in their book. Well, not a forever death anyway. What kind of story would that be?" Her melodic laugh tinkles around the room for a moment before she continues. "Come, come, a decision does need to be made soon. Our presence here won't go unnoticed forever, and I have things I need to give you should you decide to stay."

"What kind of things?" is my quick reply. Now I'm itching to know what kind of loot this lady needs to give me for my quest. Maybe a special sword like in Zelda or something?!

"Is that a yes then? I do actually need you to say you agree to all this," she gestures vaguely around, "staying here, having an adventure, and not being able to come back until you've reached 'The End.'"

"Well, of course, I agree!" I practically shout while turning to face her. "I'd never be able to live with myself if I passed on this." Throwing my hands up, I continue, "It's only what people wait for their entire lives!" My words echo and reverberate more intensely than they should, and I feel an electric weight settle over my skin. Before I can examine the sensation it's gone and the shop lady is all too quickly back on her feet.

"Splendid!" she says with a clap of her hands. "Let's get you 'geared up,' as they say. First, that outfit! Far too noticeable a color for a thief." She snaps her fingers, and my clothes morph around me, becoming black as pitch and formfitting. The fabric is unlike anything I have ever felt before, sturdy yet thin and flexible. Damn! I wish I had a mirror because I bet I look as sexy as Catwoman right now!

"Next, the footwear. I believe these shall serve you nicely." Handing me a pair of black knee-high lace-up boots that came from nowhere, she gestures at one of the closed chests. "Sit down, and I'll demonstrate how to lace them quickly." I sit as instructed, wondering where the chair and ottoman went. I get one boot on, and as promised, she shows me a fun back and forth technique that is fast and surprisingly easy. Why have I never seen this before?!

She watches as I do up the second boot and tells me, "These boots will help significantly with your sneaking around. No one will be able to hear you in these."

"Are you serious?! Are these like Boots of Sneaking, or do they have a muffled movement charm on them?" Hopping up, I start walking around, testing the fit, feel, and sound. Sure enough, not only do they fit like a glove, I hear no sound at all while I walk, jump, and jog in place. This is fucking amazing!

"Oh, it's not just the boots that are silent, my dear. While wearing them, no clothing shall rustle nor keys jingle. Your entire being will be as muted as the abyss. Barring any words spoken." She laughs lightly. "Wouldn't be good everyday wear if you couldn't verbally communicate if you wanted to. Now come here. There is some knowledge I need to pass on to you as well."

I walk back over to her, and she places two fingers gently onto my forehead. I experience another bright flash of white light, quickly followed by a splitting headache and the sensation that my brain is too full.

"Ouch, lady! You really need to warn people before you do things like that." My eyes squeeze shut as I rub my temples in an effort to alleviate the pain and pressure that suddenly rounds my skull.

"Hmm. You may be right about that, little one. I'll see what I can do." Her tone gives me the impression that she won't be trying very hard and she may in fact enjoy surprising her victims.

"So, oh magnificent one," I say sarcastically as I open an eye at her, "what exactly did that just do to me?"

"Flattery will get you everywhere, Lexi dear." The way she says it, and her wicked smile, makes me flush a little. "That was me passing off some key information you will need in order to live in this land. The language known as the Common Tongue, both written and spoken forms, how the money system works,

and a little something extra I'll let you discover on your own."
Winking, she then hands me a crossbody bag. Again, manifested
from nowhere. "Inside, you will find two sets of everyday clothes,
a sleeping gown, a bag of coin, and some toiletries. And this," she
pulls a simple gold cuff bracelet, about two inches wide, from her
skirt pocket, "is a Menstruation Cuff. While wearing this, you shall
never find yourself with child." She begins to hand it to me, but I
hold up my hand and gesture it away.

"I actually don't need that. Got my tubes tied back in my
twenties, as soon as I could find a doctor who would do it for me."
Which was no easy feat, let me tell you. "I've known all my life that
giving birth wasn't for me." Not with how I grew up. Not with
what my family went through...what my father went through.

"Ah, well, it does also put a pause on your cycle, so there would
be no more bleeding while you wear it, but if you're sure-"

"Well, why didn't you say so?! Pass it over, lady!" I'm prancing
in place like a kid on their birthday waiting to open presents.
"Gimme, gimme!" The lady may chuckle at my antics but she
hands me the bracelet all the same.

I eagerly put it on and watch it resize itself to fit snugly but
comfortably a few inches above my wrist. It's pleasantly warm for
a few moments, before settling. The gold gleams beautifully next
to my darker skin tone. I've always looked good in gold, which is
good because I will NEVER be taking this little treasure off again.

Just as I'm going to ask about the mystery knowledge she's
given me, I hear muffled voices and movement coming from the
only door I can see in the place.

"Ah, and there is my cue to leave. I hope you have yourself a
marvelous adventure. Remember, I won't be coming back for you,

no matter how much you shout to the heavens for me. You will not be seeing me again until your story is complete." I nod my head in acknowledgement. "Oh, and you probably shouldn't tell them how you really got in here. Far more impressive if you leave me out of it."

"Yeah, I hadn't planned on telling these people that they are all just fictional characters in a book." I can hear the sounds of several locks unlocking, and my heartbeat starts to pound in my chest. This is it. The start of my very own magical adventure. I have the same jitters that I get when I'm about to spar in the ring or climb an unfamiliar rockwall.

"Well, come on! They're almost in. Assume a position! Unless you want them to find you standing awkwardly in the middle of the room? Strike a pose, dear." She gestures around the chamber, and I instantly realize she's right. This will be my first impression, the scene where the vault is opened to find a stranger casually waiting inside for them.

"Right, right!" I say as I wildly scan the room, searching for the best spot. Muttering to myself, "Okay, okay," when I decide to perch on the chest I used earlier when putting on my boots. Hopping up, I put my weight on one arm and lean back, cross my legs, and peer at my nails giving my best 'I'm so over this' face, then glance at the bookstore owner to ask, "How's this?" but she's gone. Completely vanished. Damn, I wanted to tell her to say bye to Harvey for me.

I don't get much time to regret not getting any final words before the last of the locks are undone and the door knob is turned. Quickly, I assume my best nonchalant appearance as the door flies open and several people burst into the room, stopping short when they see me sitting there waiting on them.

"About time," I manage to say in an exasperated tone, even though my nerves are a wreck. "Feels like I've been sitting here for ages waiting for you all to discover me." I held off until this moment to turn my head to see them all. And I'm glad I did, or else I may not have gotten my lines out. What stands before me—and slowly coming in closer to surround—are honest-to-gawd fantasy creatures. I see what look like twin elves both with orange-red hair, a lilac woman with iridescent dragonfly wings, a guy that could be David the Gnome's goth cousin, a TMNT-looking dude with a Friar Tuck haircut, a woman with a human torso but a sapphire blue snake's tail, and an older guy who appears to be as human as me.

The human guy flashes a glance over to the snake lady, which must communicate something as she begins to slither around the room tapping the walls. Each time her fingers touch the stone, blue symbols of light I didn't notice before flare to life, then dim again once she lifts her fingers. She continues to do this in the background as the others circle around me fully. I try my best to keep up my nonchalant facade.

"Well?" the regular-looking dude asks while folding his arms over his chest. He appears to be older, I'd say in his sixties, with stringy dirty brown graying hair that falls to his shoulders. His frame is wiry in a way that could sway to be either malnourished or agile. Seeing as how he is in the Thieves Guild, I bet he could play the unassuming beggar on the street with ease, then quickly disappear before you even knew what happened.

"Well what?" I ask sweetly, feigning ignorance as to what his question implied. This makes him narrow his eyes at me.

"Why are you sitting in the middle of the Thieves Guild loot vault as pretty as you please just waiting to be discovered? Were you after something? Are you from another guild? Do you have a death wish?" The turtle monk to my left cracks his knuckles at the last question, while one of the redheaded twins leisurely tosses and catches a knife in the air to my right. The snake lady, having come full circle, makes her way over to us, giving a short shake of her head to the questioning glance from the old man. "And how did you manage to get in here without tripping or breaking any of our wards?"

"I didn't steal anything. You can check my bag to make sure," I take my bag off and offer it up. The unoccupied twin quickly snatches it. "The coin you find in there I came here with, so paws off. And no, there isn't anything in here that I particularly want." The twin quickly checks my bag and even sifts through all my coins.

"Nothing of ours in here, Gav," the twin tells the old man. "And nothing distinctive to hint at where she's from either. Even the coins are the most common." This twin gives me an appraising look as he hands me back my bag, almost like he appreciated the effort of concealing anything about myself. Not that I did that on purpose, but I'm not about to admit it. Gav nods at the twin in acknowledgment and moves his hands to rest on his hips.

"Care to enlighten us as to how," he takes an audible sniff and is surprised, "a full human managed to make her way down into the depths of our hideout, undetected by any? That is no small feat."

"Oh, a girl has got to have some secrets." I bat my eyes prettily at him, which does elicit the smallest hint of a smile to tug at the corners of his mouth. Seizing on the favorable reaction I continue, "And I thought the reason for the break-in would be obvious..." I pause for effect. "...I wanted to impress you, the Guild." I use both hands to motion at the group around me.

"I think this human wants to join our ranks, Gav," the snake lady says with a full smile. A smile that is made only slightly disconcerting by the fangs she sports. "I'll admit that I'm impressed. Not many could get past a Naga or her wards, especially mine." Her slitted eyes scan me from head to toe. "I would never have even known she was here if she hadn't been shouting." She arches an eyebrow at that in question. I laugh kind of nervously in response and quickly make up a plausible lie.

"Uh, yeah, that was me trying to sing." The Naga's eyebrows instantly shoot up. "I was bored! Thought you guys would never find me." Both twins burst out laughing, doubling over and smacking each other. "What are you two laughing for? It wasn't that bad! You didn't even really hear me."

The twins answer, back and forth between the two:

"You snuck in-"

"-past all the thieves-"

"-past all the traps-"

"-silent as the grave-"

"-past Neela-"

"-to get into our vault-"

"-and were so successful-"

"-and waited so long-"

"-that you got BORED?!" They finish in unison and explode into laughter once again.

"Yes, yes, boys," Gav interjects, "very funny." They continue their antics, one even pretending to fall asleep on a pile of treasure while the other fake yawns. Gav loudly clears his throat. "Come. I think we need to have a real conversation, and they could be at this for hours." Turning to the Naga, he continues, "Neela, could you secure the vault? I'm going to have a talk with this young lady." She nods and begins pushing the twins out with her tail. They have both begun singing off-key and loudly.

"Come." He gestures for me to follow him out the door. "Let's get somewhere quiet where we can talk about who you are and what joining the Thieves Guild entails."

Eager to begin, I follow hot on his heels out the door. I'd say everything has gone quite well so far. Could have been way worse. I'm not dead after all! Main character energy over here.

Chapter 3

Stone

"If I'm not mistaken, you were told to drop this, Stone," Chief Metis chides me as I struggle to sit in a too small chair in her office. She had instructed me to sit, to better tower over me, even though this chair was not made with Gargoyles in mind. "It was never even your case to begin with. You're on the Patrol Guard, not an Investigator." Something my superior has reminded me of countless times.

"Chief Metis, how can we possibly let this stand? That abduction ring set up shop in our city. It is our duty to bring those involved to justice." I am still unable to wrap my head around the fact that no one else is as upset by these turn of events as I am.

"As I've explained to you before, that was a Goblin matter, and the Grath Goblin Family handled the situation. No one was killed or dealt life altering damage," the black-coated Centaur recites to me once more, pinching the bridge of her nose. "The Goblins involved were punished according to their family law. We could not intervene as it was not our jurisdiction."

"But that's just it!" I rebut, swiftly standing. "It wasn't just Goblins involved. There is significant evidence to support that another unknown party hired those Goblins to abduct all those people. If you would inspect what I've found, I'm sure-"

"Enough, Stone!" she yells at me, slamming her hands on her desk. Metis does not often lose her temper, but when she does it's best to back off. "I need you to drop this before you force me to drop you from the Order all together." I'm so stunned by her threat that I sink back down into the chair with an audible creak. Taking a calming breath, she continues.

"You understand that I took a chance even putting you on Patrol. You know your grandfather greatly disapproves of your chosen path. He holds much sway in Avenston as head of the Gargoyle Clan and wants you to fail so you'll return to where he thinks you belong." Her brown eyes find mine for an instant before I look away, but I see the pity there all the same. Shifting my gaze over her shoulder, I catch my reflection in the glass of the window.

My ebony black horns are perfectly symmetrical on either side of my head, curling up and back with the dulled point resting just behind my long pointed ears. A two inch strip of inky colored hair runs back from my forehead in a braid, leaving the sides shaved to the scalp to show off my Clan tattoos that encircle the base of my horns. My skin, a shade of indigo my Aunties call Mystic Midnight, is muted in the dirty opaque window. I scowl at the filth, thinking Metis needs to have someone clean that for her.

"Stone, you are smart, clever, and notice things most others don't. And while I acknowledge you'd be an asset to the Investigative Team, I can't put you there. Not yet at any rate. This path you've chosen, to defy tradition and your family, will be a long and arduous one. You have to be patient. You can't make waves or push too hard too fast." It's nothing I don't already know, but it's still a hard tonic to swallow.

"I understand," I finally admit after a long pause. "It's just....I find it difficult to drop something that is so unjust. There is more to this, and it pains me that we are doing nothing about it, Chief." Bringing my eyes back to hers, I boldly add, "It feels like us letting a crime family handle something so egregious, that took place in our city, marks us as disgraced. It makes me feel ashamed of the Order." I instantly realize I pushed too far by her stiffened body posture, flanks twitching, eager to kick the wall behind her.

"The only thing I see disgraceful here," cold venom seeping in her tone, "is a Patrolman who doesn't know his place and thinks himself better than his superiors. You are done with this," she tells me with all the finality of death. "If I see so much as a chicken scratch note anywhere in this building regarding this case, you are done here. Do you understand me, Patrolman?"

"Yes, Chief."

"I expect a formal apology by the end of today to the Grath Family on your behalf for continuing to meddle in their affairs. That is, if you wish to maintain a position here." Her demeanor has already dismissed me as she brings her focus back to the paperwork on her desk. "As far as we can prove, the Graths are upstanding pillars of this community, and they are to be treated as such. Now, get out of my office. I have real cases to attend to."

Standing from the small squeaky chair, I offer a curt, "Chief," before walking out. It takes everything within me to contain my anger as I stride through the halls of the Order Unit 15 building. I make my way straight to the top floor launching balcony, then angrily leap to the sky. I need to fly! I need to feel the wind against my flesh, to be alone to process my torrent of emotions, and to have time to arrange my thoughts.

How can I be the disgrace?! I, who have chosen a path not just to serve, but to solve, to truly help by using all my talents to aid the people of this city. The Chief was correct about my mind. I am better than most when it comes to putting pieces of information together and seeing things that others do not. This is the whole reason I diverged from my familial path, why I do not simply guard a singular structure in this town as is tradition amongst my people. I want to do so much more!

Though my grandfather does not see it this way, I believe I am still upholding the values of our Clan. Why guard and protect only a building, a family, a place? I feel it is my duty to protect all in need. While this argument is what finally convinced grandfather to release me from the Clan's duties and allow me to be a Patrolman, it did not convince him, or anyone else, into letting me become an Investigator. Not yet anyway.

Others may push my true goals to the side, but I will not lose sight of them.

I breathe in deeply, the crisp evening air filling my lungs, its coolness a balm to my anger and mind. Once my temper is allayed, I reflect on the interaction more closely. Metis was correct about the Graths. They skirt the laws well and give back to those in the city. They grease all the right palms and take care of those in need, when it's advantageous to them. So I'll write that letter and even ask if I can deliver it myself to apologize in person. I'll let them think I've dropped this too, and if I happen to get the chance to scope out their headquarters, all the better.

Noticing my surroundings for the first time since I took off, I'm not surprised to find myself near the Clan's tower. Once my home and still the place of my ancestors, I am often drawn to its heights when seeking solitude and comfort. Within the pinnacle of the tower rests the statues of Clan members who have passed. When a Gargoyle dies, our remains return to the stone from which we were created.

Since boyhood, I found myself confiding in the stone effigies of my forebears. Talking to them helps to calm me, as I work through my thoughts and feelings, in a way no living being has been able to do.

Landing deftly, I walk the familiar open space where my ancestors rest. Here they are able to gaze out at the city that we've protected since its founding, though many on the lowest floors are so old that details have been erased with time and erosion. Once we crumble completely the Clan removes them, each of us carrying a piece to a nearby mountain, so that they may return to the earth from which we all come. It's a beautiful ceremony and one that gives me peace in knowing my fate. That I will rest alongside my family for decades, before eventually becoming one with the mountain we all came from, makes me feel connected to something much bigger than myself.

I walk amongst my ancestors for an hour or so, mulling over my plans, talking things out with a great-great-great uncle, and mentally writing that apology letter. The whistling of the winds between the statues and columns are the only sounds my brain need contend with. No chatter, no carts, no gongs or chimes or music. Just me, silence, and wind.

When I finally land back at Order Unit 15, I march right to my desk and write the letter as instructed. Once complete and checked for errors, I take it to Chief Metis's office. Knocking on the frame of the open office door, I wait for her assent to enter.

"Stone," she answers, already sounding exasperated with me, "I've told you before that you don't have to wait for me to say 'enter' when my door is open. Open means I'm available." Stepping through the threshold, I find her in the exact same position I left her in, standing at her tall desk reading over paperwork. The only difference is that her tight, black, low bun now has a writing quill sticking in it.

"Sorry, Chief. It still feels rude." She rolls her eyes and begins to stretch and pop her joints. "I have the letter as requested." As I slide it over her desk to her, I add, "If I may, I would like to be the one to deliver it. I feel it would be more genuine if I apologize in person as well as hand off the letter." I want the Graths to completely trust that I have given up on this endeavor. Don't want them thinking I'm still investigating this matter. Her eyes dance across the letter as she silently reads it before replying to my request.

"Very well written, Stone. I would expect no less from you." With a slight smirk, she slides the letter back over to me. "And I agree, it would help smooth things over and put this messy business to rest if you deliver this yourself." Quickly glancing outside, noting the setting sun, she adds, "You should have enough time to do so before your rounds begin. Make sure the Graths don't keep you too long." With that, I seem to be dismissed again as she continues to read through reports.

I offer up a, "Chief," before leaving her office once more.

Tucking the letter securely into the wide waistband of my kilt, I grab my Patrol Guard sash from my desk. A truly hideous shade of chartreuse, it helps identify me to the citizens of Avenston and shows that I am actively on duty. I decide to go ahead and put it on, adjusting it across my torso, since I am technically on Order business.

Flying high once more over the city, I quickly make my way to the Grath family manor. I land outside the iron gates and approach the two Goblin guards stationed there. Their beady black eyes squint at me in distrust.

"I have a letter to be hand delivered to the head of the Grath family, along with a personal message." They'll be getting no further details from me about it unless I absolutely have to. This is humiliating enough as it is.

They take their time scrutinizing me before they finally magic the gate open with a snap of the fingers. It swings free noiselessly as I give them a nod and enter. As I pass them, I notice one has taken out a small hand mirror, no doubt informing those within the manor of my arrival.

The lawns and hedges in the courtyard are perfectly manicured in a way that I appreciate, but there are far too many fountains. It makes it feel too crowded, and their placements aren't in alignment with how it ought to be. They're too haphazard in arrangement and size. As I walk up a brick-lined path to the front of the manor, I glance up at the Goblins patrolling the upper two balconies, noting their weapons and watchful eyes.

The large front doors to the mansion swing open before I reach them and the head of the Grath family himself steps out. This I had not expected! I had thought to be kept waiting and eventually shown to an oversized and gaudy office. I had anticipated a male eager to show off his power and finery to a lowly patrolman who thought himself better. I had expected a male who wanted to put me in my place by showing off. It seems I was wrong on all counts, and instead I find a male who may already be on his guard when it comes to me.

"My cousins tell me you have a letter for me," a gruff voice that's all business addresses me, "along with a message." The head of this family is dressed in the 'suited' attire that the Grath Goblins have adopted. They aren't the only ones who wear this newer style of dress, but they are the most consistent, wearing this fashion almost exclusively. The tailored coat and pants are a sapphire blue that shines in the fading light of the day, almost like a beetle. Chains of gold peak out from under a crisp white button-up shirt, while gold and jeweled earrings line both of his long pointed ears. This Goblin dresses to impress while showing his wealth and status. Too bad for him my respect is earned, not automatically given or swayed by such things.

"Yes, sir," I answer, keeping my personal feelings out of my voice. "I have written you a letter apologizing for prying further into a matter that was deemed a family situation. I let my curiosity and drive for unanswered questions push me into a situation that was no longer a concern for the Order." I hand him the letter in question as I continue. "I asked my chief to let me hand deliver it to you so I could offer my apologies in person as well." I dip my head, lower my eyes, and bring a fist to my chest. "I am sorry for any offense that I caused while investigating this abduction situation."

Releasing my hand, I bring my eyes to rest on the largest gold loop in his right ear, keeping the letter he's holding in my periphery.

He hasn't made a move to open it but is instead playing with it, moving it effortlessly around his fingers while leaning against the doorframe.

"I didn't realize they were letting members of the Patrol Guard investigate the goings on in Avenston these days," his eyes pointedly on my sash.

"They do not, sir. It was an action I took upon myself without authorization." I detest having to admit that part out loud, though I did include it in my letter, suspecting it was an aspect Metis would want. Needing me to take the blame, which is technically mine.

"Ah, yes, I've heard about the Gargoyle who has aspirations of being an Investigator despite his Clan's, and grandfather's, objections." I can feel my jaw tick at this statement, at his knowledge of me and my situation. "So you decided that you'd use an unfortunate incident involving a few outcast members of my family to assist in your dreams and raise your station, is that right? And what better pawns to use in your climb than a family you see as beneath you, hmm?"

"That's not it at all!" I blurt out before I can stop myself.

"Oh, is that so? Well then, Patrolman, enlighten me." He crosses his arms and legs, waiting for an explanation.

"I didn't choose this case for any personal feelings regarding your family. It just felt so...off. Things didn't add up to me. The coordinated and wide sweeping actions of these Goblins does not match up with the drugged-up Iynk users responsible. I felt like there was more to this, that they were hired by an outside unknown entity, and that this may just be the tip of the leviathan's tail." I probably shouldn't have told him my suspicions, but I still feel the need to be heard about this. Maybe he's the one who can actually do something about it? That is, if he isn't in on it. Silently, he regards me for a moment, his shrewd eyes boring into me.

"Seems the gossip was right about you being smarter than you look. Too bad you're wasting it on the Order, stuck in a dead end Patrol Guard posting." He clicks his teeth and stands straight once more, turning to go back inside. "If ever you decide you want to put that brain and brawn of yours to real use, come back here and ask to speak to me again." I'm glad his back is now to me so he doesn't see the ripple of surprise, mingled with disgust, flash across my face.

Upon hearing the door click closed, I launch myself into the air, my face frozen in a scowl. I don't know what to be more offended by, the fact that he thinks so little of the Order or the notion that I would ever work for him or his family. It will be a cold day in Muspelheim before I work with a criminal.

Chapter 4

Alexis

G av walks us through several underground tunnels. At least I'm assuming we're underground as that's what it feels like: low ceiling tunnels, no windows, slight dampness in the air, and that inexplicable feeling of depth. After passing through a much larger chamber where other members of the guild are chatting, laughing, and eating, he opens an old wooden door, then directs me inside. It's a smaller room that only contains a table, a few chairs, and a bookshelf. Closing the door, he rounds the table, taking a seat as he gestures for me to do the same.

"Now that we're away from those laughing idiots, let's have a real discussion." Looping my bag on the back of the chair across from him, I take a seat. "So you want to join the Avenston Thieves Guild. Why?" Setting his elbows on the table, he steeples his fingers, patiently awaiting my answer. Knowing that the best lies are founded in truth, I offer up the most factual answer I can conjure up.

"I've recently found myself to be incredibly bored with my life, eventually realizing I needed a drastic change. I knew nothing would happen for me if I stayed at home, so I set out into the world." Since he's nodding his head at me, I continue. "As a kid,

I'd always play the thief with my brothers in our silly little games. I've had many, many hobbies in my life, but I've only just spotted that most of them align with my childhood fascination of being a thief. Hell, my older brother even got me a lock picking kit as a birthday gift this year."

"Is that so?" Gav asks with an arched eyebrow. "And where is this kit? It was not in your belongings."

"Yeeeaaaahhhh," I string out the word. "I kinda left on a whim and totally didn't pack it." I offer him a sheepish grin. "I knew if I didn't leave right away, I'd never get my chance. Not getting any younger after all."

"I'm inclined to let you try given what you just pulled off. Though it is a decision left up to our council, you'd have my vote." I grin in excitement, wiggling in my chair. "However, this doesn't mean you'll automatically become a member, no matter how impressive your entrance was. All must train and prove themselves, with many challenges and tests." I nod, showing I understand, knowing full well I need the training...as much training as I can get actually. "Alright, if this is truly a path you wish to take, I'll go speak to the other council members." He stands and begins to walk out, but pauses after opening the door, staring at me in astonishment. "Huh, I almost forgot. What's your name?"

"Oh, sorry. It's Alexis, but everyone calls me Lexi."

"Well, Lexi, come out here and wait in the main hall. I'm sure everybody is dying from curiosity. Your first challenge: seeing if the other members scare you off," he says with a teasing smile before turning to walk out.

I follow after him, then choose an empty table to wait at. I only get a few moments to myself to think about how weird it is that not only have I understood a whole new language, but have also been speaking in it fluently. That shop lady sure knows her stuff; I'll give her that.

"So how'd it go?!" the twins ask in unison as they plop down on the bench on either side of me. "Guessing well," the left one says. "Since you're still here," the right one follows up. Now that I'm paying attention, I notice some differences between the two. Yes, they both have long straight red hair, light green eyes, pointed ears, and look remarkably like the same lean muscular person. But the one on my right has a slight scar through his left eyebrow, while the one on my left has a line of gold piercings up his right ear. They both exude the same playfully mischievous energy though.

Soon I find myself surrounded by people, asking me questions, joking with one another, laughing, drinking, and telling their stories of how they got the guild's attention. Sounds like it's not uncommon to do something daring to get an invitation. Most are really impressed by what I've done, though somewhat disbelieving given the fact that I'm a 'full human.'

I get quite a surprise as a haughty translucent figure floats through a wall and over to the table. Is..is this guy a ghost?! White as the palest moon and slightly blurring at the edges, this guy is thin in a way that almost looks delicate and has a large nose that is the defining feature on his face. Seriously, if he wasn't a ghost, I'd say it was the most interesting thing about him.

"So it's true then?!" the ghost begins. "A mere human broke into our vault. Neela must be losing her touch if that's the case." My hackles instantly raise at the ghost's dismissive tone.

"I wouldn't let her hear you saying that," the purple woman with dragonfly wings chimes in. "Her wards are still good enough to trap you, should she wish it." But the ghost merely dismisses her words with a wave of his hand.

"So then, human, I suppose you have given your choice a great deal of thought. What have you narrowed it down to? Perhaps we could help you decide what would be best for the guild and your career as a thief." I stare at this specter in evident confusion.

"What are you talking about?" The question comes out a little sassier than I intended. "What choice?" It's the twins who answer excitedly.

"What you want to become of course," says the right.

"You've got loads of options since humans are such a blank slate," chimes in the left. Gesturing at himself and his redheaded duplicate, "We're Fox Shifters."

"I'd love nothing more than to sink my teeth into you, sweetcheeks." The twin to my right adds with a wink and mischievous smile that dances up into his eyes.

"Vampire is also a great option." The lavender woman adds with a thoughtful expression on her face. "We could use another vampire in the guild. Though having a succubus could be an asset as well. I once knew–" Before she can continue, the twins burst in.

"Yes, yes, a succubus!" they chant in unison.

"Oh shut up, you two!" a bull-looking dude speaks over the twins while rolling his eyes. "This is a serious and life-altering decision here. Stop trying to make it all about what your cocks would like." The massive bullman brings his attention back to me. "Don't let the likes of them influence your decision. Look at me," he opens his hands wide so I can indeed get a good eyeful of the massive creature standing before me. "I'm not what one would typically picture as a thief, now am I? But I didn't let that stop me.

In fact, I often use that to my advantage." He's got a smile that beams with pride, as he hooks his thumbs into his belt.

I'm starting to get incredibly excited. I hadn't thought about this part of my adventure. Getting to choose to become a fantasy creature! Oh, I can't fucking wait! It's all a dream come true. I need to start making a list of all the things I could be turned into before I decide. This is a big deal and does deserve some real consideration.

"I would suggest becoming a ghost, as it truly is the best option," the asshat floating around the table interjects, "but not everyone is prepared for that kind of commitment." He peers down at me like he thinks I certainly wouldn't be committed enough. "And of course, there's no guarantee that you would be able to come back as a ghost at all. Then there's the years of training and waiting for your abilities to strengthen and improve." He's begun strolling through the center of the table with his chin up in the air, while all those around us are rolling their eyes and groaning, clearly having heard all this shit before.

"Please spare us, Valda," the right twin groans.

"Nobody even wants to be like you," Lefty gestures at the ghost in the table who has stopped to glare at them.

"Yeah, so stop talking like it's some grand prize," Righty follows up. "Not like you even set out to become a ghost, and you certainly didn't do it just to be a good thief."

"A good thief," Valda sneers. "My boys, I am the best thief this city has ever known or will ever know." At this, both twins make farting noises at him. I admit, it does make me giggle. Only slightly put off, the ghost continues.

"Anyway," he starts loudly, "back to the question at hand." Valda scowls at the fox twins before peering down his nose at me once more. "What are your plans? What do you want to become? Since staying a human is obviously out of the question." This statement makes my whole body rigid.

"Excuse me?" I ask through gritted teeth.

"Oh, come now. You must have realized that a human couldn't possibly be a decent thief, let alone a thief good enough to be a member of this guild." He's waving his hand in the air like he can fan away my obvious ire. "I mean, the very idea is laughable to say the least. You can't possibly succeed here as a human."

White hot rage has risen within me in a matter of seconds. Who the fuck does this guy think he is? He doesn't know me! How dare he think I am incapable of doing this. I had been on board with becoming some kick-ass mythical being, but now...oh, now I have to prove this asshole wrong and wipe that smug expression off his stupid transparent face. Quickly, I get to my feet and am satisfied to see that we are eye level.

"Watch me." It comes out like a growl as it passes through my gritted teeth. Challenge accepted, motherfucker!

Fuck that fucking ghost! It's been three months and he still swaggers around, tsking at my every mistake, waiting for me to fail. Waiting for me to give in and admit that I can't do this as a human, that I need to change, to become something else. Well, I don't! I have met every challenge, passed every test, and succeeded in all my training. It's actually been quite a fun and rewarding experience. Each day there is something new and interesting to learn. These months haven't been easy, but damn they sure haven't been boring.

Between the daily exercises, practice drills, tests, fake heists, and tag-alongs, I've found myself in my element! Learning how this new world works and discovering how old and new skills intermingle has been thrilling. Not to mention the high that comes from overcoming a challenge. Priceless.

I often reflect upon my time here and this supposed book that's being written based on my adventures. At this point, I'm pretty much convinced that my book will actually be a trilogy. I mean, Book One has to contain all this training. My ups and downs, trial and errors, and the fun little dalliances I've had thus far. The twins...oh boy, that was an amazing few weeks to be sure. Just thinking about what we three got up to, and where we got up to it, gets me all hot and bothered. If I keep thinking along these lines, I might just have to pay them a little visit later. Then again, my time with Neela was quite thrilling as well. That snake lady really knows how to satisfy a gal, no doubt about it. But she wanted more than I was willing to give her. I'm not ready for a relationship just yet, still having way too much fun testing out these new waters. All the different fish I've caught have been so unique and thrilling in their own ways. I'm not nearly satisfied yet.

So you see, dear reader, this has just been the tip of the iceberg of my story, and I hope you've enjoyed the read so far. But soon, very soon, I'd bet Book One will be over. I've only got one more test left, one final challenge before I am finally considered a full member of the Thieves Guild of Avenston. Then off to Book Two, where my famous exploits as a real thief will unfold. Along with finally choosing and living as a fantasy being.

Fuck that ghost. It's his fault that I haven't become some awesome fantasy being yet. Couldn't let him think I couldn't do this as my good old human self, now could I?!

"What delicious thoughts were you pondering over here, sweetcheeks?" Aiden asks smoothly. "We could smell your desire all the way across the room." He and his twin, Brayden, have joined me at the work table where I'm timing myself picking a lock.

"You wouldn't believe me if I told you," I reply while keeping my focus on the lock. To my happy surprise, I discovered the locks in this world are easier to pick than at home. Well, the non-magicked locks are anyway. The locks with the colored light symbols have to be handled a little differently first. Thankfully Gav, my mentor, has a wealth of expertise in the art of thieving and has shared his knowledge openly. Once he realized I had the ability to actually see wards, the surprise gift that shop lady gave me, any lingering uncertainty he had in me becoming a full member faded away. Apparently, this is not a gift possessed by most and gives me a definite upper hand.

"Oh, I don't know, Lexi," Brayden states with playful lust in his voice, "we might be persuaded to believe any number of things you tell us."

"Stop distracting me, you two. Can't you see I'm busy?" I've successfully picked this lock twice while they hover around tempting me with a good time. But I won't be swayed! I'm getting in the zone, and tonight will go off without a hitch.

I'm actually quite proud of myself for even getting to this point and also for staying focused on repeatedly picking this lock while these two men—er, males is what they prefer to be called here—try to entice me. It wasn't long after arriving in this land that I realized I didn't have my ADHD meds. At first, I was being stubborn about asking for help, but thankfully the twins also have my brand of neurodivergence. Flickermind, they call it here, and after a little visit to an apothecary, I've been a-okay.

"We could help relieve some of that nervousness you may have flittering around..." Damn, these fox boys will not give up.

"Yes, we know exactly how to calm your nerves," Aiden whispers in my ear. My body instantly heats as visions of our past sexcapades dance in my mind. I have no doubt they could do exactly as they claim, but at this moment, it's focus I require, not distraction.

"Sorry to disappoint you, boys, but what you're offering is not what I need right now." Finally glancing up at them, I add, "But maybe later," with a wink. After I succeed tonight, I'm due for a little reward, and being tied up and played with by these two sounds like a damn good reward to me.

"Good luck," they say in unison as they finally depart. But before I can resume my lockpicking, Gav takes a seat across from me, giving me a bit of a start. Even though I know he's a Cat Shifter, his ability to move silently still gets me sometimes.

"I'm surprised to find you here, doing that. I'd have thought you'd be pouring over your plans and the layout of the building," he offers by way of greeting.

"Oh, I am," I confess. "This is just to keep my hands busy. But up here," I tap my head with a slender tool, "I'm walking my route, going over my plans again and again while also coming up with different scenarios in case things go sideways." Looking up at him, I offer a guilty smile, "I may have taken a bit more Flickermind elixir than usual today, and I think it may have been too much." He gives me an exasperated sigh. "I know, I know," I offer before he can scold me. But instead of telling me that probably wasn't a good idea, he touches my hand to still me.

"You're going to be just fine. You are prepared, you are skilled, you have trained, and you are ready for this." He says it so earnestly while holding my gaze that I almost get choked up...almost. "Everyone gets the jitters before their first solo mission." He smiles as he removes his hand. "I threw up three times!" he confesses while laughing at himself.

"You?! You're always so calm and nonchalant. I can't imagine you getting that nervous."

"I'll have you know it took years to develop that. And one day, you too will be as old and crotchety as me."

"You're not crotchety." I roll my eyes at him. "Trust me, I've met my share of crotchety people, and you ain't it."

"Be that as it may, I want to reassure you that you are going to do just fine tonight. You've been on several missions with many members and haven't been caught yet. And we'll be around in case things go awry. So you aren't totally alone, not really. You are ready, and I'm proud to have had you as a pupil." He clears his throat, "Now, go get ready, and don't forget to use the scent-killing soap this time." He eyes me, making me remember when I showed up once for a heist reeking of human, Naga, and sex. I was instantly sent away, unable to join that mission.

"Will do, boss!" I stand, grab my tools, and leave the common hall to get ready for my first ever solo heist, the final test for becoming a full member of the Thieves Guild. I offer a silent prayer to whatever gods can hear me that nothing goes wrong tonight. Though I understand that 'main characters' don't typically die in their books, that shop lady never did answer any of my questions about it. And I've got no desire to find out the hard way.

Chapter 5

Alexis

My head is killing me! And why is the world upside down?

I squint and blink my eyes at the too bright room, trying to make out my surroundings. The taste in my mouth is disgusting, and the crick in my neck is uncomfortable to say the least. Moving my head cautiously, I realize I'm hanging off the edge of a bed. Well, that would explain the upside down part. Finally opening my eyes fully, my gaze comes to rest on a towering figure looming in the corner, arms crossed over a massive chest, scowl etched across his face.

"Who the fuck are you, and why the fuck were you watching me sleep?" My voice sounds like a bullfrog croak. I need some water, bad. Before the living statue can answer, my foot grazes across the flesh of another person in the bed with me. Turning my head, I see a woman who looks vaguely familiar. The barmaid? "Oh, shoot, bro, is she your girl or something? I don't think she said anything about you last night?" Sitting up in the bed, my body reminds me that I'm getting too old to party like that. Cautiously, I bring my hands up to massage my temples.

"She is not my female nor is she the reason I am here." His voice is all gravel and frustration. "I'm here because you–" He instantly stops talking, quickly turning his head away the same moment I feel the bedsheet fall from my chest, exposing my breasts. They're small—I'm a B cup—but still perky and perfectly adequate in my opinion. I haven't envied larger chested women in a long time, not after hearing about all the hassle and back trouble.

But it was polite of him to look away, so I pull the sheet back up with an "Oops," of apology. I mean, he is standing in my room after all. Well, I think it's my room? My eyes quickly scan the space as I try to remember where I am and what happened last night. Glancing around, I piece together that I'm in a room at the tavern I chose to celebrate in last night. That's right, and this lady here is the barmaid that was serving us. We had been flirting all night, and after her shift, we came up here and–

"Please put some clothes on," the gruff voice rudely interrupts my pleasant memories of my time with the barmaid. This guy, who I'm pretty sure is a Gargoyle, is holding out a dress to me with his head still turned. He's tall, like really tall, with great big bat-like wings, and I think I see a tail back there. His massive hands could palm my face, his body musculature is so perfect that it appears as if it was carved from stone. Hmm, given he is a Gargoyle, makes me wonder if it actually was. His strip of black hair is in a Viking-looking braid and framed by two ebony horns that curve back. He's wearing a black-and-green plaid kilt and his exposed chest is covered only by a sash. A sash of a truly unfortunate greenish yellow color that clashes horribly with his entire vibe. At least his skin color, a purply blue hue of some kind, suits him.

Unfortunately, the sash also renders this tall drink of water un-fuckable. He's a cop. Gav went over the sash system with me, and this guy is a member of the Patrol Guard. Two guesses as to what he wants from me. Time to have a little fun with this beat cop who interrupted my sleep. Putting on a roguish grin, I begin to play.

"Oh, that's not my dress, big boy. It's hers." I slink from the bed, letting the sheet fall from my form as I effortlessly walk over to a sink in the small bathroom. Grabbing a glass, I tap the blue gem for cold water. Once the cup is full, I stride back out and lean against the doorframe, fully nude and uncaring, as I drink my fill.

"Would you please put some clothes on, ma'am? I have an important matter to discuss with you, and I'd prefer–"

"AAHHHH!!!" a scream erupts from the direction of the bed. The barmaid has woken up and seems to be none too pleased to find a strange Gargoyle standing in the room with us. I understand her feelings, given that we are both naked, but I do wish she hadn't screamed. My head throbs all the more now.

"Sorry, ma'am. I mean you no harm," he begins, head once again turned. He tosses the dress in her direction. "Here's your dress. I would ask that you put it on and leave, as I have a matter to discuss with your bedmate. I have already confirmed with your boss that you were here working during the time the incident occurred and only just met this female during your shift last night. If I have any follow-up questions for you, I will find you later, but for the time being I think it's best if you leave us."

The barmaid—sure wish I remembered her name—quickly dashes out the bedroom door while clutching the dress to her body, so hasty to leave that she didn't even bother to put it on. I doubt I'll be getting a second 'date' with her after this. Yet another negative mark to this Gargoyle.

"Thanks for scaring off my 'bedmate.' I should tell your superior about you breaking into my room and scaring the daylights out of two helpless, naked females who were sleeping." Still determined not to look at me, the Gargoyle strides over to the bed and flings the sheet at me, hitting me square in the face. "Ooph. Hey!"

"Cover yourself before I do it for you," he warns, voice cool as steel. Glaring at him, I wrap the cloth around my body like a toga. Because I'm cold, not because he told me to.

"I did not break in here either. I spoke to the owner, and he gave me permission along with the key to this room." With my naked body all wrapped up, he turns to glower at me before continuing. "Seems you haven't actually paid for this room yet, though your friends did settle the bar tab for your celebration last night. What were you and your group celebrating so earnestly?" Yeah, like I'm about to tell this cop that we were partying because I passed my final thieving test by stealing a ruby comb all by myself. Meeting his eyes, I cross my arms over my chest.

"Is that why you're here, to ask me about my party habits?" my tone laced with sarcasm. "What, did someone call about the noise level last night and you're finally getting around to it? I knew the Order was slow to respond, but damn."

In a single stride, the Gargoyle is towering over me, his face as hard as granite. Fuck he's tall. Tall and big in all the right ways. With a face so stern that it makes me want to push all his buttons.

"I am not here regarding a noise complaint nor will I be goaded into forgetting my true purpose by your slanders against the Order." His voice is as stern as his face. "A thief entered the home of a prominent family, broke into said family's vault, and stole a priceless heirloom last night. I tracked the thief all the way here. A thief who meets your description." Before I can make a wiseass remark about my skin color, he plows ahead. "Now tell me, where were you last evening before you arrived here?" He takes a step back while pulling a small notebook from his waistband, pen posed to write.

"Are you kidding me right now? I'm naked and you want to interrogate me?"

"You are not naked. You are wearing a bedsheet. And if you recall I urged you several times to put your own clothes on. Answer the question." His voice is flat with no feeling, all business. For some reason, that gets under my skin and it really irks me. I quickly adopt a disbelieving face, hoping he didn't catch that moment of frustration.

"You think me, a little ol'human, broke into a rich person's house. How would I even be able to do that?!" I fling both arms up in the air, feigning outrage and frustration. It's not my first time playing the human card, but it's quickly becoming my favorite as I watch him. "I'm not strong or agile, I don't have any special abilities, and I certainly don't possess any magic." I place my hands on my hips and cock one out. "So tell me, how exactly would I be capable of doing such a thing? Me, a poor, weak, defenseless human. Are you making fun of me or something?" Just as I'm gearing up to really turn the tables, he steps in closer once more, flaring out his wings as he does.

"Anyone is capable of anything if they put their minds to it, even you, human. So if you think for one instant that I will disregard you as a suspect simply because of what you are, you are sorely mistaken." I'm so taken aback I'm left speechless, completely stunned by his reaction. Everyone underestimates me here because I'm a human. It's been equally frustrating and useful. I narrow my eyes, searching his face more closely. These feel like the words of someone who's also been underestimated before. But who would ever underrate this guy?

"Search my room."

"What?!" He's so stunned that he actually rears back at my statement.

"If you really think I might have stolen something last night, search this room for it. I give you permission to toss it. My bag is hooked on the chair there at the desk, and I'm sure my clothes are around somewhere too."

He won't find anything. After my daring heist, I met with some guild members in a graveyard, presented the ruby comb, got my congratulations, and changed into some party attire I stashed in a tomb. I've been taught to always change my clothes right after a gig, and since I planned for success, I packed my finest outfit. Glad I even opted for sandals instead of keeping my Boots of Sneaking on. This cop won't find anything that ties me to thieving, but I'm hoping this will get him off my back.

"What is your name?" He's eyeing me intensely, like he suspects I'm tricking him.

"Alexis, Alexis Callaway, but everyone calls me Lexi." He scribbles on his notepad before tucking it back into his kilt.

"Very well, Alexis. I will search this room and your belongings. You may wait in the hall or downstairs at the bar." I pointedly look down at my bedsheet toga, then back at him. Letting out an exasperated breath, he offers, "I'll search your clothes first, then you may put them on before you exit the room."

"I'd prefer to stay and watch you toss my things," I counter, throwing my chin high into the air. "Don't want you planting anything incriminating and claiming it's mine." He bristles at my accusation. "Actually, maybe you should strip too so I can check your things." I put a mischievous smirk on my face while I tease him. "Just to be sure. It only seems fair." I give his body a long and obvious appraisal. He only huffs at my words. Plucking my skirt off the top of the wardrobe, he quickly searches the pockets, then feels the seams before passing it to me.

"You may stay, if it would put your mind at ease," he hisses through gritted teeth before grabbing my top from under the bed frame. He gives my shirt the same treatment before handing it to me as well.

"Soooo, that's a no on me searching your things?" I ask coyly. "I guess I'll do my best to contain my disappointment." Wow, I can't seem to stop myself from teasing this guy! It's probably a bad idea, but damn it's fun. Glancing up, I find him standing with his arms across his chest once more, like he's waiting for something. "What?"

"The sheet," he answers while extending a hand towards me.

"You've got to be kidding me!"

"You gave me permission to search your things and this room. That includes the sheet you are currently wearing." He continues to stand there, still as a statue, waiting expectantly.

"Unbelievable!"Bending over, I step into my skirt, then shimmy it up my body under the make-shift toga, bringing it all the way up and over my boobs. If I don't get a free show, then neither will he. Ripping the sheet off, I throw it at his stupid chiseled face, but he deftly catches it before it hits him. "You must think pretty highly of me if you believe I was able to hide something in there. Seeing as how you are the one who gave it to me." I've put my top on during my tirade, muffling some of my words in the process, before shimmying my skirt back around my hips where it belongs.

In the meantime, he has searched and folded the sheet, placing it atop the wardrobe. He moves to the chair, removing my bag from the back and setting it on the bed. Deftly, he lifts said chair, looking all around and underneath it, before setting it in the middle of the room with slightly more force than necessary.

"Sit," he commands.

"Sir, yes, sir," is my mocking reply as I prance over, sitting down prettily like a little lady. I fan out my skirt so it falls perfectly around me. Glancing back up, I find him leaning over me. He's so unnervingly close that it takes my breath away for a moment.

"Stay." His low calm command whispers across my cheek. Whoa! Why has my heart rate increased? I find myself swallowing hard as he straightens to continue searching my room. I watch in stunned silence as he thoroughly searches my bag, laying every item out in a grid pattern on the small desk, before putting it all back in it. After searching the desk, he turns to the bed, stripping everything off, then folding it once checked. When he's done with the main room, he disappears into the bathroom, offering me a stern glare as he goes that clearly communicates I should stay put.

I'm silent for the whole process in awe at his thoroughness and care. The room actually looks better now than it had before he started! Real methodical, this one. He searched places I never would have considered. They certainly train their cops differently here, that's for sure. Stalking out of the bathroom, he appears somewhat disappointed that he was unable to find anything. Good, now we've both had a bad morning.

"You are free to leave, but know this Alexis, I will be keeping my eyes on you. If you are indeed a thief, as I suspect you are, I will catch you." He's confident, I'll give him that. My only reply is a smirk as I lean back into the chair. Game on, copper, game on.

Chapter 6

Stone

That human, Alexis, is bold, I'll give her that. A liar and a thief, but bold nonetheless. I know she was involved in the theft of the ruby comb. Her scent was on the window ledge, though it was the barest of whiffs. Everyone else missed it, and even I only caught the scent for the briefest of moments. I had almost thought I'd imagined it until I caught it again in the street below. Unfortunately, the rest of the Order only got the scent of that masking soap criminals like to use. Well, not only criminals, to be sure, but they do often use it.

I had scoured the city, going to all the notorious hot spots for the Thieves Guild, including places known to be sympathetic to them. I knew it had to be a Guild hit. Too quick, too organized, and too bold to be a lone thief. The family targeted is under Gargoyle protection. Not many would even dare to steal from a building under my Clan's protection, let alone succeed. I do not envy the poor soul who was on watch there last night. Grandfather does not accept failure well. My body gives a slight shiver at the thought.

I had almost reached the end of locations to search when I found her. Finally taking in a full breath of her unique smell was surprising in many ways. Not only did I then discover that she was simply a human, but I also realized that I enjoyed her scent. At first, I told myself that it was just the effect of finally getting a good sample of the smell that had eluded me all night. But when I came face-to-face with her and fully took her in, I knew that was incorrect.

Her scent reminded me of the mountain side in autumn after the stone and leaves have soaked up the warmth of the sun all day. It was light and familiar, and it upset me that it should belong to a criminal. Especially one that was so bratty! She does not deserve to smell so good. She had no regard for decorum, and she was quite the slob. How could a person get a room so messy after a single night's use?! Just thinking about the state of her bag grates me, everything was thrown in haphazardly and mingled together. She didn't even use the side pockets in it!

"Stone," a coarse whisper from the desk next to me snaps me back to the here and now, "incoming!" I glance up to see my grandfather, the head of my Clan, marching directly toward me. Placing my pen back in its holder, I stand up, bracing to meet this force of nature I call family.

"Hello, Grandfather," I offer flatly.

"Well, did you catch them yet?" He flings the question at me. Nice to see you too.

"No, but I'm sure the Order will inform you when we do."

"Not good enough. I expect to be kept in the loop on this, boy." I try not to let my face show the irritation I feel. I hate it when he calls me that, and he knows it. I underwent the adulthood rites many years ago, yet he still calls me boy. "What's the point of you being in the Order if you can't stop a theft or find the ones that did it for your Clan?"

"That is not my purpose or position–"

"You will not disgrace your family further. You will catch this thief as is your job," he spits the word out at me like a curse. "Then you will bring them to me." Before I can interject to point out all the things he is wrong about, Chief Metis steps in.

"Keir, I think you'll find that Stone is doing his job and has been all night. When we catch the thief and/or retrieve the stolen goods, I'll be sure you are made aware." My grandfather sets his jaw tightly as he offers her the respect he has never offered me. "Your Clan's purpose is to discourage and prevent a break-in or theft from occurring. Since your Clan failed at *its* job, I request that you allow us to continue with ours. Good day, sir," she offers courteously before quickly turning to me. "Stone, I'm ready to hear your report. Follow me into my office."

I will keep the memory of this moment, Metis putting him in his place and my grandfather's expression, locked up tight forever in my mind to be revisited and replayed for the rest of my days. He stepped into her territory, and she let him know it. I can hear him growling as I turn my back to him and follow Metis into her office, closing the door behind me as instructed.

"Thanks for the rescue, Chief."

"Oh, Stone, it was all my pleasure," she replies with a savage smile. "Well, since you're in here, what did you find?" She must catch me looking longingly toward my desk where I was writing up my report. "Just give me the gist of it. I'll read your full report later." I catch her chuckling at me under her breath but choose to ignore it.

As thoroughly as I remember, I give her the breakdown of my findings. My theory on the Thieves Guild involvement, confirmation that I did catch a slight scent that no one else did, what locations I checked, and that I found the person connected to the scent on the scene.

"Wait, wait. You seriously think a full human pulled this off?" Metis asks, disbelieving. "Come on, Stone. How would that even be possible?" Her face reflects just how skeptical she is about my theory. "I believed you to be a rational male, one who thought everything through."

"I also understand that people are not to be underestimated. It is a clever set up, to be something that most would dismiss as impossible. She even tried to pull the human excuse with me, something I could tell she's used before." That human is clever, but I saw through her ploy.

"Hmm," Metis hums, still unconvinced. "Well, I'm going to trust you on this. If you say she should be a suspect, I'll let Thorn and Rekker know to not dismiss her outright. I'll also give them your report." She must be able to see my disappointment. "Investigators," she emphasizes the word, "Thorn and Rekker will be handling the case from here, Stone, and I expect you to accept that." Her arms are crossed, her tail is swishing, and an eyebrow is arched on her stern face. I force a calming breath through my nose before I reply.

"Yes, Chief. I understand. I will leave the ruby comb case in their capable hands." She squints at me but eventually must decide to take my word.

"Good. Quickly finish that report, then head home. Your shift ended some time ago."

"Yes, Chief."

"And leave the door open. I have a feeling I'm going to be needed a lot today." She swipes a hand down her face before sorting through a fresh pile of paperwork.

Quickly, I finish my report and hand it off as instructed. But before heading home, I duplicate all the information collected about this case, including my notes. I was clearly instructed to not investigate this theft, but nobody said I couldn't investigate this human. Thorn and Rekker are good investigators, but they will dismiss Alexis Callaway quickly and focus their attention on more plausible suspects. So I will continue to focus on Alexis. And if she is the thief, I will be the one to catch her.

Once I get home, I organize the documents and information about the case before creating a profile for my suspect.

```
Name: Alexis Callaway (aka Lexi)
Race: Human
Age: Unknown (possibly 30s)
Gender: Female presenting
Hair: Close crop, possibly growth
from shaved
Eyes: Golden amber (~~like the turning
of an autumn leaf~~)
Skin: Golden brown
```

Scent Profile: Of stone and earth on the mountain side once warmed by the sun. ~~Intoxicating~~

Height: 6ft 1in

Body Type: Lithe & slender. Graceful & fit. ~~Moves with ease and self assuredness. Unashamed of her form and figure~~.

Other Physical Description: Slight gap in front teeth. Tattoo of peacock feather on left upper hip and thigh. Dimple on left cheek when a real smile appears. ~~Perky breasts~~.

Personality: ~~Brat~~. Confident, cocky, quick witted. Thinks herself funny. Cautious, defiant. ~~Occasionally obedient and likes being given commands. Heart rate kicks up when I~~

Stop that, Stone! That is inappropriate. She is a suspected criminal, a thief, and I should definitely not be thinking of her in any other way. I should not be replaying our encounter in order to hear again that sharp intake of breath she took when I ordered her to 'stay' in that chair for me. I should not be focusing on how her scent enveloped me, how I couldn't keep myself from standing too close to her to breathe in more of it. Hearing how I made her heart rate increase made my cock...

No, no, no! Abruptly, I get up from my large kitchen island where I currently have my notes and papers spread out over its surface. I've put them here in an attempt to get everything about this case—about her—in order, but they're just as disjointed as my own thoughts. That's it! That's the problem. I've been focusing on her for too long. I need to step away for a moment. She's not even here, and she's throwing me off.

Leaping from my balcony, I instinctively turn mid-fall in the direction that will take me where I'll find my solace: the top of the tower where my ancestors slumber forevermore. I beat my strong wings hard, trying to quickly reach the upper air currents where I hope the coolness will relieve the heat in my veins. It does not. Nor does the quiet peace and whispering wind that resides around my family statues. They have never failed to calm me, to ease my thoughts, but tonight I find no escape here.

That female! What has she done to me? No, no, this is not her doing but something wrong with me. She has done nothing to entice or lead me to these unwanted feelings...desires. Perhaps they truly just stem from my need to catch her? To prove myself. Only one thing will cure this apparent obsession, I must prove that she is a thief. I must catch her in the act!

Eventually, I make my way down the tower stairs and head to our Clan's temple. There are many altars here to different gods, but the main one is for Inera. Legends say she started out as a Goddess of Shifters, but over the centuries, she has become a Goddess of Change and Transformation. Gargoyles took her on as our Goddess when we acquired the gift of life for ourselves. What bigger transformation is there than from stone to flesh and back to stone? My Clan has honored her above all others since our formation, so her altar is the most used here.

A thirteen-foot statue of a female, carved from onyx, her face left blank since it's said she often changes her own form. Candles, flowers, stones, and gifts litter the base of her statue. I learned long ago that it's rude and unwise to tidy up altars unless you're a priest or priestess. So I resist the urge to straighten up the space as I kneel before her visage. But, before I can begin to beseech our patroness, a familiar shuffle approaches me from my left.

"Thought I might end up seeing you here today, young Stone," a warm, kind voice reaches me. A priestess of this temple and my Auntie Sel. "Not that you've been the only one, mind you. Many have been here today, and it's no wonder, given the theft that occurred and your grandfather's wrath over the incident." She chuckles as I stand to greet her. "Poor Danbur was trembling the whole time they were here, bless them."

"Oh, no. I didn't realize it was Danbur on guard," I say before bending down to touch foreheads with my auntie. "They're too kind and sweet to have to deal with Grandfather's temper."

"Indeed they are. That old coot is all iron." She shakes her head. "Ah well, what are we to do but wait for time to change all things in due course. Now, don't let me interrupt you any further. Just wanted to say hello. You don't have to be a stranger to all of us, you know," she offers with a wink. Not many of my Clan choose to live outside the Clan tower, even fewer stay away as much as I do.

"I know, I know, Auntie Sel. It's difficult sometimes, but I do come to our ancestors often. So I'm not entirely without family." I grin. My statement has her slapping my shoulder repeatedly.

"Oh, you! Back to your prayers before I drag you to a family dinner." She wouldn't force me, but she chuckles at her threat as she shuffles away.

Kneeling before my goddess once more, but with my mind clearer than before, I begin to speak to Inera. I offer the usual pleasantries before coming to my point.

Goddess, I seek your assistance in an important matter. I ask for your aid in catching a human. Alexis is her name, Alexis Callaway. Any support in this endeavor would be greatly appreciated. You have my greatest and deepest thanks.

Opening my eyes as I stand, I gaze at the face devoid of features. Bowing my head to her quickly, I retreat back upstairs and into the sky, more confident that I will expose this human for the thief that she is.

After a bit of house cleaning and chores, I decide that I will encase myself for the remainder of the night. I haven't rested in a while, plus I have tonight off. I shall become stone and awaken renewed, ready to begin the hunt.

I've dreamed before, but never while encased in stone and never this vividly. I find myself flying over the city I know so well, feeling the wind under my wings and listening to the chatter of life that hums around me. Then I spot her, my bratty thief. She's wrapped in a black velvet cloak, but that doesn't hide her form or scent from me. As I watch her, a glint of red flashes from her hand. She's got the stolen ruby comb with her!

"I've got you now," I say to myself with a smirk on my face as I dive down.

She doesn't see me above her, leaping from building to building, as she makes her way through dark alleys. She's nervous, as she should be, and trying to get somewhere quickly while remaining undetected. But I've found her, and she is mine. I wait until she makes it to a more secluded spot, away from the main streets, people, and noise. I don't want anything to distract me from my victory, from claiming my prize.

Finally, I pounce, leaping down I land with a boom in front of her, blocking her path as I stand to tower over her. Her eyes are huge as she looks up at my face. At first, surprise with a hint of fear molds her features, but she recovers herself and glares at me in anger instead.

"What. The actual. Fuck," she begins, but I catch her wrist before she can continue. "Hey! Let go, you asshat!"

But I don't let go. Instead I force her to walk backwards until her back hits a brick wall, surprising her. I only briefly notice that the wall wasn't there a moment ago, before my focus comes back to the bejeweled item she has clutched in her hand.

"Can't deny it this time, thief. I've caught you red–" but my accusations die in my mouth. Her cloak opened fully when I raised her hand, which revealed her naked form underneath. I'm shocked into silence to see her bare flesh before me. "Why?" My question comes out shaky and low. The temptation is a surprising burden.

"I didn't do it on purpose, or for you for that matter. I guess I was just in such a hurry that I forgot my clothes?" She seems earnest in her confusion of her current state. I can't seem to resist raising her hand a little higher to expose more of her. She trembles slightly but does not try to stop me. And when I slowly reach my other hand out to gently undo the ribbon holding the cloak at her throat, she bites her full lower lip. I briefly think about adding 'plump lips' to my profile, before every thought I've ever had empties out of my head. The fabric she wore has slipped from her shoulders and fallen upon the ground, leaving my prey naked before me.

The hand that hovered above her throat slowly moves down to a beautiful little breast. A full rumble escapes my chest as my knuckle gently grazes a peaked nipple.

"Oh, fuck. That's hot!" is her response. "Do it again." I tense my body and give her a look of displeasure. "Please?"

"Good girl," I rumble as I step in closer to her. Inhaling that intoxicating smell of hers, I take my thumb and stroke it back and forth over her raised nipple. Needing to submerge myself into her light scent, I bury my face in her neck and graze my fangs along her flesh.

This earns me an, "Oh sweet geezus!" and a wave of a new aroma.

"I need you," she pants. "Please, please! I need you!" I nip her neck, which makes her body tremble under me.

"You can't handle me just yet, pretty thief. But I'll give you a reward for asking so sweetly." Carefully, I wrap my arm around her back and lift so her breasts are even with my mouth. She wraps her legs as best she can around me while I bring my other arm around to support her ass. I rub my nose along one nipple, then the other.

"Oh please, please," she chants at me, but I plan to take my time now that I have her. My first lick begins under the swell of her breast and ends in a flick upon her nipple. This makes her grab my horns as she shouts the word, "Fuck!" Looking down at me she asks, "What's on your tongue?!"

Females typically enjoy the texture of my tongue. Well, all Gargoyles have it, but I cannot speak for them. All I know is that my partners always appreciate the sensation of the granules that are embedded within it.

Some say there are bits of rock that always remain within us, and these within our tongue are an example. Whatever the case, they are making my thief squirm and writhe in the most alluring way. I split my time between her two lovely breasts, making sure they get equal attention. Eventually I lower and flatten my wings in anticipation of hoisting Alexis higher.

"Would you like to feel my tongue upon you somewhere else? Somewhere that's currently burning with heat upon my front." I've been aching to bury my face there since I nibbled her neck.

"Yes, yes, yes! Gawd, yes, please," she pleads while nodding her head emphatically.

"Yes, what?" I growl at her. She said it once during our last encounter, and I need to hear her say it again.

"Yes, sir!" As soon as she finishes saying the word, I lift her higher, placing her legs over my shoulders, holding her ass with both hands, and resting her back along the wall. Gently, I bite her inner thigh while deeply inhaling her aroma. Oh, yes, I plan to take my time here. She's wiggling while panting wildly, then tries to steer me where she wants me using my horns. Impatient little thing.

"Steady, Alexis." My command sends a shudder through her body, and I can see her pretty little pussy slicken even more for me.

Slowly, oh so slowly, I draw nearer to her, intending to reward us both.

Firmly, I drag my tongue within the depth of her entire slit. Her rich taste bursts upon my tongue. As I hear her erotic moan, my own moan creates a chorus with hers, vibrating my tongue for her pleasure. When I reach her clit, I drag my tongue fully across it and flick it with the tip of my tongue, as I did her nipple. My own sounds of pleasure are overshadowed by her sudden cry of ecstasy. I knew she'd come upon my tongue, and soon I'll have her come again upon my fingers. I have to get her ready to take me. Because I plan to fuck her right here in the alley.

Then suddenly she's gone! One moment she was shaking in her euphoria, the next disappearing entirely from my clutches. I roar my rage and frustration out into the world, breaking out of my rocky shell and finding myself standing in my apartment. Breathing heavily, I wildly scan my house, instinctively searching for her. Soon my wits come back to me as I realize it was a dream, an actual dream, a vision while I rested encased in stone. It was so real, realer than any other dream I've had before, and I swear I can still taste her release in my mouth.

Chapter 7

Alexis

"Oh, no, did our little Lexi get caught by the Order after all?" the twins ask mockingly as I make my way back to the guild hall. It's like a maze down here with several entrances around town, and I'll admit I've gotten lost a time or two during my tenure here.

"No, I did not, thank you very much," I answer. "I was merely suspected for a moment this morning. I let the Gargoyle search my stuff, and when he found nothing he went on his merry way."

"Whoa, a Gargoyle? In the Order?" Aiden asks. "That's weird."

"Yeah, you remember, it caused a bit of a kerfuffle when he was allowed on the Patrol Guard. His gramps was not happy." Brayden laughs and slaps my back like I'm his brother. "He fancies himself an Investigator."

"Investigator?! A Gargoyle wanting to be an Investigator? Really? Why don't I remember this?" Aiden looks indignant.

"Probably because you were so focused on getting into that Siren's good graces that it took up all your brain power," Brayden teases. They begin slapping and poking each other right in the corridor. I quickly leave them behind. Gav told me to report to the

Council's chamber as soon as I woke this morning, so that's where I'm headed.

"I hear you handled yourself quite well with Stone," Gav says as soon as I enter the chamber. He's the only one in it, which surprises me. I had expected a big ceremony or something. Gav must notice the disappointment on my face, "There will be a proper initiation tonight, so don't look let down. Unfortunately, we've got some things to settle before the grand hooplah."

"Oh," I say quietly. "Who's Stone?"

"The Gargoyle who cornered you this morning. Got a report from the tavern owner as soon as Stone left you."

"The Gargoyle's name is Stone?!" I almost can't believe how ridiculously silly that is. A Gargoyle named STONE! "What, was Boulder taken already or something?" If I ever see him again, I'm going to tease him ruthlessly. I can already feel the wicked grin spreading across my face. Oh, is he going to get it! Then the rest of Gav's answer sinks in.

"Wait, the tavern owner is with us? Then why did he let that ass into my room?!" I'm quite indignant, but all Gav does is smile crookedly at me.

"Thought it would be a good opportunity to test you a little more, see how you handle yourself around the Order. Tig said you were quite feisty and kept him on his toes. Said she stifled her laughter a few times while eavesdropping." Tig! The barmaid's name was Tig. Looks like I might not have lost my chances with her after all. Oh, she was good! With that scream and running out of the room, totally fooled me.

"Alright. Let's get all the paperwork out of the way, then I'll take you to your new private residence." Gav does indeed begin to lay out piles of paperwork, which I half thought he was joking about.

"Wait, private residence?! I get my own place, and the guild provides it?"

"That's right! What, did you think you'd continue to live down here? I mean, you can if you want–"

"No, no! I'd love my own place! I've been missing the privacy, to be honest. Just didn't expect to get one so soon is all." Gawd, I'm so relieved. Totally planned on saving as much as I could, as quickly as possible, to get a place of my own. This whole time I've been sleeping down here in a shared bunk room that random members use to crash in. Well, when I wasn't having a naughty sleepover, that is. To have my own space again, to decorate and nest somewhere, to have my anonymity and privacy back is the greatest gift I could possibly receive today. I could hug Gav right now!

"Well, I see it's true then," a haughty and unwelcome voice interrupts my pleasant glow. "The human is to become a full member of the Guild." I almost break the pen I'm holding in irritation. "I suppose congratulations are in order." He offers me a small clap of his hands that feels patronizing.

"Yes, Valda. As you were made aware last night, Lexi passed her final test with flying colors." Gav offers me a genuinely proud smile. "We have lots to do before the ceremony tonight, so if you would kindly–"

"I heard she had a run-in with our local law enforcement this morning. So you can understand why I had to drop in and make sure nothing went amiss there." Gritting his teeth in frustration, Gav continues.

"Nothing amiss, Valda, she handled herself skillfully in that situation, as well. You may speak with Tig if you want a firsthand–"

"So human, are you finally willing to end this farce?" the transparent asshole asks me directly, blatantly ignoring my mentor. I just stare at him as blankly as my temper will allow. "Come, come, girl. You must understand that you can not possibly continue in this way. Now that you are to officially become one of us, you must choose what you want to transform into. Preferably something that will be beneficial to the Guild in some way."

This fucking asshole! Does he have to ruin everything?! I worked my ass off to earn my place here and did it all as a human just to prove to them, to him, that I could. And finally, in my moment of victory, when I was about to ask Gav to go over my list of possible options for me to be transformed into, this fucking ghost has to ruin it all! Now if I do change myself, he'll think it's because I'm giving in. He will issue me a big fat 'I told you so,' and he will have won!

"That's quite enough, you senile old ghost!" Gav shouts at him, startling us both into silence. "If Lexi makes that kind of decision, it is up to her and her alone. We do not pressure anyone here to change their entire being just to suit us." We're both staring at Gav in astonishment. "And if you do not drop this ridiculous notion that a human cannot join our ranks just because you believe they are inferior, the Council will be convened to discuss if you truly belong amongst us yourself." Speechless. I'm left completely speechless. "As you can plainly see, this human earned her place just as she is. Now, if you will kindly leave us, we have work to do." Gav holds out an arm in a clear gesture of 'get the fuck out.'

The ghost clears his throat, not that he physically needs to, and wafts out through the wall he came in from.

"Gav, you're my hero," I say with a chuckle.

"You say that now, but just you wait till I make you sign all these documents in triplicate. Then you may be singing a different tune."

After what feels like hours of paperwork and signing my name, I finally find myself standing in the middle of my very own apartment. Do I have a major hand cramp? Yes. Was it totally worth it? Oh yeah. The place isn't huge, but it's big enough for me. There's a wall of windows with a balcony to the right just as you enter the front door. It's fully furnished with an open floor plan. The living room, kitchen, and bed are all in one large room that flows from one space to the next. The bathroom, which is much bigger than I would have thought, is all the way in the back. Thankfully, it at least has its own room with a door. No closet, but there is a large wardrobe that looks like it could lead me to yet another magical land.

"This space is yours, so feel free to decorate as you like," Gav informs me. "If there are any issues with it be sure to tell Rey at the guild. He can be reached by calling-mirror if it's an emergency, but he's usually at the guild hall."

Ah, yes. The super cool magical compact mirror that Gav gave me as part of my initiation loot. It looks like a makeup compact but inside are two mirrors facing each other. Apparently, this is the magical version of a video call. You open it up, tell the mirror who you want to talk to while picturing them in your mind, and their mirror will vibrate to let them know someone is calling. He told me it still works if you've never seen that person but have their full name. It also works for businesses or companies if you picture their logo.

Apparently, there's a texting-type thing called a message book, but Gav warned me off them saying, "We don't want to have anything that may be incriminating written down anywhere, now do we." Setting up my calling-mirror was easy enough; I just had to tell the mirror that I was its new user, state my full name and nickname, show my face off, then walk back to get my full body in the mirror frame. Gav advised me to also show the mirror whenever I change up my appearance in any meaningful way. I'll do my best to remember that, but no promises.

"Speaking of mirrors, this is the calling-mirror for your home." He gestures at the large full-length mirror that's hung on the wall across from the dining table. "Think you can set that up yourself? I do need to get going but can stay and help if you need."

"If it's just like the compact, I'm pretty sure I can handle it myself."

"Excellent!" He claps his hands, then rubs them together a few times. "I'll be off then to prepare for tonight. Why don't you settle in, walk around your new neighborhood, and buy yourself a little something for your new place. You scored yourself quite a coin haul with that comb, and you should treat yourself for this accomplishment. Something grander than the hairstyles you usually get, perhaps?"

So far, I've been pretty sparing with spending my money. The only splurges thus far have been to the beauticians when I passed a big task or skill test. When I found out how easy it was to get my hair magically altered, then attach that alteration to something like an earring, I was hooked! No more hot wigs for me! Only my real hair going forward. All I have to do is go to a parlor, tell them what I want, they make it happen, and enchant an item so I can rock or remove the style anytime I desire. I was shown this as a way to make a quick change, but who says I can't use it for fun too.

One of my favorites so far is one I attached to some gold hoops. It's a straight, hip-length dark blue that transitions to gold with a blunt bang. Makes me feel like a celestial goddess. That one was worth every penny, but Gav is right. I should find something different to gift myself for this major milestone.

Having taken Gav's advice, I find myself strolling along the streets near my new home. I've loved Avenston since the first time I set foot into this bustling metropolis. From the shops to the people, there's always a feast for my eyes to gorge upon and I find them constantly darting around, trying to take in all the sights. Nothing boring at all about this place, that's for sure.

The rain that must have fallen earlier has the glistening cobblestone streets reflecting the warm glow of the shops around me and the overcast sky really adds to the picturesque scene. The horseless carriages, literally carriages being pulled by magic, pass up and down the middle of the lane. I discovered these are like taxis, and if you see an empty one, you can just get in and tell it where you want to go. There are also larger versions that run more like buses with a set route. All are free to use and kept clean, something the city itself provides.

There's also a wide array of personal vehicles and ways to travel. Of all these, I've decided the magic carpets look the most scary to ride, though I wouldn't decline if ever given the chance, just to see if it is as horrifying as it seems. There are arches that are like portals to other parts of the city that are further away, but those always have long lines. I've been told that there are portal stations that can take you to different cities and regions, but those do cost money. After a few gigs, I plan on traveling to a sunny beach somewhere as a vacation. Why not, right?!

I find several promising dining locations close to my studio and grab some lunch at a neat little corner vendor selling samosa-type food. Eating it as I window shop, I stumble upon a farmers market situation set up in a big open courtyard space. Who could pass that up?! So I walk around, buying myself some fresh produce here and there, but find nothing gift worthy. Moving on, and deciding to take some smaller streets and alleys to head back to my place, I find an old person struggling to get up a few steps into a shop.

Old might not be the right word here. My grandmother was old, but this person is ancient! Bent over at an almost ninety-degree angle, gnarled fingers gripping a wooden cane, with white wisps of hair jutting out from under a tattered graying cloak. She looks like a storybook version of an old wicked witch who lives in the woods, eating children for supper.

"Dearie," her wizened voice calls out, "would you mind helping me up here? These old bones of mine aren't cooperating today. Must be the weather." I hadn't even realized she'd been able to see me, her face still covered by her hood.

"Uh, yeah, sure." I mean, yes, it seems like a bad idea to get that close to a fairytale villain. But it seems like an even worse idea to piss off a potential evil witch. So I opt for being a helper and offer my arm. Her worn and weathered hand clasps my forearm with amazing strength. Like I might have a bruise after this.

"Thank you, dearie. Such a sweet girl." She finally turns her face to me, staring with cataract white eyes in a face with more lines than a subway map. "They're having a sale today, and I don't want to miss it." Her excitement for a sale has me trying to hide a smile. Glad to see the thrill of a good sale stays with us as the years pass.

She releases her death grip once we are up the stairs and through the door. Patting my arm with a, "That's a good girl," before wandering off on her own. It's as I look up, chuckling at her, that I finally notice what kind of a shop I'm in. It's a sex shop. Well, that was unexpected. Get it granny, I guess.

Standing to my full height, as I was hunched to help the old woman, I lock eyes with the person behind the counter. She's a slight little thing with a pixie cut and colorful tattoos everywhere skin is exposed.

"Is that Crone with you?" Her voice tinkles, like there's a bell behind it. She has a lopsided grin on her face, and her eyes are full of questions.

"No, no!" I answer while gesturing my hands for emphasis. "She just needed some help up the stairs, and I happen to be around."

"Ah, well, if you need any help or have any questions, just let me know. We have a sale today on our bee-boxes. You'll find a display," and she points where the Crone took off to, "at that end of the shop." We glance at each other and giggle.

I've been in one shop like this since coming here, but I was with the twins and they knew what they were after, so it was a quick in and out. Since I'm already here, I decide I might as well take a good look around, for science! Leisurely walking down the aisles, I eventually find myself in a big area with shelves of dildos featuring so many shapes and sizes that I'm stunned for a moment. Stunned, but intrigued.

After closer inspection, I notice that they are grouped by style...type...kind? Has me wondering if they were modeled after real fantasy creature cocks. As I'm making a metal note to ask the shopgirl about them, I find my gaze locked onto a beautiful specimen carved from stone. It gleams from its high polish and is an awfully familiar color of purply blue, only slightly darker. About the length of a ruler, with a handle carved into the base, its girth would have one questioning if it would actually fit comfortably. The head is the shape one would expect, but it's the nodes that really draw me in. They run along and around the entire length, and are of various sizes. Makes a girl curious about how that would feel inside, what sensations it would cause at her opening.

"Now, that's a real thing of beauty, that one," comes the crackling voice of the Crone, startling me from my imaginings. She actually cackles at me upon seeing me jump like a cat. Recovering, slightly, I sheepishly chuckle.

"Yeah, maybe."

"No. No, maybe about it, dearie. When a cock calls out to you, you gotta grab hold of it." She cackles again while gripping her cane as if it was the cock in question. "Not every cock calls out to every gal, you know. So when you find one, why not splurge? Don't we all deserve a little treat from time to time," she says with a wink. Turning back to the dildo I was ogling, I consider her words.

"It is quite lovely and well made. Plus, I've never had a stone one before, though I've heard good things. Like you can change the temp–" But as I turn around, I find that she has disappeared and I'm talking to myself. Okay. "Well," I go on to thin air, "I was shopping for a gift for myself. Considering that I have a private space where I'm all alone..."

I snatch it off its display, feeling the weight of it in the hand, and the coolness of the stone upon my skin. Oh yeah, this is going to be fun. It's been too long since I've had a chance for a little self-love. Partners are great, but sometimes you need to take yourself into your own hands and spend a little time on you.

I decide to grab a bee-box as well, since they're on sale and all, then take my toys and some lube up to the counter. The tattooed cutie gives me care instructions for the stone dildo and explains what a bee-box is. Turns out it's like a vibrator, and no there aren't any bees in it...anymore. Apparently, that's how they were originally made way back when, but magic rocks are what provides the vibrating sensation these days. What an amazing world I find myself in! If that bookshop lady ever thinks I'm leaving, she's got another thing coming.

Chapter 8

Alexis

Holy shit! I think that dream made me come in real life! Which is impossible, right? I'm not one of those women who come from the briefest of effort. It takes a little work to get me there. But in that dream, all it took was a fun scenario, some magnificent nipple play, then one lick from that incredible tongue, and I fell apart. So much so that it snapped me out of the best dream of my life! Now I'm laying here in my bed, panting, grumpy, and confused.

Of all the people my dream could have conjured up, why him? It had started off as a normal naked-in-public dream. Then boom! Full-on sex dream with the domineering cop I just met. That makes two days in a row he's responsible for waking me prematurely. Ass!

Throwing the sheets off myself in frustration, I find that I'm not alone in my bed. My new bumpy toy is here with me. That's right! After my formal initiation ceremony into the Thieves Guild, we partied a bit in the Guild Hall with all members present. Then I came home alone—despite some incredibly tempting offers from the twins—and began to familiarize myself with my new favorite toys.

I started with the bee-box, and—oh baby!—it did not disappoint. I might even get myself a couple more to have that stimulation in other tantalizing places. Then, I moved on to my new glorious stone dick. I had discreetly left it near the balcony windows to get infused with some of the autumn coolness while I was at the Guild. The cold was a sensation that took my breath away. Running those chilled bumps through my slick folds was a new kind of heaven, and one that I may need to repeat very soon. Memories of last night, coupled with that dream, have me reaching for that stony cock.

It's not as cool as it had been that first time, but that's ok, I can still work with it warmed from my body. So glad I cleaned it last night after my happy playtime session. It's my first stone toy, and I want to make sure it's well cared for.

I wasn't able to get it all the way in last night—not even close—so I've given myself a personal mini-challenge! To work myself up notch by notch till I can take it all. I'm not in a hurry, but one day I'll get this bad boy all the way to the handle! It's actually kind of thrilling to think about. Grabbing the bee-box as well, I use it to work my nipples as I drag the dildo along my slit. The sensations are similar to how his tongue felt in my dream, and with it so fresh in my mind, I find myself picturing him again. I'm back in that alley, pushed up against that wall, him playing with me, me begging him to...

No, no I don't want to think of him that way. I should dream up Neela, Aiden, Brayden, or even Tig. Possibly even all four of them. But instead it's Stone that I come back to as I begin to slide the lubed up dildo into myself. It's Stone's tongue, it's Stone's fingers, it's Stone's cock. I can even hear his graveled voice in my head. "Beg for me, Alexis," he orders.

"Please," I utter breathlessly to the empty room. "Please. Please, please."

"Such a good girl." I can practically hear it in my ear, feel him so close to me, his eyes watching me pleasure myself. "Do you want to come, pretty thief?"

"Yes, yes!" I whisper as I continue to work the shaft in and out of me, every node a beautiful sensation around my sensitive opening. I bring the bee-box to my clit. I'm so damn close. Then the voice of Stone in my head turns stern.

"Yes, what?" he demands, just like in the dream.

"Yes, sir. Yes, sir!" I supply as my knees quake. I do like when my male partners take on a more dominant role, but this is next level. A level I didn't realize I could enjoy so much.

"Good girl," the praise back in his voice. Wow, that has never turned me on before, but here I am, imagining it and getting off on it. I'm so damn close; I'm right on the edge. I need this stone cock deeper, but I'm already so full. I need more, I need something to push me over the edge into the heaven I've been chasing. Then it happens, my own daydream supplies exactly what I need. "Come for me, Alexis."

My breath catches at the command, at the use of my real name, and I'm falling. My back arches. I have to hold the dildo in place as my body tenses and tries to push it out. But I won't let it, instead I push it in one more notch, the sensation only prolonging the orgasm. The bee-box continues to buzz upon my clit as my body spasms again and again.

Eventually, I let the bee-box tumble down to my side. Then I, oh so slowly, pull the dildo out one nodule at a time, involuntarily making a sound of pleasure as each one passes. I'm sprawled out on my bed, panting as I recover. Hot damn! That was definitely among the most mind blowing orgasms I've ever achieved on my own—up there in the top three at least—and I almost hate that it was because of him.

No, no, it wasn't because of him. It was my own mind, my own fantasies that did it. It conjured up those images, the whole situation, really. My mind wanted to play around with the whole 'being told what to do' thing based on our previous interaction. The real Stone is too uptight to do anything like that. Plus, I'm just a suspected criminal to him. All of this is only in my imagination, and that's exactly where it is going to stay.

Here I thought it would get easier after being initiated into the Thieves Guild. Boy, was I wrong! True, I can take on gigs at my leisure, picking things that sound interesting or meaningful in some way. There's the expected greedy requests, the spite requests, and those who wish to have family heirlooms restored to them. There are also a surprising amount of requests for returning items of cultural significance to their people. I was sad to discover that even here things like that happen or have happened in the past. But unlike at home, there are ways other than petitions and red tape to recover such items. One being to ask a sneaky little thief like me, which I am all too happy to oblige.

But way too often, that fucking ghost comes around to piss on any victory I achieve with his little taunts and backhanded compliments. That is, when he isn't just wafting in and taking the request I had my eyes on. It's like he knows what I'll pick and he nabs it first. He's even more infuriating than that Gargoyle, who has begun to pop up far too frequently in my day-to-day.

He's been riding my ass, and not in the fun way! I go to the market to buy some food, then I spot him on the roof of a nearby building. While hanging out at a tavern with friends, I catch him looming in a corner. Hell, he even caught me casing out a joint I had planned to loot one night. So I obviously had to tell Gav and pass that gig on to someone else. I gave it to the twins so Valda couldn't have it. You can bet your ass I made sure to be seen out and about on the night they broke in and stole what was requested. Stone came and questioned me all the same, but my alibi was rock solid. Considering he was watching me on a date, flitting from place to place with Tig the barmaid, he knew damn good and well it wasn't me.

I can't even escape this Gargoyle in my dreams. Literally! I don't have them every time I sleep, but when I do they follow a similar pattern. He stalks me, he chases me, he catches me, then we have an almost-satisfying sexual encounter. That first time I dreamed of him, I blamed our meeting and me buying that dildo, which is so close to his coloring. After that I rationalized the dreams by thinking it was because I had come so hard that first time upon waking. Now I think it's happening because he's popping up so much in my real life that my dreams just supply him there too.

Yeah, that's definitely it. It's not because I find him sexy or anything. I mean, I certainly don't look forward to these dreams. And I, for sure, am not disappointed when they don't happen. Damn, it's getting harder and harder to lie to myself. If only the real Stone was as wonderful as Dream Stone. Wait, no, no, that would be terrible. I can't have a thing with a cop. Absolutely not!

Shaking my head, I bring my thoughts back to the task ahead. I've got myself a big heist planned today. I was in the right place at the right time at the Guild Hall and was able to snatch it up before anyone else even saw it. Apparently, there's been some kind of feud going on for centuries between two vampire covens as to whom a dagger belongs to. Every so often one coven steals it from the other, hides it for a time, then the other steals it back.

I think it's hilarious and an intriguing challenge. To steal something from the top of a tower in broad daylight will be no easy feat. I decided right away that I'd do it during the day instead of at night. True, they have familiars and most vampires can go about in the sun these days, but many vampires still prefer to sleep during the day and prowl at night. So daytime will still be the best option for me. Anyway, the take on this is very much worth it. Bonus to be given if the rival Clan doesn't notice it's been taken. What a score!

I've studied the tower's floorplan extensively. Even mapped out the best side of the tower to climb with its possible footholds. Just because I'm using a rope to get up the side doesn't mean footholds wouldn't come in handy. I've gotten a cloak to match the shade of the tower's exterior. I found out where most of the wards are, and the ones I didn't get from intel I'll be able to see. I've greased the palms of a disgruntled familiar and learned the schedules of all the staff, including their private watchmen. But most importantly,

I've planned the heist on that Gargoyle's day off! That's right, I've got his schedule too. With the way he's been following me, I can't let him foil this gig. Neela knows my plans and will be my lookout and pass off person. She plans on using this time to sun herself on a nearby roof. From there, she'll be able to watch me, get some sun, and maybe even divert some watchful eyes to her instead of me. So it's a win-win-win.

This is so fucking boring! And my knee is killing me. I'm too old to be in this position for so long. I knew it would be a lengthy wait, but this is agony. Why did I think hiding in this little alcove for a watchman's whole-ass shift would be fine? Have I never met me?! On paper, yeah, it was the best option. Get up to the window and sneak in during shift change, then sit and wait till the next shift change, at which point I'd be able to get into the room the dagger was in. Then I'd have a whole other shift to find the dagger and snag it before finally making my escape during yet another shift change. It was, and still is, the safest option, no matter how much I am now regretting it.

I'd kill for some music! That's one of the things I miss most about my world, earbuds and the limitless supply of music or podcasts at my fingertips. But here I am, sitting in absolute silence, picking at my nails to pass the time. I've already totally mangled three of my cuticles...okay, maybe four.

At least I can see the stretch of hallway with the door I'll be breaking into later. So, I've gotten to learn this watchman's routine pretty well already. All he does is jiggle the handle of the doors up here to make sure they're still locked. He walked around and checked inside all the rooms at the start of his shift, but since then he hasn't entered a single one. Fingers crossed the next guy follows the same routine since I have to spend a whole other watch within that one room. Unless...I can get in, get the stupid dagger, then get out again all during shift change. No, no, no, stick to the plan. Even if it is dull as fuck.

I've had to talk myself out of the quicker option several times already, and I'm getting less convincing each time. However, my closing statement of 'the reward is too big to waste on impatience' is still winning me over...for now. We'll see how the next hour plays out.

About half an hour later, as I pick at a loose thread in my cloak, a familiar ghostly presence wafts into my field of vision. Right up through the hallway floor, just behind the watchmen, Valda emerges like a weed. What the fuck is he doing here? Has something happened? Is he here with an important message? Do I need to abort?

Those thoughts are quickly dashed from my mind, however, as he slowly turns his head to face me and a truly wicked grin spreads across his face. No! No, no, no, no! He wouldn't dare?! But as he sinks into the wood of the door I've been watching for hours, he offers me a little wave. He totally would, and he absolutely is. He's taking my gig!

But that's against the codes! I was tested on and had to sign, in triplicate, that I understood and would follow the Thieves Guild

Codes of Conduct to the letter. And chief among those codes is not taking another member's job once it had been accepted. Which I had done well over three weeks ago! Yet here he is, flagrantly breaking the rules of the code.

Wait. Calm down, Alexis. He hasn't taken anything yet. Maybe he's just here to rile you up? To get your goat, to try to make you fail. Maybe he's just—

The door—my door—clicks open softly, and a bejeweled dagger comes floating out of the partially open door. I watch, open mouthed, as the dagger begins to float over to the window, which also opens by unseen hands. That fucker's invisible, and he is most definitely stealing my big score. That slimy little thief!

Just before disappearing out the window, Valda makes the dagger do a little dance before making it leap from the sill. I'm frozen in place with a mixture of anger and surprise. Why would he do this? He knows he'll get kicked out of the Guild, so why would he...Then I finally take in what he's done. He's left the door and window open. Shit!

Boots of Sneaking, don't fail me now! As silently and quickly as my joints allow, I hobble over to the door and shut it before kneeling down to relock it as well. If by some miracle I'm not caught in the next few moments and I do get that dagger back, I'm getting that bonus! Plus, I don't need to give this watchman any reason to start looking around as I attempt to make my escape.

I hear the tale-tell sounds of a lock setting into place right as I begin to hear the pitter-patter of footsteps coming closer. Lurching up, I sprint for the window, thankful to find my rope still coiled up under the ledge. I shake it out, haul my ass out and over, then gently close the window before popping my head out of sight. I don't know how close of a call that was, but whatever it was, it was too damn close.

I survey the area for the ghost or dagger, but neither are to be seen. Must be nice to float around wherever you want, while I'm stuck making a slow descent shimmying down this rope. Halfway down I catch Neela's eye and give her the ABORT hand signal. Thankfully, nothing seems amiss so far. When I get my hands on that backstabbing ghost, there will be hell to pay! All the way down, I ponder different things I could do to that ghost. For the moment, my mind has settled on having him bound to the rattiest, creepiest, and ugliest doll I can find. Shove his supposed soul right in there and throw it in the ocean.

Finally back down on the ground, I shed my grey cloak and throw it in a recycling bin I moved here just for this. As I close the lid, I hear it. Alarms begin to sound in the vampire's mansion. They've discovered the dagger's been stolen. Fuck!

Chapter 9

Stone

"**G**ot any fun plans for your vacation?" Chief Metis inquires as I hand in my end of shift reports. "Looks like you've been getting a lot of rest lately. Makes me curious if you were gearing up for something special?" I freeze and widen my eyes at the Centaur. She's right, I have been sleeping and stoning more often than I ever have before. Far more than is common for me as I typically only do so as needed. I hadn't realized it would be so noticeable.

"Uh, ah, I am planning to visit my parents, but spend most of my two weeks up in the mountains. I'll be heading out in time to catch the sunrise. It's truly beautiful up there." Aside from my ancestor's keep, Mt. Dern is one of the best places for me to clear my head and find peace. "There are some old ruins up there that I'll be staying at."

"Oh, that sounds amazing," she groans as she audibly cracks her neck. "I could use some time away out in nature myself. I might just do something similar next time I get a good clump of days off. Didn't your Clan used to live in those mountains before settling in Avenston?" She takes a sip of hot tea, waiting for my response.

"Yes, Chief. My Clan lived in the ruins I'll be visiting. It's also where we lay our ancestors when it's time to return to the earth." She nods as if she's about to ask more questions when Investigators Thorn and Rekker barge in.

"Chief, we've got–" Thorn pauses when he notices I'm in the room. I make a motion to leave, but he stops me. "You can stay, Stone. As I remember you had an interest in this case." Turning to the chief, he continues while his partner gives me a curt nod. "We've discovered that the theft of the ruby comb was carried out by the Thieves Guild." He looks over at me as if waiting for my reaction, but this is information I already suspected. When I give no sign of surprise, he continues, "Seems that a group of Basa-Andre have been claiming for years that it belonged to them. Thought we'd pay them a visit soon, see if perhaps they were tired of waiting and took matters into their own hands by hiring the Guild here."

"Hmmm. The Thieves Guild, is it? Could make this trickier than we'd hoped." Metis rubs her chin in thought for a few moments. The Thieves Guild does have their own exemptions and recovering stolen artifacts on behalf of their rightful or original owners would make this tricky indeed. "Don't go talk to any Basa-Andre just yet. Find out who their representatives in town are, then examine their financials. See if any large withdrawals were taken out during the window of time before or after the theft. Also, research their evidence and any claims previously submitted of their ownership. Let's get our hydras' heads all facing the same direction before we move forward on this one."

"Yes, boss," they chime in unison.

"Sorry, Stone, but it looks like your sassy human wasn't the culprit after all," Thorn says with a chuckle. I knew they wouldn't believe the claims from my report. Not that they are the only ones who've ridiculed me for my suspicions.

"How so?" I ask. "You have only concluded that the theft was carried out by the Thieves Guild. It is still entirely possible that Alexis Callaway is a member of said guild and took on the request herself or in accompaniment of other members. Therefore, she has yet to be completely ruled out as a suspect." The two investigators glance at each other, stunned, then begin to laugh.

"This guy." More laughter. "Are you serious?" The laughter continues. "You really think they'd let a human join as a thief? Come on, Stone. You can't be serious?" I'm starting to get a little miffed on Alexis's behalf. I'm all too familiar with the pang of always being doubted in your capabilities because of assumptions.

"Enough, Investigators," Metis interjects firmly. "I believe you have a lot of research to be getting on with." Leveling a stern eye at the pair, "You are dismissed."

"Yes, Chief." They do leave her office, but they are still snickering and flashing glances at me through her office windows. I take a quick calming breath before looking back to Metis. I'm surprised to find an indulgent smile on her face.

"You can't blame them, Stone. Your hypothesis is a bit far-fetched." I begin to interject, but she stops me with a hand. "I said it was far-fetched, not impossible." She walks around her desk, hooves clopping on the old stone flooring and gives my shoulder a pat. "I actually think it's kinda cute, the way you won't dismiss her because she's a human. One, because it's a mark of a good investigator to not dismiss something out of hand because it might be improbable. And two, because I know you have faced some similar difficulties yourself." She walks over to her door and closes it while continuing to hold the knob, before bringing her eyes to mine.

"I am aware that you've been tailing this Alexis from time to time. And I've been allowing it since she isn't really a part of this investigation and it is a Patrol Guard's duty to watch out for crimes and criminals. Just don't let your obsession for this female side-track you, Patrolman." I bristle at the accusation of being obsessed with a suspected criminal, but Metis only smiles wider at me.

"Go home, Stone. Get some good mountain time in. I'm hoping the fresh air up there will help clear that stubborn head of yours." Opening the door fully once more, "Off with you, before I take the trip for you and make you do all my paperwork while I'm gone. Though knowing you, you'd probably love that."

"Yes, Chief," comes out more forlorn than I expected.

Why can't I get this female out of my head?! It's infuriating, really. I made it to the mountains in plenty of time to set my things inside the old ruins before the sunrise. But all I could think of during my flight was her! Setting up my campsite, her. Making a fire, her. Settling in to watch the colors of the sky shift atop my favorite boulder, HER!

I've decided my new found 'obsession' with this human is based on my need to prove for certain that she is indeed a thief.

I know she was at or around the area where the ruby comb was stolen. Her scent tells me that much, but I need something more solid. I confirmed with the manor staff that she wasn't employed or invited there, nor could any recall having ever seen her before. So how did her scent get on that windowsill?

She is a thief, and I will prove it. Then I'll be rid of her and these maddening dreams. I've felt almost compelled to watch her during my waking hours, to seek her out and see what she is up to. Her days are so random that I find no discernible pattern. She doesn't even sleep at any regular time! One day she could sleep at night, the next during the day, while other times she'll cat nap at random. She meets different people in different places. She has a talent for making friends easily and travels around the city discovering new things. An excited expression on her face tells me when she's found something new that intrigues her.

I know I've almost caught her several times in something nefarious, but she spots me before anything really happens. I'm getting pretty good at reading her facial expressions at this point. When she sees me watching her doing something mundane, she squints her eyes at me like an auntie silently scolding a child. Unfortunately for her, it doesn't have the desired effect as it makes her nose crinkle in an adorable way.

Oh, but when she finds me watching her when she's doing something she shouldn't be, her eyes go wide in surprise with a quick involuntary inhale. This sets her mouth into an incredibly delicious-looking O shape. Then the scowl and squint come out before she flips me off and storms away like an impetuous child. When that happens, I catch myself thinking of different ways I'd like to punish her, before quickly shaking my head to clear such thoughts.

These dreams certainly aren't helping in clearing inappropriate imagery from my mind. They come every time I sleep or encase myself in stone. Metis wasn't wrong in her assumption that I've been doing so more often recently. It's not something I need to do regularly, but something I've been wanting to do more and more often. The lie I've been telling myself, about it being my need to catch her in real life just being played out in dreams, is wearing thin. Even I realize at this point that it is becoming more than that. Chief Metis is right; Alexis is becoming an obsession, one I'm enjoying far too much.

Though I have to say I did not enjoy watching her flaunt around on her little date with the fawn barmaid Tigarith. How did she know it would upset me? Has she learned about the dreams?! No, that's impossible as I haven't told another living soul about those. Have I let my unconscious desire for her slip out at some point? We haven't had any real interactions since I searched her room at the tavern. She realizes I follow her sometimes, but that's for work. Alexis understands that's for work, right?

I slide a hand down my face in frustration at myself. I'm missing the sunrise while consumed in my thoughts. I came out here purposefully to not think about work or other work-related things, and Alexis is definitely a work-related topic.

I wonder why she hasn't bought any curtains for her windows? She knows I've been watching her around town and must realize this also occasionally applies to her residence. Maybe she's voyeuristic? I mean, I am not the only being in town that can fly or see well at night. Perhaps I should add voyeurism to her profile?

"Stop it, Stone!" I chide myself with a growl. Shades of light pink are already beginning to form along the horizon. I will not let that thief steal the first sunrise of my vacation. Breathing in deeply, I ground myself with the mountain of my Clan, feeling its stability underneath me. Continuing to take big deep breaths, I push my thoughts and energy deep into the mountain, down past its base and far below the earth. I pull up the calm and fathomless energy I find there, bringing it into my being.

Once the sun has cleared the horizon, I turn my mind to its energy. Fresh, new, and bright. I still feel the coolness of the night upon my skin, but the sun's warmth is already starting to affect the atmosphere. I seek out the sun's renewing heat and pull it into myself as well.

The song of the mountainside changes to welcome a fresh new day. The birds and animals wake and begin to move about around me. The sun's brilliance sets the morning dew aglow upon various flower petals and a few spiderwebs.

For the first time in weeks, I am completely calm and content. My mind blank as I sit and enjoy the changing scenery around me. I allow myself to be utterly immersed in the beauty and tranquility of nature. This is exactly what I needed. Perhaps after spending my days like this I will return to the city, my post, more clearheaded and–

Everything that has piqued my curiosity in Alexis over the past few days clicks into place in a flash of clarity. Secret meetings with a vampire familiar, the on-location drawing class around the city where she concentrated the hardest in one particular location, and the new cloak that was a dull shade of grey. I hop up to my feet as the pieces slide to form a complete picture. The buildings she took the most pains to draw and study belonged to a vampire coven. The same coven that the familiar belonged to.

"The Tower!" I say out loud, startling some deer. The cloak matches the shade of the tower perfectly. I knew that color didn't suit her. It was made to hide her! Oh, you clever girl, you planned it all right under my nose, and I didn't see it.

She mixed it in with her other erratic behavior, but I see it now. She's going to steal something from that vampire tower, but when? I pace around the boulder in thought. The cloak has been ready for days, so what was she waiting for? Me! She needed me away. I was the thorn in her side that delayed her plans. It's no closely guarded secret when our days off and vacations are scheduled, and Alexis is so personable. I have no doubt that she'd be able to get that information out of someone.

I glide from the boulder over to my campsite and quickly pack up everything —it wasn't much anyway—then thoroughly put the fire out. If I'm wrong, there's no harm to anyone but me if I use a few of my days off to covertly follow her around. But if I'm right, I'll finally have my little thief right where I want her.

Chapter 10

Alexis

Fuck, fuck, fuck! I chant under my breath as I run. That bastard must have messed something up in the room where the dagger was kept. What an asshole!

When the alarms started, I darted and hid here and there, scurrying around as covertly as possible before making my way to a secret entrance of our underground passages. But I can't stay down here.

One, because we're warned that if we even think there is a possibility of someone following us or our trail, we are not to lead anyone to the inner sanctum of the Guild's hall. Two, I wasn't able to make it to my clothing stash. So if someone finds me running down here, I'm looking suspicious as hell in my thieving gear. Three, I'm not one hundred percent sure I even remember how to make it back to the hall from where I am right now. And four, I need to be seen at home, chillin' in real people clothes in case any of Stone's crew show up to pester me.

Not sure who else is on the 'I'm gonna catch Lexi in the act' train, but I can't take a risk that he hasn't sent someone to check up on me in his absence.

Running as quickly as I can through these dark tunnels, I decide I'll talk to Gav from my place. I'll tell him about what happened and see where we go from here. I still can't believe that fucking ghost. What was he playing at?

I make my exit from the tunnels, quickly deciding that taking the rooftop approach to my place will be the quickest and least noticeable option. It's far too crowded down here on the street.

With a little less haste, I make my way up to, then along, the rooftops. I've slowed as to not arouse any suspicion or notice, totally not because I'm winded and tired AF. Finally getting to my building, I enter the rooftop access, taking the stairs down at a snail's pace, holding the stitch in my side while breathing heavily. The fire of rage and adrenaline is all burned up at this point, leaving me exhausted. Damn, I need a good sit-down for sure! But first I'll change...well, shower, then change as I am currently completely drenched in sweat.

I let out a long audible sigh as I close my apartment door behind me, locking it out of reflex. Leaning against said door, I work up the will to walk any further while fighting the urge to sit. If I sit down now I won't be getting up for a while, and I need to get this sweat and clothing off. Boots first!

As I bend over to unlace them, my studio gets noticeably darker out of nowhere. Turning my head, I look out my windows to discover the silhouette of a large winged creature standing on my balcony. Great! Could this day get any worse? What is he even doing here anyway? He's supposed to be out of town, so he certainly shouldn't be following me. I hear his claw-tipped finger tap my glass three times.

I ignore him and continue to unlace my boots. He taps three times again, but I just move on to the next boot. However, I lose it when he moves on to a stream of constant taps in a steady beat. I kick my boots off, letting them land wherever, and violently yank my balcony door open.

"What do you want?!" I shout as I glare up at his face...area. The sun is behind him, casting his form, including his dumb face, entirely in shadow.

"The door to your balcony wasn't even locked?!" He sounds appalled and angry. "There are many who can get onto your porch with ease and walk right in. This is dangerous."

"Thank you for the heads up. Now, if you don't mind, I need a shower, and I'm sure you have countless other balconies to check." I move to shut the door, but he stops me by placing his hand upon it.

"That was not my purpose for being here. I was merely surprised."

"Oh, you mean the Order doesn't have the time or resources to check its citizens outside doors for security?" I taunt, my voice dripping with sarcasm.

"Of course, it doesn't. That would be a waste. This is something that is your responsibility." I'm a little surprised by his earnest answer. What is with this guy? "I'm here, Alexis Callaway, concerning a theft that recently took place. A theft I believe you've planned for several weeks, then executed this very day." He steps through the door, his serious and imposing demeanor making me retreat. As nonchalantly as I can muster with him invading my space, I reply to his accusations.

"Not that again. When are you going to drop this persecution of me? I'm no thief." He's backed me up into the side of a chair, and I sway as I try not to fall into it.

"Then why are you currently wearing thieves' garb? Why did I see you running along the rooftops just moments ago? And why are you sweating so profusely? Must have been a long run from that vampires' keep to here." Damn, how did he find out about my heist and where I just came from?

"I was exercising," is the first thing I can get out.

"Exercising?" he asks in a blank tone, not at all fooled. "By running on roofs?"

"Yeah," I hang onto the lie, "you know, parkour!" At his arched eyebrow, I add, "PK, freerunning, urban acrobatics." Unphased, he pointedly glances down at my clothes, then back at me, clearly waiting for me to explain them. "These are my workout clothes. Can't very well use my regular clothes when I'm running and jumping around. These are form fitting so they don't get in my way and black so they don't get stained." These are some pretty good lies right here. Totally going to use them if ever questioned about these clothes again. "And obviously I'm sweaty because I was working out. You saw me at it up there." He does not appear to be convinced.

Stone takes a step back, giving me a bit more breathing room, then folds his arms across his chest. My heart rate has kicked up to full force under his scrutiny, not to mention his proximity. If this were one of those dreams, he would...

"What of the alarms that I heard going off at the vampires' keep, hmmm? Got a clever lie for those too, Alexis? What about the familiar you met with several times? He is connected with that coven, Alexis." Sure wish he'd stop saying my real name; it's doing things to me. "Where's that new cloak you had made? The one that's suspiciously the same color as the tower that was just robbed." Fuck. "What about that drawing class? I remember you took considerable pains when sketching a certain location, a location that had an amazing view of the aforementioned tower."

Fuck, fuck, fuck! How did he know all this? He must have been following me more closely, and more often, than I realized. Was his time off a ploy to catch me? No, no, if that had been the case he'd have been waiting around that tower for me. I would never have made it home if that were true.

"I would like to see those drawings, Alexis," he says coolly as he extends a hand as if expecting them right this moment.

"Fine," I hiss. "You want to see them? Have a look." I gesture over to my dining table where my drawings from that class are strewn all over it. I thought I might go back and try to fix a few or add some details, but I never did. "In fact, why don't you just go ahead and search my whole place while you're at it?!" His brows lurch up in surprise. I wish I could appreciate it, but I'm so over everything. This has been a truly terrible day.

"Go ahead!" I screech. "I know you want to." I flop onto the floor, remembering how he searched the chair last time. And I'll be damned if I'm made to move off my comfy couch once I get onto it. "Well, go on, big boy. Search around to your heart's content." I start rubbing my poor aching feet as I continue. "But after you find nothing, I expect to no longer be harassed by you. Ever again! And if I see even a wingtip of yours following me around, I'll march down to your office and tell your superiors, you got that?"

"No." It's the deepest I've ever heard his voice, aside from in dreams, that is. I'm so shocked by the word, and it's timbre, that all I can do is gape at him for a moment.

"No? What do you mean, no?" I finally snap back. He steps closer and squats down, still looming over me, but nearer. His kilt parts in a tantalizing way, but it's too long to see anything fun.

"I will not be tricked into taking this loaded deal," he answers. "You would have been too clever to have brought the stolen item back here, and the cloak isn't with you either since I watched you make your way inside. While those drawings," he nods his head in their direction while maintaining eye contact with me, "only show that you took more care and time on certain subjects."

I swallow audibly as he leans in even closer to me, his demeanor so intense I feel like I'm trembling. But I'm not the trembling kind, am I? What is this Gargoyle doing to me?!

"I know you were a part of at least two thefts. I know you are a member of the Thieves Guild," I keep my best poker face on at that little tidbit, "and I will not stop in my pursuit or surveillance of you until I have the proof I need. You may have others fooled with that 'I'm only a human' ploy, but I see through it." He stands and offers me a hand up.

"Come, I'll be taking you into Order Unit 15. There you will be questioned about–" he suddenly cuts himself off as I come to stand in front of him. At first, I thought it was because I didn't use his offered hand to get up, but then I notice his eyes are locked on the kitchen counter behind me. I mean, I'm aware that it's a mess but it can't be that bad. I glance over and am instantly mortified. My stone dildo is sitting as pretty as you please right out in the open on the counter. I forgot I left it there to dry after I washed it this morning.

Stone is staring straight at it, frozen, as if his mind can not compute.

"Is...is that yours?" His question is hushed. So I roll my eyes and scoff.

"No, a neighbor wanted me to babysit it for her. Yes, of course, it's mine, you prude. I'm a grown woman, and I wasn't expecting company." Before I can continue, however, he interjects.

"You use this?" His focus finally comes back to me. "How many notches? How deep can you take it?" The highly inappropriate question is practically asked in a growl. His voice has turned so low and gravely, his eyes upon me have become an inferno, his expression remarkably similar to how he looks in my naughty dreams right before he pounces on me.

"Umm," is the only reply I can give at the moment, and even that comes out shaky.

"I do hate to intrude on this clearly private moment, but I fear I may see things I'm not prepared to if I don't interject." An all too familiar voice chimes in to my right, making me jump and squeak in surprise.

"What the hell, Valda?! What are you doing here?" I end up covering my chest with my arms like he's caught me naked or something, even though I'm still wearing my extremely sweaty clothes.

"Are you familiar with this apparition, Alexis?" the Gargoyle asks as he slightly positions himself between me and the ghost. Guess even he is picking up on how uncomfortable I am at this moment.

"Oh, I've been a thorn in Lexi's side for longer than you, I dare say. Isn't that right, human?" Valda has hovered over and is passively inspecting my drawing on the table. He sneers at my work and arches an eyebrow at me. "I think you need more practice, dear. I can barely tell what these buildings are supposed to be, and I've resided in Avenston longer than any other."

"That's it! I'm done!" I shout while throwing both of my hands in the air. "You two pricks can get the hell out of my apartment. Now." They both just stare at me. "I mean it. I can't take anymore of either of you, and I certainly can't deal with you both at once. The nerve of you guys, invading my home, is remarkable!" I stride over to the table, hurriedly stacking my drawings in a pile. "This is my space, and you are messing with the vibes. I want you both gone," I glare pointedly at the ghost in my table, "and I'll be dealing with you later."

"Oh, well, that is a truly marvelous glare. If I were alive, I'm sure I'd be shaking in my boots." Valda floats into the living room area and plops down onto the couch, in a very uncharacteristically easygoing manner. Not at all like the normal stick-up-his-ass grace I'm used to seeing him exhibit. "If I leave now, I won't be able to tell you both about a case I wish to hire you for, and it would be so much easier to just explain it all once."

"A case? What kind of case?" Stone has been silent, simply taking it all in, but I guess the bait of a case is too much for him. Valda leans forward on the edge of the couch, placing his elbows on his knees and steepling his fingers.

"I would like you two to solve a murder."

Chapter 11

Stone

"What murder? Who's? When did it take place? Where? Why ask us? Which investigators are on the case?" I can't seem to stop the flood of questions that have leaped to mind from spilling out.

"I knew you'd be intrigued," the ghost—Valda she called him—replies instead of answering a single question. "You have a true investigator's mind, even if you are a Gargoyle. It's too bad the Order is holding you back because of it. Well, that and your grandfather."

"For someone I've never met, you seem to have an awful lot of information about my situation, ghost." I let some of the anger his words evoked seep into my tone. "Are you going to actually explain anything about this supposed murder, or do you just like to hear yourself talk?"

"It's probably the second one," Alexis chimes in as she undoes the top of her suit while collapsing onto a chair. "He's a major asshole who thinks he knows everything. But at least I see he isn't only bigoted towards humans." Crossing her arms, she sinks deeper into her seat and asks, "What do you have against Gargoyles anyway?"

"I'm not bigoted towards anyone, and I'll thank you for keeping such opinions to yourself." Alexis scoffs at his words. "You have to realize that some beings and creatures, having possession of certain abilities or attributes, are more suited to certain things...Look, I'm not here to wax poetic about ideology with you. Do you want to hear about the murder or not?"

"Yes," I interject before they can continue a discussion I have no desire to be a part of. "Explain yourself or be off. We were in the middle of our own situation before you wandered in, uninvited."

"Mmmm, yes, and quite a situation it was too," Valda quips while shooting a smirk at Alexis.

"Enough!" I shout. It's clear there is no love lost between these two, and I have no wish to be caught in the middle of it. I have my own agenda here, and if this apparition does not get to his point soon, I'll find myself a necromancer who will make him talk. A murder is no thing to be teasing or messing around with. "Tell us, who's been murdered and why are you coming to us?"

"Why, it's my own murder, of course, and I would like you two to solve it." He beams at us like he's bestowed a great honor.

"Pass!" Alexis declares as she stands up from her chair. "Why the fuck would I ever help you with anything?" She quickly strides over to the door I came in from, pulling it open with more force than needed. "Now, if you two would kindly leave, I desperately need a hot bath and an entire bottle of wine."

"Tsk, tsk. Ushering me out before finding out what's in it for you." His tone is condescending, and I don't care for it at all. "There are many benefits for you, should you succeed. Firstly," he reaches an arm through the couch and pulls out a jewel-encrusted dagger, "I'll give you this." Alexis's eyes are wide with rage. "You see, Patrolman, Lexi didn't steal from the vampires' keep today, I did."

"You little weasel, you–" but she stops herself with a quick glance at me, clearly not wanting to divulge too much in my presence.

"Yes, I stole your prize. I thought it would be a nice little added incentive to get you on the case." I can practically hear her grinding her teeth. "You see, Stone, this was supposed to be her job, and she did an awful lot of work to complete it. But alas, I am the better thief and took it right in front of her."

"You're a cheater is what you are. Using your ghostly abilities to take what was mine." Seems as though Alexis no longer cares about admitting things in front of me. "You broke so many Guild rules today, Valda, and I'm going to get you kicked out." She walks right up to him, her furious face inches away from his pompous expression. "Then I'm going to find somebody to put you into a glass jar and hurl you into an abyss!" The ghost only chuckles at that.

"And there is yet another reason for you to solve my murder, human." I've decided I hate it when he calls her that. Sounds far too condescending from him. "If you solve my murder, I'll finally be free to move on. Thus I will be gone forever, completely out of your hair at last." Alexis seems surprised by this fact. Perhaps she had been too upset by him to realize. Needing their murder solved before they can cross over is highly common amongst ghosts. Mostly due to their own stubbornness.

"To sweeten the pot for you, not only will you be rid of me and claim the dagger for yourself, but I will also leave you and the Gargoyle all the possessions I have acquired over the centuries.

Not to brag, but they are quite...substantial." He flashes the dagger at her, moving it so it glints and glitters from the sun's rays. "Of course, the offer is only good if you both agree," he adds while turning back to me.

"What does he get out of it?" Alexis asks while gesturing towards me. I haven't moved or spoken the entire time, instead opting to watch and listen to them, taking it all in.

"You mean, aside from half of my afterlife's work? Why, Stone will get to solve one of the oldest murders in Avenston. Proving to himself, and all his naysayers, that he is more than capable of being the investigator he has been aspiring to become." The ghost comes to float closer towards me. "He'll finally be able to show his grandfather that he can do more than just stand watch, demonstrating that his mind is his greatest asset, not his brawn."

I only grunt in response. So he turns back to Alexis.

"Since I've let the cat out of the bag in affirming your thief-hood, he no longer has the need to solve the riddle that is you, Lexi. And our dear patrolman here needs a conundrum for his brain to mull over." He smirks back at me. "In truth, he'd probably take the case solely to have the puzzle. Simply solving my murder for the sake of solving it. Isn't that right?" I make no reply, remaining as still as granite. I'll give him nothing, that is until he adds, "Plus, given what I've seen, I'm guessing spending some time in closer proximity to you, Lexi, will be an unexpected boon."

My eyes, and the fact that my breath may have hitched for a moment, must confirm something for Valda as he begins to chuckle.

"Why?" Alexis asks, sparing me his taunting laughter. "Why do you want to pass on? Why now? And why the fuck have you asked us?" Unexpectedly, all signs of his mirth fade in an instant.

"I'm tired," comes a haggard reply. His being reflects the truth of those words by his change in body language and tone of voice. Almost like he's dropped a performance, his ghostly form alters. Shoulders slump where once they were squared, chin falls from its lofty position, his translucent outline blurs when just moments before it was crisp. Moving slowly to sit on the edge of the couch, the ghost bows his head to rest in between his hands, gazing at the ground for a moment before he continues.

"I've been this way for far longer than even I can remember, and I can't stand it anymore," the last part comes out so dejected. "As a ghost, one always feels diminished, but I now feel like the barest whisper of myself. I can't....I just can't do this anymore. And pretending that everything is fine feels more taxing by the day where it once helped me persevere." Finally he looks up at us, "I need your help. I need you to succeed where so many others have failed." Turning to me, he explains further.

"I chose you because I see your abilities and wish to use them. You focus so intensely on any investigation you undertake, even going so far as bringing such work home with you." He knows about the files I keep at my residence? I must react because he adds, "I've had my eye on you for some time. You have the drive to push yourself into being what you want, even when others are trying to hold you back. I need your insights and your perseverance." Turning to Alexis, he continues.

"I'll admit, I severely underestimated you when you first came to the guild and began your training. But you really proved yourself with everything you have accomplished while remaining human. It impressed me. I was going to tell you so myself at your official ceremony into the Thieves Guild, but then you had a run in with Stone." At this, he gets up and begins to pace in front of the couch, seeming to have gained more energy.

"I had gotten my hopes up so many times before, which is one reason why I never approached Stone. Then it was like the Fates themselves had brought you two together for me. One who perhaps had the ability to solve my murder coupled with a desire to advance in his career. The other with the gumption to achieve things despite the odds, who also has an extreme dislike for me. Both having something to prove to the world."

He turns toward us, excitement etched across his face. That's when I realize Alexis and I have gravitated towards each other during his admission. We are standing surprisingly near now.

"I decided that if you two were to use your individual talents and skills together, that maybe this time..." he closes his eyes as he takes a moment, "...maybe this time it will work."

"So I set my plan in motion!" The ghost has reclaimed some of his initial vigor and poise. He's back to pacing but with a straighter spine, nose in the air, and swagger in his gate. "Instead of congratulating Lexi, I would drive her even further into her hatred of me. I would provoke and goad until she would be truly motivated into being rid of me."

"Mission successful," Alexis angrily murmurs at my side, though Valda doesn't seem to hear it.

"Stone, you will never comprehend how truly giddy I was when I discovered you already had an interest in our human." The ghost actually chuckles. "He's even made a profile of you, Lexi, and taken vast notes about your movements, your habits." I can practically feel her glare upon the side of my face. I decide it's in my best interest to keep my eyes on the ghost. "Which means I didn't need to find ways to push you two together. Goodness, Lexi, now that's a death stare! You know, Stone, I think she might hate you almost as much as she hates me." At this, she turns her death stare back to the ghost.

"Is that why you stole the dagger? To make me want to murder you so much that I'd agree to damn near anything to get rid of you?" Her questions are full of venom, but Valda doesn't seem to care.

"Exactly, my dear girl! Glad you're catching up." An involuntary rumble comes from my chest. "You understand it wasn't personal, of course. I simply needed to push you over the edge. Though the expressions that flittered across your face as you watched me do it–" My rumble is more audible this time. "Yes, yes," he waves at me. "I also couldn't have been happier that you planned your heist around Stone's little vacation, a truly perfect time for you two to fully devote to my murder. Though I was a bit anxious when you flew off to that mountain. Thankfully, you came back just in time. It all couldn't have been more perfect." He's beaming at us both, while we gaze back at him in silence.

"Pass!" Alexis quickly turns, marches right into her bathroom, and slams the door shut.

"WHAT?!" The ghost shrieks in disbelief. "Come now, don't be ridiculous. You must see reason here. If not with anything else in your life, you have to be reasonable here!" He begins to waft after her right when the bathwater kicks on.

"If you enter that room while she's bathing, I'll also turn down your case." I growl out in warning.

"Wha-, bu-, now see here," Valda sputters out indignantly. "She can't be serious. I mean...okay, perhaps I went a bit too far in my prodding, but I had to be sure, you see." I'm not sure who he's trying to convince since Alexis isn't even in the room anymore.

"You...you will try to solve my murder, won't you, Stone?"

"I thought you said we both had to agree," I counter.

"Oh, well, something is better than nothing, I suppose."

"Mmmm, a glowing recommendation. But yes, Valda, I will take the case and investigate your death." Before I can continue, he interrupts.

"Excellent! Excellent. I knew you were better than those other riffraff one typically finds in the Order."

"However," I interject harshly, "the dagger will be going back to its rightful owner, along with any other 'treasure' you've stolen that I find in your collection. I also want you to understand that my main reason for doing this is to get you, a spectral thief, off the streets. You pose too much of a hazard to be left to your own devices, especially since you seem to be using your gifts primarily for theft and spying on the people of this city."

"I'm sorry to say that you'll be hard-pressed to discover who the rightful owner of this dagger is." He gestures to the dagger that is currently lying on the table. "The two vampire covens who claim ownership have been stealing this little bobble back and forth for quite some time. I know I've helped one or the other 'reclaim' it at least five times myself."

"Just another mystery for me to solve then," I answer while reaching for the dagger.

"Don't you dare take that dagger, Stone!" Alexis shouts from the bathroom. "That is part of my payment." She must be able to hear us now that the water has stopped running.

"Does that mean you'll help me leave this plane of existence?" Valda shouts back.

"I haven't decided yet. I hate being manipulated into things. I'm trying to decide what's worse, that or you." There's a long pause before, "Could you two please leave? Geezus! Can't a girl get a little peace and quiet alone? It's been a stressful and tiring day!"

"I'm not leaving that stolen dagger here," I respond through the door at her. "Especially not in the care of two confirmed thieves." She makes an overly exasperated sound, quickly followed by a loud splash of water. I can almost envision her hitting the water in frustration.

"Well, at least get us some food. I'm starving!"

"I'll pop out and grab you two something. Give our human some more time to mull things over. There's a curry place nearby I've noticed she frequents." Fast as a falling rock, the ghost disappears into the floor, eliciting a startled scream from below.

I pinch the bridge of my nose and take a calming breath. This is not how I intended to spend my vacation. Peering around at the disarray Alexis lives in, I decide I can't think with all the chaos around me. I'm just starting to clean up when I realize the dagger is gone. That thieving ghost!

Chapter 12

---◄O►---

Alexis

The nerve of that guy! Stealing my prize, almost getting me caught, confirming to the Gargoyle that I am indeed a thief, informing me he's been an asshole to me on purpose in an asinine attempt to manipulate me into doing him a favor, then confessing it all like I should be grateful to be chosen.

I slap the water a few more times before fully submerging into the tub. I stay there till my lungs can no longer stand the burning need for air. How could this day have gone so sideways?

As I finish attacking my skin with salt scrub, I hear my pocket mirror buzzing in the pile of discarded clothes. With some effort, I manage to stretch and reach just far enough to snag it without having to leave my warm watery refuge.

I open it to see Gav's name and image upon the surface of the mirror. Awesome. Now I have to explain what happened to my mentor. Tapping the mirror, I accept his call.

"Hey, Gav." Ugh, that sounded more exhausted than I intended.

"Hey. Wanted to let you know Valda just dropped off the dagger for you. Sorry the Gargoyle from the Order is still on your case." I'm stunned into silence, but Gav must not notice my surprised expression. "The ghost also informed me he was the reason the alarms went off. The client is disappointed that their rivals knew so quickly about the theft, so no bonus from them. However," Gav eyes me suspiciously, "Valda told me to transfer the lost bonus amount from his holdings into yours, stating that since it was his interference that cost you the bonus, he should instead be held responsible and pay it himself."

All I can do is stare in confusion at him. Valda turned in the dagger and gave me credit for its theft? Valda admitted that he was the reason for the alarm? Valda paid out the lost bonus from his own funds?

"Given your surprised expression, I'm assuming he didn't tell you he'd be admitting that." Gav's got a crooked smile on his face. "To be honest, I'm surprised and intrigued myself. What exactly happened in the tower, Lexi?" He's waiting for my response, but I don't know what to say exactly. I don't want to be a narc after Valda took the fall, as he should, and then paid the lost bonus, which he also should totally be responsible for. I decide to give the ghost a chance to get our stories straight before telling Gav anything.

"Can we discuss this later? As you can see, I am bathing. Plus, the Gargoyle in question is currently in my living room." Gav's mood instantly shifts at that. "Don't worry. I'm not in any trouble. We have a little business matter to discuss that he was impatient to get on with, while I refused to continue to do so covered in sweat. I promise I'll give you the skinny when I can."

"The what?" comes his perplexed reply.

"You know, the skinny? The lowdown, the deets, the 411, the scoop, the dirt, the tea..." I trail off as he looks at me like I've lost it. Note to self, learn more lingo that applies to this world. "I'll tell you the whole story later. Promise."

"I'll accept that, for the moment," he answers with an arched eyebrow. Before he can change his mind and start asking more questions, I quickly end the conversation.

"K, thanks, bye!" I rush before snapping the compact shut. Hastily, I rinse the salt scrub off as the water drains from the tub, opting to finish cleaning myself in the shower. I wash up, lotion my body, then grab a red silky robe to wear for now. I need to get back out there quickly because if Stone's noticed the dagger's missing, he's going to be one angry monster.

"Is Valda back with the food yet–" I'm shocked into stillness in the middle of tying the robe's sash, the sight before me is completely unexpected. Not only is my apartment cleaner than it has been since moving in, but the Gargoyle is standing in my kitchen washing dishes by hand. There is a cabinet-type box in the kitchen, similar to a dishwasher, that he could be using instead.

"Why are you washing those?"

"Because you had so many dirty dishes piled up that they wouldn't all fit in the dish-cleaner! And we need something to eat off of...and with." His reply is so grumpy that it's almost cute. Reminds me of my eldest brother.

"Dinner is served!" Valda stands at the front door, a bag in each hand held aloft as if in victory. He wafts over to the spotless table to set the bags down. "Goodness, looks much better in here, I must say. You've been a busy boy, haven't you?" Stone turns to face the ghost, drying his hands with a dishtowel.

"Where's the dagger, Valda?" he questions through gritted teeth, anger etched into his face.

"Oh, at this point, I should think it's with those who claim ownership and hired the Thieves Guild to retrieve their once-stolen treasure. Seeing as how the Order wouldn't dare interfere with a reclamation request, I'd say the matter is quite resolved." I try to hide a smile at the seething stance currently being displayed by Stone. "Now, if you are quite done brooding over there, I suggest you bring over some dry dishes to set the table."

Since I don't want a very angry Gargoyle breaking my plates, I step in to grab what we need off the drying rack, snatching the dishtowel Stone flung onto his shoulder along the way. The food is filling my place with the most delectable smells. If I don't eat right this second, I might pass out. Burned way too many calories today! Time to replenish.

"We'll see about that," Stone finally replies before coming over to the table and plunking into a chair, arms folded over his chest. That is one grumpy fella. I empty the bags of food which nearly fill up my large dining table.

"Got enough food there, Valda? Geez!" I'm not mad about it, just means leftovers for me!

"Well, it has been some time since I got food for anyone. Too much? I assumed our flying mountain here would really 'pack it away', as it were." Instead of his usual position of floating to stand in the middle of a table, Valda has opted to sit in a chair at one end of the table. I take a seat opposite Stone, in order to better reach all this delicious food. Not because I'd rather look at him than the ghost. With an exasperated sigh, Stone reaches to begin filling his plate.

"Alright, ghost, give us the details of your case. Tell us why you believe you have been murdered." I'm actually kind of glad

Stone has brought it back up. Despite myself, I have been curious. Plus I've currently got my face stuffed with this world's version of Vindaloo curry. This stuff has the perfect fiery hot spice level I love. If Valda was trying to butter me up with food, it just might be working.

"Unfortunately, what I have in the way of details is very limited indeed. It appears I have been dead for so long that not only do I no longer remember when I died, but even my own name has been lost to me. Valda is but one name in a long list I have chosen for myself over the years." Eyes wide, I stare at Valda. Stone only hums and nods his head, taking out his notepad to scribble down information as he chews.

"What do you mean you can't remember your own name? That's...that's terrible. I didn't even realize that could happen." Against my better judgement, I find myself feeling a little sorry for Valda.

"Yes, tragic, isn't it? I'm sure it was a truly spectacular name too. A terrible shame." He says it with such earnest arrogance that I instantly feel less sorry for him. "I believe it's pretty obvious I was murdered. What Fae dies as young as I from 'natural' causes?" And of course, he uses air quotes. "Furthermore, why would I stay around, unable to move on, if it wasn't murder?" His condescending tone instantly removes any sympathy I had for him moments ago.

"You recall for certain that you were a Fae? Any idea if you were a particular type of Fae? Seelie or Unseelie?" Glad Stone knows what kinds of questions to ask. I've never even heard the word 'sealy'.

"Well, I…I may not exactly remember being a Fae. But one assumes, with my visage and countenance…"

"It would be more beneficial if you stick to facts only and leave out your conjectures." Stone eyes him until Valda makes a reply.

"Yes, yes. Alright. Fine. I will try to recount everything to you as factually as possible." Valda crosses his arms and turns his head so he doesn't have to face either of us.

"Thank you. So, where are your boundaries? Knowing where you can and cannot travel may help us locate where your death took place or, if you are attached to an item, where the item may be found for further inspection." In between questions, Stone has been eating steadily but methodically. While I, on the other hand, grew up with three older brothers and am eating like someone may come along at any moment and take all this food. Food was a competition with a 'you snooze, you lose' mentality. I slow down a little, somewhat embarrassed by my caveman-like eating style.

"Ah, yes, that would be another sticking point, I'm afraid." Valda's response has me turning back to him. "You see, I can go anywhere within the city limits of Avenston. As the city has expanded, so too have my boundaries. I can vaguely recall a time when the area we are currently in was out of bounds to me." Valda is looking both proud and sheepish simultaneously.

"How is that possible?" Stone questions. "As far as I knew, ghosts were either tied to their location of death or an item that was near to hand at death. Occasionally it can be a highly treasured item. Though, even in the case of being linked to an item, there was still only so far they could travel. Yes, the distance could increase with time, but to have the run of a sprawling city such as Aventson…" Stone has drifted off into thought.

"Indeed, I am quite the unique specimen," Valda boasts. "I've come across many a fellow apparition in my day, but none have had the freedom I possess. As lovely as it has been to traverse our great city and explore new places as it expanded, it has made things rather difficult over the years as I've asked others for help in solving my murder." He chuckles nervously, glancing back and forth between us. Dropping my fork on my plate with a clatter, I pin Valda with my eyes.

"Do you have any useful information, like, at all? Damn, man. This is sounding more and more impossible by the minute." At this point, I'm so full I could burst, not that I'm done eating. Just need to give my stomach time to adjust.

"Of course, I have useful information, human. No need to snap at me."

"Well, get on with it then." Before I can continue to berate the ghost, Stone interjects.

"What can you tell us, Valda?"

"For starters, there is a place, deep within the city, that I get transported to yearly. I typically find myself coming back into consciousness there without even realizing I had lost it to begin with." Valda's eyes unfocus for a moment, the edges of his form going hazy before snapping back into sharpness. "It is presently underground, as the city has grown up around it. There used to be many passages to it, but over the years they have been blocked up or caved in. However, there is yet one tunnel that remains," he looks triumphant for a second, "though it is tricky for corporeals to get to," he adds sheepishly.

"But there is a way, and you can lead us there, correct?" Stone asks while scribbling in his notepad.

"Of course! In fact, I can take you to its entrance tonight." At Stone's quizzical expression, he offers, "It's located in a special members-only club that typically only operates at night. But fear not, each evening a unique passcode is created in case members wish to invite guests. I shall listen at the door and provide the code so you two may enter." Eyeing me up and down in an uncomfortably critical way, Valda continues.

"Though you two will need to blend in if you wish to reach the secret passage, as it is all the way in the back. Lexi, dear, what is the sluttiest outfit you own?"

Chapter 13

Alexis

Valda told me to wear my sluttiest outfit, so I did. But now, I'm standing out here freezing my ass off as we wait for that ghost to get the secret phrase for tonight. I didn't think we would have to wait this long, so I didn't bring a coat, even though Stone suggested it. So he gets to look all self-satisfied as I shift from heel to heel, rubbing my arms in an effort to keep warm.

On the plus side, I clearly chose the right fit judging from what I've seen others wearing who enter this place. And I thought I wasn't afraid to show some skin. Damn!

Tonight, I opted for my inky black blunt bob hair, the spell connected to a gold ear cuff. I've added little touches of other gold jewelry, including a thin belly chain. It all matches my gold period cuff perfectly. My short black skirt sits low on my hips. Its sides have wide open lacing, to show off even more skin along my thighs. My top, if you can call it that, is really just a long piece of silky black fabric that's placed, twisted, and tied strategically. I've got it done up in a halter-top fashion. My heels, which I had spelled to feel like I'm walking on clouds, are also black with strings that wrap up my leg to just under my knee. In keeping with the theme, I've painted my lips black and my nails gold.

I was feeling pretty sexy too, with my eyeliner winged to perfection and a sway in my stride. Even managed to get an appreciative, slow up-and-down lookover from Stone when I met him up here, the kind that made my skin tingle. That was until now, where I find myself hiding on a parapet, shuffling around to keep warm, with only a stoic Gargoyle as company. I feel like we've been up here forever! Stone has been still as a statue, watching the door to the members-only club with laser focus.

Unable to stand the waiting anymore and needing a distraction from the chilly weather, I attempt to engage Stone in conversation.

"Has anyone shown up yet who didn't flash one of those silver pins?" All the people I've seen enter so far have shown off the same brooch to the slit in the door after knocking. Guessing you get one as a member. "Or have you seen Valda at all?"

"No."

Okay, that didn't seem to work. Let's try some open-ended questions, the kind I had to learn when I worked retail. Nothing that can be answered with a simple yes or no.

"Wonder why Valda didn't make you dress in something sexy? All those guys have been looking pretty nice from what I've seen."

"Kilts are already sexy," he replies flatly. Can't really argue with him there; he's not wrong.

"Well, you could have put on a fancier one or something. Maybe an all-black version to match me."

"These are the colors of my Clan. I only own one kilt with a different tartan, but that was for a special event. I never felt the need to explore other patterns or colors." He surprises me by finally glancing my way. Unfortunately, I'm not quick enough to hide my warming efforts. I inwardly prepare myself for an 'I told you so,' but he only scowls at me as he stands from his crouch.

Wordlessly, he walks over to stand next to me, snapping a wing open to hover near my exposed skin. Not touching but still blocking most of the wind. I'm surprised to feel that he, and by extension his wing, generates heat. Sometimes I forget that he isn't actually made of rock.

Not willing to go back to waiting in silence, I continue my questions.

"What kind of a secret club do you think this is? Have you noticed any details or seen any clues? Think it's just for the super rich or something? Oh, wonder if there are, like, illegal cage fights going on in there?" At first, all I get is an "Hmm," before he eventually replies.

"From what I have gathered, they are not all 'super rich.' They are, however, from a variety of backgrounds and social status. I've seen a baker, a lawyer, a Clan leader, and a maid. There are many different kinds of beings entering as well. Several Fae, a Basilisk, Centaurs, Nymphs, a Yokai of some kind, Pixies, a Siren. I've recognized a few that don't even live near here, so it's not area-based either." We watch in silence as a group of three, two guys and a woman, approach the door. After a knock two of them show off silver pins and gesture at the third. I'm assuming he's their guest for the night. "Mated Wolf Shifters have brought a Hedge Witch as a guest," he answers before I can ask.

"Wait, I thought guys were called wizards and witches were women?" He gazes down at me like I'm an ignorant country bumpkin.

"Where did you hear that? Wizards are a completely different thing, and a witch would take great offense to that statement." His face morphs to one of concern, "In fact, it would be best to never call anyone a Wizard unless they themselves claim to be one. They–"

"I have a delivery; Hathor sent me!" Valda exclaims as he appears from thin air to float in front of us. I'm so startled I end up clinging to Stone's side. Just like a damn damsel! Immediately, I back away from him.

"What the fuck, Valda?! You scared the shit out of me!" Despite the cold, I feel noticeably warmer after that start. My cheeks are red from embarrassment. Definitely from embarrassment.

"It's the secret code for this week," Valda answers me like he's talking to a silly child. "Apparently, the club only changes it once a week nowadays." He rolls his eyes at the laziness of it. "If anyone asks, an Orc gave it to you. He's out of town but has given this week's code to a few other," the ghost pauses to look Stone over, "larger males. To make up for his absence." He's smiling wickedly, and I wish I knew why. "I would suggest Stone deliver the code to sell the story. Better safe than sorry." Stone nods his head in agreement.

"You're keeping something from us, Valda. I can practically smell your lies of omission." I point a gold-tipped finger right into his chest, "Spill!" He's been smirking at the two of us since we agreed to come here, and I want to know why.

"I don't know what you mean, silly human." Before I can push further, he swiftly continues, "Be sure to do your best to blend in, you two. This is the only entrance left to the underground section I'm taking you to, so if we have to come back, you need to be able to get in again. And do please try to not make it obvious you aren't here for fun. No going straight to the back to find the secret door either. Mingle, observe, partake..."

"Understood," Stone interrupts while walking back to the edge. Turning slightly, he reaches a hand out to me. "I'll glide us down so they can see us arrive together." I take a half step back, toward the stairs I used to get up here. "And it will be quicker. I will not drop you. It will be a very short glide." Ignoring his hand, I walk up to the edge to peer over. It does not look short to me! It's at least four stories up. That's a lot of faith I'd be putting into this Gargoyle.

"Come now, Lexi. Don't tell me this scares you." Valda's tone is mocking, back to how he spoke to me as I was training.

"I'm not about to fall for that, ghost. I know that's your tactic for getting me to do what you want. Well, not this time! And no, I'm not scared. I've scaled much taller buildings. Thank you very much!"

"Though you were in control then," Stone interjects, "and this takes trust. Depending on somebody else, especially a stranger, can be difficult." Oh man, why does that statement give me a sudden spike of emotion? Right in the feels! Moving in closer, he faces me, fisted hand on his chest. "I swear, by the stones of my ancestors, that I will not drop nor harm you." Not sure what it means, exactly, but he says it with such vehemence that I decide to take a little leap of faith.

"I'll hold you to it, big boy. How do you want me?" He doesn't answer. Instead, he picks me up like I'm a bride going over the threshold. Instinctively, I grab hold of his neck. Searching my face, he waits for my nod before he steps up and hops off the ledge.

Curling up tighter into his embrace, I'm pretty proud that I don't utter a peep. Not even when his wings snap open suddenly. The glide over to the door does turn out to be short, and I'm surprised by how disappointed I feel about that. It was actually quite nice. Equal parts exhilarating and terrifying with a dash of calming weightlessness mixed in. I felt a little out of control, yet safely secure in Stone's arms.

Setting me down gently, Stone goes to knock on the door as I pull down my skirt. If anyone had looked up at us, they would have gotten a little show.

"I have a delivery; Hathor sent me." Stone's voice sounds rougher than it had on the roof. The door swings open, and Stone steps aside for me to enter before him, then offers his elbow once within. Such a gentleman.

The hallway is wide enough for us to walk side by side without issue, which is impressive given Stone's size. He doesn't even have to tuck his wings in tightly. One is hovering enticingly close at the moment; I can feel its nearness along my back and shoulder. It feels...nice. Right for some reason.

The corridor we've been walking down isn't long, but there's enough room for a few paintings and torches to break up the rich mahogany walls. I think the paintings are of landscapes, but I only see them through my peripheral vision. My focus is on the door ahead of us, which mirrors the metal door we entered the building through. At the end of the hallway, there's an elegant desk, and in front of the door stands a Legolas-looking dude, if the fellowship went to Downton Abbey. Is he dressed in a maid outfit?

"Welcome and good evening," the tall blond drink of water greets us. "I hear we have some visitors tonight. Have either of you been here before?"

"No," Stone answers for us.

"I see. In that case, I will need you both to read these rules," he hands us a glossy black tablet with words carved into it, "and sign this waiver." Two scrolls appear out of nowhere, and he hands one to each of us to fill out, along with a quill. Stone reads the rules first while I fill out the info on the waiver. Name, race, age, height, weight, sexual orientation...what kind of place is this, a doctor's office?

Stone had stiffened upon receiving the tablet. Clearing his throat uncomfortably, he hands the smooth stone tablet to me. Is this obsidian? Yeah, I think these rules are carved into black obsidian while the words are silver inlaid. I eagerly read the list of rules to see if I can figure out what made this Gargoyle flustered.

1. Consent Is Mandatory & May NOT Be Magically Coerced
2. No Means No—Without Question
3. Ask Before Touching
4. Respect Personal Boundaries
5. Be Polite, Not Pushy
6. Know Your Limits
7. Respect Staff and Hosts
8. No Shape-Shifting Mid-Encounter Without Consent
9. Elemental Magic in Designated Zones Only
10. No Summoning Without Staff Permission
11. Energy Draining & Feeding Is Consent-Based
12. No Breeding

13. Healing Spells Require Permission

14. The Club Has Final Say

No, no, this club can't be what I think it is. I glance over to see Stone signing his waiver. See, he wouldn't continue into this place if that were the case. There's got to be a magical thing I haven't learned about that accounts for these rules. I sign my waiver too, then hand it over.

"Excellent! Please, do enjoy yourselves, and don't worry about cleaning up as that will be taken care of by the staff. If you have any issues, questions, or concerns, don't hesitate to ask anyone in today's uniform." He gestures at his maid outfit, and I mentally prepare myself to see other fantasy creatures in such attire.

Once the waivers are placed inside a desk drawer, the metal door swings open on its own. A red velvet curtain is on the other side but swings away as we near it. At last, I get to see inside this mysterious secret club, and boy what an eyeful I get! As I take in the sights before me, an excited, awkward giggle bubbles up unexpectedly. I'm in an honest-to-goodness sex club! Not only that, I'm here with the most uptight, straitlaced being I've ever met. This is going to be fun!

Before I can make any teasing remarks, another person in a maid getup approaches us. I clock three fox tails before she speaks.

"I understand that this is your first time here. Welcome." She gives a low bow, then smiles wide. I notice some cute little fangs before she continues. "Feel free to partake of the bar." As she gestures to our left, I see a long bar up a few steps on the other side of this big room. "All drinks are enchanted to assure no one overindulges. We must keep our wits to consent." A polite ripple of amusement follows. "This is the main area, but we have smaller rooms for different activities and abilities down the hall to your right, while private rooms that may be reserved for more intimate adventures are in the hallway to the left."

She's been pointing out locations as she talks, but I'm having a real hard time paying attention to her. There's some majorly freaky stuff happening behind her. People chained to walls, tied up on furniture, writhing on the ceiling & in the air. Butts everywhere! And is that a bear being led around on a leash? Stone must see my eyes wandering because as his wing gently taps my shoulder, bringing my attention back to the foxtailed lady.

"The entrance straight ahead has spaces for washing and relaxing only, so please no sexual activities in those locations." I nod that I understand. "There are signs throughout, but you may always ask any member of staff for clarification if in doubt. Of course, the house rules are also posted in most rooms." She gestures to a wall that has the rules I read earlier painted beautifully upon it. "Any questions so far?"

"Nope. You've been very clear. Thanks." Stone had only shaken his head no, so I felt the need to say something.

"Wonderful! Behind you, you will find the costume and toy rooms. You may take what you want yourself or ask staff to get what you require. As with everything else here, all are thoroughly washed, then cleansed of energies between uses." I'm nodding my head, super eager to see what's inside these playtime closets. "Tonight maid costumes are only for staff and have been removed as options. Sorry if this is an inconvenience to either of you." She bows again slightly before continuing.

"You may check your items and clothing with me or inside the costume room. If you toss any items about in your fervor, understand that they will be picked up and checked in for safekeeping. We do not want anything lost or becoming a tripping hazard. With that, I believe my long introduction is done. Any further questions or concerns?"

"Yes," I pipe up. "The costumes, what if there's one we want but it doesn't fit?" I eye Stone up and down with a smirk.

"A valid concern, but let me assure you that we have taken all body shapes and sizes into account with clothing options that magically resize to fit you. But if anything is amiss, the costume attendant will be happy to assist."

"That's wonderful! Right, sweetie?" I ask as I glance up lovingly at Stone. He doesn't reply, so I look back at the attendant. "Thank you. We really do appreciate it. You certainly know how to make new visitors feel more at ease." I pointedly gape at the main floor. "It does all feel a bit intimidating and overwhelming at first glance."

"Of course, miss. We understand completely and do our best to help."

"I think we'll take a little trip to that bar to get our bearings." Stone hasn't moved or uttered a single word since entering. Eventually, I actually have to tug him a little to get him into motion.

Finally, he utters a gruff "Thank you" before moving with me up to the bar. Standing outside in the cold was totally worth it! I expect I'm about to have a supremely interesting night. Can't wait to tease the shit out of this Gargoyle.

Chapter 14

Alexis

The bar itself is pretty empty, considering. We take two stools as I grab the attention of the bartender. Not caring to ask Stone what he wants or to pursue the menu myself, I ask for two of whatever the house special is. The bartender winks at me and deftly sets down two cobalt blue crystal goblets with a pinkish bubbly liquid within. Taking mine, I turn in my stool to see the large space, sipping as I gaze around. The drink is sweet with gin-esque undertones. It settles in the belly nicely and sends unexpected tingles to my joints.

I think I could sit here for hours watching the scenes before me! It's a chaos of different bodies and toys, sounds and sights. There's a circular sunken pit pretty close to the bar. Lining the circle is a continuous couch, and scattered around the floor are various sized pillows. Right in front of us, a woman is getting absolutely railed from behind by a Minotaur. I don't know how she's taking that monster cock of his, but she's clearly enjoying herself.

"What do you think of the show, Lexi?" a disembodied voice asks to my left. I'd recognize that damn ghost's mocking tones anywhere.

"A show is the right word for it," I say in a low voice before taking another sip.

"You should have given us a warning," Stone grits out.

"Oh, but where's the fun in that? Your face in the hallway, then when the curtain was pulled back, priceless!" I can hear Valda chuckling and try not to laugh with him. Wish I'd gotten to see it better myself. Stone only rumbles in response.

"Now, enough fun and games," Valda states as if he weren't the one messing around. "The entrance is in the back in a broom closet near the shower area. The shower that's only for showering, mind. Not the fun kind." I can almost picture Valda's grin.

"Obviously, since the back areas are a no playtime zone," Stone sneers. Grabbing his goblet in a chokehold, he downs the whole thing like a shot. "We got the visitor information as we entered."

"Yes, yes, of course." Valda needlessly clears his throat. "You two, mingle and try to fit in. I'll go scout ahead to make sure there aren't any issues. Meet me in said closet in one hour. That should be enough time." An invisible hand pats me on the head, in a way that feels condescending. "Have fun," is accompanied with a snicker as he leaves. We sit there in silence for a few moments before Stone takes an audible calming breath.

"I'll have another, please." Stone addresses the bartender who immediately provides. Then he directs his words to me. "If I had known this was a sex club, I would have warned you. This isn't the type of thing one springs on a person. I am sorry." I only laugh.

"Oh, I'm having a great time! Don't you worry about me. Yeah, a heads-up would have been nice, but this place is pretty amazing. I've always wanted to visit a place like this, so check that off the bucket list." I take another sip as Stone does the same.

"Heck, if I can, I'll totally come back here sometime." Stone only hmm's in thought at that.

Looking back at the pit, I see that the Minotaur and woman have changed positions. They've moved to a pouf on the floor with him on his back while she rides him for all she's worth. You go, girl! Giddy-up! The Minotaur notices me watching and offers a wink before leaning up to lick the woman's nipple. He continues his eye contact with me as he lavishes her breast with his large tongue. I'm feeling tingles in all kinds of places now, and it's not just the booze this time. Unconsciously, I have gotten closer to Stone, placing a hand on his impressive thigh.

"What are you doing, Alexis?" Stone's voice is low.

"Just playing along. You know, blending in." Moving my hand from his thigh, I gently trace my finger down his wing. "Wasn't that what we were supposed to do?" I try to make the questions as innocent sounding as possible.

"What is the third rule of this club, Alexis?" As I didn't memorize them, I turn my head in search of the rules painted on the wall. There, in a bold font, number three is 'Ask Before Touching.' Oops!

"Well, I didn't think that applied to us. We're here as a pretend couple, so we need to act like it. You think couples ask each other to touch?"

"You want me to treat you as if you were my date here this evening?" He asks it almost like a warning.

"Well, I mean, that is what we are supposed to be doing, right? You're the one who wanted to land at the front door together so we'd be seen, you know...together." I've whispered this as much as

I can, while scanning over the rules again. Don't want to make any other mistakes and get kicked out.

"That is not an answer, Alexis." His tone is so collected that I turn back to face him. His eyes are focused intensely on me, making me go silent for a beat.

"Well, yes. Within reason, of course. I think a couple on a date here would be touching and–" My words are cut short as two strong hands grab my middle, lifting me onto Stone's lap. A hasty 'Hey!' is all that I can get out before Stone whispers near my ear.

"This is where my partner for the night would be sitting. Especially while another male eyes her lustily." I try to swallow, but my throat has suddenly become dry. "I would want to show the whole room that she was here with me. Is this 'within reason,' Alexis?"

"Yep, yeah, this is fine." I answer, trying to say it as cool and calm as possible. Pretty sure it doesn't come out that way though. One of his hands slowly moves over my stomach to play with my belly chain, while the other picks up his goblet to casually take a sip. When did the tables turn on me?! I was supposed to be the one messing with him, not the other way around. I've got to get the upper hand back.

I search the room for inspiration. The Minotaur currently has his head between his partner's thighs, spreading her legs wide open with his horns. After seeing his tongue, I'm going to assume she is a very lucky girl right now. Against my back, I feel a rumble in Stone's chest. He bends down again, touching the tip of his nose to the shell of my ear.

"I like you in chains, Alexis." His rough whisper washes over my flesh, the words making me squeeze my thighs.

"Wha-what?" comes out breathy, embarrassingly so. He pointedly drags a clawed fingertip along the chain on my belly. "Oh!" I try to laugh like he's made a joke. "Very funny." I've got to do something to regain the upper hand, he's got me wiggling on his lap for crying out loud! Wait, wiggling on his lap...perfect.

I scooch up his thighs a little further and lean back into his chest. Placing the back of my head into his shoulder, I turn my neck so I can see the painted rules on the wall clearly.

"Rule number one," I begin, doing my best phone sex operator imitation, "consent is mandatory and may not be magically coerced." I grind my ass into his lap, just a little. "Rule number two, no means no, without question." I grind a little harder and arch my back. His hand on my belly stills. "Rule number three," arching further I reach a hand up to touch one of his horns, "ask before touching." I add a cute little moan when I finally feel him beginning to harden beneath me.

"What are you doing, little thief?" The whole of his hand is clutching my stomach, points just beginning to dig in.

"Me?" I switch to a coy tone. "Oh, I'm just playing."

"Playing?" He's back to speaking into my ear, his warm breath dancing across my exposed neck. "Do you really want to play, Alexis?"

"What?!" My eyes snap open. I hadn't realized they were closed.

"Do you consent to playing? I'll play with you, if that's what you want." My heart rate has kicked up significantly, my chest rises and falls as my breath quickens. He...he can't be...is he serious? Could he be teasing me, or is this for real? "Alexis"—I must have been quiet for too long—"do you want me to play with you?"

"Yes," I answer automatically while visions of him from my dreams dance in my head. Plus, we have to act the part, right? I have to play along so we can hide our true motives. Though at the moment, I'm having a hard time remembering what my real reasons for being in his lap are.

"Yes, what?" His cock has gotten noticeably harder under my ass, and that voice makes my whole body shudder.

"Yes, sir," I whisper.

"Good girl." Why does that make me melt into him?! "I see just the place." Stone lifts me off his lap to set me down on my feet. My legs wobble a little as he places a hand on the small of my back, guiding me. No, I won't show him how he's affecting me! I bring forth all the poise I ever learned in ballet, and I walk gracefully beside him.

My eyes go wide, however, when I see where he's leading us. Not to one of the more private rooms like I had assumed. No, he's directing me to a corner of this very open room where an interesting chair sits. It looks like a more comfortable OBGYN table, but with straps for your arms, legs...well, all over the body, really.

Stone confidently steps up on the platform, circling the seat while testing the straps, while I remain at the edge of the dais that this chair sits upon. There are a few cushions, chairs, and loveseats angled towards it for people to watch the show.

"Yes, I think this will do nicely." He glances over at me with an arched eyebrow. "That is, if you still want to play?" There's a smug little smile tugging at the corner of his lips, a challenge in his tone. If he thinks for one minute that I'll be the one to back down first, he has another thing coming. Lifting my chin, I strut onto the stage, leaning over into the raised chair once I reach it, showing the room at large my ass.

"Of course, I still want to play, big boy. What did you have in mind?" The heat in his eyes is searing as he walks closer to me, around me. I straighten to stand at my full height, made considerably taller than my normal six-foot frame due to these heels. Even with the added height, this Gargoyle still looms over me. Eventually, he comes back to face me, arms crossed.

"I'm all yours." At my words, he signals an attendant to come over.

"We would like a pleasure wand, a bee-box, chilling lube, and a training dildo. My partner here still isn't quite ready to take me." Stone has ordered these things like he's at a drive-thru and already knew exactly what he was in the mood for. Who is this guy? I'm starting to think some of my assumptions about him were very, very wrong.

It takes no time at all for the requested items to appear. The hostess sets the tray of toys on a little table near the chair. Stone inspects them before approving the selection. As the host steps away, I notice what Stone currently has in his hand, a stone dildo that bears a striking resemblance to the one I own, the one he saw earlier today.

"Alexis Callaway, do you consent to me using these items on you while you are strapped to this chair?" Taking a moment, I peer at the items on the tray.

"What is a pleasure wand?" I mean, if he's asking, I might as well know exactly what I'm getting into. It straight up looks like the Fairy Godmother's wand or something, but it's fluorescent pink.

"A pleasure wand is an item that, when touched to the skin, creates a sensation of pleasure in the area in question. If you hold out your arm, I will demonstrate." Stone picks up the wand while I extend my forearm toward him. He gently touches the wand tip to my skin, and I instantly feel that the name is a hundred percent accurate.

"Ho, boy, yes, absolutely you may use that wand on me!" Perhaps tomorrow I'll be heading back to a certain sex shop to buy one of my own. Cost be damned! Stone nods as he places that magnificent wand back onto the tray. "What about the icy lube? Can I feel that too before I agree?" Don't want to go freezing off my naughty bits.

"Of course." Using his tail, Stone dips the tip into the glass jar the lube is held in. I'm impressed by how prehensile this tail is as it moves up to rub the lube onto my forearm. It's pleasantly cold, not like an ice cube as I feared. More like something from the back of the fridge. That, I can handle.

"Okay. That's not bad. You may use that too." I eye the bumpy dildo. "You may use all these items, in fact. But I do reserve the right to change my mind later," I quickly add in.

"Certainly. What are your hard no's for this session?" My mind instantly goes blank for a minute. What are my hard no's with this Gargoyle? Truthfully, I hadn't expected it to get this far. I glance at him with an expression of worry and confusion. "Take your time, Alexis. I am a patient male." From under the restraint chair, he pulls a stool out that I hadn't noticed before, then sits, simply waiting for me to answer. In response, I start pacing around to think.

"No anal. I'm not prepared for that." He easily nods in agreement. "No kissing." Another nod. "I'm not ready for that either," I mutter more to myself, though I think he caught that as I hear him stifle a chuckle. I choose to ignore that as I pace this little stage. It's only two steps up and has two walls, behind and to the right, but it's still more visible than anything I've ever done, even in my high school days. I'm sure at some point someone saw me back then since you take a lot of risks when you're young and horny. Which reminds me...

"Absolutely no tickling! I hate it. It's not funny, and I will scream bloody murder if you tickle me while strapped to that chair." My body shivers just thinking about it.

"Understood. No tickling, no kissing, no anal. What is your safe word?" I stop my pacing to look at him. He's made this whole exchange so serious that it's almost taking the fun out of it. So I decide to test the waters and tease him a bit.

"Oh, I don't think a safe word is necessary." He sits up straight at this, narrowing his eyes. "I mean, I get that you're big and strong, but I don't think you'll push it with witnesses around. Plus, if I don't like it, I'll tell you 'stop' or 'no' or 'ouch, that hurts' or whatever." Hearing the stool's legs being violently shoved back makes me turn around. In seconds, I'm face-to-face with a remarkably angry Gargoyle.

"You will have a safe word, Alexis Callaway, or this will go no further. Do you understand me?" His eyes are boring into mine, unblinking. Okay, note to self, do not play around with safe words. I mean, I understand they're important, especially with a monster that is so much stronger than me. Stronger than any man I've ever been with for that matter. I was just trying to yank his chain.

"Yes, of course. I understand. I was just playing with you. Obviously, I have a safe word. It's 'mimic.'" I offer him a wicked little smile to reiterate the fact that I was just messing with him. But he still does not look pleased.

"Hmmm, perhaps I should have included a paddle for us to play with? A little stinging punishment." Why does the thought of Stone taking me across his knee to spank me send a thrill up my spine? "Speaking of punishment," standing to his full height once more, he circles me. "Alexis Callaway, do you consent to follow my orders and to be punished if you do not comply?" I stare at him wide-eyed. What is he asking? Does he...does he want to play dom and sub? I stand there frozen. I mean, I've done a little of that myself with my femme partners, but no one has really been empowered enough to really dominate me. Am I ready for that? Because I get the feeling that this man—oh this man—could do it properly, for sure. I must look like a deer caught in headlights because he comes closer, his tone changing to a softer one.

"You will have your safe word if I push you too far. If something I ask is beyond what you are willing to do, I expect you to use your safe word, Alexis." Voice stern once more, he continues, "Rule number six, know your limits'." Feeling more confident, with only a little unease, I square my shoulders.

"I agree. I will let you attempt to dominate me." I cock my hip and head, offering up as much sass as I can muster. But this only makes him grin. I recognize that look; I've used that look. I might be in for a little surprise if he's as up to the task as he seems. Guess I'll be playing the role of brat tonight.

Gently, he runs a bluish purple knuckle down my arm.

"Strip for me." It's said with such a naturally easy command that my hands automatically come to the tie at my hip. Slowly, I pull the string as he stands near. "Hmmm, good girl." My eyes flutter at the praise issued in such a bass tone. What is it about a deep voice?! "But leave this on," he says while fingering the gold chain around my middle. He takes a few steps backwards, watching and waiting for me to follow his orders.

Oh, I'll do it, because I'm curious AF what this experience is going to be like. But I'll do it in my own damn time. Cocking my head once more, I pull on my string painfully slow. I unlace the skirt in the same methodical manner, watching him as he watches me. Eventually the skirt falls to the floor around my feet revealing the fact that I have no underwear on. There wasn't really a way to wear them in this skirt.

Stone's body shows his surprise in little ways. His nose flares ever so slightly with a quick intake of breath. His body leans in just a little bit closer, and his spine straightens a fraction. Wonder if he's more surprised that I've gone commando or by the fact that I am au naturale down there. That's right, full 70's bush, baby! I lick my lips, biting my lower one. Getting him to react is a reward in itself, and it's got me hot with power.

I kick the skirt to the side, as I reach my hand behind my neck to undo the bow I have there. Just as slowly, I pull the black fabric until it's undone as well, dropping the piece I was holding to let gravity pull the wrapping on my chest off and down. With its silky texture, it doesn't take long before it too is fluttering down to fall at my feet. Resting one hand on my hip, I bring the other to trace a line between my breasts and down my stomach.

"Sit in the chair." With a grin that would rival the cat who ate the canary, I saunter over and sit my naked ass down. It's only when I turn around that I remember we're in a big open room full of people. And to my amazement, we have a little audience. An audience that includes that Minotaur and his fuck buddy. She's sitting on his lap as they watch us. Turnabout is fair play, I guess. There are three others seated around too, but before I can focus on them, Stone steps right in front of me.

With the back of his finger, he traces my jawline all the way to my chin, where he tilts my head to look right up at him. "What is your safe word, my sexy thief?" I swallow thickly before answering.

"Mimic." It's more of a whisper, having lost some of my confidence after facing an unexpected crowd.

"Good girl." That does bring a genuine smile to my face. Mostly because I recognize what he just did for me. He noticed my discomfort, stopped it before I could spiral, and gave me an out. Or at least reminded me that I do have some control here, and we can stop whenever I want.

"Now, lay back. I'm going to strap you in." Tentatively, I lean back as he assists in placing my legs in the stirrups. Magically, the ties bind themselves snugly around my ankles, knees, and thighs as he guides them into place. Stone caresses my legs softly, feeling around the straps. "How do these feel? Not too tight?"

"They feel just fine, but I'll pipe up if they become too much." He nods and begins to walk round to my left side, leaving me wide open to our little audience, but he maintains eye contact with me all the while.

"Oh, I almost forgot to ask, how many climaxes is your limit?" The question is so absurd that I laugh out loud.

Chapter 15

"What?" I ask while laughing in disbelief.

"I asked, how many orgasms is too much for you?" O.M.G. I...I think he's dead serious! He has continued to strap me into the chair, securing my hips, my ribs, and my shoulders. Now he's checking on my left arm.

"Bold of you to assume you can get one orgasm out of me, let alone several." I've had male partners let me down before, which was always a downer. "You're going to have to work to get me there, big boy." Another deep rumble comes from him, which gets louder as he leans down to my ear.

"Challenge accepted." Oh sweet geezus!

He straightens, having finished checking both my arm restraints. There is a head strap too, but he's left it undone. While strapping me in, he had put the chair in a flatter position, but he angles it up slightly once done. This means I can look out at the sex room and our audience, if I want. Or I can choose to focus on the ceiling. I'm super grateful for this choice as I don't know how ready I am to acknowledge just how vulnerable and exposed I am at the moment.

"Breathtaking." My eyes instantly snap to his. "I knew I'd catch my little thief someday, but I hadn't realized how mouthwatering she'd be all tied up for me." Another gravely rumble escapes him. "And now, I'm going to punish her for how much she's vexed me." My whole body shudders. From nerves, from anticipation, from lust...who knows?! So I do the only thing I can think of to keep from shaking, I play along.

"You think you have what it takes to punish me, Patrolman?" I wiggle in my chair. "So far it's been a whole lot of talking and not a lot of action. Quite frankly, I'm having my doubts."

"Two."

"What? Two what?" I'm thoroughly confused.

"Two orgasms. You will not be leaving this chair until you've climaxed twice for me." He's picked up the pink wand, eyes roaming over the landscape of my exposed body.

"Haha, very funny, Stone." He's come back over to my left side, glowering down at me.

"You want to go for three, or are you going to be a good little thief and accept your fate?" He's just standing there, still as a statue, as if he's waiting for something. I furrow my eyebrows at him in question. "Do you accept your punishment?"

"Y-yes?" He takes in a breath of displeasure. "Yes, sir." I grit it out through my teeth. Instantly, he touches the tip of the wand to my skin, gently dragging it along the length of my belly chain. The sudden sensations of pleasure thunders across my flesh, sinking deep into my core. It's over just as quickly as it began. Opening eyes that had closed on their own, I peer back up at Stone.

"Yes, sir. I-I accept my punishment." This time I say it more earnestly as my body begins to quiver with desire.

"Good." He looks so smug, so self satisfied that I can't help myself.

"If you can." I give him my most wicked smile. Oh, I am liking this game. However, before I can truly enjoy the expression that passes over his face, he leans down so close our noses are almost touching.

"Three." Before I can react or respond, he brings the pleasure wand's tip to rest on my left nipple. The immediate ecstasy that washes over makes me moan loudly, right into his face. A peekaboo of a fang is exposed for a moment when he smiles.

Face passive once more, he straightens, moving the wand tip down the curve of my pert breast. He continues the line down, down, down to my belly button. But instead of going further he circles it, going back up to my right breast. I'm torn; while I wish he had continued down, I'm also eager to feel that pleasure on my nipple again. But even that he teases. Instead of going right for it, he circles my breast with the wand, slowly spiraling in toward my peak.

The reward when it finally makes contact is worth it. Perhaps the torturous anticipation made it even better. I can feel myself getting wet. My pussy wanting its turn. That thought has me glancing at our audience, imagining what they must be seeing. It's grown since the last time I glanced out. My Minotaur friend has his partner's legs wide open across his lap, while a thick finger leisurely plays with her slit as she squirms.

Stone removes the wand, leaving me panting for breath. Coming to stand behind my head, he places the wand just under my ear, running it down my neck.

"Your lovely moans have started to attract others, little thief. Even now, you steal their attention." The wand tip is quickly placed back onto my left nipple. I can't help the cry that comes up. "Hmm, your sounds of pleasure are even more delicious than I'd imagined." Wait, what?! He's imagined me moaning for him, imagined me in a sexual way? Before I can continue thinking about that he continues speaking. "Let's see if we can make them even sweeter."

Slowly, oh so slowly, he walks down my right side trailing the pleasure wand lower as he moves, removing it briefly once he gets to my hip. Beginning anew, he traces a path that starts at my ankle and moves up the inside of my thigh. My legs are shaking, held in place for him as he teases me, plays with me, just like he said he would.

Stone doesn't lead the wand where I hoped he would; instead he stops right at the crease where thigh meets torso. Lifting it, he begins the same slow journey from ankle to crease on the other leg. Only this time, he continues the path upward, tracing the crease onto my pelvis. Once there, he begins to pass the tip back and forth, following the hairline inches above my clit. I'm starting to feel the punishment aspect of all this, and it's frustratingly delicious.

Using his tail, he moves the stool near my legs.

"Now, let's start working on your first orgasm," he says while taking a seat on the stool. NOW?! Now we'll start working on it? What had he been doing before? Once he removes the wand from my skin, I get a real chance to catch my breath. My whole body feels wound up tight, needing to spring. Taking a moment to glance at the room, I clock the Minotaur getting a blow job from his lady friend, while he's fingering a new woman who has turquoise skin that glistens like scales.

Next to them is a thruple doing an Eiffel Tower situation. It's the Shifter couple and Hedge Witch we saw enter earlier. Her mate seems to be taking her from behind while the male witch has his cock down her throat. The Shifter is watching his mate give a blow job, while the witch is watching me...watching us.

I'm instantly brought back to myself when Stone's wingtip touches a nipple. Suddenly it's cold and remains that way. Eyes back on Stone, I see him dip his wing into the chilling lube before he brings it to my other nipple, rubbing the cold slick gel onto me. He gives his wing a little flick once done, sending air racing across my skin, which enhances the effect to my nipples greatly. Meanwhile his tail has taken hold of the bee-box. I bite my lower lip as my hunger builds.

Stone turns on the box—well, it's shaped more like a river rock, really—with the tap of a finger. The familiar buzz has me antsy in anticipation. I catch another glimpse of one of Stone's fangs. Seems he enjoys having me at his mercy.

Before I can make a troublesome remark, he lowers the vibrating box to my left nipple while simultaneously placing the pleasure wand just above my clit.

"Oh fuck!" It's the first words he's gotten out of me. I didn't even mean to say them. But he hums in satisfaction. Rocking the bee-box around one nipple, then moving it to the next, all the while he's using that glorious wand to trace the outline of my slit. I can't believe I'm so close already. I definitely need to buy one of these wands, maybe two so I can have a backup, or better yet for two pleasure points at once! I realize my hips are rocking of their own accord, as much as they can being strapped down and all.

"Look how wet you are for me already." His breath skates across the inside of my knee as he speaks. "What a beautiful sight, to see you straining against my bonds." He rubs his nose along the same knee. "I can't wait to watch you fall apart and accept your punishment. Tell me, Alexis, did you go out on a date with that fawn to make me watch you?" He moves the bee-box down the plains of my body until it's just above my pussy. "And your curtains, do you leave your curtains open so others might see you?" The wand moves up again to my tortured nipples. "So I might see you?"

"Ahhh!" I scream as the vibrating object is finally brought to my clit. My hips are trying so hard to buck, but they're held fast by the restraints. I'm so close, I'm so fucking close! Without warning, he removes the bee-box, and I can't help the "No!" I plead in response.

"You knew I was watching you, little thief. Did you do those things to tease me, to tempt me?" I hate how calmly he asks me questions. It's a stark contrast to how I'm feeling.

"Yes!" I shout. "Yes, I knew you were watching. How could I not? Yes, I wanted to mess with you a little. I wanted to flaunt my date with Tig to show you I was having fun, that I was carefree under your surveillance. You were a thorn in my side, and I wanted to get back at you." I'm practically writhing in pleasure and rage that he took that building orgasm away from me, but I need him to continue.

"And, the curtains, why do you leave those always open?"

"I...I..." I've never admitted this to anyone, and I'm not sure if I want to admit it now, to him.

He removes the wand from my nipple, and I actually whine in protest.

"I...I..." he places the wand at my belly chain, sending sparks of pleasure through me once more, but not nearly enough. "I..." My whole body is quaking as he leisurely strokes the tip higher and higher but never to my breast again.

"I like the thought that people might see me, okay?!" I hurl my confession at him, somewhat ashamed of admitting that private fantasy out loud. He brings the wand to play with the underside of my breast. With only the thought of further pleasure in mind, I continue to admit more of the truth.

"I..I hoped that you might see." The wand is moved to run circles around my areola. "I wanted you to watch me," I cry in frustration. Instantly, I'm rewarded with the wand upon my tight cold nipple. Ripples of pleasure began to ramp me back up. Through my haze of renewed pleasure, I can hear him make a tsking sound with his tongue.

"What a naughty little thief I have here, trying to steal my focus. I think it's time for your punishment, don't you?" This time I know exactly what he wants to hear.

"Yes, sir. I'm ready to accept my punishment." And I am. I am so damn ready.

"Then break for me, Alexis." The bee-box is back to my clit, being worked and rubbed with new fervor. The wand moves to circle the other nipple, before eventually trailing back down my body, hitting new places along the way. He works me back up so well, too well. I'm already near the precipice again. So close, I'm so very close.

"I need...I need." Fuck, I don't know what I need, but I need something. Something more to push me over the edge. Staring straight out at our audience, I see the Minotaur has his lady friend back on his lap, bouncing on his cock, while their new turquoise partner is on her knees in front of them, using their own bee-box on the impaled woman's clit. The Shifter threesome are all snuggled together on the floor, intensely watching me as they caress each other's skin.

A dangerous growl brings my focus sharply back to Stone.

"You will look at me, and me alone, as I make you come, Alexis. This punishment is mine. This orgasm is mine. Mine alone to give." Something new touches me, right at my entrance. I glance down to see it's his tail. The tip of his tail is teasing my opening, and it was exactly what I needed.

"Yes, sir!" rips from my mouth as I begin to come. My orgasm washes over me like a tidal wave. I couldn't stop it now even if I wanted to. All I can do is hold on and enjoy the ride. My cries of pleasure keep coming as he works me through this. His tail enters me slightly as I shake in ecstasy. I keep my eyes on him, just as he wanted. I watch him lick his lips in hunger before smiling at me, exposing both of his fangs. Boy, do I want to feel them on my skin.

Eventually he removes the wand and the box, leaving me a quivering mess. But his tail, he leaves that slightly inside me, gently and slowly stroking in and out.

"Outstanding, Alexis. You took your first punishment so well." His voice is even deeper than before; that alone tells me he's being affected by this too. Well, that, and the huge boner I can see pushing at his kilt. I lick my lips wondering what it would feel like. Thankfully, he didn't see that since he's gone back over to the tray, staring down at it. A shudder ripples through my body as I remember what else is on that tray.

"Do you need anything before we continue, Alexis?" He turns to stare right at me, scanning my face and body in a systematic way. "Something to drink perhaps?" With this tail still playing with me, how can I think about anything else? I realize the audience must be getting a great view from us at the moment, but all I can look at is him. Him, and what's sitting on that tray.

"More." Thankfully, it doesn't come out in a croak like I feared after all that shouting. "All I need right now is more." If he can give me another orgasm like that one, I want it.

"Exquisite." This one word, and the look he's giving me, has me preening. "But, let's get you a sip of water first." He motions to an attendant. "I want to hear more of that sweet music you make. It's even better than in my dreams." I'm about to ask about that statement, but he turns to speak with the host who instantly brings me over a glass of water.

"May I?" the hostess asks. I nod, and she moves the glass to my lips. I down it in three big gulps. Damn it, he was right. And he knows it too, given the shit-eating grin he has plastered on his face.

The hostess quickly steps aside, grabbing my clothes off the floor before dashing away.

"Ready for your second punishment, Alexis?" I don't get a chance to answer before his tail spears deeper into me. Stretching my opening wider, the tip curling to rub my G-spot. My quick inhale actually makes him chuckle.

"You've done this before, haven't you? Been to a place like this, played like this?" A wicked smile is all the answer I need. "But I thought...I mean, you seemed so..." I trail off not sure where to go with this and not wanting to admit outright that I assumed he was a prude or something. He pushes his tail in deeper, rubbing my spot with more pressure.

"Seems you don't know me nearly as well as I know you, Alexis Callaway. But I would still like to learn more. So much more." He pulls his tail out, which elicits some embarrassing sounds from me. My mind instantly blanks as I watch him bring that tail to his mouth, licking my juices off with a tongue much longer than I expected. "Hmm, yes, I would like to know you much better." And I'd like to know that tongue much better!

Noticing movement to my right, I glance over to see that more people have come to sit on that side, wanting a better, or different, angle. Stone must notice as well because he pushes a button which turns the chair slightly in that direction. I didn't know it could do that!

Stone moves the stool over to the wall, out of his way, preparing for whatever he's about to do to me. Blessedly, his tail finds me again. Instead of plunging back in, he begins rubbing its length along my slit, the tip teasing my clit along the way.

"Do you know what this is, little thief?" He holds up the dildo that is surprisingly like my own, except this one is jet black. Other than that the handle, the size, girth, and lines of nodes are the same. I feel like this is a trick question, but I answer anyway.

"It's a very interesting phallus," I state. He only nods, so I continue. "That resembles the one I own, the one you saw in my apartment." He nods again, but his face seems expectant, like he's wanting something more. "Um, I know that it feels amazing, and I wish it was inside me right now?" For some reason, this answer makes him react, like a tiny little tremor moved up his spine. Interesting.

"This is a training dildo among my people. It is meant to prepare our sexual partners to accept our cocks." I blink at him rapidly, processing what I've just learned. Pleased with my reaction, he continues with a half grin. "This," and he holds it up, "is the approximate size and shape of a Gargoyle penis. We count the notches a lover takes," he taps a claw down the length, "to determine if they are ready to accept the real thing." I can't help but run my eyes down to where his cock bulges against the fabric of his kilt. I swallow in an effort to moisten my mouth.

"So, so you're saying that your cock looks like that?" I can't believe it. I can't believe I have been pleasuring myself with a Gargoyle penis. And the worst of it is, it's been the best dildo I've ever used.

"Actually, Alexis Callaway," he steps in right between my legs, leaning down over my naked body, resting his hands on either side of my waist, "my cock looks exactly like the dildo you own. Almost as if I had commissioned an artisan to craft one of myself." Oh gawd, my whole body is trembling. His nearness, the revelation that I've practically been fucking myself with Stone's cock, that nimble tail still rubbing inside me.

"Given your reaction, I'm going to believe that you didn't know, and that you did not do that on purpose." He backs away, going over to the tray once more.

"No, no, I had no fucking idea! There wasn't a sign or anything that said it was a Gargoyle dildo. And I've certainly never seen a Gargoyle cock in my life." Removing his tail, he uses it to dip into the lube jar, rubbing said tail along the stone dildo to smear the lube all over it. Muttering, I add a quick, "Though I certainly wouldn't mind..." My eyes once again trace the outline I see along his kilt. Having heard me, he chuckles.

"No, Alexis, you are not yet ready for my cock. But we'll see if we can get you closer tonight." Stepping nearer, he holds the stone cock by its handle. At least I now know why the end was made like that, for this exact purpose. Resting the head at my opening, I can feel the slightest of chills from the lube beginning to stir. "You never did answer me, how many notches can you take, Alexis?" He's twisting the head there, not pushing it in yet, only teasing.

"I don't know." A lie. I know exactly how many I can handle. It's been a little competition with myself. I'm about four nodes away from taking it all. Stone only arches an eyebrow at me. It appears as if he can't tell if I'm lying or not, so he chooses to say nothing more about it. Thank goodness.

"Guess we'll be finding out together." Finally, he begins to work it into me slowly. Once the head passes through my opening, he pulls it back out before slowly pushing it back in. This time after the head makes it, he pushes till the first row of nodes are in as well.

"One." He pulls it all the way out before pushing it in again. "Two," he says when the second row enters me. As he's pulling it back out again, he swipes the leftover lube from his tail across my chest, making sure to cover both nipples in a fresh coat. "Three." My body is shivering from the cold sensations that are tormenting me inside and out. "Four." A blaze of pleasure hits my inner left thigh. The pink wand is back in the game. "Five." I'm moaning in earnest again, the cold stone nods are beginning to rub my primed G-spot. The bumps are a magnificent experience as they pass in and out of my opening. "Six." My body has begun to squirm against the restraints.

"You're doing better than I expected, Alexis. Taking this toy so well." Fuck, why do I like his praise so much? "Tell me, how often do you use my facsimile on yourself?" I refuse to answer that question! Not that I can really talk at the moment. He doesn't take the dildo out, instead leaving it there, six notches in. He does, however, move the pleasure wand to touch my clit. The sound that comes up out of me has lowered at least one octave. "How often?" he repeats, removing the wand.

"Almost daily!" I shout. He moves the cock out one node but no more. "S-Sometimes more than once, depending." He crouches down, squatting in between my wide open legs. Now, I can fully see my audience, and they can fully see me. I don't get a chance to focus on them before Stone thrusts the cock back inside me.

"Seven." His tail has taken the bee-box and placed it upon my nipple. "Where? Where do you use my cock?" I can feel the breath from his questions whisper across my skin. His face must be very close for me to feel that. Again, the wand touches my clit, exploding sensations throughout my body.

"Fuck! Everywhere!" He moves the dildo in and out with gusto, but leaves the wand where it is. I continue answering the question unprompted. "On my bed, in the shower, in the tub, once on the table." I try to breathe, but the sensations are overwhelming: my nipples being assaulted by the bee-box in turn, the bumps passing in and out of my opening, the same bumpy texture rubbing all over my insides, being filled and filled by this massive dildo, and that wand now making smooth circles around my clit.

"Eight." Oh fuck, the stretch of it. "How diligent of you. I appreciate your dedication."

"On the couch!" I shout, continuing to fully answer his question. "And once, oh fuck, once..." My whole body is shaking, straining against the straps. "One night, I turned off all the lights...layed in front of that open window...and fucked myself with it hoping someone was watching...hoping you were watching!"

"Nine," comes out in a growl. He's properly fucking me with the dildo at this point. No longer slow and testing as before. Faster, deeper, the rhythm exquisite. I'm about to come for the second time, and I can hardly believe it. "What a naughty little tease. Are you ready for your second punishment to be fulfilled?"

"Yes, yes, yes," I chant. "Please!"

"You beg so sweetly, Alexis," he practically croons. "How could I deny you?" Suddenly, the tip of the pleasure wand is back directly onto my clit, making my eyes roll and my toes curl.

"Please, please, please." It's a whisper now, but I know he can hear it. A fang gently nips my inner thigh, and I'm lost. "Yeeeesssss!" I scream as I convulse, held in place by my bonds. He continues to pump the stone into me, milking this orgasm for all it's worth.

Once I've calmed down, he removes the bee-box first, quickly followed by the wand. But the dildo—oh the dildo—he keeps deep inside me twisting it, turning it. I feel him stand to lean over me, but I'm unable to open my eyes or turn my head at the moment.

"Ten."

Chapter 16

Stone

I'm almost stunned that she can take so much of the training tool already. Only two notches left before she can handle it all. With another session, I have no doubt that she could take it all. Her diligence in using hers has paid off.

Evaluating her exhausted form, I determine another orgasm might be pushing it. That last one was big, and this is our first session, after all. But I'll have her make the call, the right call. Her eyes flutter open too slowly for my liking.

"How are you feeling, Alexis?" All I get is a hum in reply. So I walk over to the side her head is facing. Unable to stop myself, I stroke a knuckle down her cheek. Goddess bless me, she's gorgeous. I actually had to stop looking at her at the end of the session. Her twisting, moaning, pleasured form was making it difficult to focus on what I was doing. Crouching next to that mouthwatering slit may not have been the best choice in retrospect, but at least it was one thing to focus on. I'll be replaying the vision of me using that dildo on her for years to come.

"Alexis, I need you to answer me." I make my voice stern but caring.

"Fubbada...hmmm...yep." Oh no, I might have broken my sexy little thief. Time to shock her into reality.

"Are you ready for your third punishment?" Her eyes fly open in alarm, but I only smile down at her. She's made me smile several times this evening, a feat in itself.

"Um, maybe more water first." Her eyes are darting around, mind racing to think of something to stave me off. "A slight break perhaps." Slight break, my ass. Judging by those sluggish blinks, she'll need a full night's rest before she can even attempt to continue this game.

"Are you sure that's all you require?" I understand her enough by now that, if I claim she can't do anymore, she'll try to prove me wrong on principle alone. And I'll not have her harming herself. "You did just give us all a magnificent performance." There's a slight questioning furrow to her brow. "It was truly breathtaking." My earnest answer removes the lingering doubt on her face. Coming to stand again, I walk over to the tray, placing the items back upon it.

"Maybe some time out of the bindings?" A good call on her part. So I nod my head as I push the release crystal on the chair's panel. "Think I'd like to sit up too. Clear my head." I press the appropriate crystals, and the chair responds, back straightening, feet and legs lowering. She rubs her wrists, then moves her hands down her thighs as if trying to wake them. I grumble in displeasure. She glances at me, but I do not respond. Instead I flag a hostess for more water.

The same hostess comes quickly, maid outfit neat and crisp, clear glass of water on a silver tray. I let my eyes roam over the little crowd we have around our stage. Most are caught up in their own joys now that our show has paused. A few chat to each other or comfort each other or both. I wonder what drew my thief's eye back to the Minotaur time and again. At the moment, he's whispering in his female's ear. Sweet nothings, I presume.

Looking back at the languid Alexis, I marvel at the odd turn of events. This morning I was high upon my mountain, trying desperately not to think about this female. Now here I am, giving into the temptation of her allure. She admitted some surprising things to me, and I'd be lying to myself if I too didn't admit some things to her. Things that I had been trying profoundly hard not to realize.

Once done with her water, she stretches her body to and fro, beginning to rally herself for what she thinks is coming. I do not want her to rally. I want her to know her limits, I want her to let me take care of her, I want her to let me hold her. No, no, stop that. We have business to attend to, a murder to solve. I have given in to my desires for long enough this night, time to set the hunger aside.

I should never have given in in the first place, assuming that my cravings for her would only increase if I did. As soon as I discovered that I'd brought Alexis to a sex club, I knew I'd give in despite myself. Her taunting only gave me the excuse I longed for.

Wait, an excuse. That's exactly what she needs in this moment, a way out. I step up to her side, my headstrong little thief, and give her the out she needs. As silently as I can make my voice, but still be heard by her, I begin.

"Do you know how much time we have left?" Her brows furrow slightly. "Before we meet up with Valda?" Realization starts to spread across her face. Gently, I take hold of her arm, inspecting it. "We have created a perfect excuse to make our way into the back.

There are typically healing waters, or at the very least warm mineral waters, for patrons to soak in." Full realization hit her eyes. Her mind is quick, even after having shattered moments before. I try to ignore the feelings that surface in my chest.

"You think it's been an hour?" she mutters under her breath while she plays along, offering up her other arm for inspection, continuing our little performance. "I mean, you were good, but I don't think that took an hour." It is an effort to suppress my smile.

"There was the time we spent playing at the bar," I counter. She pulls both lips into her mouth in an effort not to smile as well. Kneeling down, I inspect her legs. "We should also be seen in the spa area for a time. Plus, you could use the relief they provide." She begins to bristle, so I continue quickly. "As we are uncertain what we might face in these tunnels, or how long we may be in there, a respite would not go amiss. Especially since you did fight against your bonds during our session." I flash her a fanged half-smile. Her fascination with my fangs has not gone unnoticed. "The warm waters would do your strained muscles good." I begin to untie the strings of her heeled shoes. "Didn't you scale a tower today, little thief?" I try to lace my tone with disapproval, but it only makes her gloat.

"Up and down, then a race back to my apartment." She pauses a moment before she fully concedes. "Okay, you're right, my body is pretty exhausted and could definitely use some TLC."

"What is TLC? Is it something the hostess could get for you?" She actually giggles, the sound pleasant yet surprising.

"Sorry," clearing her throat she explains, "TLC stands for tender loving care. Well, that, and it's the name of a singing group, but I'm referring to the care version."

"I see, well, let us get you some of that TLC." I stand, leaving her shoes on the ground. "What is the sixth rule of this establishment, Alexis?" I ask, bringing my voice back up to the volume it had been during our session, in case anyone is listening. She searches the space beyond for a moment, finding the list etched into a nearby wall. She then hangs her head, reciting the rule as dejected as possible.

"Know your limits." No, I do not like this posture on her, even if it is an act. So I lift her chin with a finger, forcing her to look up at me.

"Good girl. Not everyone is wise enough to know their limits, then to act accordingly." This earns me a little smile. Glorious. "You were absolutely radiant, my graceful little thief." I let pride lace my compliment, hoping she realizes how much I mean that. She laughs nervously, looking around. Leaning down, I continue in her ear, "And if you think I've forgotten about your third punishment, you are sorely mistaken." I straighten in time to see her eyes widen in shock. "We'll continue this another time."

I scoop her off the seat, carrying her again as I did when we glided in. She utters a faint little "Whoa" but doesn't protest further. Marching us back into the no playtime zone, I read the helpful signs, in search of what we need.

"Ah, perfect. They do have a heated healing pool. If I'm not mistaken, I believe I also see the closet door we'll need later." Alexis nods in response, seeing the closet as well.

The healing pool is empty, save one other, but it appears as if he is on his way out.

"Pool's all yours," he offers as he walks past us. I nod in acknowledgment.

"Was that a sasquatch?!" Alexis hisses excitedly into my ear, craning her neck to gawk at the being behind us.

"Yes, I believe that is one of the names his people go by. Never met one before?"

"No, of course not. There are rumors and some fuzzy pictures..." She trails off.

"They are pleasant enough company." Unwilling to set her down just yet, I use my tail to remove my kilt, hanging it upon a hook before walking into the pool.

The waters are warm, a slight steam rising from its pearlescent surface, reminding me of a unicorn's horn. Walking us to a deeper section, I set her upon a seat so the waters come up to her chin before backing away to find my own.

"Are you naked?!" Alexis practically shrieks when her eyes settle upon me. I am confused at her surprise.

"Of course, I am. Why would I walk in here in my kilt? I don't want it dripping wet as we lurk around in underground tunnels." For some reason, she's covered her breasts with her hands, as if she hadn't just spent time on full display for me moments ago.

"But why are you in here at all?" Taking a moment, I attempt to instill patience into my tone. It still comes out somewhat annoyed, however.

"Because, while you were busy scaling vampire towers and running upon rooftops, I was flying back to Avenston in all haste, trying to stop you." I give her a stern look. "Since you planned your little heist while I was away, I had to fly all the way back from Mt. Dern, after only arriving there hours before, a journey I also took by flying." Grabbing the end of my braid, I hook it on the point of the right horn, behind my ear, so it doesn't get wet. I sink deeper into the water, up to my chin, then close my eyes. "As you can imagine my muscles are sore too and would greatly benefit from a warm healing soak. Now, shhh and relax."

It doesn't take long before I can hear her fidgeting, though I try my best to ignore it.

"How much longer do you think we have?" she asks.

"At least ten minutes."

"What about clothes? They have mine up front, and I'm not exploring naked."

"Ask an attendant for a costume next time you see one." I growl out.

"Oh, yeah, that's smart." I only grunt in reply.

"Are we not going to talk about what we just did?" I open my eyes to look at her. Alexis's tone was a little too weary for my liking.

"Of course, we will discuss what happened. It is a conversation I expect to have with you." Closing my eyes once more, "However, in this moment we are resting, healing, and mentally preparing to move forward with our murder investigation."

"You're right, you're right. We'll talk about that later." There's only a short pause before she continues. "It's just...I just don't want you to get the wrong idea or be confused at all by anything I might have said....or, or admitted to–"

"Alexis." I throw as much command in my voice as I can.

"Yes, sir!" I open my eyes with a grin and see that she's clearly flustered by her response.

"Be still, and focus on healing. We will talk about our session later, I promise you." Closing my eyes, I let the waters buoy me, feeling them work upon my back and wings. I'm only slightly perturbed when I hear Alexis singing under her breath, something about not chasing waterfalls. This is going to be a very long ten minutes. Resigned to my fate, I take a deep breath before opening my eyes to drift closer to her.

"Oops, sorry, I'll be quiet." Obviously, just now realizing she had been singing under her breath.

"I find that to be highly unlikely." Taking one of her legs under the water, I begin to massage it. "I had expected you to nearly fall asleep once in here, as you almost did within my bonds." I'm pleased that she isn't fighting about me kneading her leg. Instead she hums pleasantly.

"What can I say, I recover quickly."

"Hmm, yes. And for the record, I meant everything I said." Locking eyes with her, "Everything." I hold her gaze for a few beats, letting the weight of my words sink in, before looking down to grab her other leg.

"You think I was exquisite and radiant?" It's asked in a teasing tone, but I reply seriously.

"All that and more." Alexis is stunned into silence. Finally. "Turn and I'll get your shoulders." She complies, seeming eager to no longer face me. "You are also a vexation, a rule breaker, sassy, a tease," she laughs, "graceful, clever, adaptable, and underestimated far too often, I suspect." Using a claw, I move her hair so I may whisper, "and a captivating adversary."

"Oh, I, uh," is all she can muster as I turn her body to work on her other shoulder and arm.

"Well, aren't you two just adorable." Valda's voice echoes off the walls making Alexis jump in surprise.

"Fuck, Valda! What the hell, man? I thought we were going to meet up in the closet?" she hisses in the direction his voice came from.

"Over here, darling." He's become visible, standing in the water near us. "I got tired of waiting. So I thought I'd come let you both know we can begin, seeing as how you are no longer tied up." I can practically feel the rage that rises off Alexis at that comment.

"You were watching us?! You...you...pervert!" This, however, only makes the ghost laugh. "How much? How much did you see?"

"Calm yourself, human. Such sights no longer tempt me or bring me any pleasure." He rises to float above the water, still in a seated position sans chair. "I can remember a time when lurking in such places was fun. I even joined in occasionally, touching only, of course. Apparently the touch of a ghost can be a pleasurable sensation." I am over this conversation.

"Is the way still clear, Valda?" From his expression, I can tell that there is an issue.

"Yes. Mostly." His answer confirms my suspicions. So I stand and start to walk out of the pool. "There's just one, tiny little section where a few rocks have fallen into the path." I grab one of the larger towels provided, not entirely convinced that the ghost is being truthful. "But after that, the rest of the way is clear, I assure you." I hum in response.

"Chop, chop, missy," Valda says behind me, "you have a murder to solve!" I turn, expecting to see Alexis near me, but find she's still in the pool.

"I don't have anything to wear! An attendant hasn't come by yet." She's covering her chest again, even though you can't really see anything under the healing waters.

"Already taken care of, Lexi." Valda waves a hand dismissively. "I've stashed a cleaner's uniform in the closet for you, shoes as well. So, out you get!" The ghost claps his translucent hands.

"I am not getting out of this pool with you watching me, you Peeping Tom!" I've mostly dried myself during this whole interaction, so I walk over toward my kilt.

"Oh human, if I wanted to see you naked, I've had no shortage of opportunities. If it wasn't you and the Naga in the treasury, it was you and the fox twins all over the damn sanctum." I had reached up to grab my clothing but froze in place at his words. "I swear, for a few weeks there, I couldn't go anywhere without encountering you tied up and naked with those two." I clutch my kilt in a death grip.

"I thought you were seeing that fawn, Tigarith?" I'm trying really hard not to sound angry. "Who is this Naga? What fox twins? What happens in that Thieves Guild of yours?" I glare over at Valda. "You said she was tied up?"

"Oh yes, astonishingly intricate knotting too. Why, this one time, I found her practically on the ceiling–"

"Stop! Stop right there!" Alexis marches out of the pool, dripping water all over, not even taking a nearby towel. "That was none of your business, Valda. And as for you," she turns her ire towards me, "all that took place before we ever crossed paths. Before I met Tig, even." Standing there in all her naked glory, she places both hands on her hips. "I am a grown-ass woman, and I can fuck whoever, however, I damn well please. You got a problem with that? Tough titties." She roughly snatches a towel for herself, brutally wiping water off her skin.

"Yes, well, I'll, ah, I'll see you two in the cleaning closet." Valda promptly vanishes from sight. Under her breath, I can hear Alexis muttering.

"Fucking ghost. Sticking his gawd-damn nose where it doesn't belong. Ooo, how dare he spy on me while I was..." she trails off as she looks towards me. "You got a problem, Stone?" The fire of rage is dancing in her eyes. Why do I find that to be so...beautiful?

"No, there is nothing wrong with consenting adults having sexual relations. I merely thought I had missed a vital part of your current relationship situation." Peering down, I rebuckle my kilt as I had done so incorrectly the first time.

"Uh-huh." I can practically feel the burn of her eyes upon my skin.

"And I may have been disappointed to discover that I was not the first to have tied you up. It was a foolish response that I realize was selfish." I roll my shoulders finding they are no longer stiff. "I am glad you have found such pleasures before and that it is something you enjoy."

"That better be all there is to it, Stone. Because I do not go in for that whole 'I better have been the only one to have ever touched you' macho bullshit." She's wrapped the towel around herself, standing with one hip cocked out.

"No, of course not. That would be hypocritical of me. Not to mention the fact that I'd rather have a partner who knows what she's doing. Only..." She arches an eyebrow at me. "Earlier, you seemed resistant to the use of a safe word. Did they, those that tied you up before, not encourage this? Not insist upon this? Having a safe word for those types of activities is–" I'm cut off by her sweet laughter, though she's tried to stifle it behind her hands.

"Stone, oh gosh, I was messing with you. Teasing you." Searching my face, she adds, "I was trying to get your goat, playing with you but in my own way. I assure you, I have always used, and insisted upon having, a safe word. Especially with that kind of play."

"Ah, I see, yes. That makes more sense, upon retrospect." I can feel my cheeks heat in embarrassment at having misread the situation. In good spirits once more, Alexis walks closer to me and pats my chest.

"Come on, big boy. Let's meet a ghost in a closet."

Chapter 17

Alexis

"Are you serious right now, Valda?" I've got the clothes he stole for me crumpled in my hand, waving them at him in the supply closet. "This! This is what you got me to wear to explore unused underground tunnels?" I'd throw them in his face if I thought they'd actually hit him.

"Why are you acting so irrational, Lexi? I told you I got you a cleaning person's uniform, and so I did." His stupid face tells me he knows exactly why I'm upset though.

"These are the maid uniforms that the hosts are wearing tonight, Valda. They are a costume, not what a cleaning person actually wears. I thought you had gotten me a jumpsuit or something." I'm exasperated beyond belief. How can I do what I need to do in this frilly dress?!

"Poppycock! People clean wearing these all the time. Or, at least, they used to. Not sure what servants are wearing these days to be honest. I don't really pay attention to them." I could strangle this ghost!

"Enough, you two," Stone commands. "A member of staff might hear us. We want to be able to come back here in future, remember." Pinching the bridge of his nose, he turns to Valda. "Can you grab her something else to wear? Something more appropriate for the task at hand."

"That, I'm afraid, would take needless time and effort. These are perfectly good clothes. She'll be able to walk down the tunnels in them without issue." I'm about to lay into Valda again, but the ghost quickly continues. "There's only so much time you can plausibly stay back here in the 'no playtime' area. So unless you want to dally around and possibly get discovered, I suggest you get a move on. I would like to remind you that you weren't actually invited here by a member and only have so much leeway."

"Why–" Stone begins, but I cut him off.

"Fine, fine. I'll put the damn maid costume on. But I'm not wearing the hat. Or the apron. Turn around, both of you. I've shown you two enough of my skin for one evening, and I'm in no mood to show you anymore." Thankfully, they do both turn without opposition. Throwing the towel in a random direction, which Stone automatically picks up to fold and place on a shelf, I put on the black dress.

At first it feels like it's going to be way too big, but once on, it molds to fit me perfectly. That foxtailed lady at the front wasn't kidding. Next come the stockings along with some short-heeled black shoes. Fortunately, they also fit to size. This is actually amazing! Totally wish I had gone into the costume closet first and had some fun trying on clothes. I'm definitely going to find a way to get back into this club.

"Okay. All done. So where's this entrance?" Scanning the small room, I don't immediately see another door.

"No, no, this won't do," Valda chimes in upon seeing me. "You've got to at least wear the apron, Lexi. You look like you are

going to a funeral, and it will help pull the whole outfit together."
He tries to hand the white apron to me, but I refuse to take it.

"If you don't stop pestering me, there WILL be a funeral.
Yours!"

"Where is the entrance, Valda?" Stone is clearly over this bickering.

"Right behind this shelf here. You will have to scooch it out of
the way." Without any effort whatsoever, Stone moves the shelf in
question. "If you examine the base of the wall closely, you should
find a small carving upon it. Tap the carving with your foot, and
the secret door will open."

"Wait!" Thankfully, I catch Stone right before his tail touches
the carving. "There's a ward on it." Narrowing my eyes at Valda,
"Why didn't you warn us?" Getting down on all fours, I inspect
the ward in question. Faint sparkling green, easy enough to dispel.
"This would have caused a cave-in after we passed the threshold."

"Oops. Must have slipped my mind. I was wondering why
I never had anyone else use this entrance. Well, mystery solved, I
suppose." I can hear Stone's grumble as I work my magic.

Taking the golden ring from my middle finger, I remove the
false stone from it. Crushing it with my hands, it quickly turns into
fine red powder. Collecting all the powder in one hand, I blow it at
the carving, effectively dissolving the ward in a few short moments.
Standing, I dust the dirt off my dress.

"That should do it. Ward's all gone now." Pressing the carving
with the toe of my borrowed shoe, we hear a few groans before
the stone wall eventually moves to the side, revealing a pitch black
opening.

"How did you do that?" Stone asks, eyeing my empty ring.

"Tricks of the trade, big boy, tricks of the trade." Motioning to the void in front of us, "After you, Officer." I'll be damned if I'm going down into that darkness first, especially with Forgetful Frank as our guide. Stone peers inside, wary.

"It's too dark for even my eyes. Here," he reaches into the band of his kilt, "I have some Fairy Lights." He hands me a small round quartz-looking crystal. Thankfully, I know how to use it now. Gav was equal parts confused and horrified when he handed me one, fully expecting me to know what it was, but instead finding he had to explain it to me. Setting the ball into the middle of his palm, Stone brings it close to his mouth.

"Time to shine." Instantly the crystal turns into a glowing ball of light, about five inches around, and moves to float above his head.

"Really? You left the activation phrase at factory setting?" I tsk at him.

"It's a perfectly adequate and acceptable phrase. What do you set yours to?"

"Twinkle, twinkle, bitches." All I get is a 'humph' in response. "Oh, come on, at least mine's fun."

"Yes, very amusing, Alexis. Now, come inside so I may put the shelves back in place before we descend." Quickly, I whisper the activation phrase so my little ball lights up too. Once it's hovering over my head, I walk in and move a few steps down, giving Stone room to maneuver the shelf.

"Marvelous, you two. The closing trigger is just there." Valda points at a small protruding square in the wall. "Press it, and I will meet you at the bottom. Have fun!" With that, the ghost is gone, and we're faced with stairs straight down into an abyss. Great.

As a woman, I'd never thought I'd say this, but I wish I had my heels to walk in. These borrowed ones are not nearly as comfortable as mine, which I had spelled specifically for comfort. Not only is there no Cloud Walking enchantment on these, but the backs are rubbing on my Achilles tendons. If this goes on for much longer, I'll get blisters for sure.

The zig-zaggy stairs took us pretty far down. I'd say we're probably even further under the city than the Thieves Guild sanctum. There have only been two turns so far within the tunnels, but at least Valda seemed confident in them. I'm just glad this tunnel is huge, like subway-tunnel huge, and not cramped like I feared.

"How much farther till this cave-in you spoke of? From how you described it, I thought it would have been closer." I'm so glad it was Stone who asked and not me. If I had spoken up, it may have sounded more like a whine. I've had a very long day, I'm exhausted, and now my feet hurt. Plus, that curry we had for lunch is long gone! I'm surprised my stomach hasn't sent echoes down these halls with its growls.

"Quite near, quite near, indeed. In fact, I believe it's just up ahead." He floats off further in front of us, turning down another corridor. "Ah ha! Here we go. See, it wasn't far into the tunnel at all." Turning down the same tunnel, we soon see a wall of giant rocks blocking our path.

"You have got to be kidding me! Valda, you call this a little cave-in? These, these are boulders, brother." I sit on one of the massive rocks that must have rolled down the corridor after falling.

"Nonsense! For a big strong Gargoyle male like Stone, this should be nothing." The look on Stone's face clearly says otherwise. Valda must see it too because he continues, "It only appears to be bad, but in truth, it's not much rubble at all. Simply moving one or two rocks will clear a space for you two to pass through."

"Which ones?" Stones asks in an unamused tone. Valda perks up in excitement, while I'm in shock.

"You can't be serious, Stone. This is too much to do alone, and I do not trust that it's only going to be a few boulders." I glare daggers at the ghost.

"I'll only move a few, then reevaluate. If it seems dangerous or impossible, we'll return later with a plan and maybe some tools." He's eyeing the wall the way a dad surveys a lawn he's about to mow. "I won't know what we're dealing with until I get in there."

"Fine. I'm too tired to argue with you. Be a big strong man and move some rocks." I remain sitting on my boulder, taking off a shoe to dig out a pebble.

Valda and Stone get to work. There's lots of talking, pointing, and headshaking before Stone even moves the first boulder. I'm not gonna lie, the effortless way he moves all that weight is awfully impressive. Impressive and just a little sexy. I'm not ashamed to admit it. Mmmm, those muscles. But when I lean back to enjoy the show, I hear an odd noise. At first, I think it's a monster in the tunnel with us, so I race over to Stone's side. Once next to him, I realize it's something much, much worse.

Before my brain can tell me what to do, Stone pulls me towards the wall, sandwiching me between it and his body, taking the full brunt of the cave-in.

There's so much dust that it's hard to see, and breathing only makes me cough. Stone's Fairy Light is lost, but thankfully mine is still active above my head.

"Stone, Stone! Answer me!" I'm smacking his chest frantically, but he's not responding. "Come on, Stone, you idiot," I slap his jaw as best I can, which is kinda hard from this angle.

"Ouch."

"Not funny, that is not funny. I thought you were dead! What happened? Are you hurt? Why did you do that?!" I should be grateful, seeing as how he probably just saved my life and all, but at the moment, I'm far too frantic.

"Not dead. It appears I may have moved a supporting boulder which in turn caused more to fall from above." I can feel him wince. "My wings are damaged." More wincing. "And I think my left ankle took a hit."

"Valda, Valda, where are you, you piece of shit?!" I can't see around Stone's massive form.

"I'm here, and I had no idea that would happen. Truly. I'm so sorry–"

"Shut up and tell me how it looks out there." I'm in no mood to hear any of that ghost's platitudes. "Is there a way for Stone to get out? Can you move anything to help?"

"Let me assess the situation." Valda's reply is muffled, but I can tell he's pretty close.

"Are those tears for me?" Stone asks in a weak voice. Tears? What tears? Oh.

"Don't be silly; they're obviously from the dust." His chest rumbles as I dash them away.

"Good news all around," comes Valda's far too chipper voice. "First, congratulations, you have successfully made a path forward through the rest of the tunnel." I can feel my body vibrate with rage.

"Seriously! Are you fucking serious right now?! That's what you lead with, Valda? If I die, I'm going to haunt the shit out of you. And if I live, I'll make sure you never sucker another living soul into helping you." I'm shaking, but for some reason, Stone chuckles. This is no laughing matter. I am dead serious.

"Apologies. Yes, of course, you're right. I should not have begun with that. It was in poor taste." His voice is nearer this time, right behind Stone. "The actual good news is that I believe Stone can get out once I shift a few things. Thankfully, the exit back up to the club is clear, so you two should be able to get out of here without any issue. Just give me a moment to move some things for you." Mentally, I try to calm myself when I hear rocks moving behind Stone.

It happened so fast, it all happened so fast! Panic starts to rise in my chest, my heart fluttering like a captured butterfly.

"Are you hurt, little thief?" At least his voice sounds stronger this time.

"Me? No, yes, I'm not sure. I think I'm in shock, to be honest." I feel a new tear roll down my cheek. "It all happened so fast," my voice breaks.

"Shhh, we are okay. We are alive, and we will heal. Thankfully, there will be no need to waste your afterlife tormenting Valda." This makes me laugh a little, a very little. "Now, take a moment to assess your body. Is there anywhere you can feel pain or numbness?"

"How are you so freaking calm right now? I think I am about to lose my shit." He chuckles, but I'm not lying.

"I am a Gargoyle, surrounded by stones. I am in my element. One day, I will return to stone, though I am glad it is not this day." He winces again when I hear a bigger shifting of rubble. "I am calm because I have to be, and we will soon be out of here."

"Well, I'd like to be out of here sooner rather than later. No offense, but you are crushing me." He laughs, then winces in more pain. "Sorry, sorry. Too soon?"

"No, no, it wasn't your fault. I just realized my ribs are bruised."

"Alright, I've done all I can do." Valda finally pipes up. "I am still a ghost after all and therefore have my limits. However, I think, if Stone pushes back, you two will be free." Without warning, Stone begins to push against the mass of rocks at his back. He doesn't make a sound, but his face tells me how painful this is for him. Another tear rolls down my cheek.

After what feels like eons, I hear rocks clatter to the ground, releasing Stone and I from our earthy prison. We have to make our way up and over some rubble, but we're free and we're alive. Once fully out, I look over at Stone, his back and wings are a wreck. He broke himself, to save me.

Chapter 18

Alexis

"Oh fuck, Stone, your back." My hand hovers near his wings, not daring to touch. With a grunt, he lowers himself to sit down on a boulder, favoring one leg.

"How bad is it? What does it look like? Cuts, tears, breaks?" He's trying to sound fine, but it's not working.

"All of the above," I answer on an exhale. "May I touch? Promise I'll be as gentle as possible." Stone nods, so I begin to examine. "There are many smaller cuts and two long gashes. One along this shoulder, another near your spine." His blood—I assume its blood—is a dark gunmetal gray. "There are a few holes in your wings, and one longer tear through the membrane." I move his wings around as gently as I can, but I feel each twinge of pain down my own spine when I see him flinch. "Given the angles, I believe you have at least three breaks along your phalanges, which will need to be reset." Cursory examination finished, I turn to Valda who is hovering nearby. "You, go up and tell someone at the club to send for a healer."

"That won't be necessary," Stone interjects. "I merely need to encase myself for a time to be healed. What we really need to do is get back up and out of the club as inconspicuously as possible."

I can feel my mouth hanging open. "Alexis, I need you to reset those bones if they appear noticeably unaligned." I can't believe I'm hearing this.

"You still want to keep up our charade? You intend to continue helping this prick?" I start walking around in frustration. "Unbelievable. Unbelievable!"

"Alexis." Stone's voice is annoyingly calm again.

"No. He almost got us killed, Stone."

"He didn't cause the collapse, Alexis."

"Can you even walk? Stand? No, no, there is no way we can waltz back through the club. Hell, I don't even think you'll make it back up to the closet like this. I mean look at you, look at us. We are a mess of blood and dirt."

"Then it is fortunate that the exit above us is so near showers, baths, and a healing pool." His response stops my frantic pacing in its tracks.

"You're dead serious, aren't you? You're actually planning it all out? You're thinking about how we can achieve this ludicrous goal!" I let out a 'grrr' in frustration.

"All we need do is set my wings, go back up, then get into the healing waters." He's speaking so calmly, voice monotone. "I will sit in the waters until I am able to walk more normally. Then we will exit together as if nothing is amiss, and I will find a place to rest." I just shake my head at him the whole time.

"Sounds so simple, so easy," my voice is laced with sarcasm.

"It will not be easy, but it is what we must do." I point my finger at him, about to start arguing, when he adds, "I want to come back to this establishment and play with you again, Alexis. We've only just begun." The heat in his eyes as he scans my body tells me he's not kidding. I mean, yeah, I want that too, but at what cost?

"Can't you 'encase' yourself here? Seems the easiest and quickest way," I counter.

"They are sure to notice if a guest enters but doesn't leave tonight. They will search for me and question you."

"Then, I'll stay down here too." I sit on the floor to prove my point. "Later, we'll sneak out when the club is closed. They can assume we left some other way." Stone's been shaking his head since I sat down.

"Given my injuries, I will be stoned for days. You can not wait down here for that long. No, we must leave, and soon. I can already feel my body wanting to shift, to encase me in order to heal these injuries. Please, Alexis, help me do this." I sit in silence for a time, staring straight at him.

"Fine!" I shout, throwing my hands in the air in surrender. "We'll do your stupid plan instead of the smart thing." Standing, I march over to him. "What first, oh great mastermind?" Before he actually answers me, "Ah, yes, that's right, I'm supposed to put your bones back in place. Let me just go ahead and do that real quick. Easy peasy." I hastily move around to his back.

"I would appreciate some delicacy in this." He sounds worried, like I'm about to just yank them in place.

"Obviously. I'm not a complete idiot nor am I a sadist." Assessing the damage on his back again, I mutter, "Wish I had some water."

"I can help with that," Valda chimes in for the first time. "There is a small pool just over these rocks in the direction you were headed. I could show–" I begin to rip the ruffle off the bottom of my maid dress, shoving it out towards him when it's off.

"Here. Take this, get it wet, bring it back." He doesn't move. "Now!"

"Yes, yes, of course. I will be but a moment," and he silently glides away.

Turning my focus to Stone's back, I gently feel around the three breaks with my fingertips, figuring out what I need to do. Valda quickly returns with the fabric, trailing water along the way. I snatch it without a word, wringing the excess water over Stone's wings and back, before gently wiping dark blood off the break points. Again I thrust the cloth at Valda.

"More," is my simple command, to which he quietly obeys.

Searching the floor, I find two suitably sized rocks. Kicking them towards Stone, not wanting to get my wet hands dirty, I manage to get them near him.

"Pick those up, one in each hand. You're going to want something to squeeze when I begin setting bones." Slowly, he leans down, following my orders. Valda has returned with the water-laden ruffle, and I let some water drip over my hands as he holds it. "Show me your ankle." Stone complies without qualms. Taking the fabric, I wring some water over it, then clean off the wound I find there. His ankle is already beginning to swell. Thankfully, it seems his wounds aren't bleeding too badly, starting to crust over instead. With a few more water trips, I wipe down Stone's entire back, along with his wing tears.

"Once more, Valda, and try to wash out as much blood as possible." Eagerly, he nods before leaving.

"You are genuinely good at this," Stone says in a mildly surprised tone. "Assessing, moving me about, ordering us around." He turns his face, and I can see he's arched an eyebrow.

"Yeah, well, I grew up with three older brothers who constantly got into scraps. Not to mention all the sports we were in at one time or another." I move his wings to better attend the break I plan to tackle first. "In my last job, I was a massage therapist. So I'm used to working with other people's bodies."

"You mean, you weren't always a burglary aficionado?" There's a little teasing tone in the question.

"Oh goodness, no," Valda inserts himself into our conversation. "She's incredibly new at that. Came to Avenston for training in the art. Why, you two met the day she passed her last trial and became a full member of the Guild."

"Shut. The. Fuck. Up. I'm not ready to talk to you." Cracking my knuckles, I prepare to move some bones.

The mini surgery went well enough, though Stone did end up crushing both the rocks he was holding. We cleaned up as much dirt, dust, and blood from ourselves as possible before heading back up. The journey was slow, and Stone had to stop a few times. Something about concentrating to stave off the stoning process. But here we are at the secret entrance once more.

"We should leave the maid outfit in the passage, so no one finds it and starts asking questions." Stone advises. I nod in agreement and start taking off my borrowed shoes and stockings. "Valda, go check to see if the healing pool is occupied. If it is, check other shower or bathing rooms till you find one that's empty. We can't be spotted this dirty and wounded. At least a shower will get us ready to be seen in the healing waters." Valda zips through a wall to follow Stone's orders without question. Turning to me, "The towel is still here, so you can wrap yourself in that." He tries to hand it to me, but I stop him.

"Actually, I think you might need it. Your kilt is filthy, and you shouldn't be seen in it the way it is now. If you take it off here, I can at least shake it out in the passageway for you." He hums in agreement before starting to undo the little buckles along the waist band. As curious as I am to see him naked, this doesn't feel like the right time. I did catch a glimpse when he stepped out of the pool earlier, but I didn't see anything fun. Too obscured by his wings and tail.

"What will you wear?" His eyes start searching the closet as if an article of clothing will appear.

"Nothing. I've already been seen naked in this club, and being in my birthday suit will help me blend in better. In case you haven't noticed, most people around here are naked. And to be honest, I am way too tired to care at this point." Vigorously, I shake and smack the kilt he hands me as he waits, holding the towel in place at his hips. "I think I could sleep for twenty-four hours." Stone hmm's in reply.

"Alright, I've got the lay of the land," Valda begins talking as soon as he passes back into the room. "While there isn't anyone in the healing waters, there are two people chatting just outside of it. Unfortunately, they don't appear to be in any hurry to move.

But there is a free private shower room just around the corner. I've taken the liberty and locked it for you two. I believe, if you wash up first, you can walk by the pair without drawing any unnecessary attention."

"Thank you, Valda." Stone offers.

"Happy to help, happy to help. Oh, I could take that kilt to the staff washroom. They have quick high-end laundry devices. I could pop it in, then bring it back to you in no time."

"You're being extra helpful, ghost." I interject as I squint my eyes at Valda. "Trying to get back into our good graces after the disaster that took place down there?" Pointedly, I thumb back toward the dark opening. "You remember, where we both almost died." Stone might be able to move past the incident quickly, but I sure as hell am not ready to let Valda forget.

"It was not my intention...You must realize that I had no idea...Obviously I don't want you two dead. I need you both alive to solve my murder."

"Oh, I think you mispronounced 'I'm sorry' in your little speech there, asshat."

"It goes without saying that I'm sorry. I would think–" but I cut him off.

"Some things still need saying, Valda."

"Enough," Stone cuts in sounding as tired as I feel. "We can deal with that later. At present, I need to heal, and we need to get out." Gazing up at Stone, I feel somewhat ashamed of myself.

"You're right. Sorry. Let's get out there." In one smooth motion, I pull the ruined dress over my head, tossing it onto the tunnel stairs. Tapping the wall carving with my big toe to close the secret door, I hand Valda the kilt before turning to Stone.

"Got it in you to put the shelves back in place, big boy?" Stone stares at my newly naked body, as if surprised, before my words finally sink in.

"I'm injured, not crumbling to pieces." Just as smoothly as before, he puts the shelves along the wall. Turning on my heel, I crack the door to check no one is around to see us exiting out of this off-limits closet.

"Left or right?"

"Right," the ghost whispers. "I'll leave the kilt here, then come back for it once I've unlocked that shower. Meet you both in the healing pool?" At my nod, he drops Stone's kilt, heading out the door to take the lead. I can practically feel Stone's struggle to not pick up his kilt from the floor.

The trip to the shower room is uneventful, as is the shower itself. I help Stone carefully wash his back while being as quick as possible. It's all very matter of fact, though I do notice a few stolen glances at my ass. I don't blame him, since I totally tried to get some peeks in myself. I need to see that cock of his. I'm dying to know exactly how much it resembles my favorite toy!

Arms linked, we strut down the hall towards the healing pool. Well, I strut. Stone tries not to limp. Seeing the two chatterboxes, I attempt to act as natural as possible. Well, as natural as I can walking around naked in front of complete strangers with a damaged monster cop at my side. I smile at the moth creature when we make eye contact. Then I watch in horror as his eyes travel over to Stone, brows furrowing. Busted!

"Hey, you alright?" the mothman asks. What is it with cryptids in this place?!

"Oh, don't worry," I walk ahead of Stone, trying to block him and take up their attention. "He just pulled something while we were playing." I pull out all the stops to make them focus on me. As I approach, I sway my hips, trace my hand down the middle of my chest, look him up and down, lick my lips, then bite my lower one before continuing. "He'll be good as new after a soak." With one hand behind my back, I motion at Stone to enter the pool room. He doesn't take the hint, however, choosing to stand right behind me instead of going through the open doorway.

"A little slip of a human like you, giving a Gargoyle a run for his money? Now that would have been a show to see." The stranger's friend, a fanged Fae of some kind, has turned his eyes to me as well.

"What can I say," I continue the conversation, all the while frantically motioning Stone to GTFO, "we like to play cops and robbers. I might be a little too nimble. Resist arrest a little too well." The two guys smile and nod at me, but Stone is just standing there like a statue.

"Say, could you two help a girl out? We're first time guests here tonight, and I can't remember where they said to pick up our clothes." Nothing like playing the 'damsel in distress' card to get a man to do something for you. "I remember they would pick them up if we dropped them in the heat of the moment," I step closer into both men, praying the Gargoyle sees my waving hand and leaves. "But I just can't recall where they are taken."

"We'd be happy to help you out. The first time here can be overwhelming." The Fae tongues his right fang while perusing the plains of my naked body. "You can pick your clothes up in the costume closet at the front. You simply tell the attendant at the back desk in there; they'll have a cubby with your name on it. Any

clothes lost in the midst of passion will be stored for you there."
My stomach erupts in an embarrassingly loud growl.

"Oh my," I try to laugh sweetly, "must have worked off my
meal," while batting my eyelashes prettily at them.

"We can show you where you can grab a bite to eat. The bar up
front has snacks if you ask. But if you want something more...sub-
stantial, there's a place back here with fruits, veg, protein. We can
take you there first if you like, then show you where your clothes
will be."

"You hear that, sweetie? I can get something to nibble on while
you rest up." I turn my head back to him, mouthing the word,
'GO,' before turning back. "People here have been so nice and ac-
commodating." Instead of leaving, Stone steps in closer, bending
down to my ear.

"Don't have too much fun without me, little thief." Gently,
he runs a finger down my arm, making me shiver. Finally, he walks
into the pool room where he should have gone to begin with. I
ignore the feeling I get when we part. We have a plan, and this was
part of it, so why do I feel disappointed? Do I like spending time
with Stone?

Chapter 19

Stone

I'm brooding. I know I'm brooding. I know why I'm brooding, and it's stupid. I shouldn't be brooding. Yet here I sit, all alone, brooding.

She wasn't really flirting with those two males. She was faking; she was being clever. Distracting them from my injuries, obtaining any excuses we may need about our whereabouts, being seen openly with other members, being remembered by other members, and getting her clothes as we planned. Also, finding herself some food.

I should have been the one to realize she hadn't eaten since lunch. Much time has passed since then. It made me feel embarrassed when her stomach growled so loud in front of those males. Ashamed even. I had not been taking care of her or seen that she had taken care of herself. Through watching her, I've seen how she can be forgetful when it comes to her own needs. While working together, I could have been more mindful of that fact, been a better partner. Because we are partners in this case after all.

Her reaction to me wasn't fake though. Her intake of breath when I spoke lowly in her ear, the shiver when I stroked her, the goosebumps on her flesh. I can feel myself getting hard, and not from the stonification that's trying to take over.

"Tada! Kilt fresh and clean, as promised." Valda hangs my kilt on a peg along the wall. "I assume everything went off without a hitch in my absence? That our dear human has scampered off to get her clothes?"

I only nod. I'm in no mood to speak to him.

"Good, good." I remain silent, allowing the healing pool to do what it can as I stave off stoning. "I do wish to formally apologize to you. I thought the cave-in had settled, I didn't realize...Well, I am sorry, truly. It was not my intention to cause either of you harm."

"I know, Valda."

"I may have been too hasty in insisting you go down there straight away. I was just so eager, you see. I really feel like this time, with you two working together, things can be different. Resolved." He's quiet for a time before he continues.

"Perhaps I should have you two search through my personnel effects next? There could be something of import in items I have collected over the years. There are some diaries that may be of interest. After you've thoroughly rested, of course."

"Why do you think–"

"I'm back!" Alexis bursts in. "How are you feeling? Are we able to leave yet? Because I am so ready to crawl into bed."

"Yes, I believe I am sufficiently healed to walk out of this establishment without anyone noticing my condition." I flex my wings and wince. "Though flying is out of the question at the moment. Would you check my back?" She walks to the edge of the pool, heel clacks filling the room with echoes.

"Holes and tears are closed up, and the deep gashes look like faint scars at this point. The area around the broken bones are swollen, but only noticeable if you're really looking. How about that ankle? Think you can walk on it without limping?" I test the weight in the water and all seems fine, not entirely healed but I can manage the short walk out of the building without showing strain. "We can hang out in here a little longer if it would help."

"No, what I really need can't happen here. I am well enough to move on." Walking out of the pool, I fight the urge to inquire about her time with the two males. There's no reason to ask, no purpose will be served by its answer. A burp resounds throughout the room.

"Excuse me!" Alexis laughs. "I ate an apple while those dudes told me more about this place. There are all kinds of rooms here! Rooms for every elemental, sets to play out fantasies, rooms that look like outdoor gardens that you can change from day to night. This building has to be magicked to have this much space." She kneels down, playing her fingers across the surface of the water. "Apparently there's a kraken here tonight, and he was using his tentacles to play with willing partners." She gives a wistful sigh, like she would very much have liked to be one of those partners. "My new friends bailed on me when they found out, wanting to go watch. Can't blame them honestly."

Relief spreads unbidden across my chest.

"Anyway, I found my clothes just fine. Oh, and you'll never guess. They know I'm a member of the Thieves Guild. The host who greeted us walked me into the costume closet and said they were honored to have a member amongst them this evening. She told me that if I was interested in joining she would send information about a trial period to my home. I said yes, of course. Which means we might have a more legitimate means of coming back here. Apparently me being a human was also a boon as they don't have any human members at the moment. They like to keep it as diverse as possible here." Her smile is beaming, and I'm glad of it.

"Congratulations, Alexis. This place would be lucky to have you as a member." Kilt on, I turn to her. "Shall we?" Without hesitation, she links her arm in mine.

"Well, then, I'll be off too," Valda interjects before promptly disappearing.

"Good riddance," Alexis mutters under her breath as we exit the room.

The walk back to the front is uneventful. I'm able to keep my limp in check, and no one stops us about our prolonged absence. As we approach the exit, the three-tailed Kitsune politely stops us, stepping in our path with a bow. I can feel Alexis tense at my side.

"Patrolman Stone, member of the Gargoyle Clan of Avenston, the proprietor of this establishment would like to extend an invitation to you." She proffers a small silver tray that holds a sealed red envelope. I take it as she continues, "Your skilled demonstration upon Alexis Callaway this evening did not go unnoticed nor does the reputation you hold amongst our brethren houses. We would be most honored if you would consider joining our club." She bows again. I glance at Alexis, who is wearing a mask of polite indifference upon her face, but her hand has tightened its grip on my arm.

"Inside the envelope you will find more information, a few forms, and a temporary pass of entry. You may return here at any time to test the waters, as it were. We understand that you have many options but hope that you consider us." With a final bow she steps aside.

"Thank you. Your offer is most appreciated. I will be sure to give it full consideration." I tuck the envelope into my waistband while tipping my head to her. We exit the building without any further disruptions.

"What the hell, Stone?!" Alexis erupts as soon as the door closes behind us. "I get a 'probation period' while they practically beg you to join! What kind of a reputation do you have? Why do you even have a reputation in the sex club circles? How often do you go to these places?" We walk down the alley as she hurls her questions at me.

"You know how I love rules." I try to joke with her. It's somewhat successful as she does turn slowly to eye me incredulously. "Such establishments are my preferred place for sexual relief. Everyone is there for the same, or similar, reasons. There are rules, codes of conduct, and clear expectations. Just as you know what to expect from a library or an art museum, I know what to expect at such places. It is like going to a restaurant when one is hungry. Yes, you can make dinner at home, but it is both more efficient and eventful if you go out." She is being silent, listening to my words, and I think trying to understand.

"So, do you still date and stuff?"

"Yes, of course." I can't help rolling my eyes. "I have courted females before in the traditional manner, but I recognize quickly if a person is not for me. Having no desire to waste my time, or theirs, I end a relationship if I see no future. There are different expectations when one courts, and thus far I have yet to meet a person who holds my interest, whom I can see spending lots of my time with, not to mention my whole life." As we turn a corner, I can feel myself limping, short sharp pains starting to return.

"No. No, you don't have to explain yourself. Here I am being a hypocrite when you didn't press me about my sexual exploits. Sorry about that. It just took me by surprise is all. You've surprised me a lot today actually. I'm kinda reeling from what all I've learned about you." She smiles wickedly at me, playfully even.

"I am not ashamed of how I scratch that particular itch nor of the reputation I have cultivated. I...I like you learning more about me, showing myself to you. If you haven't gathered, I can be a little closed off." This makes her laugh, a beautiful dancing laugh.

"You? Closed off?" She laughs again, the sound skipping down the lane. I can feel my body trying to turn to stone, trying to cocoon me, to heal me the way a Gargoyle does. But I don't want this conversation to end. I don't want to stop our interaction.

"You hold my interest far more than any paramour ever has." I didn't mean to say it out loud, the sudden realization hit me and made its way out into the world unprompted. I'm not sorry I said it, because it is the truth, but I do wish I hadn't said it just yet. Alexis stops dead, looking up at me.

"Wh-what?" Purposely, I stride into her, making her back up into the wall.

"I said, you hold my interest far more than any paramour ever has." Lightly, I trail a knuckle down the side of her face. "You perplex me, intrigue me, play with me, push me." I lean in, placing a hand above her on the wall to steady myself, taking the weight off that fucking ankle.

She must like it because she utters a silent little "Oh" when I cage her in. Even now, I learn more about her. She's staring at my lips, like she's expecting…does she want me to kiss her? I take her chin in hand, holding her in place as I inch forward, giving her time to refuse me. Instead her chest heaves up and down with excited breaths. She licks her lips in preparation, and I rumble deep in my chest in excitement.

"Ouch!" Alexis exclaims. I instantly back off, letting go.

"What happened? Where did I hurt you?" Looking her over, I chide myself. I've got to keep in mind how fragile humans can be.

"Your fingers, it's like they– Oh fuck, your hand!" Glancing down, I see the cause of her alarm and pain. My body is beginning to turn, whether I'm ready or not.

"I need to get somewhere safe immediately. I'm turning to stone and will be thus for at least two days, possibly more." Searching our surroundings, I run through options near where we are.

"My place is close. Think you can make it there?" She's right, we are nearer her apartment.

"I will try."

"Just a few more stairs, Stone. We're so close!" She's been coaching me along the way, saying words of encouragement as more and more of my flesh begins to change. I'm moving even slower now, limbs heavy and rapidly losing their responsiveness.

"Run ahead and unlock the door." Even speaking is difficult.

"Yes, right, right." Leaving my side, she takes the remaining stairs two at a time. Once unlocked, she enters, and I hear the sound of closing curtains. Wonder if that was for my benefit or her own? "Two more stairs, you're almost there. And you're sure there's nothing I need to do?" She's asked this question, in different variations, several times at this point.

"No, just keep me safe. No clubs or maces to any of my digits please." I'm only half joking with her.

Finally making it, she actually claps as I shuffle into her apartment. I make it as far as her balcony door before I run out of time. One moment I'm looking at her and her apartment beyond, the next my muscles seize and all is lost to blackness.

Sometimes there are dreams of her. But mostly I am only aware of blackness, a nothingness where there is no time or senses. I cherish the dreams more than I ever have before. For the whole of my life, the void of stoning has not bothered me. It's simply a part of my existence. But now, I feel the long stretch of time keenly between my visions of her. My pretty little thief.

I dream of her, bound once more upon that chair, accepting her punishment. There's a larger crowd, something that excites my captive. This time, I do not use the training dildo, but my own cock. She accepts all of me with sweet cries of pleasure.

I dream of her in a garden, under the stars. I chase her through a hedgemaze, catching her before we reach the center. I toss her over my shoulder, knuckles playing with her delicious slit as I walk her to the center of the maze. There I find a statue of a Minotaur upon a pedestal, surrounded by large red roses. I push the statue off, setting her ass upon the flat stone surface. I spread her legs wide and eat my fill of her pussy. Her moans music to my ears.

I dream of her being held captive in a faraway tower, her cries for help drawing me in. She pleads with me to rescue her, to save her from her wicked mothmen captors. I do, holding her close as I leap from her window, soaring to my own castle where I claim my reward. Her. I play with her, teasing climax after climax out of her until she is spent, laying in my arms as I rock her to and fro. That was the dream I was most loath to part with.

Eventually I roar back into consciousness, breaking the stony prison around me. Stretching, I take in my surroundings. Morning light is streaming in from the windows of Alexis's apartment. The place is an absolute wreck again. How long have I been out, weeks?!

Getting my bearings, I notice that there are clothing items strewn all around me. Glancing up at my wing, I see a green breast-covering hanging off the tip. Alexis peeks her head out of the bathroom.

"Did you hang your laundry on me to dry?!"

Chapter 20

◄◆►

Stone

Alexis steps out of the bathroom, hair back to its typical close shave, tying a red silken robe in place as she walks towards me. She was clearly about to take a shower before I awoke. My fury, and my desire to be near her, have me quickly crossing the small apartment.

"Did you hang your wet clothes on me while I was stoned?!" I'm growling, holding the green article of clothing clutched tightly in my fist.

"Hey, hey, don't scrunch it!" She's hopping up in an attempt to snatch it out of my hand. "That's my favorite bralette."

"Then why did you hang it on me?"

"Because, you oversized doorjamb, you blocked the way onto my balcony." She stops trying to reclaim her clover green 'bralette,' planting both fists on her hips in defiance. "I couldn't get outside to hang my delicates to dry in the fresh air. So I hung them on you, using the sun from the window to dry them." Smirking at me, "I made you useful."

In a smooth, quick motion, I take hold of one of her wrists, spin her around, planting her back upon my chest. Clutching our hands over her belly, I wrap my other around the long elegance of her throat.

"Hey! What the? Oh!" She inhales sharply as I hold her throat a little tighter.

"What a naughty little partner I have here. Whatever shall I do with her?" I walk us over to her dining table, passing a wing over its surface to clear off the mess. Kicking her legs open wider, I press her hips into the edge of the table. Her breathing has quickened, but she hasn't said a word yet. Slowly, I glide my tail up the inside of her leg.

"What is your safe word, Alexis?" I ask while running my nose along her cute little rounded ear.

"Oh sweet geezuz, yes!" Her eagerness makes me chuckle.

"That is not your safe word, little thief."

"Mimic! Mimic! My safe word is mimic!" The answer is frantic in her eagerness.

"Good girl," I purr into her neck. "Are you ready for your punishment?"

"Yes. Yes, sir." Keeping hold of her wrist, I extend it out to the side as I ease the hand at her throat down her chest to her waist, deftly untying her belt.

"Let's see, you owe me one punishment from the club," I open her robe, keeping the silken tie in my hand. "And you earned another from that little laundry stunt. Does that sound right?" Releasing her wrist, I use claw-tipped fingers to slide the robe off her shoulders and down her arms. I am more than pleased to find her naked under it. She shivers as my points gently skim over her flesh.

"Yes, sir." She leans into me as her closed eyes turn to the ceiling.

"Ah, but there is the matter of the state of this house to deal with." Tossing her robe into a chair, I bend her over the table, bringing both her hands behind her back. "It's an absolute disaster." Taking the silken tie, I bind her forearms together. The red sheen of the fabric looking magnificent around her dark golden skin. "And after I cleaned it so thoroughly for you."

Stepping to the side, I place one hand on the back of her neck, caressing the round of her ass with the other. Without warning, I give it a resounding smack! A lovely 'ah' escapes her throat. Gently, I rub the skin I just hit.

"Is this a fair punishment for the mess you made?" I smack her ass again.

"Yes, sir," she whispers into the table as I massage her ass cheek. Another smack.

"Good girl." Smack! She whimpers. Smack! "You take your penance so well." I bring the tip of my tail to begin running along her slit, light and teasing.

Smack! This time I get a louder 'Ah!' so I decide to move to the other cheek. Smack!

"The mirror behind you provides me quite a view." Smack! "I get to watch my tail play with you as I spank your sweet round ass." Smack!

"Oh!" she moans. I feel the wetness of her pussy increase, so I reward her with more tail pressure. No longer teasing, but fully running along the inside of her folds, grazing her clit along the way.

Smack! She's wiggling her ass under my ministrations. It's tempting, so very tempting. Smack! I caress her ass cheeks as I stare down at the pink blossoming upon them both.

"Beautiful," I growl. "You took that incredibly well, Alexis. Are you ready to begin working on your punishment?" I can see the buds of tears at the corners of her eyes, but I can also see her grin. Pride warms my chest, causing me to rumble.

"Yes, sir," she answers emphatically.

"Knee on the table, I want to taste that sweet pussy of yours." Her whole body quakes at my words. Helping, we move her right knee and thigh along the top of the table. I kneel down behind her, leveling my face with her reddened ass. Gently, I trace my claws down the round of her cheeks before parting them further for me. Languidly, I lick my tongue all along her wet folds.

"Oh, whoa! Is that your tongue?!" She's surprised, but not upset. "Are those, are those bumps on it?" Her response makes me smile.

"Yes, a Gargoyle's tongue has little granules just under the skin. It appears flat on the surface, but just underneath lurk little pebbles. Mine has three rows. Is it not pleasurable? Would you like me to stop?" I would be greatly disappointed if she didn't want me to continue. Most females enjoy it greatly.

"Don't you dare fucking stop!" She clears her throat. "Sir. I was surprised was all. Carry on." She wiggles that ass again right in front of my face. "Please carry on?"

I attack her pussy with gusto, running my tongue along it, making her feel all the little bumps my tongue possesses. She's moaning and panting in earnest as I trace the circle of her opening before plunging deep inside. Moving to sit cross-legged under her,

I use my hands to lift her ass higher, causing her to stand on her tiptoes. When the tip of my tongue finds her G-spot, her knees jerk in surprise.

"What! How?" She pants her questions as I continue to fuck her with my tongue. Bringing my tail to play with her clit, I remove my mouth from her in order to answer.

"My tongue is longer than it looks." Unable to stop myself, I bite her ass before returning my tongue to her core. I leave my tail-tip to rub her clit as I attack the G-spot within; flicking, rubbing, and pressing it. Her legs are shaking as she begins her chant.

"Yes, yes, yes, don't, yes, please." I do not halt in my efforts, knowing she is close. Taking a knuckle, I graze the pucker of her asshole. "Aahhhhh!" her cry resounds as her body clamps down around my tongue. I do not let that stop its movements, however. Pushing, writhing, forcing, I continue to work her as she rides her orgasm.

When she's past the fall, I slow my efforts, back off in pressure, and remove my tail. I lick her all over, drinking her in before lowering her back down. Her shaking knee buckles as she puts her full weight on the table.

"Oh my. Oh my, oh my, oh my. That's my new favorite tongue ever in existence. Wow, wow, wow." My chest rumbles at her praise. Standing, I run my claws up the backs of her legs, loving the shuddering I feel from her.

"Glad you enjoy it, little thief, as I plan to taste you as often as possible." I bring both hands to either side of her torso, folding my body over hers. "You have the most delicious pussy." I nuzzle her neck before standing. Playfully I tap her ass. "Prepare for your second punishment." She laughs at my statement.

"Sir, yes, sir." She stands and rolls her shoulders. "Think I'll walk around a second." I nod in agreement as I take a seat on the corner of her table.

"Need anything to drink?"

"No, just need to move my hips and legs." She does an interesting high-kneed march back and forth. "I think my tie loosened up too, if you want to check." Prancing over to me, she turns around. My thief was correct, it had loosened somewhat. I take my time, binding her forearms more securely. "All good! Where do you want me, Officer?" Her question is playful, wiggling her eyebrows as she asks. I bring a claw-tipped finger to tap on my chin, giving signs of heavy thought.

Standing from the table, I move to the short side, pushing it forward till the edge is seen fully in the mirror. I motion her over with a finger to which she eagerly obeys. I catch her before she bends back over the table, wrapping my hand around her throat once more.

"I want you to watch yourself as I fuck you with that training toy you have." I can see half of her smile in the reflection as her body wiggles against mine. "Now, bend over, and get comfortable." I release her so she can follow my orders. "Such a good girl, eager for her punishment." Moving away, I walk over to her bedside, where I put the dildo when I cleaned her space. Opening the drawer, I find only the bee-box there.

"Alexis," I say, my voice sounding angry, "where is your training dildo?" I slowly turn my head to face her in the mirror where she's watching my reflection. "Did you play with it while I was healing?"

"Maaaaybeee?" Her smile is coy, butt moving back and forth.

"Where is it now, little thief?" My tone is dangerous.

"In the fridge," she answers as she glances at the chill box. I growl as I stalk over to it. "Just getting it ready, sir." Yanking the door open, I find it in a clear box resting on a shelf alone. "It's all clean, sir. Ready to use." Unfastening the tight lid, I take the toy in hand. It's cool to the touch.

"Oh, Alexis, you are about to pay dearly for using this while I was here recovering." She giggles in anticipation. "Stand." She glances up at me confused but obeys my command. "Turn your head to look at yourself in the mirror." Again, she obeys. "For the entirety of this next punishment, I want you to keep your eyes on that mirror, to watch yourself and what I do to you. Understand?"

"Yes, sir," she answers the mirrored me who is now right behind her. I wrap my tail around her thigh and snake it up to play with her wet slit. As her eyes trail down to focus on that, I take the cold stone dildo and touch its head to a peaked nipple. Gasping in surprise, her body tries to move away, but I keep her in place using my own like a wall. I quickly move to the other nipple, eliciting an 'oh' as she stands on her tiptoes.

"Bend over, and spread your legs wide for me." As she starts to bend forward, her eyes flick to the table. "Look at the mirror, Alexis." Eyes back to mine via the mirror, she slowly bends over. Taking the stone toy, I set its head at her opening, the cold of its stone making her gasp and squirm.

"Mimic!" I instantly remove the head and step back.

"What do you need?" My question is quick as I inspect her body.

"It's just...I've never," she licks her lips. "I've never used that without lube before." She looks at me a little worried, but I smile at her.

"Understood." I nod, smiling wider. "You did well to speak up. I shall remember this for future sessions." She grins at me, worry faded completely. "Where do you keep your lube?"

"It's in the bathroom at the moment. I..." she trails off.

"Were you about to use this," I hold up the dildo, "on yourself in the tub?" I tsk at her as I walk to grab the lube. "Answer me, Alexis," I shout before I enter the bathing room.

"Yes, sir. Well, actually, I was about to use it in the shower." Lube in hand, I stride back to her, grabbing the bee-box on my way back for good measure. I toss that onto the table as I stand behind Alexis once more. As before, I use my tail to apply lube, but only along one side of the toy.

"Better? Ready to resume?"

"Yes, sir." Her eyes are full of emotions, but I can't tell which ones.

I bring the chilled dildo to run it along her pussy folds. She writhes at the contact, but I continue, twisting it to make sure the entire length is covered in lube before leveling it to her entrance again. Slowly, I begin to work it inside her, in and out. Her feet move about as I set to work, so I hold one in place by the ankle with my tail. I've got her at three notches already.

"Tell me, Alexis, where did you use this toy as I rested in stone?" Her eyes in the mirror are watching me press the phallus into her, just as I ordered. Good. I still my movements at notch four, turning the dildo in place. "Where, Alexis?"

"In front of you." Intriguing. I continue my slow movements in and out, but stop once more at notch five when she doesn't elaborate. She whines before continuing.

"On the floor at your feet on the second day." Moving again, she continues. "I..I...oh gawd that's hot...I braced my feet on your stone knees, holding myself open I as fucked myself with it. I imagined it was your cock, that you were fucking me." She is up to seven notches, more than halfway. "Ooohhhh!" Eight notches.

"I imagined, I hoped, you'd wake up and find me there, spread wide open for you." Nine. "Oh fuck! And then you'd take me, hold me down, and have your way with me." I grab the bee-box off the table, turn it on, and kneel down. She deserves a reward for this full confession. "Fuck me!" she shouts as I bring the vibrating box to her clit. Ten.

"Is that what you wanted, little thief? You wanted this monster to wake up and fuck you?" Eleven.

"Oh fuck, oh fuck, yes!" Her hands are grasping at nothing, her eyes enraptured at the mirrored image of me fucking her with the facsimile of my own cock. "Fuck, I'm so full!"

"Yes, you are," I croon to her. "Only one more notch, and you'll have taken it all. Such a good girl, getting herself ready to take my cock." She's nodding her head in agreement. "Is that what you want, little thief? Do you want me to fuck you with my monster cock?"

"Yes, yes." Leaving the dildo in at notch eleven, I twist the handle. "Oooooh, fuck! Yes, sir. Yes, sir. I want you to fuck me with your monster cock."

"Then relax for me, and take one more notch." I push and pull the stone cock three more times before I feel her body ready to take the last bump. The one that lets a Gargoyle know our lover is truly ready to take the real thing.

"Magnificent, Alexis." I say enraptured. "You took it all, and now you are ready." I stand, leaving the dildo inside her all the way, twisting it so her body becomes accustomed to the size. Turning the bee-box off and setting it aside, I unbuckle my kilt. Throwing it on the chair with Alexis' robe, I let her get a good look at my cock in the mirror. It's bigger than this training toy, but only a little. I notice her eyes have gone wide though.

"You still want this, Alexis?" I take the toy out of her slowly before bringing it next to my length for comparison. "You still want to be fucked by this monster cock?" She's blinking at the image of me in the mirror. "I need an answer, little thief. We can continue with just–"

"Yes," she whispers, cutting me off. Licking her plump lips, she looks me in the eyes via the mirror. "Yes, I very much want to be fucked by that monster cock, sir." I rumble in pleasure. Walking to the longer side of the table, I place a chair facing the mirror. Sitting down, I meet her eyes in the reflection once more.

"Then come over here and sit on it," I order, tapping my thigh.

Chapter 21

———◆O◆———

Stone

"You may look where you need in order to safely make your way onto my lap, Alexis."

"Thank you, sir." She stands, arms still tightly bound, and makes her way in front of me. Grabbing her waist, I help guide her down to sit on my thighs, cock jutting up between her back and my front. She glances at the mirror again in question.

"We'll get there, little thief. First, hook your legs over mine." When she does so, I open my legs, spreading her wide open for me in front of the mirror as she gasps in surprise. "Look at how beautiful you are. What an amazing view." I work my tail up to play with her folds, my hands come around to fondle her breasts, her nipples. "We're both going to watch you take my cock in that mirror, aren't we, Alexis?"

"Yes, sir," she answers breathlessly.

"Then, we are going to watch you get fucked by my cock in that mirror."

"Yes, sir." Her hips are rocking on my lap as I work her nipples and clit. I can't wait to watch her break upon me. A growl of anticipation escapes me as she moans.

Taking my hands from her breasts, I place them under her thighs, lifting her up. Instinctively, she leans back into me for stability. Removing my tail, I position her right above my cock, the head finding her opening.

"Keep watching, Alexis. I want you to see how I fill that tasty pussy of yours." Slowly, I begin to lower her, my shaft disappearing into her core. When I feel any resistance, I lift her slightly before letting her fall further down. It's a sweet agony to go this slow, to watch as she takes me. I can feel myself stretching her, the sounds she's making are a sweet melody. More than halfway down, I decide to reward her with the bee-box.

Using my tail, I grab it, then tap it on. Draping my tail over her thigh, I hold the box atop her clit, so as not to obscure the view. Her hips are moving in earnest, helping the friction, the glide of my penetration.

Up and down, in and out, her pleasure builds. She's almost taken all of me; I'll make her come when she does.

"You're doing so well, my little thief. You've almost stolen all of my cock deep inside you." Up and down, I pump her. "Look how open you are for me; look how exquisitely you get fucked by this monster's cock."

"Oh fuck, oh fuck, Stone." I growl when she says my name, unable to help the thrust of my hips up into her. "Ah! Yes! Stone, yes. Fuck me." I thrust a few more times letting her fall to meet it. She's there!

"You've done it, my beautiful thief." I still my motions so we can both see her sitting upon my lap. "You've taken it all." I gently bite her neck. "Now, I'm going to make you come while I'm deep inside you."

Angling the bee-box to its narrower side, I play with her clit, building her up even more. She rocks and moves her hips upon my lap, moving my cock around inside her. I keep her here for a time, using my claws to play with her nipples, running my tongue along her neck and ears as she tries to fuck herself with my cock. This is a punishment after all.

"Please, Stone, please," she begs. "I'm so fucking ready for my punishment. I'm so fucking ready!" Nuzzling her neck, I ask the question I know the answer to.

"What do you need to make you come, Alexis?" Without hesitation, she answers.

"Your cock! Your cock fucking me!" she yells, but I don't move just yet, leaving her here panting and undulating. "Please sir, I need your monster cock to fuck me!"

Giving in to her demands, I lift her up, then let her fall down over and over again. Her screams of, 'yes, yes, yes,' tell me she's close. Right as I feel her starting to clench around me, I begin to thrust up to meet her. It only takes three good thrusts before she crumbles completely.

Wrapping both arms around her body, I hold her in place with me deep inside, gently moving my hips as she bucks and cries in sweet agony. It is a sight to see. When the time is right, I remove the bee-box, setting it back on the table.

Coming down from her high, she trembles and shakes all over in my arms. Lifting her off my cock, I turn her and set her back down on my lap, legs to the side. Gently, I untie her bonds as she leans into me, head resting on my shoulder.

"Breathe, my radiant Alexis, breathe." She begins to deepen and slow her breaths at my command. "You took your final punishment so beautifully. You were absolutely perfect." I'm stroking her arm, her face, her legs. Bringing her back, calming her down. Taking my claws, I run them delicately over her scalp as I rock us.

"Oh boy, that was something," she finally says.

"I couldn't agree more." I rumble in satisfaction. "What do you need, Alexis?"

"Just a moment. Well, maybe something to drink too." Tenderly, I kiss her head before I stand with her in my arms. I set her down on the table before walking over to her 'fridge' to take out some juice I saw in there earlier. Pouring two glasses, I walk back over and hand her one. She gulps it down greedily. Taking the glass from her once she's finished, I set them both in the sink.

"How are you feeling?" A giddy laugh erupts out of her at my question.

"Oh, I'm doing amazing." She thinks a moment as I place my hands on either side of her hips on the table. "I can feel a little stretch, but I ain't complaining. You?"

"Eager."

"Eager, for what?" She furrows her brows at me.

"My turn." I lick my lips as I look her body over, my hunger palpable.

"Oh my," she whispers, eyes round in surprise.

"That is, if you're up for it?" I arch my eyebrow. "I don't want to break you so soon. We've only just begun, you and I."

"I didn't say I wasn't up for it!" she snaps back, rising to the challenge I accidentally just set.

"That wasn't an insult, Alexis." I smooth her shoulder down. She bristles like a cat, this one. "We can stop right here, if you are not ready or simply done. I am a patient male. I can wait for you."

Taking her chin, I make her look up at me. "Tell me the truth, thief of my cock." She smiles at that. "Do you want to continue, or is this session over?"

She instantly opens her mouth, but I stop her with a kiss. A slow, deep, tender kiss. The kind that makes me feel tingles all along the tops of my wings. I nibble her lips, glide my tongue over hers, and growl into her mouth. When we part, her eyes remain closed for a time.

"I want you to think before you answer, Alexis." She nods her head, eyes still closed. They finally open when I chuckle.

"Sorry, what was the question again?" she asks, dazed.

"Do you want to continue?" I ask, running a knuckle down her cheek. "Will you let me fuck you to completion? Or are we done for the moment?" I hold up a finger. "And I want you to think about it."

"Oh yeah, I've definitely got more in me after that kiss. Which was amazing by the way." She stretches up to nibble my jaw. " But maybe leave my clit alone? She's way overstimulated now."

"Agreed." Grabbing the back of her head, I bring her in for another kiss, even deeper than before and laced with hunger. She moans into me, hands grabbing my horns. Eventually she breaks the kiss, panting.

"Where?" comes her question.

"Right here!" Taking her neck, I pull her down to lay on the table as she places her feet on its edge. Lining up my cock, I push all the way in using one slow movement, basking in the feel of her wrapped so tightly around me. Pulling out all the way, I slowly sink into her once more. This is not going to take much longer. I continue my long strokes, enjoying every moment of them. Alexis has begun rocking her hips in time to the pace I have set.

"Look at you, my beautiful thief, taking my cock like it was made for you." She moans at my praise, so I ramp up my thrusts. "For this perfect," thrust, "tight," thrust, "pussy," thrust. She brings her hands to her nipples, playing with them as I watch, as I fuck her. Lifting the bee-box with my tail, I hand it to her.

"Mind reader," she praises me as she turns it on, bringing it to a nipple. That leaves one nipple all alone. I return to my slow thrust as I bend over and lick that lonely nipple. "Oh, sweet mother of, ugh!" she exclaims as I dragged my pebbled tongue across her entire breast. Focusing my efforts on the nipple itself, I ramp up my thrusts once more.

"Oh my, I might….oh man, I might…" She never finishes the thought, but I have a feeling I know what she's trying to say. And if I can make it happen, I will.

"Switch." I order as I move the vibrating stone aside to attack her other nipple. I've grabbed hold of her hips, pulling her down as I thrust into her. I rumble against her breast, so close to coming myself. "Alexis, I…" Seems I also can't finish my thoughts.

"Yes, gawd, yes! Come for me, come for me, big boy! Make me feel it!" I've snaked my right arm under her side, grabbing her shoulder as I begin to yank her down upon my thrusting cock. "Make me feel it! I want to feel it, Stone!"

Forehead to forehead, I'm growling into her face as she moans and cries out.

"Stone, I–" Both hands grab my horns as her back arches into me, pussy holding so tight I start to come along with her. My movements are jerky as I pump, both hands pulling her into me by her shoulders.

I lift my head and bellow as my own climax rips through me. Rocketing into her as I finish, holding her tightly to me as I stay buried deep inside. We remain this way for a time, each catching our breaths.

"Stone," she begins while gasping, "you are my new favorite toy." I want to growl at that statement, but it turns into a laugh to match her own. We laugh for a time, as I shake my head.

"I should punish you for that." I say as I nip her earlobe.

"Maybe later, big boy. After that, I'm one hundred percent done with our session." She slaps her hand upon the table. "I tap out. You win. I know my limit."

"Good girl. Now," I straighten up, cock still buried deep inside her, "let's get you that shower I interrupted." I slowly pull out, making her arch her back and moan one last time. "Then, some food because I am starving!"

"Pussy not filling enough for you?" She asks, smiling up at me while still laid out upon the table.

"Unfortunately, this Gargoyle can not sustain himself on pussy alone." Her laughter in reply has me realizing that I enjoy playing with Alexis in this way as well. Grinning, I bend over her to lift her over my shoulder.

"Hey, put me down!" Lazily, she struggles while hitting my back. "Oh! You're all healed."

"Indeed. Though I am concerned that you hit me before checking." Hefting her into place, I march into the bathing room.

"Ha, ha, very funny."

"No, it's not funny at all. I was quite injured." Opening the shower door I start the water. "Not sure if you remember this, but I took an avalanche of boulders for you." She lets out a 'grrr' in frustration.

"Put me down, you oaf! I can walk, you know." She feebly swings her legs. "And yes, of course, I remember. It scared the shit out of me. You scared the shit out of me." I set her down just outside the shower, taking this opportunity to undo my braid before getting wet.

"Thank you, by the way. For saving my life." It comes out small, just above a whisper. Looking down at her, I see her eyes are turned away from me. No, that will not do at all. I like Alexis proud and cocky, sure of herself and determined.

"Anytime, little thief. It was an honor to protect you." As she glances back up at me, I continue, "But please, try not to make it a habit. It did hurt quite a bit after all." Fire back in her eyes, she slaps my chest.

"Shut up, you! Get into the shower."

Chapter 22

Alexis

I am never going back to the real world! These monsters fuck different. I thought sex with Shifters was fun, I thought sex with a Naga was great, but sex with this Gargoyle was amazing! My body shivers despite the warm water cascading down my skin.

"Water too cold, Alexis?" Stone has taken it upon himself to join me in the shower, washing me himself.

"Must have just been an aftershock." I grin over my shoulder at him, as a small rumble comes from his chest. I'm starting to think of those like a purr, except they don't only happen when he's happy. It's almost like they happen when he's feeling new or strong emotions of any kind. Turning to face the shower wall again, I smile to myself. During the three days he was a statue in my house, I realized I kind of missed him.

Which is absolutely ridiculous on so many levels. For one, he was still right here in the apartment with me, sort of. Then, of course, just a few days ago, I would have given anything to have him off my back. He was a constant menacing shadow that followed me around, trying to catch me in some unlawful act. It was really fun to mess with him at a distance though. Ugh, I barely know the guy! So what if getting to know him, if peeling back the layers kept getting more and more interesting, more intriguing. He's a cop, an adversary, and spending time with him shouldn't be so much fun.

"Arms up," Stone orders.

"No tickling!" I warn.

"No tickling," he agrees.

During those three days alone, I couldn't decide if I missed him because I was lonely or if I was lonely because I missed him. Other than a check-in with Gav and a quick convo with Valda, I didn't interact with anyone during that time. Even that fucking ghost had kept his distance after a brief peak-in at Stone. Probably because I made it known I was still royally pissed at him.

"I need to get the bottoms of your feet, Alexis." Stone is crouched down, washing my lower half. "I promise not to tickle you there either."

Maybe I was only lonely because I spent three days cooped up in my house?! He said he needed to be kept safe while encased in stone, so it felt wrong to leave him. Like watching over a patient in the hospital. So I hung around. I listened to music, tried to read, attempted to sketch him, and ordered a lot of delivery food! I spoke to him too, like a lot.

"Could you hear me, while you were...stoned?" I still can't believe that's what he calls it. My inner teenager snorts every time he says it or I think it.

"Did you talk to me, Alexis?" It's his playful voice that replies. He's spun me around to clean the front of my legs. Oh, I think I like having him on his knees in front of me.

"Well, yeah. Felt weird to just ignore you." He doesn't need to know it was more like a running commentary and not just a few words here and there. "I blasted my music too. Did you hear any of that?"

"Blasted music?"

"Jammed out, cranked it up, blared some tunes, rattled the windows, shook the walls, blew out the speakers..." Yeah, I've totally lost him. "I turned up the volume real loud. The music box doesn't do the songs of my homeland justice, so I make up for it in volume!" I came across the enchanted music box while I was planning my daring vampire heist. It can play any song the user remembers. It was a gawd-send for my sanity! Not being able to listen to a song you have stuck in your head is torture.

"No, I did not hear your music nor your voice." Stone seems to be taking extra special time cleaning my nether region.

"What's it like then, while you're a statue?" Finally he stands again, bringing the Everfresh Sponge to clean my chest. They say it's self-cleaning, they say it never molds, but I still buy a new one every few weeks. It does do wonders for my skin, which is why I keep using them.

"It is blackness; it is nothingness. There is no sense of time or feeling. Usually I have no consciousness there, but sometimes I am aware of it." He sure is taking his time cleaning my breasts. "I've recently started dreaming occasionally while encased."

"That sounds terrible! Well, not the dreaming part, the being aware while trapped in the dark nothingness part. How do you stand it?" It sounds horrifying to me, like worse than sleep paralysis even.

"It has always been so." Gently, he strokes the sponge over my throat. "Knowing it is temporary helps."

"Bet the dreams are a relief." There's a quick glance to my face before he nods. "What do you dream about? Can you remember any?" I had assumed they would be about catching bad guys or something, but the way he stiffens at my question has me curious.

"I don't remember them," he answers in a rush. Did...did Stone just lie to me?! Wow, must be real embarrassing then. He did say they are new, so he might not understand what they mean yet. I've had far too many dreams that involve me showing up to work in a bikini or having a test in a subject I've never studied. Oh man, the teeth falling out dream I hate the most! I'll leave him to his own psyche then.

The topic of dreams has me thinking about my own recent ones. One detail in particular has really got me thinking since Stone went downtown on me. How did my dream brain know that he had bumps on his tongue?! I thought I had made that up since I certainly hadn't known that little tidbit before. His tongue has been that way in my dreams from the very beginning. But how? The only thing I can think of is that I had to have read or heard somewhere that Gargoyles have bumpy tongues. Then my conscious forgot while my unconscious put it into play when it started to give me sexy dreams of Stone. Speaking of sexy Stone.

"My turn!" Snatching the sponge from his hand. "You washed me, so I get to wash you." He tries to take the sponge back, but I move it out of reach.

"There is a lot more of me to wash than there is of you, little thief."

"I've got nowhere to be. Do you?" He grumbles, which I take as a sign of resigned acceptance. Refreshing the soap on the sponge, I begin with his chest, since we're facing each other anyway. Having a big shower with multiple shower heads has never been more handy.

"I think our next steps should be to find Valda and see what he's got," I begin. "He seemed to think his collection could help us in some way." Stone has been sporting a semi all throughout the shower, and I plan to do a little fake-out with him. Get him thinking about the case, bringing out his inner investigator, then boom! I'll play with his cock. I haven't gotten to inspect it up close yet, and I'm curious just how alike it is to my dildo.

"Agreed. I assume you can get a message to him somehow via your Guild connections." I've finished his chest and one arm and begin to work on the other arm as he continues. "I am curious what all he has been collecting, why he has been collecting it, and why he thinks any of it will help solve his murder." Beginning to kneel down as I wash his thighs, his cock jumps slightly at my nearness.

"He did say something about diaries, but I wasn't interested in hearing anything about his damn 'murder' at the time," I offer right as I take hold of his quickly hardening cock. Bumpy texture and color almost exactly like my toy. The only difference being the size, and one other little detail I discover when lifting his cock with my left hand as I prepare to wash.

"Your balls!"

"What balls?"

"Exactly?! Where are your balls?" I had expected to find big monster balls just under his cock, but instead I find...nothing. He's laughing low, genuinely amused at my surprised horror.

"Gargoyles don't have balls, Alexis. We have no need of them."

"What do you mean you don't need them? Where do you keep your baby gravy?!" I'm frantically searching his undercarriage. He's got to be messing with me!

"Baby gravy?" His rumbling laughs are cavernous.

"Yeah! Your jizz, spunk, cum, seed, ejaculate, sperm!"

"Gargoyles do not have this. And given the way you are describing it, I've never been more glad of this fact." Standing up, I watch him shake his head. "Spunk?"

"Well, how do you make little Gargoyles then? How does your kind procreate?" I am so damned confused. He did say that the training toy was made to look like a Gargoyle's dong, but I had still expected balls! I just figured they left them off the toy.

"Alexis, do you really want the 'where do babies come from' talk right now?"

"Yes! Yes I do!" I practically shout while throwing my hands up.

"Very well. Since it seems to be causing you great distress, I'll elaborate." Clearing his throat, he continues in a voice you would use with a child, "When a Gargoyle and their mate, or mates, love each other very, very much," I glare up at him, "they go to their Clan's Maker."

"Maker?" I am even more confused.

"Yes, a Maker is the person in the Clan that carves new Gargoyles." Thankfully, he has dropped the condescending voice. "Well, the eggs at least. They mine the stone we are created from out of our home mountain. Ours is Mt. Dern. Taking the essence of the parents," I must make a face at that because he explains further. "It's usually blood but not always. My father used his 'baby gravy' when making me."

"Wait. So your dad isn't a Gargoyle?"

"No, my father is a Minotaur, while my mother is a Gargoyle. No matter what essence is used, a child created this way will always be a Gargoyle," he answers before I can ask. Leaning against the shower wall, I attempt to take this all in. Thoughts of a BJ completely vanished. Wait, his dad is a Minotaur! I try really, really hard not to think of the Minotaur I kept watching at the sex club. I'm not one hundred percent successful in my efforts.

"The Maker will infuse the essence provided into a stone egg, while the parents place their hands upon it. There's a whole ceremony that involves a basin, the parents holding the egg together for a time, while the Maker has them think of different attributes and project different feelings mentally at the egg. I've never witnessed it myself. It's a deeply personal experience."

"Huh. So no growing a baby inside you?" Absently, I play with my tubal ligation scars. "No physical childbirth?"

"No, the egg gestates for about three months and can be kept at the parents home or within special rooms at the Clan's tower. Typically one or all parents stay with the egg during gestation. To bond, to protect, to speak with, or to fuss over." Stone smiles sweetly as he resumes washing himself. "Father says that my mother fussed endlessly over my egg. Turning it, caressing it, putting blankets on or around it. While he read to it, to me, tales of adventure and daring, Mother opted for poetry and textbooks. She wanted me to be well-rounded."

"Turn around, I'll get your back." I did say I'd wash him after all. "You don't look much like a Minotaur. Not even your horns."

"No, I take after my mother a great deal, though I did get my size and bullheadedness from my father. I'm large even for a

Gargoyle. My grandfather," Stone takes a deep inhale before he continues. "My grandfather had been so hopeful at my creation. Having both parents be strong and inclined to watchful protection, he thought I'd be a great asset to the Clan." His chuckle holds no joy. "Instead he got me, a great disappointment. Not being satisfied with guarding and protecting as I ought."

A disappointment? The Gargoyle I know is anything but a disappointment.

Chapter 23

Alexis

"Well then, your grandfather is an idiot," flies right out of my mouth before I even think. "For one thing, you watch and protect just fine; I can attest to that. You watch a little too well in my opinion. What's he got against the Order, anyway?"

"He doesn't have anything against them personally. The Clan works and coordinates with them well and often. What he takes issue with is the fact that I would rather use my talents to protect the whole city, to stop criminals wherever I can, or to bring them to justice when I can't. To actually help the people in Avenston, not just one family or one building who can afford it, but any who need me." He's become so passionate during his speech that his wings end up flicking soap all over me.

"Apologies, Alexis."

"No, no, it's fine." I sputter as I wipe soap off my face. "If anyone gets it, it's me. I can't stand it when people tell me I can't do something, especially if they think I am incapable. I like that you are going after your dreams, despite your grandfather's wishes." I have him turn so he can stretch out a wing. "What about your parents? How do they feel, what do they think?"

"Like good parents, they are happy as long as I am happy. They never discouraged me, though I suspect Father may have been disappointed that I won't be taking over the family maze once he retires. I have Minotaur cousins aplenty who are more than capable of taking over that task. No pressure there, and he never let any disappointment show."

"Where are they now, your parents?" I'll ask about that maze later.

"They are both in The Basin of Rowshall, working at the maze." Ooo, my chance to ask came sooner than expected.

"What do they do at this maze?" asking as I move to the other wing. He was not kidding, there is so much of him to wash.

"They are the Maze Guardians. A god, or possibly a demigod, has placed a magical hammer within the maze's center to be claimed by a chosen one or someone worthy. The usual." Yeah, sure, the usual. "They watch the maze, scaring those that try, seeing that no one cheats or tampers with the maze in any way. Basically making sure that only the one that the maze deems worthy takes its prize. They also clean up any mess champions leave within the maze." Stone glances over his shoulder to add, "You'd be surprised at the amount of litter and waste people abandon there." He shakes his head in disappointment while I'm mentally picturing a Minotaur with a push broom sweeping down the halls of a maze.

"What about your parents?" There it is, the question I've dreaded would come up during this conversation but hoped wouldn't. "Where are they? What do they do?" The shower was going so well. Having finished washing his back, I turn away to wash my face, delaying the inevitable. Stone takes this opportunity to attack his own head, starting with that long hair of his.

"Dad passed away a couple years ago but spent fifty years as a bus driver, if you can believe that. I could never hold the same job for more than a few years, let alone my whole working life." Mentally steadying myself, I move on to the next bit, the hardest part.

"Mom's gone too. Died in childbirth, my birth actually. But I'm told I take after her a lot. She changed jobs almost as often as I do." I'm trying to move past the whole 'I killed my mother part' as quickly as possible. "I'm told she found her calling when she became a stay-at-home mom. I have three older brothers, but who knows what would have happened after we all grew up. If she would have…" I hold my face under the warm current of water, letting it wash away any tears that may have appeared. "…if she would have lived. Maybe she would have pursued art more. I have some of her drawings she did of my brothers and my father." None of me though, she didn't get the chance to draw any of me. "They were really good."

"I'm sorry both your parents have passed. And to lose your mother so young like that…" I don't want to hear that, I don't want to hear any of that.

"Oh, I'm fine. Can't miss what you never had after all. It's my father and brothers you should feel sorry for. Losing my mother destroyed my dad, and he wasn't okay for a very long time. But he had to soldier on, with four kids to look after." Why am I still talking about this? I don't want to talk about this anymore. "I don't think he ever recovered though, never really moved on. He didn't even remarry, barely had any serious relationships at all actually." Stop, stop, stop! I should stop. Stone doesn't need to hear about any of this.

"It still must have been hard for you. It's always harder for those left behind." Stone has come closer behind me, not touching but a strong solid presence at my back.

"Yes, it is. It's so very hard on the people left behind." I can feel water sliding down my face; it can be water from the shower if I pretend. "That's why I decided I would never be the cause of such grief again." I trace the faint scars on my abdomen. "I made sure I would never leave behind a screaming baby or a mourning father. I will not die the way she did." I sound angry even to my own ears. "I made sure of that as soon as I was old enough, as soon as I found a doctor who would operate on a young childless woman."

"Operate? Is that where those scars came from? You let someone cut into you?" How dare he ask that! "There are far better methods to prevent childbirth, Alexis." I spin around, angrily facing him.

"Not where I'm from!" My voice comes out louder than it should have. "Where I come from, there are no menstruation cuffs or other magical means of prevention." I wave the golden cuff in front of him. "Where I come from the only real way to make sure is by surgery!" Funny how quickly sorrow can turn into anger. "So yes, I let someone cut into me. And I'd do it again if it was my only option." Breathing heavy, hot tears still streaming down my face, Stone slowly reaches out to touch my scars.

"You made a noble and honorable sacrifice in doing this." So taken aback, my anger sputters. "To have a person carve into you in order to prevent inflicting such pain upon your loved ones. It was incredibly brave of you, Alexis." No, no, I don't want to be called that. What I did wasn't brave, if anything it was the coward's way out, right? I...I didn't want to die like that.

Turning away from him to face the wall, I hug my arms tightly around myself. Why am I telling him all this? I got far too comfortable constantly talking to him as a statue that now I can't seem to stop.

"I am sorry that this was the only choice you had where you came from, but I am glad the option was available to you. Did it hurt much?" Again, he's not touching me, just a still and constant presence.

"Compared to what I watched my family go through, what I went through, it was nothing. A small price to pay to make sure I..." Don't, don't finish that sentence! "...I don't ever fuck up anyone else's happy life again."

"Alexis, you did not–"

"You were right, you know, when you called me a little thief. I am a little thief. The first thing I stole was my mother's life, my father's wife, my brothers' mother." I'm letting the tears flow freely, hunched over and shaking in my despair. "I took so much the day I was born." He takes a closer step toward me, and I fall. I fall right into his arms, and he catches me like I hoped he would. He holds me tight. With arms and wings, he encases me.

"You are wrong, Alexis. You are not a thief of life; that would be a murderer, and you are not a murderer." I sob louder. On some level, I understand I didn't kill my mother. I really do realize it wasn't my fault, but the feelings still remain. Even after all these years. They'll probably be here all my life, popping up at the most inopportune moments, just like this one.

"You are a thief who steals the spotlight," he whispers into my ear. "A thief who steals hearts wherever she goes." My dad used to say something similar, that I made it hard not to love me. That I could make friends with a lamppost or get the devil on my side given the chance. "You are a thief of my patience." Dad used to say that too. I laugh a little in Stone's arms. "Alexis, you cannot take what was freely given. Your mother gave you life, and from what I've seen, you live that life to the fullest."

"She gave me my name too," I sniffle. "Dad wanted to name me after some random TV show character, but Mom put her foot down. She said, 'I grew this little girl, and she's going to get my name this time!' Alexis was Mom's middle name. Dad already had Ottis Jr., my eldest brother, so Mom decided she would get a turn too."

"Your mother gave you a beautiful name, made all the more special by sharing it. Alexis. Why you allow other people to call you Lexi is beyond me." That has got me thinking.

"Why have you never called me Lexi, by the way?" I ask while wiping the tears from my face. "You have always used Alexis, when you aren't calling me 'thief,' that is."

"When we first met you said your name was Alexis, but that people call you Lexi. So your name is Alexis, but other people chose to call you Lexi instead. Names are particularly important to Gargoyles." His fingers begin stroking my arms. "We are given a temporary name at birth, then we all choose our real names when we come of age. Our real names are respected, so when you said it was Alexis, I respected yours." Wow, that's really...nice. I had thought he had done it to irk me, but it was actually respectful.

"Wait! Are you telling me that you actually chose the name Stone?! On purpose?" This whole time I thought his family was funny or playing a joke or something.

"Yes, I did." I'm so surprised by his answer that I push away enough to stare up at him.

"Why?! Why would you do that to yourself? You get how confusing that can be? Isn't it a little too on the nose?!"

"I am of stone. It is what I came from, it is what I shall return to being. I am Stone." He is dead serious. I guess it makes a weird kind of sense, so I do my best to stifle the laughter that has bubbled up. "I will have you know that Stone is an acceptable and time honored name for a Gargoyle."

"Yeah, sure it is, buddy." I pat his chest as I exit the embrace. "I'm, ah, sorry about the trauma dump there. Did not mean to do that. At all."

"I am honored that you shared your past with me, your suffering, and your troubles." Gently he cups my face with a massive hand. "And do not feel bad, I often have this effect on people. I find even strangers tell me the most intimate details of their lives. I do not understand why, given how unapproachable I can appear." He must really wonder about it because he has the most perplexed look on his face.

"Ah, poor baby. Must be such a burden to bear." I playfully slap his cheek.

"It is, Alexis. I know things. Things I wish I had never heard." Ho ho, now my curiosity is peaked! Wait, is this how he's been able to get so much out of me? Is this like his superpower?

"Come, I think we deserve a nice long soak in that large tub of yours." Turning off the shower, he stalks over to the tub which I really hope will fit us both. I mean it's big, but... Water whooshes on and steam begins to rise. "What do you like adding to the water for relaxation? I did just put your body through its paces after all."

I'm about to argue that point when he adds, "And reliving grief takes its own toll."

"I have a jar of lavender and rosemary bath salts next to the tub there." Pouring in an expertly measured amount, he swooshes it around with his tail before climbing in. Once settled, he motions for me to join him. Here's hoping we don't completely flood my bathroom.

The bath with Stone was pleasant. He talked about playing in the maze as a kid and his plans to advance his career. How he's being held back, but he knows if he can get a chance to show them what he can do, they'll bump him up to Investigator. We talked about my various hobbies and jobs, which took up most of the time we were in there. He was quite interested in tabletop roleplaying, which is great because I can go on at length about that. He also wheedled his way into a promised back massage at a later date. Still not sure how he accomplished that, and I was there.

The nicest part, though, was when he told me that living my life to the fullest, which is one way of looking at it I guess, is an amazing way to honor the gift of life my mother had given me. Living extra for her and for myself. I might have gotten a little choked up again there. It certainly had me feeling better about my tendency to flutter from thing to thing. I'm just tasting all that life has to offer, gaining new experiences and skills along the way.

I must admit, I'm in a happy little bubble when I exit the bathroom. A bubble that's instantly popped when I see who's sitting on my couch, pretty as you please. Valda.

Chapter 24

---◆○◆---

Alexis

"How dare you come back into my house uninvited!" I'm going to have to go out and find some wards or something to keep him from floating in whenever he wants. I walk around here naked far too often to allow that.

"Oh my, I see our human is still feeling a bit testy about that accident in the tunnels." Valda's flippant response sets me off. Stone has to physically hold me back.

"Enough, Valda." The ghost seems surprised, like he expected Stone to be on his side. Well, suck it, ghost. Stone's with me! I mean, he's my partner; he has my back. That's what partners do. Okay, we aren't just partners. We're also fuck buddies, confidantes, we make each other laugh...oh...oh no.

"You understand why she's upset, don't you, Valda? And given her reaction, I'm going to assume that you have yet to make your apologies to her, is that correct?" Stone's standing in front of the ghost, arms crossed, bare ass out. Where I quickly picked up my robe when I saw someone was in my house, Stone did not.

"Well, I, I hadn't had the chance yet, you see," Valda sputters.

"Is that so?" Stone levels a gaze down at Valda that's as cold as ice. It's kind of hot, him getting onto Valda on my behalf. "Alexis, how many days has it been again?"

"Three!"

"Three days. Are you telling me, in all that time, you couldn't find a moment to apologize properly? You made the time for me that same night, yet Alexis was not afforded that same courtesy." Stone is pacing back and forth, like he's grilling a perp in the interrogation room. "You even visited once, while I was stoned, yet no apology came then either. Even now, when you do return, an apology is not forthcoming. Instead you choose to tease and downplay the significance of the danger you put her in." Did I say it was kind of hot? No, no, this is extra spicy hot. And him being naked, swinging that big dick around, literally and metaphorically, is making it all the hotter.

"I, well, yes, I suppose I could have—"

"No!" Stone stops dead in his tracks, voice booming. "No more excuses. No more pompous or condescending attitude towards her. You will offer her an earnest and heartfelt apology, or we will walk away from this investigation." Take me now, big boy! This is a Gargoyle who has a happy ending in his near future.

"Yes, yes, very well." Valda starts to float my way, but Stone steps in his path pointing a finger at him.

"I said, earnestly." There's a menacing rumble behind that last word. Deep and foreboding. "Alexis, please take a seat in this chair." Stone motions to the chair I have in my living room area. Head held high, I strut to the seat like a queen, lowering myself into it as if it were a throne. Stone, beside me, plays the loyal bodyguard.

"Lexi, I would like–"

"Alexis," I interrupt him sharply. Valda looks at me with surprised confusion. "My name is Alexis. Not Lexi, not human. Alexis." A faint rumble comes from Stone. I kind of hope it's pride.

"Alexis, my fellow member of the Thieves Guild of Avenston, I would like to formally apologize to you for inadvertently putting you in harm's way." He glances at Stone's face. The ghost must see something that indicates he should continue. "And for downplaying the severity of the situation. If it hadn't been for Stone's quick action you may have been seriously damaged or possibly even killed." He glances up again before he pushes on, but this time it actually starts to sound earnest. "I, I had no intention of seeing any harm befall you, either of you. I had not realized the danger and felt somewhat ashamed at how recklessly I pushed you two forward."

"Thank you, Valda. I accept your apology." His expression is a little too relieved, so I add, "But that doesn't mean I forgive you completely or trust you completely for that matter. I will, however, continue working with you to solve your murder." Nobody deserves to be stuck haunting a city this long, not even Valda.

"Thank you, Alexis, I truly do appreciate it. I would also like to take this time to express my regrets for the way I treated you previously. I may have looked down on you upon your first arrival, then continued to treat you poorly in an effort to manipulate your actions. I, I am very sorry, Alexis."

"Apology accepted. But please, stop calling me Alexis. Sounds wrong when you use it." I give a visible shudder that has Stone hiding a smile from the ghost. "Enough mushy stuff. Let's get cracking into this murder case."

Once we're dressed, Valda leads us to an abandoned house in one of the oldest parts of the city. He bragged about running off every person who ever tried to live there until the city finally gave the deed of the place over to him, to be given back to the city upon his crossing.

"Only ghost in the whole of the city who owns property," he boasts. "Unfortunately, the house is not a part of our bargain as it will need to be returned to the city, should you succeed. I have, however, already drawn up legal papers bequeathing the entirety of its contents to you two." Tapping the side of his nose, "Never fear upon that score. The robbers on the city council shall have no claim upon your reward."

We enter through the front door after Valda unlocked it from within. The house itself isn't as deteriorated as I had pictured in my head. When you hear of an old abandoned haunted house, you have certain expectations. This was not it. Instead of the run-down, cobweb-filled, creaky dilapidated building, we find a perfectly lovely three story house. A house that is not only maintained, but cleaner than my apartment. There are vibrant paintings, cared for furniture, and lit candles. Even the fireplaces are roaring!

"How is it so clean?" Of all the questions, this is my most burning. I just can't picture Valda scrubbing floors or washing windows.

"Why, a housekeeper, of course. Something I suggest you may want to look into yourself, Lexi." Roasted by a ghost, ouch.

"Where are the items you've collected that you think will help?" Straight to the point, that's my...partner? That's as good a title as any at the moment, but truthfully I'm not exactly sure where we stand anymore. Too many changes too quickly.

"Those I keep in my private private study. This way," he motions us into a side room on the ground floor.

"What makes it a private private study?" Seems redundant to me.

"Well, I have a private study that's for my different accounts and bookkeeping, along with letter writing and other business matters." This guy has a surprisingly full afterlife. "But my private private study is tucked away in a secret section of the house that only I know about. That is where I keep my collection. Not even my housekeeper is aware of its existence. So you will forgive me if it's not as well kept as the rest of the house." The rest of the house being spotless, warm, and inviting.

"What exactly do you keep in this private private study?" Stone asks. "You've mentioned a collection and how you think it will help us solve your murder, but you have been pretty tight-lipped on the specifics."

"All will be revealed shortly. I promise to explain myself once inside." He has taken us into what I assume is his regular private study and closed the doors after us. When he does, I get a little excited. Is he about to open a secret passageway?! As he floats over to a bookcase, my excitement grows. Pointing at a thick blue book, he extends a translucent finger.

"Can I open the secret passage?!" I blurt, unable to contain myself. He pauses, so I continue, "It's just I've always wanted to, and what if this is my only opportunity ever?!" I can feel myself bouncing on the balls of my feet.

"By all means," Valda bows, stepping aside. "Have you never opened any of the Guild's secret passages?" I see Stone stiffen at this tidbit of information, but I'm not the one who spilled the beans there.

"Yes, but that's not the same. This," I graze my fingers over the spines of books, "is a bookshelf secret passage in a house. Very different, very cool."

"Oh ho, flattery will get you everywhere, Lexi."

"Just pull the book already." Stone is rubbing his temples, clearly over our shenanigans. Looks like Valda and I have eased into a playful truce of sorts. We are firmly on the same side, not quite friends, but no longer the rivals we were.

"Can't a girl cherish this moment? It's my first time," I say softly while offering Stone a coquettish gaze. Rolling his eyes at me, he crosses his arms over his chest. I stroke the book's spine delicately before placing a finger at its top. Gently I tilt it back like in the movies. Absolutely nothing happens. No movement, no clinking, no whirring, no groans.

"Well, that was disappointing. Nothing happened," glancing back to Valda he waggles a finger back and forth.

"Things are not always as they seem, Lexi dear." Quickly glancing back at the bookshelves, I search for anything I might have missed. But everything looks exactly the same. "Try touching the bookcase to your left." Tentatively reaching out my hand, I move to pick up a book bound in purple leather, but my hand passes right through it. "The whole shelf, along with its contents, are spelled to phase slightly into a neighboring reality. Thus allowing corporeals to pass into the secret staircase just behind."

"That's pretty cool too." I haven't stopped moving my hands and arms into various books since the first passed through.

"More secret stairs," Stone speaks up, "can't wait. I'm assuming there's a switch on the other side to bring the case back into phase with this reality?"

"Oh yes, of course. Can't have some nosey ninny falling down into it, after all. I was also advised not to keep the bookcase out of phase for too long, lest those in the other reality get suspicious." Valda taps his chin. "I always meant to ask the mage who installed it for me what they meant by that, but I never got around to it. Now he's dead. Oh well." He shrugs before quickly sinking into the floor.

"Here's hoping the switch on the other side is obvious," I offer before stepping through a very tangible looking bookshelf. Probably should've been a little more wary. I mean, what if it phases back into our reality while I'm still inside the damn thing? I'm guessing that would suck a lot, but sometimes it's best not to think about such things.

"I can't believe you just did that." Stone's voice is muffled from the other side. "I should have gone first to make sure the spell in effect was still completely operational."

"I was closest. So you snooze, you lose." The other side is alight with magicked torches that came to life as soon as I stepped onto the landing. On the wall to my right is a green stone that must be the way to open and close the entrance. Taking a few steps down the spiral staircase, I shout, "Jump on in, the water's fine."

"There's water in there?" I can't help the smile that leaps to my face.

"No! It's a figure of speech. But it is pretty cramped so you might want to–" Hearing a grunt, I turn around. While the spiral of the staircase is more than enough for my frame, it's a very tight squeeze for the Gargoyle behind me. I try hard not to laugh when I see him, shoulders bunched up to his ears, arms in front of him, wings still within the bookcase. Stone glares unamused down at me.

"Cramped indeed," he mutters as he twists himself sideways.

"Don't forget to hit the emerald crystal once you finally get inside." More grumbly mutters follow as I effortlessly descend the steps, while he has to go down the whole spiral sideways. Valda yanks the door at the bottom open for me once I reach it.

"Welcome to my collection!" The ghost ushers me in, then takes a moment to look up at Stone's progress. "I'll wait to explain until Stone joins us." Angry rumbles echo off the walls in the stairwell.

Chapter 25

Alexis

Valda wasn't kidding when he suggested that this place wasn't as clean as the rest of the house. A layer of dust covers every surface, cobwebs droop down from the ceiling, and the air feels stale. The ghost must notice my eyes move to the cobwebs because he floats up and begins to remove the major ones.

"I hadn't expected the window," I comment, beginning a conversation as we wait for Stone. "Thought we were underground?" Big windows line the longer wall to my right, letting in the noonday sun.

"Ah, yes, we are indeed underground. But I had enchanted windows installed down here. They showcase the view from the third floor." We both begin to gaze outside. The cobblestoned street below is the same one we walked up, the tree tops vivid in their autumn colors, the house across the way just as beautiful as this one.

"Are those birds chirping?" Not just birds, but the rustling of leaves and the sound of a cart on the road. "Can the windows project the sounds too?"

"That cost me extra, but well worth it, wouldn't you agree?" I have to admit, I do. Much more enjoyable, less claustrophobic, and helps to make the room feel more alive. Like it's really part of the rest of the house. We turn in unison when we hear Stone snap his wings out, stretching after his cramped descent.

"Now, explain what this collection is"—Stone is getting straight to business I see—"and why you think it could help solve your death."

"Everything here in this secret room of mine are items I have collected over the centuries due to an attachment I feel to them." Floating to the center of the long room, Valda continues. "Every single item has a sort of pull for me, a familiarity that I can't quite place. I believe that the items here were once connected to me in some way. That they belonged to me, my family, former lovers, or enemies. I have no way to be certain, but I just feel it in my heart."

"I remember working tirelessly to gain the ability to touch objects, to interact with the world that was around me once more, due to the strong connections I felt for these things." Valda gestures around the room. "That's actually how I first became a thief, taking back items I felt were a part of my story. Even the location we are in." He stretches his arms out wide. "While this home wasn't always the building that currently resides here, I felt the same pull to this place as I did with the items I had been amassing." He pauses to chuckle to himself. "I actually believed I had died or was buried here for a long time, but alas that was not the case."

"How did you discover that?" Stone asks as he begins to look the room over. A row of tables lines its center, stacked with papers, scrolls, and a few trinkets here and there. Bookcases line the other long wall, filled with more books, along with boxes that must contain items. "And what are your first memories of this location?"

"My first memories are of rubble and despair. Walking amongst ruins and crying, wailing even. So you can understand why I had assumed I'd died here." Seems a logical assumption to me. "I...persuaded the first owner of these lands to delve into the events of the building that stood here previously, to search for the names of those who had died here. But alas, the building was empty when it had burned down; no bodies were found within it."

"I'm sorry you didn't die in a horrible fire? What a shame!" Seems a terrible way to go to me, but Valda appeared to be so disappointed that I felt I had to say something.

"Yes, it really was. This whole thing would have been over long ago if that had been the case." I was joking, but Valda's reply is almost mournful. Interesting priorities. "My next thought was that I must have been murdered here or my body was buried on the grounds somewhere." He sinks into the flagged stone floor up to his shoulders. "It took a great deal of...persuasion to get the next owners to dig up the land. Not a lot of the land, of course, since I was only drawn to the small area that is this lot. But we dug and dug, then dug some more, without so much as a bone in sight. Other than animals, of course. He even had a few mystics and mages come check the land to make sure nothing was missed, bless him. Wish I could remember that man's name. He tried really hard to help me pass on."

I shoot a look at Stone that indicates I'm thinking that the man worked so hard to get rid of this pest of a ghost. His face reflects his agreement.

"Anyway, after coming to terms with that disappointing re-alization I became more discerning in who I asked to help. No longer did I need to rely upon whomever lived here or owned the property. That is, when I felt the need to ask for others' assistance at all. I did much digging on my own for a time. Researching the items I had collected, tracking down their previous owners, hoping to find myself amongst them. However, no name I ever came across jogged any memories of my past life." Stone hums and nods his head.

"And these diaries you spoke of, what are they?" Stone questions as he brings out the notepad he keeps in his waistband.

"A few are journals kept by previous assistants, marking their progress and findings." Stone looks excited by this, well, his face's version of excitement anyway. "Then there are diaries kept by two females in this city. Though I only felt a connection to one female's collection. I have no idea why, a previous lover perhaps?"

"She could have been a family member." I offer.

"I had thought that for a time as well, especially since the set belonged to the sister of the founder of this city. But my hopes were dashed when I learned she only had the one brother who is confirmed to have died of old age, peacefully in his bed. There were no male cousins, and her mate was a female." He's shaking his head, "Truly a shame."

"What of the other female you mentioned?" Stone questions while taking notes. "What of her diary?" Valda moves to 'sit' on a table.

"That is a sad tale, I'm afraid. About three hundred years ago, I had an assistant who was very near to discovering my truth. But he was lost in a collapse, not unlike the one you two witnessed. It, however, was a more catastrophic event, taking the whole city street above the ground down with it. His body was never recovered; no one knew he was down there including myself for a time. I eventually found him, his bones clutching the diary in question. I assume his journal also rests with his remains as I have been unable to find it."

"Couldn't you just take the diary back?" I ask. "I've seen you move objects through stuff before. Why haven't you done that?"

"The item in question is deep within the earth now. While I can pass objects through solid matter, it can only be done in short distances. As adept as my ghostly skills are, where it currently rests is far beyond my power," Valda admits.

"Oh, I see," my reply is somewhat abashed. Of course, he would have reclaimed the lost diary if he could.

"Anyhow, this cave-in forced the city to shore up and close many of the underground tunnels. Even the thieves' tunnels got a good overhaul, all quite secretly and involving many memory spells, of course." Valda winks at Stone. Stone is not amused. "That was why I had assumed the tunnel I took you to was safe. The city was supposed to have fixed them all or closed them off completely."

"Looks like they either missed that one or the fix didn't last." Absently, I start snooping through the boxes on the shelf nearest me. "I mean, it has been three hundred years. That might not be a lot of time for you, but it is for most things."

"If you had all of this here, why did you send us into the tunnels first?" Stones has a great point there.

"Hey, yeah," I chime in, "why didn't you lead with this stuff?"

"Ah, yes, well, you see..." He takes a deep breath to buy himself some time because we all understand that he doesn't actually breathe. "Once a year, my being returns to a location down there and my lost assistant believed that was the key to finding my body. Or at the very least, my murder location."

"What?!" we both say in unison. Stone raises his hand, clearly wanting to ask questions first.

"If you know where you died, why the misadventure with this location? The research, the digging. Why not just discover your body on your own, then tell someone?" Yep, much better than my question of 'what is wrong with you,' for sure.

"It took me a long time to even realize what was happening, Stone. When I am pulled there, I am dazed, not myself, and I stumble about for a time before regaining my mind. After each event, I come to my senses in a different location. Other ghosts have observed me, saying I moan about, walking aimlessly, hands covering my head." Valda glides over to peer out the sunlit windows. "Trust me, I have tried to retrace my steps, tried to get other beings to follow me when this happens, but it has all been in vain. I know not where my starting location is, and no one has ever been around in the correct place to see me appear." Valda is looking so forlorn.

"What do you remember about this event?" Stone asks in a less accusatory tone, obviously seeing Valda's mood shift. "Can you recall any time frame or date it happens on?"

"Ever the investigator, Stone." Valda turns his head to offer a sad smile. "My memories are muddled, but I do believe that the event happens sometime in autumn, which is why I wanted you two down there so urgently. It currently being autumn and all. I know I used to remember the date. You have no idea how frustrating that is, to realize that you've forgotten something so important." Valda takes a beat before continuing.

"There are fuzzy images of past events where I started coming to, surrounded by a mass of people. People absolutely everywhere; bumping, walking, colorful blurs of clothing all around me. But for centuries now it's been only darkness, all alone."

"Perhaps it used to be along a main busy street, square, or tavern?" I offer.

"Oh, yes, it was most definitely outside because I can remember the stars glittering in the sky above me, as well as lanterns or fires of some kind." Floating back over to the table, he points at a box of scrolls. "These are the maps of some likely places where the old city used to have major streets, courtyards, and such." Stone and I both take one to open, studying the blueprint looking images.

"Valda, where did you get these?" There's an undercurrent of menace in Stone's question that neither of us miss. I'm guessing Stone thinks these should be in some city archives somewhere, especially given the official-looking seals at the bottom corner of many of these.

"Oh, you know, here and there." Valda only chuckles at the stare Stone levels at him. "It's no use berating me, Stone, my boy. I procured these long ago. If you want to return them, you'll have to solve my murder first." Stone rumbles in annoyance but turns back to inspect the map in his hands. "Do you have any other questions for me at the moment? I really must pop off to the Guild and handle my affairs there. Oh, I do have a good feeling about all this!"

"Yes," Stone speaks up first, "where do you keep your cleaning supplies?"

Much to my chagrin, Stone was not joking about those cleaning supplies. We spend the rest of the day cleaning, dusting, and organizing the long-ass room Valda keeps his collection in. I get sidetracked a lot while looking through the items he has stored in here. It's all so random! Tea sets, hair brushes, scissors, cutlery, walking canes, knitting needles, a baby rattle, a chest of moth-eaten clothing, men's and women's jewelry. Basically, most of this stuff is everyday normal things a person or family would have. I had expected...well, I'm not sure what I expected, but it wasn't treasures of the mundane, that's for sure.

I did have a good time looking through all the paintings I found. Some were portraits, some landscapes, some scenes. I search all the faces hoping to catch a glimpse of Valda, but no luck there. That would have been too easy, I guess.

"Goodness me, are you two still going at it down here?" I fumble and nearly drop the crystal goblet I was inspecting for a maker's mark...I mean, cleaning.

"Geezus Krist, Valda! You just about gave me a heart attack!" Gently, I set the glass onto the shelf Stone designated for kitchen items.

"Well, well, well," Valda's eyes peruse over the room, "I don't think this place has been this tidy and organized since...well, since ever. Bravo, you two!" He silently claps his hands. "I should have hired you long ago, if only for this right here."

"What do you want, Valda? If it's to check on our progress, I'm afraid that Mr. Clean over there hasn't let us begin anything yet." Stretching my back and arms, I get several cracks and pops.

"For your information, I have come to tell you that there is some food up in the dining room for you two." Now he's got my interest! "I have prepared two guest rooms on the second floor for you, as well. If you wish to make my house your home for a while, I suggest you retrieve personal items, though I have what you need for the night."

"You had me at food, Valda!" Walking up to Stone, I begin to push the Gargoyle. "Come on. Put that down." I grab the silver tray he was cleaning. "Even you need to eat."

"Actually, I do not," is his reply as he reaches to take the tray back.

"I don't care what you say; we both need a break. Now out. Out!" Begrudgingly, he slowly begins to make his way out of the room.

"I thought I was supposed to be the one who gave orders?" Stone grumbles.

"Women only let men think that, lets them feel big and important." Patting his shoulder, I add, "But we all know who's really in charge of things, don't we?" His response is a rumble I can feel vibrating on my fingertips.

"I'll remember that, little thief." The look he shoots back down at me sets goosebumps loose all over my body.

Chapter 26

Stone

We spend the next few days in companionable research. I must admit, I like having Alexis around. Her presence, her quips, her questions, her dancing around, and her laughter are all a pleasant backdrop to our endeavor instead of the distraction I feared they would be. I enjoy her company more than I have enjoyed most others. It is very...interesting. I do not, however, enjoy her music.

She took Valda up on his offer to stay here while we searched his collection for clues. Returning to her home that first night to pack up some belongings, she insisted on bringing her music box. Said it was torture to work in silence while we cleaned, and she wouldn't be doing it again. Halfway into the second day, I left to buy her a personal listener, as her incessant music was tortuous to me. Who can think with all that going on?!

Thankfully, I found exactly what I needed at a local shop, a torc necklace she could link with her music box allowing her, and only her, to hear her music. They weren't bad songs, not that I could understand the words being said. The rhythms were often quite good. They were, however, exceedingly distracting for one who was trying to concentrate.

When presented with the gold-coated torc, you'd have thought I had bought her a necklace wrought by Hephaestus himself. The way she squealed, hopped about, and peppered my face with kisses made my chest warm. Now, I can focus on work, except for noticing her humming and occasionally breaking out into dance or random verses; her graceful body moving about the space we share; her scent of warmed earth occasionally wafting by; her little moans as she stretches her body...Okay, now, my only distraction is her. But it's one I welcome, mostly.

"Find anything good in that diary yet?" Alexis interrupts my notetaking. "Whose was it again?"

"It belonged to the youngest sister of the founding family of Avenston," I answer first. "The entries are from well after the founding, when her chief concern for most of the volume is mating her two children off advantageously." I close the diary, having already read it three times. "She fears her son is a layabout without any of the ambition her brother has and that her daughter has set her sights on a stable hand instead of any of the worthwhile suitors presented to her." Rubbing my temples, I continue. "Of course, knowing history, it wasn't the stable hand, but a tutor the daughter ran off with."

"Ooo, that sounds juicy. What happened there?" Deciding to humor her, I continue.

"The tutor ended up being quite the mage and scholar, becoming renowned in his time. The daughter and her mate, the scholar, came back to Avenston once his reputation was well established. The two of them founded the largest library within the city and were responsible for bringing many other scholars of the time here as well, who in turn set up arcane universities and training centers. Effectively creating quite a population boom."

"Whoa, nice! And what about the brother? He ever get his shit together and show up their mother too?" Alexis is more engrossed in this story than she has been for any of the research we've done so far.

"No," I chuckle. "It turned out his mother was right about him. He was a no-good layabout who spent years gambling and losing, never finding a mate, and was overall the black sheep of the family. Not a very good person by all accounts either."

"How do you know so much about them? Did they teach this in school or something? I have no idea who founded my town, let alone the family tea!"

"Children of our Clan are taught the founding history earnestly because it was the founders who invited us here. My Clan once belonged to a Wizard and his cohorts atop Mt. Dern. Once the Wizards were overthrown, my Clan gained their freedom and stayed to protect the mountain, keeping mostly to themselves. It was the founding family of Avenston who sought my Clan out, personally inviting us here to protect its city's families. My Clan accepted, becoming the Gargoyle Clan of Avenston."

"Damn, there is a lot to unpack there. Wizards used to own your Clan? Like own, own? Like slaves?" I can't quite read the expression on her face, but I answer.

"We were created by the Wizards there, made to protect them and their secrets. My ancestors were unwilling servants, appalled at the ways the Wizards created their magical workings. But the Wizards could turn them back into stone anytime they wished. Either for a time as punishment or forever. They also kept the

ways of making more Gargoyles a closely guarded secret. So, if my
ancestors wanted a child, you'd have to ask permission and gain the
Wizard's favor."

"That's fucking terrible, Stone!" She came to sit near me while
I spoke about the founders, but now she's on her feet pacing
around. "I hate that slavery happened here too!" She makes a few
angry sounds that aren't quite words, but I lock onto that word
'too.'

"Did your kind suffer such a fate?" I have heard stories from
the Fae Courts of old that humans were often taken as slaves. To
play with, to force into labor, to trick and torture. Is this what
happened to Alexis' ancestors?

"Yeah, yeah, we did." Alexi looks both sad and angry. "And
I wish I knew more, wish we were taught more than the white-
washed version of events." Turning back to me, "I'm glad your
Clan kept the truth of what happened alive within you all. So
how did they escape? How did your ancestors get free?" Mentally
making a note to ask her more about her people later, I continue
as she sits herself across from me once more.

"It was Inera who came to our aid, or one of her priestesses.
Seems my ancestors weren't quite sure if the person who came
was the goddess herself in disguise or an enchantress following her
goddesses bidding." Before I continue, Alexis interrupts.

"Who's Inera?" I'm surprised she doesn't know, but not everyone is familiar with all the gods, I suppose.

"Inera is the Goddess of Transformation and Change. Originally a Shifter goddess, she evolved into more. Most Shifters follow her still, as well as many magical beings who change, shift,
or transform in any way. Like us Gargoyles. She granted us the

gift of transformation for ourselves, essentially taking away the hold Wizards had upon us. My ancestors quickly dealt with the Wizards, claiming their castle as our own. Soon after, we were given the knowledge on how to procreate with certain Gargoyles being born with or seeking the gifts of a Maker." When did I absently start playing with her hand and fingers? "My Clan keeps a large shrine to Inera in our temple. In fact," I chuckle, "I went there asking the goddess for help the day you and I met. I asked her to help me catch you..."

Astonished, I bring my mind back to my prayer, the plea to my goddess. *'I ask for your aid in catching a human. Alexis is her name, Alexis Callaway. Any support in this endeavor would be greatly appreciated.'* Rumbles begin deep within myself as I laugh at my own misstep. I had asked Inera to help me catch this human, and catch her I did. Only not in the way I had wanted, expected, nor anticipated. I should have known better. One must always be clear when asking for the help of the gods or any powerful being for that matter.

"You actually prayed to catch me? Needed divine intervention to nab a thief did you?" She's shaking her head at me, unaware of the conclusions I am currently making. "You need to have more faith in yourself, my man." Bringing the hand I've been playing with to my face, I run my lips along her delicate knuckles.

"Oh, but I did need help catching you, little thief." Thief of my heart. How have I not realized it before? The dreams! They started that night, right after I asked the goddess for help. Legends say that Inera has always been good friends with, and occasional lover to Morpheus, the god of dreams himself. My goddess has been sending me messages via these new dreams, and I intend to heed them.

"Oh, I don't know," Alexis says coyly, "you seem to have been catching me just fine on your own, Patrolman." I rumble as I breathe in her scent, seeing Alexis and our encounters in a new light. My playful little thief, my vexing little thief, my–

"Don't you two have anything more important to do?" Valda's head emerges from the ceiling, soon followed by the rest of his ghostly form. "I swear you are like a mating pair in heat. Every time I pop in you're in the middle of," he waves his hands about, "this!"

"Go away, Valda," Alexis says through gritted teeth, eyes remaining on me. "We were just about to start something real good down here." Licking her lips, her eyes roam down my chest, then back up to my face. "Real good."

"No. No! I will not have you down here canoodling while you are meant to be searching for clues to my murder." He has righted himself, as he pinches the bridge of his nose. "I swear, you two. Here I thought I was going to have a hard time simply keeping you in the same room as the other, not keeping you off each other."

"You are no fun, Valda," Alexis pouts. "Plus, we've been good for two days, and a girl has her needs."

"A ghost has his needs too, Lexi. Chief among them is solving my death so I can cross over!" He's come to stand, within the table near us. "What have you found? Any questions for me?" He's trying to get us back to the task at hand, which I can understand, but I was in the middle of unraveling my own mystery.

"Yeah, I have a question," Alexis puts in, "were you always this much of a jackass? You know, before you died. Maybe you were this lady's good-for-nothing son?" She gestures at the diary. "Makes sense to me, given his attributes and the fact that most of your collection here links back to the city founders in some way." I too had had similar thoughts.

"No, I was not her son, and no you have not been the only assistant to make such an assumption of me." Valda seems rather affronted by this. "The son in question, Aristede, loved to commission busts of himself, of which I have several. And if you care to look, you'll notice that I do not resemble him at any stage of his arguably long life." He turns to me then with arms crossed over his chest, "Do you have anything useful to ask or add?"

"Yes. I know that the founders of this city were siblings, one brother and three sisters, but the youngest often makes a mistake within her diaries that I find odd." Opening to a page where such an error occurs, I show him. "Here you can see that she originally wrote out the word 'brothers,' then marked out the 's' as a mistake. I would have thought nothing of it, as she makes mistakes often, but this same slip up of 'brothers' happens six more times within this text alone." Alexis bends over to inspect the error herself, which allows me a glimpse of her lovely cleavage.

"Hmm," Valda ponders, "I suppose that is strange."

"In your research on the family, have you ever come across anyone that they would have considered a brother? A male cousin or close friend of the eldest perhaps? Did any of the sisters identify as male at any point?" Valda's been shaking his head the whole time.

"No, no males like that have come up. And as far as I've seen, each sister has only ever been female. Unless the transition happened very early in life?"

"Given the age of the youngest, if the transition did happen early in life, why would she think of a sister as a brother often enough to make this mistake?" Making a comment in my notepad, "It's unlikely, but not impossible. So no other males who were close like family to them ever pop up?"

"No. The oldest, the brother, was close with his sisters, but no one else at all, really. Even those who mated into the family were kept at arm's length." Alexis furrows her brows in puzzlement at Valda's comment. "Oh, he made a good show of working well with others, convincing those he wanted or needed to assist him in some way. From what I've gathered it was almost like a mask he wore, a facade to put others at ease."

"That does seem to be at odds with the stories we all learn about him. How he dreamed of a city where magical beings from all backgrounds could live together in harmony." I can see the question forming on Alexis's face. "In the past, most beings lived separately in villages or towns, keeping to their own kind. There were very few mingled cities, but the Avenstons pushed to create one here. They were the driving force, especially Aven, the eldest."

"Wait, wait, I'm confused by the names here." Alexis stops us. "Wonderful dream and all, couldn't agree more, but was his name Aven or was the family name Avenston? Then they named the city after them or him?"

"All of the above." Valda answers for me. "The family name was Avenston, the city was named after them, and the eldest brother was named Aven."

"So you're telling me, this dude's name was Aven Avenston." She laughs in disbelief. "You guys and your names, I swear. His parents were either mean or narcissists."

"It is a bit redundant," I concede while flipping through my notepad. "Which is probably why we just call him the founder and them the founding family." Unable to find a blank page, I change the subject before we continue. "I need to make a visit to my house. Grab a new notepad, along with a few other items."

"About time," Alexis waves her hand in front of her nose. "You've been wearing that same kilt for days." Is she implying that I am smelly?!

"I will have you know that I have been stoning every night down here. Refreshing both myself and my kilt in the process."

"Ummmhmmm, whatever you gotta tell yourself, big boy." She pats my shoulder while shaking her head.

"The stonification process mends myself and my items. There could be a tear within the fabric that, once encased, will fix itself. This includes any dirt, stains, or odors." Why am I defending myself? Both my person and my kilt are clean. Does she really think I've been down here in filthy clothing?

"I'm coming with you," she interjects before I can continue to explain my cleaning habits.

"What? Why?" Not that I don't want her to come, but it isn't needed.

"One, I have got to get out of here and see the real sun." Valda tries to cut in, but Alexis quickly moves on. "Two, I've been dying to see your place!" She...she wants to see my home?

Chapter 27

—◆○◆—

Stone

It didn't take long for Alexis to lose her fear of flying with me. She cranes around, trusting that I have her, as she looks at the city below and all around us. Her amazement of Avenston, along with its citizens, is endearing.

"What are you grinning about?" Was I grinning? I hadn't realized. I think my face has been doing that a lot more lately.

"Flying always brings me solace, but flying with a beautiful burglar in my arms is enjoyable too, I suppose." I try not to smile as I tease her. It is difficult as I find that I am enjoying myself.

"You say the sweetest things," she says with an exaggerated eye roll. "Oh, look! Can we get dumplings on our way back?" Alexis is practically bouncing in my arms as she points. "I love that place!"

"If you don't stop wiggling around, you'll get to visit it much sooner than you would like," I tease, shifting her into a better hold.

"Pish, you wouldn't drop me," Alexis offers flippantly as she continues to peer down at the street.

"Oh?" My question has her amber eyes back to me.

"Yeah! For one, you know I'd haunt your ass and be even more annoying than Valda." I nod as I believe that would be true. "Two, you're like super strong, and I'd have to really fight to get out of your clutches." A rumble of pride vibrates up my throat. "And three, you like me way too much to let me splat on the street. Admit it, your life would be so dull without me around."

"Hmmm, you're right"—a wide grin breaks her face—"I am very strong." Alexis mimics fake outrage as she swats my chest. "Do not worry, little thief. I have no intention of letting you slip away. I've only just caught you." Turning my head to whisper in her ear, "You are all mine now." An excited giggle accompanies little feet kicks. A goddess has put Alexis into my path, into my life, into my dreams, and I have no intention of letting such a blessing slip through my fingers.

"Hey, wait, aren't we going to Gargoyle tower?" She points as I veer away from the home of my Clan.

"No. I haven't lived there in some time." With a questioning arch of her brow, I continue. "Not enough autonomy nor privacy. People dropping in all too often whenever they please."

"Totally get that! With three overprotective brothers and a dad at home, I moved out with some friends as soon as I was able to." She laughs, "Family, you love them, but they can be too much at times."

Turning away from the distant dark, imposing tower of my people, I make my way to my current home, a shorter tower of graying white stone. Many winged beings live upon the uppermost floors, catering to our need for large balconies and height. The owner was more than happy to have a Gargoyle amongst its tenants.

"Whoa, your porch is huge! Makes sense. Do you ever sleep out here? I totally would." I've reluctantly set her down upon landing, finding I miss her nearness as she explores my outside space. It's sparsely decorated compared to my neighbors. I've only got a few hardy plants, a marble abstract sculpture Mother gifted me, a self-contained fire pit, and two large cushioned benches. "A girl likes to sleep under the stars from time to time, though maybe not till spring or summer. Bet it can get super cold out here."

"It can be, but there are ways to keep it warm enough out here for you. As for me, fluctuations in the weather are of no concern." Walking to my large balcony door, I add, "I've awoken a time or two to find myself covered in snow." This gets me an astonished response.

"Really?!" I nod at her question. "Whoa, not how I'd like to wake up." Placing my hand on the door, I speak the password I set the locks to. Soon, the door opens wide for us as windows appear along the whole of the stone wall. "What did you just say? How did you do that?" Alexis races over to inspect the door.

"The balcony entrances of these units are password protected. When you move in, you set the word or phrase you wish to use to lock and unlock your unit. Since I was going to be away for some time, I sealed the windows as well as the door."

"But what did you say? I didn't understand it. It sounded like gravel rubbing together." She's still eyeing the door instead of going inside.

"My password is in Gargoyle. Translated to Common Tongue it would be the word 'open.' Now please," I motion for her to enter.

"Wait, wait, wait. You set your secret code word that unlocks your door to the word 'open'? You can't be serious!" she shouts before laughing. "It's like, it's like," still laughing, "setting your password to the word 'password,' my guy. Isn't your whole family into security?"

"Only a Gargoyle can say the word correctly, and the spell only works for my exact voice and hand." Having no idea why she thinks this so funny, I attempt to explain. It's incredibly secure but she seems to think otherwise. A rumble of annoyance bubbles up at her continued disbelief. "I assure you that my home is secure, and my password is reliable."

"Oh yes, yes, very secure!" her words laced with sarcasm, "and I totally wouldn't be able to break into your place if I wanted to." Alexis swaggers inside, leaving me sputtering at the door. I'm about to argue that bold claim of hers, but she changes the subject when she looks at my home. "Guess I shouldn't be surprised that you're a minimalist, but damn!"

Glancing inside I find my home exactly as I left it. Clean, neat, with everything in its proper place. My unit is mostly one large space, with two separate bedrooms that have private bathing rooms. The kitchen is sized to accommodate me, with a large island that I dine on. I've turned the dining area near the windows into my office space, while a large ash-grey couch and matching chairs face a fireplace opposite the kitchen. The floor is made of a dark slate, with the walls and countertops carved of a white quartzite.

"I suppose it could use a bit of color. Maybe some art? I haven't put much thought into decorating it. Suppose it is somewhat–"

"Boring, lifeless, void of all feeling and color." I was going to say austere. "I'm taking you shopping the next chance we get. There's not even any art on the walls! Did you just move in here?" Something about me must give it away. "Oh.My.Gawd! You didn't just move in, did you? How long? How long have you been living like this?" Well, I'm certainly not going to admit I've been here for five years.

"My home is perfectly acceptable, thank you." Briskly, I make my way back to my bedroom to pack some things. "It has everything I need," I offer before disappearing into my room. Taking the same bag I had packed for my mountain stay, I add another kilt as I repack my belongings. If I had known we'd be staying at Valda's, I wouldn't have unpacked the night we went to the secret sex club. Looking around my bedroom, I realize just how plain this room is too. Large oak bed with black sheets and comforter, white quartzite walls, and grey slate floors. I don't even have a rug in here. Shopping with Alexis could be interesting.

Hefting my bag onto my shoulder, I enter the main room to find my thief rifling through my desk. Before I can get mad, however, she lifts an open file to a face that has morphed into fury. I freeze when I hear a heavy exhale through her nose. She must notice me though because her storm-filled eyes sear into me across the room.

"Voyeuristic, question mark!" Alexis has found the profile I made of her. "What the hell is this, Stone?" She gives me no time to answer. "You profiled me! That is seriously messed up, man. Not to mention creepy."

"It is not creepy," I scoff as I walk towards my desk, "it's my job. You were a person of interest and a suspected criminal." Snatching her file, I place it back where it goes. "And I happened to be right about that one. Question mark no longer required." I make a show of removing the incorrect mark as she fumes near me.

"What about this 'murder board' you have over here about creature abductions? That's a very creepy thing to have in your house too."

"That is my findings on a case I am no longer allowed to investigate." Under my breath, I add, "Not that I've had time while I was keeping surveillance on you."

"I heard that!" Her fists are both balled up at her sides, and she actually stomped her foot when she shouted. Maybe this little snooping brat deserves a punishment? Her body instantly reacts to the smirking grin I aim at her, breath catches and eyes widen. Licking my lips as I let my eyes roam all over her body. Today she's wearing a red choli-inspired top paired with high-waisted harem pants that have a yellow pattern on black fabric. Wonder how upset she'd be if I ripped them off?

My focus is instantly diverted when I catch sight of a form landing on my balcony. Quick as I can, I move to put myself in between Alexis and the windows. I growl when I realize who is here.

"Who is it? Do we need to make a run for it?" My little thief has caught on quick, ready to follow my lead in this dangerous situation. But the danger is only to me. What is he doing here anyway? He hasn't been by since I moved out, away from him.

In two strides, I'm at the door, yanking it open. Three more and I'm out on the balcony meeting him. I have no desire to let him into my space or near Alexis.

"Grandfather," I dip my head to him, as his position of Clan leader deserves. "Why have you come here? Has something happened?"

"Happened?" he growls at me. "No, nothing has happened, which is exactly the problem." I set my jaw, waiting for him to tell me how I've failed the Clan this time. "No reports, no news, no information on the thief of that ruby comb." He's crossed his arms over his chest. "What is the use of having you in the Order if you aren't going to do anything to help the Clan or our patrons?!"

"I'm not on that case, Grandfather. If you seek information, I suggest you contact Chief Metis. She could get you–"

"I've already learned what the Order has found and not found," he spits at me. "I'm here to find out what you've done, what you've discovered. Have you not even caught the thief yet?" Instantly, I stiffen, because yes, I technically have caught the thief. "I heard you were trailing someone, that you had your own theories about the break-in. So out with it, boy!" I barely contain a growl. "What have you to show for your efforts?" Steadying myself, I answer as calmly as I can.

"As I've told you before, I am not working that case. I believe you are also aware that I was told explicitly not to investigate the theft at all." My Clan leader scoffs while looking away from me. "And what I have been surveilling is none of the Clans' concern."

"Waste," my grandfather snaps at me. "Waste of time, talents, strength, and blood. What use are you–"

"Shut the fuck up!" I hadn't even noticed she had come outside. "What the fuck is wrong with you?" Alexis asks as she stomps to my side. "Is that really how you talk to your own grandson? You should be ashamed of yourself!" Seems I was wrong, she wasn't coming to stand by my side. Instead my brave little thief steps right up into my grandfather's personal space, finger pointed in his face. "Stone doesn't work for you, old man, so get over yourself." This must look quite funny from the outside. Two Gargoyles, frozen in place, as a slip of a human female gives a dressing down to the leader of my Clan. "I bet your mother would tan your hide if she heard how you spoke to her great-grandson, you pathetic excuse of a Gargoyle." Grandfather's eyes open wide at the mention of his mother.

"I feel sorry for you actually." She's removed her finger, but stepped even closer into him, face as close to his as possible. "Too blind to see how amazing your grandson really is." Her posturing is interesting. Close yet still able to look him up and down like he's the little one unworthing of being in her presence. Like he's the dirt beneath her shoes and may be in danger of getting hurt by her. "So why don't you"—the pointing finger is back—"march your grumpy ass back home, and let us get back to work." I've never seen anyone stare my grandfather down for so long. It's actually him who breaks first, peering over her head at me, confusion written all over his face.

"Who is this?" He's taken a step back from her, clearly uncomfortable with everything. But my sassy thief answers before I can even form a thought.

"I'm his partner!" she declares as she steps back to be nearer to me. "And if you don't like it, you can sit on it and spin."

"What?!" I am also confused, but I'm not about to say anything right now. I'll ask what it means later. "Now, see here, human, my grandson is supposed to be–"

"Your grandson doesn't work for you." She holds up a finger to wave around as she continues, "He's not on the case you're so concerned about and is currently working on something with me. So if you could bring your bitch session to a close and fuck all the way off, we can get back to our business. Which, by the way, is none of yours."

Thief of my heart! No one has ever stood up for me in this way. I knew she had quite the attitude, but I didn't realize just how much of a hellcat she was.

"Come on, Stone." She finally looks at me. "Let's get back to the discussion we were having," glaring over her shoulder, "before we were so rudely interrupted." Taking my arm she begins to lead us back inside. I let her guide me, turning our backs to my grandfather.

"Stone!" my Clan leader begins. "Are you going to let this–" Alexis cuts him off again, glancing back over her shoulder.

"Shoo!" I'm extremely grateful he can not see the smile I attempt to stifle. "Go back to your tower and think about what you've done. Disgraceful!" Without any more words, she marches us right back into my home, slamming the door once inside.

Alexis Callaway, you are in for such a punishment.

Chapter 28

Alexis

"The nerve of that guy!" I'm so fucking furious right now. Stone's own grandfather, calling him a waste! I round on Stone, "Is that how he always talks to you?! If I were you, I would have hauled off and hit him years ago. Right in that smug–" Without warning Stone has lifted me onto his shoulder, carrying me like a sack of potatoes again. "Hey, what the?" I ask as I squirm in his hold. Effortlessly, he strides to the back hallway. "What are you doing?

"I'm taking you to administer your punishment." My skin instantly pebbles with goosebumps.

"Wh-what? What did I do?!" I begin to struggle even more.

"You greatly insulted the leader of my Clan, Alexis. Not to mention the fact that he is my blood relation and elder. I cannot let that stand, little thief." He swats my ass, "So stop struggling and take what you earned like a good girl."

"He deserved every word of it and more. I have zero regrets!" I increase my struggles but in a playful way. "And if you think I'm going to apologize to that old coot, you've got another thing coming!" I'm getting very excited by where this is going.

"We shall see." Stone kicks open the door to a room. Setting me down once inside, he closes the door behind us, while I take a good look around.

"No. Fucking. Way!" Turning in a circle, taking it all in, I almost can't believe what I'm seeing. "Is this a sex room?! You have an honest-to-goodness sex room in your house!"

"Indeed, I do, little thief." I clock a slight smile, even though he's trying to stay stern. Walking away from him, I explore the room. It's bigger than I thought it would be, with a connecting bathroom. Guessing he converted a bedroom to make this. Along the walls are all kinds of toys and chains with the occasional mirror, everything illuminated by the glow of red crystal lights along the ceiling. There are several interesting chairs and things that are obviously placed where Stone ties people up or chains them down.

"This place is amazing!" He tries to hide a smile again, clearly happy by my excitement. "Is this a sex swing?!" In the center of the room, far from any walls, is a mess of leathers and rings, held from the ceiling by chains. It took me a moment to figure out what it was. Taking ahold of the chains, I lift myself off the ground an inch or two, putting my full weight on it. Sturdy, but I wouldn't expect anything less than the safest toys from Stone.

Time to play! Walking around the room, I begin to taunt my big strong Gargoyle cop.

"Awful lot of equipment here, Officer. Sure you know how to use it all?" Still by the door, his intense eyes track my every movement. "Or maybe you have all this because you're compensating for something?" His growl makes me giggle.

"Strip." I blatantly ignore his order, continuing my slow perusal of the room.

"Bet you bring all the pretty criminals here." Taking a leather paddle off the wall, I slap it into my palm, creating a nice sound that resounds around the room.

"No, I do not. Now strip." I ignore the order again, tossing the paddle onto the ground instead of putting it back where it clearly belongs. His eyes narrow at that, but I only smile wider.

"I don't think I deserve this punishment, Officer." As innocently as possible, I add, "I only did what I thought was right, sir," before laughing. Hopping up, I grab a large metal ring from the ceiling to hang from.

"Strip, thief. Or I will rip the clothes from your body myself." The thought alone sends a shiver down my spine. Releasing the ring to stand again, I walk backward into a wall, lifting my hand to the string of my pants as if I am going to untie them.

"Pass," I say as I move both hands to my hips. "I don't believe you'd actually rip them off anyway–" Quicker than I would have thought possible, he's across the room, hand on my throat, pressing me firmly into the wall.

"What is your safe word, Alexis?" With a single claw, he slowly begins to tear my top down the middle, pointed tip lightly trailing down the skin underneath.

"Mimic," I manage to whisper, having a hard time catching my breath. With a final rip, my shirt splits wide open, revealing my emerald green bralette. Stone hooks a claw under the fabric in the center. With a single flick, his claw slices the bra, exposing my pert breasts. His cavernous rumble vibrates through my soul.

"I am going to punish you like I have never punished anyone else, Alexis." I whimper at his words, I actually whimper!

Hand still on my throat, Stone begins to kiss me, textured tongue delving deep into my mouth, dominating my own smooth one. Taking one of my wrists in hand, he presses it against the wall above my head, sending an even clearer sign that he is the one in control here. I moan as his fingers direct where my jaw should go as he intensifies the kiss, setting my body on fire with need. Stone breaks from me suddenly, leaving me breathless and dazed.

Before I can recover he spins me around to face the wall, the cool stone biting my bare breasts as he presses me into it. Stone places both my hands wide above my head as he kicks my legs open, making me feel like I'm about to get the sexiest frisking known to man.

"Leave your hands right where I put them, little thief," is ordered into my neck before he runs his fangs along it. Damn, that's sexy. Why is that so sexy?

"Yes, sir."

Stepping back slightly, he gently runs his claws down the length of my entire back shredding the rest of my top off. I try to swallow the sounds this elicits. I'm mostly successful. More ripping sounds follow the trace of his claws when he reaches my kickass pants. Seriously, they are the coolest pair I own...well, used to own. With one final loud rip, Stone pulls the pants apart with force, falling in tatters at my feet. I can totally buy another pair, I remember where I got them. Having my clothes ripped off is a kink I didn't know I had, till now.

"Alexis?" My name comes as a question.

"Yes, sir?" I answer in kind.

"Do you ever wear undergarments?" Oh, yeah. Totally forgot I went commando today. They were baggy pants and I'd kinda hoped I'd get lucky today. Plus, I like going without panties any-time I think I can get away with it. "Pity, I was looking forward to tearing them off myself." Shit! Mental note, wear undies if I might get sex with Stone. He smacks my bare ass forcefully.

"Sorry, sir!" I yelp. "I, uh, I like the breeze." Stone hmm's in response. Pretty sure he likes the breeze down below himself.

"Don't. Move." Oh, I have no intention of going anywhere, so I nod as he walks away. I can hear him getting something ready, but I don't peek, wanting to be surprised. Anticipation builds as he walks back to me. "Turn around, wrists together in front of yourself." Slowly, I follow his orders, kicking my tattered clothes out from under me.

At first, I'm not sure what he's got in his hands, but then he gives me a better view. They look like black leather bracers that are bound together with a steel ring at the top. Is Stone really about to cuff me?!

"Do you consent?" Stone asks earnestly while capturing my eyes with his. "Do you have any reservations or concerns about this? I assure you that the leather within is soft with no sharp edges. Would you like to feel them?" He holds them out closer to me, so I take him up on his offer. He's right, of course; the inside is buttery soft with no hard edges where my skin will be. Handing them back, I look my lover in his eyes.

"I consent to the use of these restraints. And I consent to being punished," I flash my eyes over to the paddle I left lying on the floor, "however you see fit, Officer." Stone rumbles at what I've said and indicated. Stepping nearer, he begins binding my forearms together.

"That's Investigator to you, thief." A nervous, excited laugh escapes my throat at this, loving that he's continuing the game with me, that he's playing along too. Add cops and robbers roleplaying to my list of new kinks learned today. I'm practically giddy as he cinches me into these bracer cuffs. He tests around the edges thoroughly, asking silent questions with his face. When he's satisfied, he leads me over to some chains hanging from the ceiling, lifts my arms fully over my head, and hooks my cuffs to them. It's at a good height for me as I'm still able to stand on the floor.

"I expect you to speak up if and when you need to, Alexis." I bite my lower lip and nod. "I'm going to push you harder today, and you will tell me if anything is too much. Do you understand me? Anything."

"Yes, sir." Then add, "Investigator Stone," in a flirtatious tone. Leaning in, he kisses me again. A kiss that's sweet and tender, something I didn't expect. A kiss that causes butterflies to form in my stomach. Which is something that hasn't happened to me in a long time. Slowly, Stone ends the kiss, resting his forehead upon mine.

"Good girl." With a quick peck to my forehead, he walks over to a cabinet.

What was that?! I swallow hard as my chest warms with feeling. Oh no, am I? No, I can't be. We've only just started to be able to tolerate each other, well, more than tolerate if I'm honest. I can't be catching feelings already, can I? No, that would be ridiculous! Yeah, we're having fun. Yeah, we work and play well together. Yeah, I like spending time with him and annoying him. No, no, I will not be in a one-sided love affair. And Stone certainly doesn't have any kinds of feelings like that for me.

Well, he did save my life. But he might have just seen that as his job or his duty. Though, he did buy me that thoughtful gift. It was probably more for him though, so he didn't have to listen to my music. But he could have just told me to turn it off or removed my music box altogether. Instead, he found a way for us both to be okay while working in that room together. That kiss though. Why would he kiss me like that if he weren't feeling some type of way about me? Maybe that was just appreciation for standing up to his grandfather? Yeah, that must be it. Appreciation, not love or something silly like that.

The sound of a cabinet door closing brings me back to the here and now, breaking me from the winding path of thoughts I just fell into. As Stone walks closer to me, I can hear items moving around in the black box he's carrying. Wonder what kinds of goodies he's picked out for me?

Setting the box on a tall skinny table on wheels, he rolls it closer to where I'm chained up. Instead of taking anything out of the box, he walks right past me and over to the toy I left on the floor. Looks like we'll be starting with a little spanking. I wiggle in my chains as he stalks towards me, paddle held out in front, and irritation on his face.

"Is this how you should treat other people's belongings, thief?"

"No, sir," I respond flippantly, like a teenager.

"Then why," he begins to run the leather paddle along the exposed flesh at my thigh, "did you do so to mine?" Stone circles around me, trailing the toy over my abdomen and to my other thigh. "Why did you throw this on the floor once you had finished inspecting it?" Smack! A sting lances across my ass cheek.

"Because I knew you'd hate it," I quickly answer. "Sir." Smack!

"Why would you want to anger me, thief?" Smack!

"Because it's fun." Instantly he brings the paddle across both my ass cheeks, harder than the previous swats. "Ah!"

"Is that the real answer, thief?" Right behind me, close to my ear, he growls, "Don't you lie to me." He's brought the paddle around to rub along my nipple. "I will have the truth."

"I..." Swallowing thickly, I lick my lips. Stone moves the cool paddle to the other breast while his tail starts a lazy journey up the inside of my leg. "I..."

"You what?" Lightly, he swats my breast with the paddle.

"I wanted you to use it!" I quickly answer. "I dropped it on the floor because I wanted you to use the paddle on me, sir." My heart has started racing, eager for more.

"Just as I suspected." He glides the leather across my skin around to my backside. "My naughty thief was itching for her punishment." Smack! Right across both cheeks.

"Yes, sir! Yes, sir!" I plead hurriedly. "I very much need you to punish me, Investigator Stone." The vibrations of his deep rumble skitter across my back.

"Then you shall have it, and more." Another smack resounds as his tail makes it to my slit. "So wet already. So eager, and we've only just begun." I moan as his tail strokes me there. "Not just yet, my thief." After one last sweep of his tail, he walks away, over to the black mystery box. Turning in place, I'm excited to see what he pulls out first, and I am not disappointed. Slowly he lifts out a sparkly red pleasure wand.

"Let's begin."

Chapter 29

Alexis

Pleasure wand in one hand, leather paddle in the other, Stone begins to circle me as I hang from his chains. But he stops and shakes his head instead.

"No, there's something missing here. This is too easy for you." Somewhat confused, I watch him walk back over to the box of toys, hanging the paddle from a wingtip as he puts his hand inside. "Here we are, exactly what you deserve, the element of surprise." In his hand is a red satin eye mask. My breaths quicken automatically. "Won't you agree, little thief?"

"Yes, sir." The eyemask is over my head and covering my vision before I know it.

"Mmm, much better." A sharp slap to my ass is quickly followed by a wave of pleasure that travels down my spine along the tip of the wand. I moan in earnest as Stone drags the wand over my skin, down to my stinging ass cheeks. Leaving the wand on one cheek he brings the paddle down upon the other. Oh yeah, add simultaneous pleasure and pain to my growing list of kinks.

Stone trails the wand to my newly smarting cheek, spiraling it into the center before he removes it entirely. I'm left alone, standing here blind, as I wait for his next move. I don't know where he is, as all I can hear are my breaths and pounding heart. A flash of pleasure hits my right nipple making me rock on my feet. But the wand stays in place as I arch and moan in pleasure. Suddenly the wand is removed, replaced by a slap to the same breast. Before any real sting sets in, the wand is returned, sending pleasure rippling down to my core. If Stone thought I was wet before, it's nothing compared to what's going on now. He does this three more times, switching between breasts, before I get a little reprieve.

"I do love you in my chains, Alexis Callaway." He's brought his claws up to scrape down my trembling arms, slowly dragging them down to my neck. "Exactly where my vexing thief should be." The claws trail down my heaving chest, skating over my sensitive nipples. I shudder at the contact. "Do you enjoy being in my chains, Alexis?"

"Yes sir, Investigator, sir." A warm wet bumpy tongue licks across my left nipple before being sucked into Stone's mouth. My back bows into him, loving the feel of it.

"Your breast is so delicious, little thief. Makes me wonder what the rest of you tastes like." Oh, sweet merciful heavens, yes, please taste the rest of me! His tongue hits my other nipple, swirling around it before popping into his mouth for a good suck and a little nibble. I'm rubbing my thighs together, eager for him to taste me further south. My wish is very soon granted.

Suddenly, my knees are being lifted, placed on either side of Stone's horns as he stands up, walking back a few paces, pulling the chains tight as he holds my ass with his hands. I feel like a weird clothes line.

"Open your legs wider." It's an order. "My wings won't let your knees slide off my shoulders. I've got you." Taking a steadying breath I do as he commands. "Good girl. Showing me that pretty pussy of yours." Without warning, his tongue licks my entire slit.

"Oh, fuck me!" I shout. Hefting me closer to his face, his textured tongue begins to rub along my folds, working me up quickly. Next he moves to attack my clit; licking it, circling it, and sucking on it. I'm rocking on his face, wanting more. Needing more. "Stone, I–" But I don't get to finish my words as his tongue thrusts inside me, in and out, quickly finding my G-spot. That tongue is a fucking marvel. If he keeps this up, I'll break! Then suddenly he stops. This motherfucker stops!

I growl in frustration. Before I can start hurling insults at him, however, the pleasure wand is traced down the line of my spine while his tongue slowly enters my core again. Stone keeps up this slow-ass pace, in and out with his tongue, up and down with the wand. It's a maddening sort of pleasure. My body starts to shake of its own accord. As soon as it does, he picks up the pace once more. Without warning, the pleasure wand is at my clit, and I'm screaming! Back arched in the air, thighs clamped around Stones horns, as the sudden orgasm rips through me in force. The pleasure wand directly on my clit, his tongue stroking my G-spot, and his bumps rubbing my opening.

If I thought I was shaking before, it's nothing compared to how my body convulses after that. Slowly, Stone sets me back on my feet. To be honest, I'm mostly hanging from my chains at this point, trying to catch my breath.

"Even more delicious than your breasts." A little chuckle comes out of me at that. Coming to stand behind at my back, he leans me into his chest to rest, running his warm hands all over my body. "If I thought you were beautiful in my chains before, you are absolutely stunning now." A sigh of contentment passes my lips. "I think you should get to watch this next part." He removes the blindfold, but all I can think of is 'next part!'

Kissing the back of my neck, he leaves to deposit the blindfold in the box, before exiting the room completely. I get a little concerned before I hear him pouring liquid into a glass. Ah, yes, one must stay hydrated.

Stone has me drink some orange juice when he returns, then he checks the cuffs and chains before filling a glass of water for himself. After downing that, he sets the glass aside as he reaches back into the box of mystery toys. Holding whatever he plans to use on me next behind his back, he walks up to me. Slowly he brings both hands out in front, each holding its own pleasure wand.

"Ready for round two?" he asks as he gives both wands a shake. I can't help the snort laugh at his attempt at a joke. Taking a moment, I stretch my body out here and there, hearing some lovely cracks and pops as I do.

"Ready to rock and roll, sir!" I answer with a big-ass smile on my face. He arches an eyebrow but doesn't ask what that means. Instead, he spins me to face a different direction.

"From here, you should be able to look at yourself in that mirror," he points to one of the mirrors along the wall, "should you wish to." Glancing up, I see that he's right. I am a little further away, and it's at an angle, but if I wanted to, I could look at my reflection there. Watching, I see Stone come to stand right behind me, feeling his warm chest upon my naked back. Both arms come into view, wrapping around me, pleasure wand in each hand.

He starts on either side of my neck, moving the tips down to my clavicle in unison, around my breasts, down my stomach, and around my hips. Both wands mirroring each other's actions down the frame of my body. Two pleasure wands was definitely the way to go, the dual sensation coursing through me has my eyes rolling in my head. I tried to keep watching Stone as he played my body like a cello—I really did—but it just felt too good to keep my eyes open. Instead, my head has tilted back, eyes lightly closed, as I dance and sway to the rhythm of pleasure Stone is creating.

When he circles both nipples, I undulate in such a way that I find Stone's hard cock pressing into my back. Time for me to play with him a little too. Moaning loudly as both wand tips hit my peaked nipples, I grind into his cock. Leaning into it, and him, as much as I can as I writhe with desire. Suddenly, one wand tip is set right above my clit, shocking me to stand up straight, toes curling.

"What do you think you were doing, little thief?" The second wand is added to my clit, making me scream as I stand on my tiptoes. "So eager for cock that you try and steal it too soon." Both wands are removed, and my knees instantly buckle, making me hang as I try to remember how to breathe. "If it is cock you want, then it is cock you shall have." My eyes regain their focus as I watch him set an arched box in front of a mirror. A box that must have a hole as he sets a black training dildo just inside so that it stands erect. Blinking, I finally take in what I'm seeing. It's a sex seat!

I watch wide-eyed as Stone pours a viscous liquid onto the dildo, which I'm guessing is lube. Oh, he's going to want me to fuck myself on it, right in front of that mirror. Next, Stone slides some cushioned pads on either side of the arched box. How thoughtful of him, to make sure his partners don't get their knees all bruised up. Seemingly finished, Stone marches over to me.

"Ready for your next punishment, little thief?" He's unhooking my cuffs from the chains on the ceiling.

"Yes, sir," I answer, just above a whisper. Leading me by the ring of my cuffs, we walk to the sex seat. But instead of facing the mirror, he has me face away.

"Kneel just in front of the dildo, do not," his eyes squint at me, "touch it yet." I do as he asks, setting my knees on the padding as I straddle the seat. Walking over to a cabinet, he takes out more padding, then adds a layer to either side, lifting me up a little. "Perfect. Now, move forward, resting the head at your pussy's entrance. Do not sink down upon it." Scooching forward, the dildos head runs along my already wet slit until it hits my opening. Looking up at him, I wait for my next orders like a good little sub.

"Normally, I would let the seat fuck you, controlling it with its crystal. But since you were a naughty thief and attempted to steal my cock before it was given, you are going to ride that seat yourself, and only I will get to watch you fuck it." Damn, I am so ready to fuck this seat as he watches me! I don't think I even need the lube at this point, but he remembered my concerns from last time. Which is nice. Oops, I've been silent for too long.

"Yes. sir. I understand my punishment, Officer." A growl informs me that I've said the wrong thing. I don't correct myself yet though, wondering what the punishment will be for not using Investigator like he told me. What I certainly wasn't expecting was for him to whip off his kilt, letting me get an eyeful of that beautifully bumpy dick of his.

"Reach down, and put some of that lube into your hands." Score! He's going to let me touch him. Finally! As quickly as I can, I grab the lubed up dildo between my legs, pumping it twice to get a good amount on my palms while also coating the toy. Forearms still bound together I show my investigator my slick hands. "Sink down till you feel any resistance, then come back up." Staring up into his face, I follow his orders, making it a few inches down the shaft before returning to the top.

"Now, thief, you are going to get what you wanted to steal." Extending his hand down, he caresses my jaw as he gives his orders. "You are going to jerk me off with those bound hands, and that troublesome mouth, until I come." Licking my lips, I prepare to begin. "And you will hover above that cock until I tell you to do otherwise. Understood?"

"Yes, Investigator Stone." This earns me a half-smile. He steps up closer to me, but I wait to touch him. Which is very hard, let me tell you.

"Good girl." Removing his hand from my face, he puts them both behind his back. "You may begin." I waste no time! I've been wanting to thoroughly explore this cock since he told me it looked like my favorite sex toy. Framing it with both hands, I grab hold just below the head, slowly stroking it downward as I bring my tongue to lick his tip. I get a low rumble, but nothing more. Time to get to work then. I'm going to make him fall to pieces.

Without any preamble, I sink his head deep into my mouth, well deep for me. I have a big mouth, but not Gargoyle cock big. Thankfully, I have my hands, which pump him as I create suction around his head. Glancing up, I see his eyes are on me, so I smile as I swirl my tongue. His face remains impassive, like a statue, but his tail is swishing behind him like an agitated cat. A good sign, I think. Taking a firmer grip with my hands, I bring him into my mouth again and moan, letting the vibrations work their magic. That makes his wings snap out, excellent. So I continue to moan as I bob.

"Fuck. That. Toy." The order is given through gritted teeth. Oh, I'm getting to him alright. Popping his dick out of my mouth, I sink down, pulling his cock as I go. Then push back as I rise, cock going right back into my mouth. I do this several more times, moaning out loud as I sink the bumpy toy deeper and deeper into me.

"If you make it all the way down," his voice is so low, "I'll let you choose where I fuck you." Oh gawd, he still plans to fuck me after this. What we are doing here is just to get me ready for him.

"Thank you, sir." It's the only thing I can think to say. So, I begin to fuck this toy in earnest, keeping his dick firmly in my mouth the whole time. I've started to twist my grip as my fingers slide up and down his bumpy shaft. But when I add in some teeth scraping, oh baby, that's when he finally reacts. Head tilts back, rumble so cavernous it vibrates his cock in my hands, as his tail comes between his legs to wrap around my waist. Seems I've found the magic key.

I continue in this manner: teeth, twist, gripping hard when I fall back into the seat. I've almost taken the toy all the way. Glancing up to his face, his rapt attention is focused on me in the mirror, fucking myself with his toy. Wonder if he's imagining me riding him like I am this toy as I give him a blow job?

Finally my ass hits the top of the sex chair; the training cock is all the way inside me. Stone growls as I moan around his cock.

Slowly I come up to my knees again, my eyes lock onto his as I slam my ass down to clap into the sex chair. That's all it takes to finally break him. As soon as my cheeks meet the chair, I bite down just a little harder, and he roars. Wings spread wide, tail tight around me, cock enlarging slightly as I clamp down around it. It pulses as he comes. It's odd to not have any semen come out, but I think I like it. I'd probably drown if a monster like Stone ejaculated down my throat.

"Release," comes his gravelly command. I do as instructed but give his head a little swirl of my tongue as I do. Breathing hard, he falls to his knees before me and kisses me passionately. From the side of his mouth, "Did I tell you to stop fucking yourself?" Whimpering I comply, bouncing up and down as Stone kisses me like I am his very breath. We both moan as I continue to work myself with his toy.

"Stop," Stone orders as he breaks the kiss, just as breathless as I am. "Where do you want me to fuck you, thief of my cock?" I squirm on my seat, eager but drawing a blank. Wildly, I cast my eyes around me before my sight locks onto the contraption in the middle of the room.

"The sex swing!" I pant. Eye's back to Stone's, "Strap me in, and fuck me hard." Kissing me again, slower and deeper than before, he holds me close, wrapping even his wings around me. Breaking the kiss, he nibbles my jaw before he undoes the cuffs wrapped around my forearms, inspecting each wrist closely, before kissing them in turn. Stone lifts me off my seat, I moan at the sensation. Carrying me bridal style, the way he does when we fly, he sets me into my new seat. Before strapping me in, however, he wipes the goopy lube off my hands then fetches me some water.

I gladly gulp it down as he reaches into that black box one more time.

"These," he starts as he holds three large flat rubies in his hand, "are pleasure stones." Placing one upon each nipple he explains, "they are much like the wand but stay in place." Putting the third crystal near my clit, "And they are controlled by this." Stone shows me a clear crystal of the same size and shape. "By swiping your thumb across the flat surface like so," an instant pulse of pure rapture zings through the three stones placed upon my body. I nearly leap out of the swing! Stone hands me the clear crystal as he takes my glass.

"You will use the controller on yourself as I fuck you on this swing." Licking his lips as he looks me over. "The pressure which you apply and the speed of which you rub it controls what you receive. Test it on yourself." His eyes are locked on mine, so I keep eye contact as I gently pass my thumb over the smooth facet. Stone rumbles as my breath catches at the triple sensation. Oh, this is a dangerous toy.

"Play with it as I strap you in. I want to hear your little sounds of delight." Leaning back into the swing, I place my limbs in the area for straps as he sets the glass down in the black box. I wait until he begins buckling me in to test out the toy more. Quickly I discover that even the slightest pressure or speed will supply loads of pulsing pleasure through my body. Sooner than expected, I'm all strapped in. "Test your bindings, Alexis."

"Everything feels perfect, Investigator," I answer, slightly rocking in my suspended pose as he moves to stand between my wide open legs.

"Then work yourself up with the crystals, thief of my cock." My heart rate dramatically increases. "I want you squirming and begging before I enter you."

Chapter 30

Stone

I'm so glad she chose the swing, though I would have fucked her in a graveyard if that's what she requested. I've never wanted to bring a person pleasure more than I have on this day. After what Alexis did for me, swooping in to put a spectacular end to my grandfather's antics, I needed to reward her then and there.

She's taken her 'punishment' spectacularly. I love how she plays the game with me, the way her body moves in ecstasy, the sounds she makes, the feel of her skin, and the way she handled my cock. A shiver races down my tail. No, I won't be letting my pretty thief slip through my fingers. Running my claws down the inside of her thighs, her body trembles at the sensation.

"Begin," I order. Her first moan is music to my ears. The pleasure stones can be intense, so I wanted her to be in control of them this first time. Next time, however, I might just take the reins. Her lithe body shakes and convulses as she follows my orders, playing with herself as I watch her. Stepping out, I begin to circle her, wanting to see her pleasure ripple through her at every angle. I can't help the small touches, the gentle caresses, the clawed strokes I pepper her skin with as I watch her.

I'm curious if she would like me to use the crystals on her as we fly through the air, holding her in my arms as she loses herself in the sky. Wonder if she would let me fuck her as we glide down to earth. The logistics would be interesting, but with some straps...

Her moans become louder as she bucks in the swing, her hips wanting more. Soon, thief of my heart, very soon I will give you what we both need. Leaning over, I capture her mouth in a kiss, devouring her sounds of pleasure. I've never been so drawn to kissing a partner before, but with Alexis I can't seem to get enough. Her smooth little tongue, her plump lips, the way she matches my passion each time.

"Stone!" she cries, breaking the kiss. She thinks calling me Officer or Investigator pleases me, but it's my name upon her lips that really gives me a thrill. My name in her sweet notes of desire stirs something primal deep within me.

Making my way back to stand between her legs, I gaze down at my beautiful thief. Bound in my swing, pleasing herself as I ordered her to, the need for my cock sweeping through her body. What a rare treasure I have found. But she hasn't begged me yet. I need her to beg for my cock before I can give it to her. Those were the rules of this game, and I won't take her until she is ravenous for me. I can hurry things along though, tease her as she loves to tease me.

Taking my cock in hand, I run the head through her slick folds. She tries to position it with her hips, eager for me to slide inside, but I take it away. This makes her whimper and growl at me. So cute. Let's hear more of it. Grabbing the swing, I move her till my cock is just outside her entrance. I allow her to rub herself on me there, though it's only enough to tease that sweet open hole of hers.

Come on, Alexis, I'm begging you to beg for me. Let me fuck you hard like you requested. I've been thinking about being back inside you for days.

"Stone! Please, Stone." Almost. She's almost there. So stubborn. Releasing the chains, I let her swing away from me, only to return. Pussy grazing my cock for an instant before she swings away again. "Please, please!" Pushing the swing again, I let the action continue to tease us both.

"Fuck me! Please, fuck me, Stone. I need you–" she catches her breath, "I need you to fuck me, please! Rail me with your big monster cock." Perfection, even more than I needed to hear. Grabbing the swing I hold her, lining my head to finally enter her. "Yes, yes, gawd, please, I need, I need, so close, so close." As slow as I can muster, I push inside. Halfway in, she screams while arching her back, channel gripping tightly around my cock. My amazing thief came before I even got in all the way.

Continuing, I push in deeper, slow and steady, till I seat myself fully as she rides out her orgasm, hips bucking and grinding me within her as she finishes. When she stops, however, I begin. Moving the swing, I push her slowly away until my cock is almost out. She screams in pleasure when I let the swing fall, setting my cock fully inside her once more. Pushing the swing back slowly once more, I hold her away from me as her hips wiggle.

"Are you ready to be fucked in this swing, Alexis? Because I'm going to fuck you hard." She's moaning again, playing with the crystals once more, hips moving in a circle as she tries to get any friction from my cock she can. Good, I was afraid she might want to be done already. Instead, I see that she's still eager for more, and more is exactly what I plan to give her.

"Fuck!" rips from her lips when I let the swing fall, spearing her with my rigid cock. Taking hold of her waist, I fuck her gently for a few strokes.

"Are you ready to be fucked hard by this monster, thief of my cock?" I continue to bounce her gently on me, liking the feel of it, watching her thighs and tits jiggle as I do.

"Yes, my monster." I freeze. "I'm so very ready to be fucked hard by you." Without hesitation, I thrust into her with force, taking her by surprise. She eyes me, clearly shocked for a moment, then smirks. "Please fuck me, my monster." Quickly pulling out, I slam into her again. Her head leans back with a gasps of pleasure. "Please, my monster, please fuck me." Slamming into her, I create a rhythm as I fuck her. Pulling her by the hips as the swing gives me full rein to move her as I like. I might even go a little feral as she speaks to me, chants to me, encouraging me as I pound into her.

"Fuck!" she cries. "That feels so fucking good, my monster," she shouts. "Don't stop, please don't stop my...my...my Stone!" No, no, I wasn't feral before, but I am now. Say it again, say it again, I chant in my head. I'm holding her waist, absolutely slamming her into me, watching her face for any discomfort. Thankfully, all I see there is ecstasy, ecstasy and hunger.

"Gawd-damn, Stone, that's amazing!" Wings snap to the side, tail wrapped around her thigh, I'm so close to losing it again. "Stone, Stone, please, Stone." Growling, I set a new rhythm.

"Fuck yes, Stone!" she screams. "Fuck me just like that." I'm honestly surprised she can talk with how hard I'm ramming into her. "Stone, oh Stone, my monster, my fucking monster! My Stone!" Instantly, I begin to come with a roar as she calls me hers, Her Stone. But I won't stop, won't still my efforts, until she comes too. So I growl as I continue pulling her hard into me, to take all of my cock deep within her.

"Oh fuck, Stone. Don't stop, my Stone, please! I'm so, I'm almost! Ahhhh!" She explodes around me, body shaking as she utters nonsense words, convulsing against the restraints. Continuing, but slowing my pace, I bounce her as I prolong this orgasm for her as long as possible. I relish the fact that her words have become gibberish, almost as much as I crave hearing my name upon her lips. Though nothing can compare to her calling me 'my Stone.' That will live with me forever.

"Wow!" she finally says with a chuckle. "That was...wow." Stilling my movement completely, I caress her knee with my lips. "You...you really like hearing your name, big guy." Nipping her with my fangs, I chuckle.

"I really like hearing you say my name, thief of my heart." Alexis halts all movement at my admission. "No one else has ever claimed it the way you do." I kiss her other knee. "Until now, I never cared if my name was uttered in euphoria. But with you, everything is different." Slowly, I pull myself out, causing her to sigh in pleasure. "Let's get you out of here and into a warm bath." I don't want her to feel pressured into saying anything in reply. Just because I have admitted my feelings does not mean she needs to. If she has any feelings yet, that is.

Taking the pleasure crystals off first, I set them in the box for cleaning later. She remains silent as I undo her bindings, which I hope is a good sign. Maybe she's reflecting, maybe she's recovering, either way she hasn't outright rejected my feelings. Finding some redness, but no true injuries, I relax the tension I hadn't realized I was holding. Using cloths I keep here for such messes, I wipe off any remaining lube from her, then wipe myself with another cloth. Lifting her out of the swing, I walk us into my personal bathroom instead of the one in here. Feels more intimate to bring her into my space.

"I'll get bathwater running as you use the toilet. There's a door to close for privacy." Setting her down in my spacious bathing room, she silently turns, walking slowly to the toilet room. Did I break her? Did I stun her? Is she in some kind of shock? I do not like this quiet Alexis.

"Okay." It comes out wispy, but at least it's something. She doesn't close the door, so I turn my back to her, getting the bath ready. I'll add some lavender drops to the healing and relaxation blend I have premixed. Water running, I swiftly stride back into the playroom, gathering all the items we used. After a cursory wipe-down, I place them all in the large cleansing closet I had built in, sex swing and all. Upon entering the bathing room, I find Alexis already in the tub. I was going to wash us off in the shower first, but this is fine.

"Hey," she greets me, almost shyly. Relief spreads through my body.

"Hello, Alexis," making my voice deep and calming. "How's the temperature?"

"Oh, it's perfect." She looks around as I enter the warm pool. "This is, ah, the biggest personal tub I've ever seen. But then again, I guess a big guy like you needs a lot more space." Bless the goddess, she's talking again. I may have been worried for a moment there, but nervous-talking Alexis I can handle. "Smells really nice, whatever you put in the water, I mean. Not that you don't smell nice too or anything."

Using my tail, I pull her closer to me in the water. Depositing her in my lap with a little "eep" from her. Inhaling her scent deeply, right where her shoulder meets her neck, I rumble.

"You smell nice too, thief of my heart." This makes her sit up straight, but I wanted her to hear it again, to know it wasn't said in a moment of passion. "Let's get you cleaned up anyway, so you don't smell only of sex when we fetch those dumplings you wanted." Grabbing a clean net bathing cloth, I lather some soap into it.

"Why did you call me that?" Brave Alexis, starting with the hardest question first instead of tiptoeing around it.

"I should think that's obvious, my pretty thief, seeing as how you're the one who stole it." Her breath catches at my calm reply. It was an answer she wasn't expecting, but it is the truth, my truth. Washing her back, I continue, "You waltzed right in, as pretty as you please, and took it without me even realizing till after it happened." Gently, and with great care, I wash her arms as well. "But I've discovered your theft."

"I didn't mean to. I mean, I didn't plan...I wasn't trying to..." Flustered Alexis is cute.

"Such a skilled thief I have caught, plucking my heart from my chest without effort." I nip her rounded ear. "But caught you I have." Starting at the neck, I begin to wash her front. "I am a great investigator after all." I offer her a playful smile, letting her see my mood. There's a little flash of relief on her face at that.

"When...when did you...um." Squaring her shoulder, taking back some confidence, she finally gets the question out. "When did you realize I had taken it?" There she is, my bold playful thief.

"I put it all together slowly, the final piece fell into place when you confronted my grandfather on my behalf." Meeting her eyes, I add with a wink, "An excellent maneuver that, winning my affections by coming to my rescue." Is that a slight blush? "But I began to really put things in order when I recalled the plea to my goddess, Inera. Do you remember me telling you about her?"

"Yeah, you asked her to help catch me." There's a twinkle in her eye and a smile on her face at that statement. Without warning, I lift her out of the pool, setting her on the edge so I can wash her legs. She doesn't fight me, but I do get an indignant "hey!" before she swats my shoulder.

"What I didn't divulge was that Inera has been sending me dreams about you since that request." Alexis tenses her body, staring at me shocked. "Showing me, in no uncertain terms, that–" but she interrupts our game.

"Whoa, whoa, whoa! You've been getting those sex dreams too?!" Too? Has my goddess been sending Alexis the same messages?

Chapter 31

Alexis

Stone's face tells me that I'm right about the sex dreams. This can't be real! People don't share dreams! Surely they aren't the same exact dreams as mine, just sexy dreams about me in general.

If I wasn't halfway through a bath and covered in soap, I'd be pacing, for sure. No, no, I need to move in order to think. Stone drifts back as I slide into the overly large tub. Seriously, it's bigger than any hot tub I've been in. Though, at the moment I'm grateful for its size. Slowly, I walk back and forth within the hip deep water.

"How? How does this goddess send people dreams?" I don't understand. I thought only prophets got dreams, and not sex scenarios either. Real 'save the world' shit.

"It is not uncommon for the gods to send dreams to followers, or even non-followers, to get a message to them. Any god can do so themselves or request Morpheus to on their behalf, but Inera has a very close relationship with Morpheus." Stone keeps saying Morpheus like I should know who that is, but all I'm picturing is a bald Black guy in tiny sunglasses.

"Who's Morpheus? And why would they be sending us sex dreams about each other?" How many people know about my naughty-ass dreams?! Any number higher than just me is far too many in my book.

"Morpheus is the god of dreams. It is said that he and Inera have been friends for quite a long time, occasionally even lovers themselves. It would be nothing for him to send us a shared message." Whipping around, I face him.

"Shared! What do you mean shared?" My voice has reached a higher pitch than normal. "You don't think they have been sending us the exact same dreams do you?" He's smiling wickedly at me, "They're just similar right, not...not identical." Low in the water, Stone begins to prowl towards me.

"What have you been dreaming of, my pretty thief?" My eyes go wide, but I clamp my mouth shut. "Hedgemazes under a starlit night?" No! "Locked away in towers, seeking my rescue." Fuck! "Being chased down an alley to be caught like the thief you are?" Leaping forward, I press both hands over his mouth.

"Those were private!" I squeak, but he only laughs under my palms. "Can't a girl have a little privacy in her dreams?!" Squeezing my eyes shut, flashes of everything we've acted out, everything we've done in those dreams, floods my mind. "I don't even believe in any gods!" This only makes him laugh, then mumble something about his goddess choosing me anyway.

"Wait!" I shout. "When was your first dream? When did this start for you?" Removing my hands so he can answer, he stands forcing me backwards.

"The day I first caught your delicious scent at a crime scene." he steps closer to me. I back up. "The day I tracked you to that tavern, to find you in bed with another." A small growl escapes him as he presses forward. "The day you first vexed me, yet followed my commands so eagerly." He's backed me into the wall of the pool, a single fang showing in his smile as he looms over me. "The day you first lodged yourself into my thoughts." He pulls us both down into the steamy water so we are face-to-face. "The day that I asked a goddess to help me catch you, my thief." He's whispering now, and so, so close to my face. "That night, I encased myself in stone and dreamed there for the first time. I dreamed of you." He kisses my forehead. "I dreamed of hunting you down, of catching you with that ruby comb, only to find a very naked thief under a black cloak." I nervously giggle as he smiles, searching my face.

"Totally thought I was just having a typical 'naked in public' dream, till you," anxiously I laugh a little, "till you–" I'm spared finishing that sentence by a kiss, a wonderfully sweet kiss with a hint of passion to it. A kiss that is rudely interrupted by my embarrassingly loud stomach.

"Come," he chuckles, "let us finish our bathing, then get you something to eat. We were only running an errand before returning to work, remember."

"Yeah, yeah, yeah," I reply, lazily waving my hand in the air. "Solving a murder, and all that jazz. But first," hand on his chest, I push him back to the built-in seating, "I want one more of those kisses." Sitting him down, I slide onto his lap, straddling him as he arches a brow at me. "Just one little kiss," I say in mock innocence.

Taking his rumble as consent, I grab his head with both my hands and give him a kiss to remember. A kiss that speaks of things to come, a promise and a request. Rubbing along his front, I moan as I feel his cock beginning to harden under my ass, exactly as I hoped it would. Before it starts poking anything, however, I break the kiss.

"Now," somewhat breathless, "let's get clean so we can get those dumplings." Patting his cheek, I hop off, hearing a growl as I grab the washcloth. Humming, I clean myself quickly. He scowls as he does the same, rumbling in annoyance. I only hum louder. Draining the tub, he rinses us both off with a showerhead built-in here. The water is cold! Which I think he did on purpose. It was invigorating, however. Before I can get out and dry off, he motions to a glass bottle of oil.

"Want to oil your skin? I prefer it over lotion after a bath." He pours some in a cupped hand, so I lean in to smell it. After a whiff that smells like nothing at all, I nod.

"Sure, I think my skin would appreciate that." Moving to reach for the bottle, Stone moves it away.

"I will be oiling you," he states. Motioning for me to spin, I comply. "We didn't spend as long soaking as I would have liked after having you tied up like that." Stone works the oil into me well, massaging my back, arms, and wrists like a pro.

"If you give me some, I can get my front while you get my legs." Pouring some into both our hands, he sits to rub my legs as I work the oil into my chest. I am hungry, but there's one last thing I need to do. Once one leg is done, I put the other on the bench for him, but just as he's about to finish, I slide into his lap once more, trapping his semi-hard cock between us. Before he can say anything I take hold of his curved horns, pulling him in to claim his mouth.

His hands come to my ass as I rub his cock between us, getting it hard, getting it ready, getting it oiled. Kissing him fiercely, I work him up. I need to know, I need to make sure that it's not just the toys or the games we play. That we have more than that between us. He says I have his heart, that a faceless goddess I've never heard of has brought us together in dreams. But I need to feel what we have for myself, without anything else going on.

"Alexis," he growls into my mouth as his claw-tipped finger pricks the skin of my ass.

"I need to feel you, Stone." I whisper upon his lips. "To feel my Stone, deep inside me." Lifting, I easily glide his head to my opening, sinking down slowly when I do. "Please, just for a moment." I work myself down his cock as we breathe into each other. "Let me ride you, my Stone. I need to–" My words vanish in a gasp when I take him all the way, deep inside me. Impossibly deep.

Riding and kissing Stone leisurely, I take my time. Feel every bump upon his cock, every pebble along his tongue. Every rumble vibrates through me exquisitely. He's wrapped me in his arms and wings. Holding me, assisting my movements but letting me set the pace. Keeping it slow, the pleasure builds within me. Stone is all around me, within me, in a way that feels more intimate than ever before. Sucking on his lower lip, I sever the kiss, moving to nibble on his earlobe.

"Are you really my Stone?" The whisper is almost inaudible. I wasn't even sure I had actually asked it until he replies.

"Yes," His answer is sure. No doubt whatsoever. Biting and sucking on his neck, I rock my hips right where I need him.

"My Stone," I repeat. Is that a tear running down my cheek?

"Yes," he answers with a growl. Stone is rumbling constantly now, his chest vibrating my sensitive nipples. Moaning into his neck, I bite him harder.

These feelings are so big, too big even. But I won't run away. He's here facing them, opening himself up to me without fear.

Without pushing me to feel the same at all. Only showing me where he's at.

"My Stone," I whisper once more into his neck before returning to his lips. His kiss eagerly greets me, consuming everything I have to give. Holding his face I work my hips with more need, gearing up for the orgasm that's fast approaching.

It's not overwhelming like a tsunami. It's not a blast of fire through my veins. Instead I come like a flower opening from its bud, slow yet transformingly beautiful. Curling into him, my scream is silent into his shoulder. Gently rocking us both, he comes with me too, cock expanding slightly inside me. Clawed tips poking my head and thigh as he holds me tightly, shaking in his release.

We stay there for a time, holding each other in companionable silence. More warm tears streak down my cheeks, which I'm glad Stone can't see. I have a lot of big feelings right now. Feelings I'll need to look at later. But I got the answer I needed. What I have with Stone is not just about games and toys after all.

"That was beautiful, Alexis. Thank you." Glad he said something first, breaking me out of whatever place I just zoned out to. Nuzzling his neck, in an attempt to wipe away any remaining tears, I give him my muffled reply.

"You're welcome." I finally get the courage to face Stone when he chuckles at that. "So about those dumplings..." This earns me a real laugh.

"I was trying to get you fed before you tricked me, you needy thief." Bouncing me slightly on his lap, which causes tingly sensations all over since his cock is still hard within me. "Stealing my cock, yet again." Cupping my face, he kisses me gently. "But I will forgive you. This time." He tries to make his face look stern, but I see a smile peeking at the corners.

"Got curious to see if I could survive on cock alone. Turns out I can't." Shrugging, I add, "Not even your monster cock. Sorry, big guy, guess it will have to be dumplings after all." Unexpectedly, Stone stands while holding me, cock still thoroughly buried inside. Holding me tight, he steps out of the tub, walking us over to a countertop, where he sets my ass on to the cold surface.

"Hey, that's cold, you!" Tilting my chin to look at him, Stone slides his cock out while watching my face. I inhale a small gasp as he does.

"Perfection." How do I reply to that?! "What am I going to do with you, Alexis?"

"Hand me a towel and feed me, I hope!" Stone shakes his head and laughs as he gives me an overly large gray towel.

"Seriously, do you have something against color?" Hopping off the cold counter, I start to dry myself with the blanket he just handed me. As Stone opens his closet door, I realize the fatal flaw in my dumpling plans. "Clothes! I don't have anything to wear!" I narrow my eyes at Stone's back. "Somebody ripped everything I was wearing to shreds, including my favorite bra!"

"Well, somebody didn't strip when she was told to," comes his matter-of-fact reply. "I warned you what would happen if you didn't." I try to growl, but it doesn't sound as good as his. "I'll pick up the dumplings myself and buy you a dress or something along the way, then bring everything back so we can eat here. How does that sound?" Huffing in exasperation, I wrap the towel around myself like a cloak, hood and all.

"What am I supposed to do here all alone while I wait on you?" He's dressed in his usual kilt, of which he has at least ten of in that closet.

"Snoop around would be my guess." I hide a smile within the folds of my towel because he's not wrong.

Following him to the balcony door, I pepper him with my food order. I'm so hungry I would eat anything at this point, but I do have my favorites. Staying in the doorframe, I watch him leap off the edge into the open air below before shutting the door.

Immediately, I sprint back to the sex room, eager to snoop around his whole house. Once I satisfy my curiosity there, leaving with some tantalizing ideas, I enter his bedroom. Like the tub, his bed is oversized. It's looking awfully soft and inviting too. Throwing back the black comforter, I run my hand over the matching black sheets. Ooo, those are nice. Dropping the towel to the floor, I climb inside. Just as I suspected, they feel great against my bare skin as I make a bedsheet snow angel.

"Alexis." I think I hear my name being called, but I can't be sure. "Alexis."

"Five more minutes," I mumble under the sheets as I curl into the fetal position.

"Alexis." The deep voice is definitely closer now, but I just snuggle into my warm cocoon even deeper. The bed sinks a little near me, but I don't move, trying to capture sleep once more.

"Time to wake up, pretty thief." Is that Stone? What's he doing here?

"Go away," I groan as I feel the coolness of open air hit my shoulder. Unsuccessfully, I try to snatch the covers back over me, but Stone is clearly stronger than I am. A clawed finger traces over my shoulder and down my spine, making me shutter.

"I bought a new dress for you. Want to put it on?" I make agitated noises at him. "That's okay. I prefer you naked anyway." Turning to lay on my back, I'm about to give him a piece of my mind when a devilish tongue laps across an exposed nipple. That wakes me up very quickly!

"Come, time enough for that later," Stone declares. "Your food is getting cold." I sit straight up.

"Food! Why didn't you lead with that?" Eagerly, I slide out of the bed, striding right down the hall that leads to the kitchen.

"Wait! Your dress." I can hear Stone starting to follow me.

"It's okay. I don't mind eating naked if you don't"

"No, I don't mind at all, Lexi dear," comes the cool voice of the ghost I hate most. Damn it!

Chapter 32

―◆◇◆―

Alexis

U nfortunately, I'm unable to slow my pace in time. So Valda gets a good eyeful of my naked ass from the living room before Stone steps in front of me, holding something.

"You could've warned a girl," I hiss while snatching the green fabric out of Stone's hand. It's silky, long, and a similar shade to the bralette he tore.

"I didn't get a chance. You took off as soon as I said the word 'food.'" I yank the kaftan over my head and glare at him for a beat before continuing into the kitchen and the amazing smells coming from there.

"Why is he even here?" Randomly, I begin yanking open cabinet doors, searching for plates.

"I'll do that," Stone jumps in. "Sit, and I'll make you a plate." Can't tell if he's being nice or trying to protect his kitchen from me.

"I'm here," Valda begins, "because you two never came back. You were only supposed to be getting some new clothes for Stone."

"Aww, did you miss us, Valda?" I say mockingly as Stone sets out the food and dishes.

"Hardly." The ghost rolls his eyes as he floats into the kitchen island. "After that one went missing, I thought it best to keep closer tabs on those working with me on this. Don't want any wandering off with vital information again."

"We didn't go wandering off," I can't help the hardcore eyeroll that accompanies my statement, "we just had a little grandfather problem is all."

"Ah, I see." Valda offers before I can elaborate any further. "Yes, yes."

"Eat." Stone's simple command is one I am all too eager to obey. My feet swing happily off the large stool I'm sitting on. Stone's things make me feel like I've had a sip of Alice in Wonderland's shrinking potion. We eat in silence for a time as my eyes idly roam over Stone's house.

"Valda, did you ever search your lost assistant's house? Maybe they brought their work home with them, like Stone here does?"

"They didn't have a house. They lived at the Thieves Guild." Dismissively, the ghost adds, "Besides, why would they take any research or findings home? I have a perfectly wonderful area dedicated to my murder, with everything of note contained within."

"So, wait," I start, "you didn't search their room at the Guild for their journal or any notes about the case?" Stone and I both have stopped to stare at the ghost.

"Well, I mean, it wasn't with their possessions. I'm not an idiot. I did rummage through their boxed-up effects, but there was nothing of consequence there. Only the note about finding a new diary and checking something out himself." Starting to get excited, I press on.

"Yes, but what about their hidey-holes? Did you find them all?"

"I...I...ah...I mean." Valda stammers.

"Is it a common practice for the members of the Thieves Guild to have hidden spaces down there?" Stone asks, almost incredulous.

"Yes!" I slam my hands on the countertop. "Gav mentioned it within the first week of me being down there." Shoveling food into my face as fast as possible, I continue around mouthfuls. "The twins have at least six that I know about." Valda's face morphs into absolute disgust at my table manners. "There are rules around finding others, seeking them out, and what you can and cannot do when you locate an occupied hidey-hole. Valda! It's a big deal down there. We have to sign paperwork about it even, and you never thought to look?!"

"I don't use hidey-holes, thank you very much!" Valda says defensively. "Because I'm constantly passing though squirreled away bits within the walls, floors, and ceilings down there, I've had to sign my own paperwork about it. My own special set of rules, not that I ever cared about any of it as I've never felt a pull to anything down there. Though, I admit, you may be on to something." I can practically see the wheels turning in Valda's head as he thinks.

"Oh, I know I'm onto something." Knocking back the last of my green tea, I hop off the stool. Spinning on the spot, I wildly look around. "Where are my shoes?"

"By the door." Stone must have put them there earlier.

"Thanks!" Racing over to the balcony entrance, I slip them on. "Valda and I will go down to the sanctum, check out this lost assistant's room, and see what we can find. While you," I vaguely wave at Stone, "can work on your murder board or something. Alright, how do I get out of here?" There's got to be another way aside from leaping off the balcony, right?

"I'll drop you off where you need to go. There are some questions of my own I need answering." Stone stands, but instead of coming to the door, he begins to clean up.

"Seriously?! Come on, we've got to chase this new lead!" This is finally getting exciting for me, like a little treasure hunt. But Stone just continues to put away food and dishes.

"If there is such a notebook, it's not going anywhere. This will only take a moment, my impatient thief." Wanting to get this done faster, I march over to help clean up.

"Do you even remember which room belonged to this lost assistant?" I ask Valda as we walk down the dark secret tunnels to the Guild's sanctum. Shooting the ghost a little side eye, I add, "Seeing as how you haven't bothered to remember their name."

"My memory is a fickle thing, Lexi. And I would thank you kindly to not keep reminding me of my inadequacy." Ah, a touchy subject. "I'd like to see how much your human brain can remember after a thousand years."

"Thousand!" Stopping in my tracks, I turn to look at my transparent companion. "Really?"

"Given the age of the city, I'd guess I've been dead around a thousand years, give or take a few hundred." We continue through the tunnel as I think about that, what being a ghost for over a thousand years must be like. "To answer your question, no, I do not remember what room was theirs or their name. But," he raises a finger, "the records should show which room they stayed in. All we need do is find who went missing three hundred years ago, cross check that with those who kept rooms down here, then we shall have our answers."

"Great. Research." The excitement for this mini treasure hunt instantly vanishes.

"Lexi! Where've you been, girly?" Turning around I see the fox twins jogging up behind us. Not sure who spoke first but Aiden adds, "Haven't seen you since that vampire dagger theft." They both eye Valda suspiciously. "Everything okay here?"

"Aww, did you two miss me?" I say patting both of their cheeks simultaneously. "Don't worry about him," I jerk my thumb at Valda. "We've buried the hatchet, haven't we, V?"

"Indeed, we have," Valda answers with a fake smile on his face. Either he doesn't like the twins or he hates the nickname V. I'm betting it's both!

"In fact, I'm helping old V here out with something." Valda's head whips over to me, face clearly saying 'please dear gawd, do not tell these two buffoons what I asked for your help with.' I only smile wider, increasing his terror for a moment. "An old friend of his died about three hundred years ago, and V is trying to find a book he lent them." Instantly, the ghost relaxes. "I'm helping him look for it." The twins still seem suspicious but less threatening.

"A lost book, you say?" Brayden asks, looking amused. "And you think it's down here?"

"We hope so, anyway. They went missing, but the book wasn't in their room down here at the time. However," I eye Valda pointedly, "V here forgot that normal members keep things in hidey-holes sometimes. So we're hoping to get into the room they stayed in and search around."

"Oooo, a hunt, is it?" Aiden rubs his palms together. "What room was it?"

"That's another problem. V doesn't remember which was theirs. He's had so many friends over the years, he can't keep them all straight." My sarcasm makes the twins chuckle. "So, unfortunately, our first stop is the records room."

"Bummer," Brayden adds. "Well, good luck with that, you two." They both turn to start walking back the way they came, clearly no longer interested since it will involve some research.

"Might want to let Gav know you're here though," Aiden adds as they pick up their pace, wanting to get away before I ask for help. "Think he's got something for you." With that, the twins disappear around a corner.

"Some friends you have there, Lexi." Valda makes a tsking sound. "At least I've learned how to run them off should the need arise in the future. Hint that I might ask them for help researching something."

"For real! Not at all like Stone. He'd have been eager to do this stuff." Turning, I begin to make my way into the sanctum's records room.

"Wishing he were here, Lexi dear? Missing him already?" I know Valda is teasing me, but I can't help grumbling under my breath as I quicken my pace.

"That wasn't so bad." Valda says chipperly at my side. "It only took us two hours to find that my lost assistant's name was Olin, along with the room they lived in."

"Speak for yourself." To me, those two hours felt like twelve! I would have killed to have my music box with me. And I will never take that necklace—think he called it a torc—Stone bought me for granted again. Wonder what the range on that thing is?

"Come, come! We've finally made it to the exciting part. Aren't you itching to hunt for a hidey-hole? One that might hold new clues to my murder!"

"The only thing itching right now are my eyes from all that dust. Seriously, I think I sneezed fifty times in that records room!" I'm going to need a steamy AF shower to unclog my nose. You'd think there was some kind of spell to keep dust off things, but if there is the Guild sure isn't using it.

"Ah, here we are! How fortuitous that it's currently being used for storage." Yay, more dust. As I reach for the door handle, I get the scare of my life.

"What are you two up to?" I feel like I jump about six feet straight up. Fuck me, I forgot how quite that Cat Shifter can walk.

"You scared the shit out of me, Gav!" I shout, putting my hand over my racing heart for emphasis.

"Just means you still have a lot to learn about paying attention to your surroundings." Gav answers with a crooked smile. "Now, care to answer the question? You two have been acting odd since that incident at the vampire tower, and I'd like to know why." Crossing his arms over his chest, Gav waits for my reply.

"Like I told the twins, I'm helping Valda find a lost book," I begin answering my old mentor. But Valda interrupts before I can continue.

"Yes, indeed. Since my unfortunate prank, Lexi and I have become fast friends." Fast friends? Does he seriously think Gav is going to buy that? "I deeply regret how I treated our sassy human in the past. After many an apology, some recompense, and a few long conversations, I feel we are finally on equal footing." Valda actually beams over at me, while Gav gives us both disbelieving looks.

"His apologies really were genuine...eventually." Quickly, I decide convincing Gav that Valda and I are on good terms is for the best. "Plus, the money didn't hurt. And the groveling." I slide a sly smile at the ghost.

"Ha ha, human. Very funny. Imagine me groveling to anyone."

"Oh, I don't have to imagine it, I was there. You were on your knees–"

"Anyway," Valda cuts in, "as you can clearly see, we are getting along swimmingly these days. Why, I was the one who introduced her to her new beau." Shock! I'm in total shock that he brought up Stone that I freeze. "An old friend of mine actually. He's a rather capable young gentleman and an expert lover from–"

"Gav doesn't want to hear about my love life, V." Thankfully, I find my voice before this asshat of a ghost can continue.

"Ho, ho! Love, is it?" Damn it. "You do move fast, don't you, dear?" My cheeks are on fire. "Can't blame you for snatching up such a male. Good catch, but then again, I knew you two would work well together. Despite your differences."

"I didn't....we just....it's not." Turning to Gav, "We're not...I mean we've only just...." My brain is working too fast and too slow all at once. Valda laughs like he's our matchmaker.

"You don't owe me, or anyone else," Gav pointedly stares at the tittering Valda, "an explanation about that aspect of your life. I just wanted to make sure everything was alright with you. That you weren't doing anything under duress."

"Gav!" Valda looks affronted. "Do you honestly think I–"

"I'll leave you two to carry on with...whatever it is you are doing." Gav waves between us and the door to our backs. "Just know that I'm here for you if you need help or want to talk, okay?" I nod my head. "I'm your mentor, and that doesn't stop just because you're a full member, don't forget that." Backing up a few paces, he adds, "You'll have to tell me about your new fella sometime, kid."

"I'll tell you all about him once I finish helping Valda. Thanks, Gav."

"Anytime, Lexi. If you two will excuse me, I have a task of my own to see to." As he turns, I remember what the twins mentioned.

"Oh, the boys said you had something for me."

"More like a discussion about your future," he throws over his back. "One that can wait till you're not busy with a project. Good luck with finding that book." Turning a corner, he's gone. Wonder what he wants to talk to me about?

"Well, let's get crackin'!" Valda's excitement is instantly back, but I find my curiosity is torn. What aspect of my future does Gav want to discuss with me?

Chapter 33

Stone

The impromptu meeting with my Clan's priestess and her friend went well. After writing down all the necessary information, I shopped for and gathered the items needed for the spell. Auntie Sel offered to help me, of course, but it's simple enough that I believe I can accomplish it on my own. Also, I didn't want to invite someone else without speaking to my team first.

Standing at the end of Valda's long dining table, I realize I'm anxious as I adjust the items I collected for the hundredth time. What do I have to be anxious about? Leaving the table, I pace around the house. This seems to help Alexis think, so I decide to try it. After three passes between the dining room and kitchen, I realize this method is not for me. Instead of thinking, I found myself counting my steps. Flying, now that's how you think. Counting my steps has calmed me at least.

"We found it!" is quickly followed by the slamming of the front door. "Stone! Stone, are you here? Oh, there you are. Look, look, look!" Alexis waves a book in front of her as we rush towards each other. "Olin's journal was there! I can't believe we fucking found it!" She holds it over her head like an idol while hopping in place. Her exuberance has me smiling.

"I'm guessing Olin was the lost assistant's name?" She nods fervently while handing me the journal. "How did you find it? What does it say? Any secrets revealed?" Taking the book, I walk over to the dining table, preparing to read it myself.

"Well, we don't know yet, now do we?!" Valda enters the dining room clearly upset. "She wouldn't let me read it, beyond the first page stating who the journal belonged to."

"We couldn't read it without Stone! What's wrong with you?" My chest warms again with a slight rumble, which she must hear, "It, ah, it didn't seem right." Looking everywhere but at me, Aleixs notices my items on the table. "Plus, I can't read whatever language that is. Hey, what's all this?"

"That is what I was up to. But it can wait until we read through your discovery." Sitting down on the bench, I slide my notepad next to the journal, opening them both.

"Do you understand it?" Alexis is attempting to hover over my shoulder, but even seated she has to stretch to do so.

"Yes, it's Fae, which I am familiar with. Sit and I will read it to you." My thief only shakes her head.

"No, I'm too excited to sit. Just tell me what it says." She begins chewing on her thumbnail as she paces the length of the table. Quickly, I decide to not read it word for word, instead I'll get to the heart of the matter.

"Hmm, let's see," I begin to skim the pages. "Olin talks about Valda, whom he calls Valdemar, asking him to solve his murder."

"Oh gosh," Valda chuckles to himself, "I forgot I insisted on being called that for a time. How pretentious of me." He shakes his head like he's not still pretentious. "Carry on." Alexis and I share a look before I continue reading.

"Olin also thinks Valda was connected to the founders in some way." For Alexis's sake, I flip through the pages where he documents what we've already been through. He also notices the 'brothers' error within the sister's diary. "Here's something new, towards the end." After scanning the page, I summarize. "Olin heard, or read, not sure which they meant here. Anyway, Olin found out there were rumors of a deathbed confession made to a priestess by Aven Avenston himself. Olin thinks it must have been either the family or Clan Priestess." Scanning a few more pages, "Oh, interesting."

"What?" Alexis races over to look at the journal she can't read. "What's interesting?"

"One of the priestesses insisted on being entombed with all of her possessions. Olin hoped that it was done to hide a secret account of that deathbed confession." Translating as fast as I can in my head, "Yes, yes, he thinks he found the location of the tomb."

"Score! Way to go Olin!" Alexis resumes her pacing. "Ooo, this is getting good! Don't stop." Her excitement is infectious.

"Olin found the tomb and a sealed book with the body"—Alexis sucks in a breath—"but they couldn't read it." She lets the breath out with a disappointed sound. "Don't worry, my thief; they do not give up. The translation does seem to take some time though." Fanning through the pages to verify, "The direct translations must be with the book itself," shaking my head, "nothing like that is in here." Looking up at Valda, who kept himself back, I ask, "Where were you during all this? Olin states that they tried to get in touch with you several times. They seem quite upset as they think you could have translated the text easily yourself." Slowly, Valda drifts to stand directly across the table from me.

"I didn't know." It's a whisper. "I didn't know they had gotten so much, had learned new things, I..." Valda closes his eyes for a moment. "At that point, I had all but given up hope, having tried so many times already, asked for help that wasn't much help at all. I only asked Olin as an aside, like I was going through the motions, but didn't expect..." He trails off, lowering his gaze to the wooden table's surface. "It wasn't until they were gone, when I read a letter they left for me, that I even knew about this new diary. By then, it was far too late." Valda sounds truly remorseful about the whole situation.

"Does it say what they found out once it was translated?" Alexis sits next to Valda, moving the conversation forward. Nodding at her, I return to my quick translation.

"Wait. No. This can't be right, can't be correct." If it's true, this would shake the foundation of this city. I read it over and over again to myself, making sure I'm correct.

"Don't keep us in suspense, big boy! What is it?" Alexis is practically bouncing in her seat, while Valda stares wide-eyed.

"There was a twin." They gasp in unison. "The family priestess did indeed take the deathbed confession of Aven Avenston, the founder of this city. Aven had a twin brother, an older twin brother." I stare right at Valda. "Which would have made the brother the head of the family, not Aven." Alexis is rapidly looking between the ghost and myself.

"Valda, does that sound familiar? Do you think you might be the twin?" Alexis asks.

"I...I don't know?" Valda replies slowly.

"This is so soap opera coded. There's always an evil twin out there somewhere." I want to ask what she means by that, but she waves me to continue.

"According to Olin, Aven confessed to systematically erasing his twin from history."

"What? Why would he do that?" Alexis is shaking her head. "That's sus to me. What was he trying to hide, and where did the twin brother go?"

"Well, I see why he wanted to hide his brother. Valda, you aren't going to like it. Actually, many will find this a hard pill to swallow." Taking a deep breath, I'm about to go on, but Alexis cuts in.

"If you don't spill the tea already, I'm going to lose it! Enough with the suspense, Stone. Geez!" Her little outburst does lighten the mood, for a moment at least.

"I'll do my best, impatient little thief." Looking straight at Valda, "Aven erased his older brother from history to cover up a truth about the entire family. They were all born human." I let that statement hang in the air for a moment before I continue. "The twin brother refused to become a Raven Shifter like Aven wanted. He believed that it shouldn't matter, that they were building this city specifically for all types of beings, including humans." My eyes rest on Alexis for a moment.

"No. No, no." Valda stands, backing up.

"Aven confessed he tried desperately to convince his twin to change. That they wouldn't live long enough to shape the city, to see it grow as it should. But the twin wouldn't budge. He wasn't ashamed of being human and argued that they had done so much already while staying who they were. That he, or they, didn't need to change to earn the respect they already had."

Valda's just slowly shaking his head, not ready to accept what Olin found out.

"The confession stated that Aven told his family that the twin ran away after a fight, abandoning the family and their new city. That he told whatever lies he needed to to the rest of the people living or moving here who had already met the twins." Taking a moment, I jot down some notes, not wanting to miss certain verbiage Olin used.

"What really happened to the twin?" Alexis asks quietly.

"Aven never said, never explained what the truth was, to the priestess. But she," I take a breath, "had her theories."

"Say it, Stone." Valda says coolly. "Say it out loud."

"The priestess suspects that Aven either cursed or killed his twin brother."

"Oh, Valda, I'm sorry." My sweet thief extends a hand as if to touch him, stopping a breath away from his translucent shoulder. "I'm so, so sorry."

"Why are you sorry, Lexi dear? This family drama has nothing to do with me." Valda tries to steady himself, tries to put his pompous mask back on, but it doesn't work as well as he hopes. "You can't possibly believe that I'm a human. The very notion is ridiculous." He fiddles with his ghostly clothing. "Look at me. Why, I'm far too grand, too noble to be a mere human." He looks down his nose at Alexis. "This was a waste of Olin's time, and ours. Nothing but a red herring and ancient history."

"Valda, you can't deny the possibility that–" but he cuts me off.

"Enough! I don't want to hear anymore about this." Valda appears truly uncomfortable and I wonder if anything had began to resonate, but he's too afraid to face it. "What we really should be doing is finding my body. That is where the truth will be. Not some secondhand upon secondhand account that's nothing but hearsay."

"That is something I may be able to help with." Gently, I close the journal. "While you two were finding this, I was speaking with my Auntie Sel, our Clan Priestess." Getting up, I walk over to the end of the table where I put the spell items. "Sometimes, we guard homes that have unwanted spirits within them," I look pointedly at Valda, "which need to be removed."

"Are we going to banish him?!" Alexis is far too excited by that idea.

"You can't banish me, human. Better beings than you have tried." I do not like the way he's talking down to Alexis again.

"No," it accidentally comes out as a growl at the ghost, which surprises him. "Banishing is not a permanent solution nor do I find it to be an ethical one. Besides, we were hired to solve his death, not get rid of him."

"Fine," Alexis rolls her eyes, "no banishing. Then how do you evict unwanted ghosts?"

"We find what they are connected to, what physical item is keeping them here. It could be their body, a piece of their remains, the home itself, the murder weapon, their favorite chair, the rug they died on, a person they hated or loved."

"Wow, that's a lot of things it could be! How would you even begin to narrow that down? Then, how would you know for sure-for-sure you found the right thing?" Alexis asks while eyeing the various crystals, bottles, and herbs I have gathered.

"After consulting with various Mediums, Shamans, Necromancers, Deathwalkers, and Psychopomps over the years my Clan devised a simple spell that will bring the ghost in question directly to their item for a time." Peering up at Valda, "Similar to what happens to you once a year when you are dragged to your anchor unwillingly. I'm hoping this method will leave you cognizant instead of disoriented."

"Really? Is that possible?" Valda asks "I've never heard of such a thing." Seems like the ghost is starting to shake off his earlier shock, or repress it.

"It's not too common." I answer. "Plus, once it's done the ghost has moved on, which means they wouldn't have a chance to go around gossiping about it."

"So what's the plan, sir?" I can't help the physical reaction that occurs when she calls me sir. Given her facial expression, she did that on purpose.

"The plan is simple. We make our way back to the tunnels, around the area Valda thinks his body may be located. I do the spell, then Valda will stay wherever he appears, calling out to us until we find him. Then we'll search the area for anything of note. I have enough here to do the spell five times, should we need to."

"Yes, yes, this is what we should be doing!" Valda proclaims. "You are a genius, Stone! I never had a doubt you would come through for me. When? When can we do this?"

"We can do this as soon as we're ready and the club is open. I have my temporary pass, so we can walk right in. But Valda," I need to set his expectations to rights, "this may not be the end of our search. You only assume your body is your anchor. Even then, simply having a body does not solve a murder."

"Pish, tosh, Stone. I have a good feeling about this," Valda states while rubbing his hands together. "Yes, a very good feeling indeed." Looking all around his house, he thinks for a moment before he adds, "All my affairs are in order, so I'm ready whenever you two are."

"Tonight!" Alexis sounds shocked. "You want to go do this tonight?"

"Why not, Lexi dear! Stone has collected all the items, you've had a nap, and there'll be no problem getting in. The club should be opening soon, so all you need do is find a change of clothes." Alexis opens her mouth to argue, but Valda cuts her off. "Not that your green sack dress isn't lovely, but I think something else may be more appropriate."

"Oh, I've got just the appropriate outfit in mind, Valda." From the threatening way she's said it, I feel like the outfit in question will be anything but appropriate.

Chapter 34

Stone

After a quick change of clothes and packing of supplies, I fly us over and land near the club's entrance.

"Did you have to wear that?" I ask from the side of my mouth. Alexis insisted on wearing her thieving garb, cloak and all.

"Yes, I did," comes her sing-song reply. "If we're about to be doing goodness knows what in a bunch of dark tunnels, I want to be comfortable and prepared. I will not have a repeat of what happened last time." She's pulled down her hood to reveal her shorn hair. No wig and no jewelry, tonight she's ready to work.

"What happened last time wasn't all bad," I rumble as I snake my tail up her cloak.

"Keep it in your kilt, big boy." With a wink she adds, "Maybe later though." Flashing my pass, we're ushered in. With no paperwork to sign, the door attendant, who's dressed in a toga this time, bows as the inner door to the club opens.

"Patrolman Stone of the Gargoyle Clan of Avenston," the same three-tailed Kitsune greets us, "it is a pleasure to have you visit us this evening." Turning to Alexis, she takes in her outfit before glancing quickly at me again. "And Alexis Callaway," again the hostess pointedly looks at Alexis's clothes, then back to me.

"Oh! Yes, thank you." Whatever the Kitsune was trying to communicate seems to click for Alexis. "Stone is aware that I'm a member of the Thieves Guild, no worries there. We're an interesting couple, for sure." The hostess relaxes, smile more genuine now.

"Alexis Callaway of the Avenston Thieves Guild, it is a pleasure to have you join us this evening." Our hostess bows to us both, white toga pooling on the floor in front of her. "Do you have any questions or requests of us this evening?"

"Yes, two actually." Alexis takes charge. "First, is it okay for me to wear my own gear here?" She touches the skintight black clothing under her cloak. "You see, we would like to have a private room to play some," she looks coyly at me, "'catch a thief' games. Which leads me to my second question; do you have any rooms for that activity?"

"Of course, Alexis Callaway. To answer the first, yes, you may bring and wear your own costumes and clothing. As for the second, we have rooms for every fantasy." The hostess walks us over to a small table. "Tell me, were you seeking a room post- or pre-capture? We have dungeons and cells of several varieties."

"Pre-capture, please. I want to be caught in the act of stealing something. Either in the room itself or during a chase somewhere." I can't tell if Alexis is acting or genuinely excited by our cover story.

"Would you like to be stealing from an estate or a public building? We have an excellent museum setup, as well as a seaside chateau." The hostess glances between the two of us, patiently waiting.

"Oooo, that's a tough one. What do you think, big boy?" Alexis's hand rests on my forearm as she asks.

"I want you to steal something that sparkles. My pretty thief looks magnificent in things that sparkle."

"We will make sure the mistress of this chateau has excellent jewels, ripe for the taking." The Kitsune offers a devious grin flashing a hint of fang. "Any other requests for the room?" She has begun writing on a slip of paper, parameters for those who shape the enchantments of the fantasy rooms.

"Night time, can it be at night?! Oh, oh, a stormy night!" Our hostess laughs quietly at my thief's exuberance.

"Of course, guildsmen. Thunder, lightning, and rain?" Alexis nods emphatically. "Anything else?"

"No, that will be more than enough, thank you. I will need to visit the toy room for cuffs and such. I'd like to pick items myself this time."

"Of course, Patrolman. You will be notified once your fantasy room is ready." With one last bow, she's gone. I steer Alexis into the toy and costume rooms to choose items I would want if we were to actually use this room tonight.

"Is she really going to be able to make all that happen? How? It is a magicked room? Is all this expensive? No one has talked about price to me yet. Did you get something about it in your letter?" Alexis has a lot of questions this evening.

"Yes, I have no reason to doubt the ability of this establishment to create such a space for us. Fantasy rooms are enchanted to the specifications of the guests, usually bigger than they seem. While playrooms are predesigned rooms with little to minimal magicks involved. I would assume they have bondage playrooms, stage playrooms, bathing playrooms–"

"Wow! Really? Man, we have got to explore this place more." I chuckle as I point out the cuffs I want to the toy attendant.

"As far as payment goes, we signed an agreement that they may collect our sexual energy as compensation. They collect such energy from all the patrons here. Using it or selling it to make their profits."

"What? That's it, that's all they want?" Obediently she holds out her wrist as I test out several cuffs and bindings on her.

"Yes. Sexual energy is extremely potent and can be used in many different ways. Some beings feed on it, so they will buy as is. It can be used in fertility rites, love potions, or simply as raw magical energy." Cuffs selected, I move on to the connected room to find the various Order sashes. Tonight I chose the dark blue of an investigator, instead of the chartreuse of a patrolman.

"That's wild! And amazing. So, the more sexual energy given to a place the better. Guess that's why they wanted you so bad." She gives me a long look up and down before adjusting my sash. "You put on a show."

"Correct. Not only do I generate sexual energy for myself and my partner, but in all those who watch." Glancing down at my thief, I lick my lips remembering the show we put on the last time we were here.

"Pardon my intrusion, but your room is ready whenever you are." A new attendant has come to fetch us. This one is a short male satyr with curly brown hair and freckles.

The attendant shows us to our room, which is down a hall to the left of the main open playroom. He demonstrates their notification system by pressing the green panel, indicating the room is in play, and asks us to press the red panel once done to indicate when we are finished with the room. Once inside, we may press a yellow panel if we wish no one else to enter. Seems if we wander down this hall and see a green room, we may enter if we like to join in on any fantasies in progress.

Alexis is absolutely floored when we enter our room, stepping inside the foyer of a large elegant mansion. Thunder claps while lightning briefly illuminates the twin staircases before us. This enchantment is expertly crafted.

"It's like the damn holodeck!" she exclaims while striding over to touch a carved stone banister. "It feels so real! Stone, are you seeing this?!" Turning, I thank the attendant while closing the door, pressing the yellow panel once it's shut.

"As much as I would love to explore this space with you, and trust me I would, we have a job to do here tonight."

"Right, right, sorry." She looks around longingly as another slash of lightning flashes. "Can't we just snoop around a little?" Her plea makes me laugh.

"Before we leave, I'll tell the hostess to save this scenario for us. Claiming to have enjoyed it so much we will wish to visit it again sometime soon. How's that?" She hops up to kiss my cheek.

"Sounds like a plan." Smiling up at me, standing so near, she continues. "Speaking of plans, how do we want to get to the closet? I'm pretty sure this hall loops around to the no-play zone, opening near the food area back there. So, we should go that way to avoid being seen by that foxtailed lady." I nod at her suggestion.

"I think we should also go separately," I add, "meeting in the closet. That way, if anyone questions us we can claim to have needed a snack."

"Agreed, less suspicious to be alone. Definitely might get questions if we both leave the room we just requested." She eyes the space longingly again, "Who should go first? I wouldn't mind–"

"No. I'll not spend an hour waiting in a cleaning closet for you while you forget about me to explore this manor." I cross my arms in front of my chest, easily reading what she intended to do upon her face.

"Fine, I'll go first. Geez, it's like you don't trust me or something." She laughs, "You're totally right though, I wouldn't have been able to stop myself from wandering around. I'm dying to see these jewels!" She laughs again, full and carefree as it echoes around the foyer.

"I enjoy working with you, Alexis Callaway. It's...fun." Stroking her cheek with a knuckle, "You always keep things interesting."

"Hey now, if you keep being sweet we won't be discovering a dead body tonight like we hope." Grabbing both my horns, she brings my head down to kiss the tip of my nose. "I like working with you too, Stone." Before I can claim her lips in a kiss, she darts away to the door. "See you in a bit!" Just like that, she's gone, leaving me alone with a cock that's all too eager to play with her.

Chapter 35

Alexis

After sneaking a few apples into my cloak, I make it into the supply closet without issue. Chomping away as I wait, I get halfway through a second apple before Stone enters. Quickly, we open the secret passage and jog down the stairs where Valda is waiting. We agreed earlier to move quicker this time as we don't know how long it will take to find Valda's anchor.

With two Fairy Lights apiece, hovering above and in front of us both, we are able to continue jogging down the tunnels without issue. Soon, we find ourselves at the cave-in site, scrambling through the hole we created during our last visit. We follow Valda in silence further until we come to an area that looks like a ruined town. It's kind of eerie with broken streets and crumbling buildings.

"Alright," Valda stops, "I think this is close to the area I sometimes find myself when I come to."

"Excellent. Search around for a clearer space I can cast in," Stone tells the group. "Maybe someplace flatter than the streets?"

"Last I saw, there were some buildings holding up relatively well around the corner from here." The ghost leads us to a ruin that might have once been a shop. "Here we are. This one's not so bad!" Stone and I cautiously enter.

"So, how does this work exactly? You doing the spell? Do I need to help or something? Can you even do magic?" I pepper Stone with questions as I help clear off a patch on the floor inside.

"Alexis, Gargoyles are made from magic. We use magic when we encase and heal. Of course, I can do a simple spell with the right ingredients and instruction." Well damn, don't I feel silly. Of course, Stone wouldn't have come down here to work a spell if he thought he couldn't. "No, I will not need your energy or involvement for this. All you need do is hand me the ingredients from your cloak pockets as I ask for them." Stone looks at me then, "Unless workings make you uncomfortable? If that's the case, you do not need–"

"No, no," I wave off his concern, "I'm fine. Doesn't bother me at all. Just tell me what you need, chef!" We spend the next few minutes placing items in a circle as he mumbles some words I don't understand. Eventually, I guess he's done with the setup when he calls for Valda, who's stayed outside in the streets.

"Valda, you ready?" comes Stone's booming voice, echoing off the walls.

"Yes," the ghost replies, poking his head inside.

"What happens next?" I'm getting a little antsy, eager to get out of the creepy place.

"I will step within the circle, saying a few words and giving energy as I complete the spell. Then, if everything works, Valda will disappear from here to reappear where his anchor is." He nods at Valda. "He will stay exactly in place and yell for us, if he is able."

"So we just gonna Marco Polo this?" I ask with a smile.

"What is Marco Polo?" Stone asks. Shoot, that's a real world historical human, which means they've never heard of him or the game named after him.

"Oh, it's a child's game where I come from. One kid is blind-folded or trusted to keep their eyes closed, and calls out 'Marco' to which the other kids playing reply with 'Polo.' The object of the game is for the blind kid to find the others by sound. It's a silly call and response thing." My explanation sounds stupid. It's a game that everyone just seems to learn through assimilation as a kid.

"Hmm, this could work." Stone says thoughtfully. "Valda, you will be Polo, and I will be Marco. We will call back and forth to each other until we find you."

"Well, I think I should be Marco," Valda counters, "as I should be the one to start the game."

"But Marco is the seeker, and we do not want you moving at all. I will be Marco, as I am the one trying to find you. Those are the rules, are they not, Alexis?" Stone asks.

"Well, of course she's going to take your side; she likes you more," Valda complains.

"It is not a matter of popularity. It is about the rules," Stone growls back.

"Enough, you two!" I shout to break up this petty squabble. "Maybe I am playing with kids after all. Stone is right though, Valda. Marco is the one seeking, while Polo is to be found." Stone looks smug, but Valda looks about ready to argue some more. "Now, if you two children are ready," I eye them both like an upset auntie, "can we get started?"

Stone steps into the circle, nodding at Valda before he begins chanting. Soon, a fog forms at Stone's feet, covering the whole of the circle. Moments after that, Valda vanishes. Shit! That was faster than I thought it would be. After a few final words, Stone steps out of the circle, then onto the street.

"Marco!" he booms. There is no response. We both walk further along the path. "Marco!" Another booming call. We wait again but nothing. Walking a few more paces, Stone takes another deep breath, preparing to shout.

"Polo." It's not very loud.

"You're supposed to shout!" Stone bellows before another "Marco" erupts from him.

"Polo." Still not very loud, his reply almost sounds pissy. Is Valda really upset about being Polo instead of Marco?

"Marco!" We continue our walk down the broken street, getting nearer and nearer to Valda.

"Is this really necessary?" Valda asks, sounding closer. "I could just keep talking until you two find me, after all."

"That is not what we agreed on, Valda. Marco!" It's taking everything within me not to laugh at this interaction.

"This is absurd, Stone! I can hear that you're near me now. I could even come to meet you, then lead you to where I appeared." Valda increases his voice, "Clearly I'm fully myself this time!"

"Don't you dare move!" Stone rumbles. "We need to know exactly where you stand. Marco!" O.M.G. I am going to lose it over here.

"Fine, fine, I won't move an inch. But I'm not saying Polo anymore."

We've made our way to what must have been a market or center at one point. Many streets branch off from here, it's more open, and there's a fountain in the middle. Well, what used to be a fountain anyway.

"Oh, oh! Polo! Polo!" Valda shouts excitedly. "I can see you, well, at least with one of my eyes." I look around everywhere but don't see a thing.

"Wave your arms or something, Valda, we can't see you," I say. "What can you see, describe it."

"Well, I'm mostly in the ground, up to my shoulders," Valda begins to answer. "Then half my face is also inside something, because it's dark. I'm waving an arm. Can't you see me yet?"

Down in the ground? Makes sense, I guess. Spinning in place, I scan the ground where larger rocks and debris are. Who knew finding a mostly transparent, mostly buried person would be so hard to do in the mostly dark space? There! I catch movement at the corner of my eye near the fountain's base. Finally I can make him out, a wildly waving opaque arm, right next to half a head.

Immediately I burst out laughing! How could I not?! Valda's extremely angry face is poking out of the ground within what must have been the rim of the fountain.

"Look at your furious little face," I mock in baby talk. Stone is already at the fountain, inspecting the area, blatantly ignoring my laughter.

"If you do not stop laughing at me right this minute, I'll make sure you get no sleep until I cross over." Valda's one eye narrows at me, "I've done it before and I'll do it again."

"That's enough." Stone chides us calmly. "This is exactly how and where you arrived from the spell?"

"Well, I'm not down here for the view, now am I?! Of course this is exactly where I came to!" Valda is sounding more irate by the second. "May I get up now, oh master of the undead? As Lexi has not-so-kindly pointed out, this is very undignified."

"For this, I thank you. But, before you move, could you kneel down to see if you are standing on anything?" Stone looks reverently at the fountain and the plaque upon the ground in front of the ghostly head. "I would hate to damage this piece of Avenston history needlessly."

"What is it?" I ask while moving forward. I can tell there is something carved there, but can't read it with Stone's bulk in the way.

"It's the foundation stone." Reverently he runs his hand over the carved letters. "The first stone laid upon the cobbled streets of Avenston. It says that Aven placed this stone himself."

"Bones!" Valda's head emerges from the ground as he exclaims. "There are bones down there, Stone, right where my feet are!" Without prompting, he levitates up through the foundation stone. "To think, I've been right here all this time!" Valda floats around the fountain. "No wonder no one could ever see where I came from, I would have simply appeared within the water of this fountain." Glancing over to my frozen Gargoyle, "Well, crack to it, my boy! Time to dig up my body!"

With a resigned sigh, Stone begins to work his claws around the seam of the foundation stone, clearly trying to preserve it as best he can. Helping where possible, I move rubble from around the area. Finally wiggling it out, Stone walks the precious artifact away from the fountain, setting it down gently.

"Wish we had thought to bring shovels," I grunt as I attempt to pull up a cobblestone from around the void Stone left. "Can't believe we didn't think about that!" His rumbling chuckle behind has me craning my neck to look at Stone.

"Why would you need a shovel when you have a Gargoyle at your side?" Lifting me up, Stone walks me to where he set the foundation stone. "Stay." It's an order. Stretching his arms in preparation, Stone walks back to our excavation site. Squatting down, he gives me one last glance before he begins to tear into the earth.

Like a dog from a gardener's nightmare, Stone rips up and flings rubble, then dirt, back behind him. Occasionally around him as well. Sprays of debris fly all around! I can see why Stone put me and the slab so far away. Not gonna lie, it's impressive. In no time at all, Stone has made quite the hole in the ground. Slowing his pace, I begin to hear sweeping sounds from the hole as I see his wings dip.

"If you have issues with death or remains, you may wish to not look within this hole. Valda was right; there is a body here." As quickly as I can, I race over to see for myself. Sure enough, Stone has uncovered a full skeleton, tattered clothes and all.

"Whoa!" It's all I can think to say as I peer down at the half-covered skeleton. Stone leaps out of the hole effortlessly, choosing to stare down with me. "Valda, do you feel anything? Any new memories come up?" Looking up at our ghost companion, who's floating on the other side of the grave, I await an answer. He's still, eyes searching, for a time.

"No." Valda says reluctantly. "No, I don't feel anything. Why don't I remember, Stone? I thought...I thought that once we found..." He can't seem to continue as his face morphs into confused sorrow.

"Here, let me look the body over. Maybe there's something on it that will trigger memories for you." Carefully, I hop down. As gently as possible, I move what clothing remains, searching for pockets. Several coins fall out of a leather pouch. But aside from buttons and a small knife, there's nothing else.

"Well, I think we can rule out a mugging since all the money's here. Knife is still sheathed too, so he wasn't expecting any trouble." I scan the clothes over again. "I don't see any blood, so if there's an injury we'd have to roll him over on his back. No, wait, look at the skull." Moving closer to the head, I examine the spiderweb fissures there. "I think someone hit him in the back of the head! See how these cracks radiate out from this deeper depression." Leaning over the lip of the hole, Stone examines where I'm pointing.

"That could be." Glancing up, "Valda, how does your ghostly head feel? Any blood or injuries under your hair at the back of your skull?" Slowly, Valda lifts his hand, feeling around the back of his head.

"No, I....I don't feel anything back there. Maybe that's why I don't remember though," he drops his arm, "because I was hit in the head from behind?"

"Sounds plausible." Stone hmm's as he thinks. "We may need to bring others in on this now that we have found a body. Experts would know better." Standing, he looks at our disappointed ghost. "I am sorry we were not able to solve your murder tonight like you had hoped. But we are very close, much closer than I think you have ever been."

"Yes," Valda sounds so dejected. "You are right; this is good progress. I thank you both. Stone," he dips his head at the Gargoyle, "Alexis," head dips to me. "You have done well this night. If you can find your own way back, I might stay here for a while."

"Of course," Stone peers down at me. "You did well down there, thief of my heart. How do you know so much about this?" he asks while gesturing at the body.

"I've watched more than a few crime shows in my day." Stone gives me a puzzled look. "I'll explain later, here, help me up." As I stand, I notice a glint. "Whoa, whoa, wait!" Crouching down again, "There's something else here." Just to the side of the body, still mostly buried is a carved crystal of some kind. Gently I wipe away the damp earth. It's more than just a crystal. "It's a cane! There's a cane down here."

Chapter 36

Alexis

Taking the corner of my cloak, I wipe down the length of the cane. "I think the shaft is made from ivory or possibly bone." Eventually I work it free, holding it up to get a better look. The crystal in the end is black, like onyx, and carved into the shape of a bird's head.

"That's it." Valda whispers next to me, making me almost drop the cane in surprise. "That's what I'm tied to. This was my cane!" Slowly, he reaches out his hand to touch it. As ghostly fingers wrap around its length, his eyes drift shut. "I remember." Without any further words, he drifts up to hover in front of the fountain.

"Hey, hey, get me out of here." I hurriedly call to Stone, not wanting to miss a moment of whatever's about to happen. Effortlessly, Stone hauls me out.

"My brother and I came here alone one night to discuss final approval for the fountain. Everyone else was away celebrating Hallows Eve, but we...we were so driven, constantly working on our dreams to build a grand city. But we got into a fight." Valda begins to circle the fountain, clutching the cane. "He was so stubborn! We were so loud I feared someone would hear us, but no one did." He pauses his story after a mirthless chuckle. "No one did..."

"So your brother killed you that night," Stone fills in the rest of the story. "He then buried you here, under the foundation stone of this city, thereby making the center of the city your grave. That's why you were able to roam everywhere."

"Killed me? No, my brother didn't kill me." Before our eyes, Valda begins to rapidly age, eventually shifting to that of a wizened old man. "I...I am the killer. My twin lies within that grave." Pearlescent tears begin cascading down the ghost's face. "It's my walking stick that ended him. My name is Aven Avenston, and I murdered my brother."

The silence that follows that statement is deafening. I don't think either of us is breathing as we both process what we just heard.

"But, why?" My question is barely a whisper. "Why did you kill him?"

"He wouldn't listen to me," resounds, full of emotions. "He was adamant about remaining a human. Said it was what this town needed to be truly integrated, and my siblings would follow whatever he did. None of them would change without him. It seems so stupid now!" the ghost yells, angry with himself. "To kill him over that, to erase him from history! I even burnt our old house down before my death, in fear of his name being carved within its walls." The old man before us falls to his knees, clutching the cane close to his chest. His grief has me tearing up.

"I couldn't have anyone knowing how weak I once was, how weak...Goddess forgive me, what have I done?! My brother, my own brother." Valda—er, Aven—begins to rock as he cries. "I deserved these hundreds of years of torment, wandering the very city we dreamed of creating, a dream I stole from him. Valer, oh

Valer, I am so sorry!" he begins to wail. "You should have been the one to live, the one everyone remembers, not I."

Sniffling, Aven's head lifts up to me, mouth open as if to say something. But something stops him, his eyes dart to stare just to the right of us. Turning my head, I can't see whatever is it that has him frozen in place.

"No," he whispers, "I don't deserve it. I don't deserve to cross over." Trembling, Aven begins to back away, hand out in front as if to ward something off. "It can't be now, just as I finally remember what I've done." Clutching onto Stone, I'm suddenly afraid. Afraid of whatever it is that I can't see, of whatever is moving closer to Aven Avenston, the murderer. Stone wraps me tight in his arms as I look around wildly.

As the silence stretches, Aven's face becomes less afraid. Fear being replaced with calmness, perhaps even hope. He stops backing away, staring intensely at blank air.

"I understand." Glad one of us does! "My Reaper has finally come to collect me," Aven begins, attention back on us. "Thank you, my friends. You will never understand how truly grateful I am to you both. And Lexi, I am genuinely sorry for the way I treated you. Being human was never the weakness I believed it to be, something you proved to me time and time again." After a low bow to us both, he turns to walk away but stops after two steps.

"You two work well together. It truly would be a shame for you to stop now." Pointing between us, the old man adds, "Have you thought about striking out on your own? Taking the chance that's been denied to you, Stone. Doing something more worthwhile than simply stealing, Lexi."

"What, like becoming PIs?"

"What?" Both Stone and Aven say in unison.

"A gumshoe...a sleuth, a shamus, a dick." Blank stares all around. "A Private Investigator, guys."

"Well, whatever you want to call yourselves, you should seriously think about it. Goodbye, my PIs, till we meet again in the life beyond this." With the clatter of a falling cane, Aven turns away once more. My old ghost rival fades with each step he takes until it's just Stone and me, alone in an underground city. At least, I hope we're actually alone now.

"Damn it, I didn't expect to cry when he finally left." With tears running down my cheeks, I twist in Stone's arms, planting my face into his chest. Stone is silent as he holds me close.

"It was a very sad story, but he walked with his Reaper knowing that his brother is no longer forgotten. And we will share his story, even though it will shake the city to its core."

"Can we shake the city tomorrow?" I plead. "I feel like we've done enough for one day."

"Of course, there is time enough to rewrite history later, thief of my heart." With a final squeeze that takes my breath from me, he lets go. "We'd better head back up now if that's the case. Should they notice our absence, we'll have to explain all this before we are ready."

"Fuck that!" Taking his dirty hand in mine, "If we hurry, we might still be able to explore our room upstairs. That is, if my Stone is up for it?" We begin to walk back together, hand in hand.

"Oh, am I your Stone now? Thought you only claimed me while in the throes of passion?" The tone is teasing, but the underlying question is a serious one.

"Yeah, I guess you're mine. Suppose I like you enough to keep you around." His laugh echoes around us.

"Is that so? You like me, huh?"

"There could be some love in there too...maybe...just a little...against my will. I'll blame that goddess of yours for that." I can't help the smile that springs to my lips on admitting it out loud. It's been a long time since I felt the stirrings of love, but if Stone can admit it, then so can I.

It's been a crazy few weeks! What with the discoveries we've made and the changes that ensued thereafter, it's been wild. Once Stone reported the news to the Order, teams were dispatched, not only to the gravesite but also to the tunnel where the lost assistant Olin lay entombed. Historians, along with those higher up the food chain, were eager to get their hands on the deathbed confession of Aven Avenston.

Even after all we had done, Stone's boss, Chief Metis, couldn't promise Stone an Investigator's position. Not now anyhow, which is a song Stone had heard before. After a lengthy conversation with me, he gave up his position as a patrolman of the Order to start a business with me. Today, we signed the contracts for an office space, and I couldn't be more excited! Never imagined myself as a PI, but everything just felt right about this. True, with what Valda left us we have more than enough money to live a life of luxury for several lifetimes, but neither of us is near ready to retire.

"How did we get roped into helping you move furniture around in here?" Aiden complains.

"Yeah, don't you have a big strong Gargoyle to do this kinda stuff?" Brayden adds. I learned early on that curiosity can get these Fox Shifters to do all kinds of things.

"Stone's busy finalizing some paperwork, and I couldn't wait to get in here. I've got a vision that can't be denied!" I make a motion with my hands so the twins scooch the desk to the left. "It's your own fault for showing up, really."

"We just wanted to see what this whole private investigator thing was all about," Aiden says while shifting the desk he's holding.

"We didn't expect to become interior decorators." Brayden adds while setting the desk down.

"Don't be ridiculous. I'm the interior decorator. You two are my grunts." I laugh at the look they give me in unison.

"Well, these grunts are leaving! Good luck with your 'vision,' dick." Once hearing that term for PIs, the boys preferred that name to all the others. "Oh," Aiden adds while inching towards the door, "Gav says you better not be late to your Shifter training today. Still can't believe you chose cat over fox." The twins shake their heads disappointedly, but the cat within me only purrs.

"If you can't believe that, then you don't get me as well as you think." Walking them out the door, I wave them off with a reply, "Tell Gav I promise not to be late...this time." Closing the door, I get the surprise of my life when turning around. The bookstore owner, the woman who trapped me in this book so many months ago, is here sitting in a chair that definitely isn't mine.

"How did you get in here?!" Seriously, how?! Since becoming a Cat Shifter, no one has been able to sneak up on me. Let alone with a piece of furniture in tow!

"The same way you did, my dear. Through your book." My heart thumps wildly as she just sits in the winged back chair, cool as a cucumber. Nervously, I lick my lips, still plastered to the closed door, as I ask the question I already know the answer to.

"Why are you here?" Her melodic laugh fills the space as she stands, gliding over towards me.

"Because you've reached the end of your story. Your tale is complete, so it's time to come home." Silently I'm shaking my head, unable to speak. "Oh yes, I'm afraid we have finally made it to your," she emphasizes the last words, "happily ever after." Frantically, I try to open the door at my back, but the damn thing seems to be locked!

"Goodness, are you trying to run away from me?" More tinkling laughter. "No, this won't do at all. Come." Slowly she backs away, sitting in her chair once more. "Let's all calm down and have a nice civilized conversation. I understand this must seem jarring for you." She gestures at an ottoman that is suddenly across from her, but I sit on the desktop instead, not wanting to be too close.

"The story isn't over yet!" I begin, ready to argue with her. "We've only just signed the contract for this place–"

"Today," she cuts in. "Today, you have signed the last of the paperwork needed to start your new endeavor with the Gargoyle you were destined to love." I swallow thickly as she continues. "Now the book fades to black with the promise of future success in career and romance. The end."

"No, no, not the end!" Tears began to sting my eyes. "It's only the beginning. We've only just opened and...and I'm moving in with Stone next week." Hopping off the desk, I begin to pace. "So this can be the end of one book," I add, trying to bargain, "and the next can be about another harrowing case as we find our PI groove and discuss the next stage of our relationship." The shop owner is already shaking her head.

"I'm afraid that's not how it works, my dear." She continues sympathetically, "Only one book, only one adventure is available to you. The magic—"

"I'm not leaving!" I shout defiantly. "You'll have to kill me first and drag my corpse out of here!" The cat within me bristles, ready for a fight. I wish I had become a Shifter sooner. If I had, I'd be able to change right now and dart out an open window or something.

"Whoa, whoa, no one is killing anybody." She's come to the edge of her seat, hands raised in an attempt to calm me. "I have no intention of dragging you out of here, dead or otherwise. So calm yourself, child."

"You," my breathing is heavy, eyes darting all around still searching for an escape, "you won't make me leave?"

"Goodness no! I don't make people do anything." She sounds indignant while straightening out her skirt, sitting back more comfortably. "Honestly, the reactions I get sometimes. Many are relieved to see me, I'll have you know," she says while shaking a finger at me. "Now sit!" She points to her ottoman. "So we may have a serious discussion about your options and the choice you are making." Slowly, I sink onto the ottoman, keeping my eyes trained on her.

"If," she looks pointedly at me, "you decide to stay, you must understand that you will never be able to leave. This, right here, is your only chance to ever return to your world. So I need you to really think about what that means." Nodding my head to show her I understand, she continues to drive the point home. "There will be no second chance, no future opportunity to return."

"I understand." The face she makes clearly suggests I don't. "Once you leave, you'll never come back to fetch me again. This is it, and I get that. But lady," her brow arches at that, "I never intended to leave here anyway."

"Pardon?" Clearly she hadn't expected that.

"Are you kidding? This is like a dream come true!" Standing again, I wave my hand out towards the city beyond my windows. "I knew almost as soon as I arrived here that I'd never be leaving. And the longer I've stayed, the more certain I've become that this is the place I'm meant to be." Walking back over, I take her hands. "So please, please let me stay. I promise I'm not doing this for some man, though he is amazing. I'm doing this for me. This is where I want to be; this is the future I choose." Smiling down at me, she nods.

"I hear you, I believe you, and I wish you all the luck." She squeezes my hands affectionately.

"Really?! I can stay?!"

"Who am I to deny your truest wish? Yes, of course you can stay. I, however, cannot." Releasing her hands, I step back, letting her stand. "Do you have any questions or concerns before I leave you?" Whoa, where did the stool and chair go?!

"Um, yeah..." I look around behind her for a second before coming back to the question. "Yes! Can you take a letter to my family?" Frantically I search for some paper in my mostly empty office. "Just want to tell them that I'm finally going off on that wild adventure to unknown lands I kept threatening to take for most of my life."

"Sounds reasonable enough." Suddenly, paper, quill, and an envelope appear atop the empty desk. Quickly, I scribble out a message full of my love, asking them not to worry and that I'm more excited and happy than I've been in a long time. After perusing its contents, the shop owner folds the letter, placing it within the envelope.

"This means a lot to me. Thank you." At my words the shop owner smiles and pats my shoulder.

"Oh, it's just a letter, dear."

"I mean, for everything. For bringing me here, letting me have this adventure, allowing me to change my life completely." Don't cry, don't cry, don't cry. "Thank you."

"Of course, my darling." She wraps me in one of the best hugs I've ever had. "It's my truest calling in life." With an unexpected rap on the door, we break the hug.

"Who could that be?" I ask. Facing her, "Let me answer that real quick, then I'll get you an address." Striding over to open the door, I find myself facing three green Goblins in...suits? Are these creatures actually wearing suits?

"It has come to my attention," the Goblin, who's clearly the ring leader of the bunch, "that you, along with the Gargoyle, Stone, are opening up an independent investigative service, is that correct?"

"Yes, we're in the process of opening for business. We plan to start taking clients very soon." Before I can continue, the leader cuts in.

"Excellent. I believe I have a case that your partner would be incredibly interested in assisting me with. May we come in?" Not wanting to turn away our first prospective client, I wave them in.

"Of course, please step inside. Sorry about the lack of furniture, sir. Let me wrap up my business with...huh." Turning back to the rest of the office, I find it empty. The bookshop owner, and her furniture, have disappeared without a trace. "Looks like I'm all yours, gentlemen. What can we do for you?" Hopping back up to sit on my new desk, I try not to worry about the fact I never gave that woman the address to my brother's house. Not sure if I should be impressed or worried about that? Guess I'll just have faith that my farewell letter gets delivered nonetheless.

Epilogue

Harvey

The Woman appears from the back room with a letter in her hand.

"I've got a little errand to run, Harvey, my dear. I trust you'll mind the shop while I'm away." A long plum-colored cloak appears in her hand before she makes it to the front door. Twirling it around herself, she looks back at me perched on the wooden counter.

Reluctantly, I meow at her, confirming that I heard what she said. Obviously I did since we were in the same room when she said it.

"Fantastic. Thank you, Harvey." The bell tings as she opens the door to leave. "Don't do anything I wouldn't do." With a wink, she's gone, bell sounding around the empty store.

Lazily, I stretch my body, preparing to have an unobserved exploration around the stacks. Not wanting to appear too eager, of course. That would be quite unbecoming for a feline of my caliber. Taking my time, I walk the length of the counter, away from the front door. Despite the oddness of my new home, it still belongs to me, so I am confident in my walk, strutting with my tail held high.

Leaping gracefully, I land expertly on the floor before continuing my leisurely strides to the back staircase, the one that leads to the second floor. The floor that is never for visitors, only for the changed books they leave behind. This is where I found the book that smells like my Silvia. Well, mostly anyway. At first, it primarily smelled of her as she was, but as time passes it smells more and more of an altered version of her.

Finding my human's scent so strongly upon a book confused me at first. That is, until the first visitor came. Then I saw what happens here, humans going into books. The Woman assured me everything was fine, that all those who entered chose to stay and were even given a second opportunity to leave later.

I didn't believe her at first, of course. But I've come to learn she speaks the truth. Some humans immediately return, scared and running away babbling how they're going crazy. Others come back after some time has passed; some sad, some terrified, and some in shock. Then there are those like my Silvia who never return at all.

What really convinced me that those who stayed were well was the scent of happiness that drifted from the used books. Silvia's scent was easy to discern, as I knew her smells well. Eventually I discovered similar tangs upon the others who stayed within.

For the moment, I am content in knowing my Silvia is happy. Not that I didn't try to join her at first. Once I knew what was going on, I knocked her book off the shelf and tried desperately to jump into it. The Woman only laughed at my 'antics' while explaining it was impossible to get in that way again. Seems once a book is used, that's it. I also tried a few blank books, but the result was the same.

So here I will remain until I can find a way to get to where my human is. It's not so bad here though. The Woman, I really should give her a name, gives me food and treats aplenty.

I also enjoy the unique individuals who come here. Many lavish me with praise and affection. I always knew I was a handsome cat, something my time here has reaffirmed.

Finding Silvia's book, I sniff it. Checking it, as I often do, to make sure she's still happy. Hers is a forest green with gold lettering framed by gold bees. This makes me glad for her, as she did once have such a fondness for bees and honey. Moving on, I find the newest book in the collection up here. This one is a nighttime shade of purple with silver words framed by silver chains. This is the woman who knew the meaning behind my name, Harvey.

Sniffing it to make sure she's happy as well, I get a surprise. Somehow she smells strongly of feline. Why would this human smell like a cat? Just as I think I find the answer to one riddle, more always appear. Hearing the ting of the door's bell I know The Woman has returned. She's never gone long.

"Harvey dear, I brought home tuna," she sings out. The involuntary meow of happiness embarrasses me. I try not to seem too eager with her, but it's tuna! Vaulting down the stairs, I race through the shelves, springing up onto the counter. I offer her another meow as I impatiently await my tuna. Once the plate is set before me, I attack it with gusto. This Woman knows my weakness.

"How is Silvia today?" I pause long enough to meow. "Good, good. And Alexis, our newest arrival?" A questioning meow this time. "I was wondering if you would pick up on that." The Woman strokes my back twice as I eat. "Your nose isn't wrong, my fine feline friend, she has become part cat herself." Another meow full of questions before I lick the plate clean. "Oh, you don't want all the answers right away, now do you, Harvey? Where's the fun in that?"

Taking my empty plate, she glides into the back room, a room that holds its own mysteries. She goes in there sometimes, then just disappears. Perhaps that shall be the next thing I seek to discover more about within this bookshop?

The bell above the door rings as I am cleaning my face. Today, it's a younger man with hair the color of a golden retriever, though I won't hold that against him. When she greets the man, I witness the same expressions of shock and awe they all show at first. He is no different. No doubt she will offer him the same deal she offers the rest. I know she gains something from this exchange with humans, and I mean to find out what that is. Someday.

The End

Review

———◄○►———

T HANK YOU so much for reading my silly little adventure.

If you enjoyed *The Tale of Alexis & the Straitlaced Gargoyle*, please leave a review anywhere you like to review books. Even if it's just some stars.

You have no idea how important your reviews are for a self-published and indie author. Just a moment of you time to rank a book is crucial for others to take a chance on an unknown author or book. You will never know how much we truly appreciate it.

Author Notes

A lexis's book has been a long time coming, and I'm so glad I've finally gotten to share her story, especially since she's been yelling in my head for many years now. Alexis and her Gargoyle and ghost companions were actually going to be my first book. I understood her character inside and out before I even knew who Silvia was. But at the time I didn't feel like I was quite ready to write Alexis's...spicier scenes. Seeing as how I had never written one before, you may understand why I was nervous. That's when Silvia stepped up to the plate for me. She and Torbin were so sweet and felt easier to attempt. So I decided to be gentle on myself and put Alexis on hold.

Personally, I think it was the best choice I could've made. However, this did upset Alexis a bit. So when it was finally time to write book two, she was silent in my head, which was a little perturbing, considering how insistent she had been two years before. But even that turned out to be a blessing in disguise. With her silence, I was finally able to hear Stone, my Gargoyle. Getting to know Stone and uncover who he was fully before I wrote my outline was much needed.

Then like the contrarian she is, Lexi finally came out again, not wanting to be overshadowed by Stone. Having a firm grasp on my two main characters did end up changing the story a bit, but I think for the best. There were definitely times where one of them was supposed to do something, but when I got to that part, I realized their character would simply never. An example being when Stone comes to Alexis's apartment after her failed mission. He was supposed to search her apartment. But when she offered, I realized he wouldn't fall for that trick. So I had to quickly scramble to keep the story going because he simply refused! Within the same chapter, I had no idea that Alexis would yell "pass" when Valda came to them asking to solve his murder. She was supposed to listen to him at that point, but Lexi was in no fucking mood.

Needless to say these characters certainly kept me on my toes, and I'm very glad I had them be my second book instead of my first. As a first time author, choosing the sweeter, nicer option of Silvia & Torben was definitely the way to go before dealing with the whirlwind that was Alexis.

Not going to lie, I was very nervous writing a FMC who was a POC. I know, as a white woman, I could've easily fucked this up, but I don't want this entire series to be filled with only white women MCs. So fingers crossed that I portrayed Alexis's POV well enough so in future, I can introduce other POCs as well. Because I have plans. Oh, I do have plans.

Speaking of plans, I'm so glad that I got to write Harvey again! Not just in his POV but right up front in chapter one. I hope you'll all be happy to know that Harvey will be in every book. And we will learn a great deal about this mysterious shop owner, her plans, and what she's doing through the eyes of our feline friend. Rest assured that I know exactly how her truth will be revealed, but, like a good burlesque, revealing too much too soon just wouldn't be nearly as satisfying. Gotta keep you on your toes and weave in some red herrings along the way ;)

Acknowledgments

A huge shout out to my work friends, Lauren & Levi. Without them this series would still just be a dream in my head. Their initial and continued encouragement is truly the foundation of this writing endeavor of mine. Not to mention their comments, suggestions, and laughing emojis within my manuscript keeping my imposter syndrome at bay. Blessings upon you both!

My sweet partner, James, most definitely deserves a shout out. He's always there to support me in anything I do and has been such a rock throughout my author journey. Thank you for all the random times you've told me how proud you are of me.

Thank you so much to my amazing beta readers; Letha, Consensultea (aka Thai), and Rio! Your comments, points of view, suggestions, and encouragement helped to shape this story into an adventure I'm proud of.

Since this book is from the POV of a badass Black woman, I decided I needed a little outside perspective to make sure I didn't misstep anywhere along the way. So, thank you, Tierrani, for being my first ever sensitivity reader.

Enough cannot be said about the efforts of my copyeditor, Jesslyn. They asked all the right questions and pushed me to truly polish this little gem of a story. I swear that one day I'll learn where commas do and do not go...hopefully. Till then, I'll rely on your keen eye.

My friend and cover designer, Lisa, you've done such an amazing job with the look and feel of my covers. You nail the vibe every time, girl! It's always a pleasure to see what you come up with.

Lastly to my readers. Your reviews, comments on social media, and shares are what keep me going. Thank you for your dedication to this series. There's so much to come yet, and I can't wait to share it with you all.

Ella Outlaw Books

The Magical Bookshop Series

About the Author

Ella Outlaw is a nerdy, witchy, neurodivergent girlie, with one of those invisible chronic illnesses. Currently living in the DFW area of Texas, though desperately seeking to leave as it's far too hot here! She loves to game, cross-stitch, and read smut. While her love of writing may be 'new,' her joy of storytelling has been with her since childhood. Who knew her maladaptive daydreaming would be turned into such works of art!?